BABY & SOLO

LISABETH POSTHUMA

CANDLEWICK PRESS

Copyright © 2021 by Lisabeth Posthuma

First edition 2021

Library of Congress Catalog Card Number pending
ISBN 978-1-5362-1303-4

21 22 23 24 25 26 LBM 10 9 8 7 6 5 4 3 2 1

Printed in Melrose Park, IL, USA

This book was typeset in Adobe Garamond Pro.

Candlewick Press
99 Dover Street
Somerville, Massachusetts 02144

www.candlewick.com

To JLB

Part 1

Prologue

Royal Oak, Michigan — August 1996

"I think Joel is ready," Dr. Singh concluded.

I was on the couch, sitting up because it was only my brain and not my whole body being examined. There weren't enough chairs for us all to have one, and since I was technically still the patient, I followed rank.

"I don't know how I feel about this, Dr. Singh," my mom said. "It doesn't sound like there are safeguards in case of a relapse."

I hated that word. *Relapse.* It made me sound like a druggie.

"There haven't been any occurrences in almost two years." He glanced at my chart to confirm this timeline, but he was right. I hadn't had a major flare-up of What Was Wrong With Me since I was fifteen. "I think it's time we let him try life out, Mrs. Teague."

Mom scowled. "Shouldn't we try another medication?"

"I'm ready, Mom," I assured her, though she wasn't asking me. I was used to that — being discussed instead of participating in the discussion.

My dad said nothing, but he squeezed Mom's hand. She sighed. "What does it mean to 'try life out,' exactly?" she asked. "We're not talking about backpacking across Europe, are we?"

"Is that something that would interest you, Joel?" Dr. Singh mistook my mother's absurdity for a legitimate suggestion. "An adventure could be highly beneficial to Joel's recovery."

Both of my parents looked horror-struck.

I thought about making light of things and pretending that I'd always dreamed of running with the bulls in Pamplona, but Mom and Dad had already been through enough. The Bad Thing That Happened had happened to them, too. Besides, I disagreed with Dr. Singh. What Was Wrong With Me had been adventure enough.

"I'm good to experience life on a smaller scale before becoming a world traveler," I said, to my parents' obvious relief.

"How so?" my dad asked. If anyone invited my opinion in discussions about my mental health, it was always him. "What sounds fun to you? Would you maybe want to join a sports team?"

The genericness of his suggestion proved how little my dad knew about me.

"Maybe," I answered. "We'll see."

"It's important to set concrete goals as you fully integrate into normal life," Dr. Singh cautioned. "We need to have a plan in place before you all leave here today. And I'll be following up to make sure you actually take whatever we decide the first step is." Then he recited the words printed on the motivational poster hanging on the wall behind him: "It's never too late to become what you might have been."

Motivational posters were staples in child psychiatrists' offices.

These posters typically featured cheesy advice splashed across scenic mountain photographs, puppies and/or kittens, or, for reasons I will never understand, Charlie Brown.

Charlie Brown. The kid so mercilessly bullied by his so-called friends that *he couldn't even grow hair* was somehow the (literal) poster child meant to rally the mentally ill youth of this world. His picture was usually paired with such pandering catchphrases as "Anything is possible with determination!" and "Success is up to you!" and, worst of all, "Never give up!" The "Never give up!" poster featured that heartless bitch Lucy yanking the football away from Charlie just as he's about to kick it. In the history of Peanuts, Charlie Brown has never gotten to kick that goddamn ball because Lucy always, always pulls it away. But, you know, "Never give up!"

My father turned to Dr. Singh. "What do you think of him getting a job? Something part-time with other kids his age?"

"That's a great idea," my mom agreed, shockingly.

Without consulting me, the doctor said, "That sounds perfect. Let's aim for it!"

"OK." I shrugged, climbing onto the bandwagon. A job did appeal to me more than sports. For one thing, I'd be getting paid. Plus, a job felt like less of a commitment. If you quit a sports team, you were considered a wuss, but people quit jobs all the time, and no one cared. That was Normal, and let's be honest, Normal was the ultimate goal. I used to be Normal, after all. Maybe all that remained between me and being Normal again was providing goods or services to my peers for minimum wage for a while. It was worth a try.

"I'll spiff up my resume."

Everyone was all smiles after this, though I knew my mom's was forced.

The doctor gave me a two-week deadline to set up an interview.

5

He wrote this on a prescription pad and handed it to me like it was an antibiotic for a bacterial infection.

I thanked him, and we left his office. It was the first time in seven years that I thought that someday I might not have to come back anymore.

Chapter 1

"So, what makes you want to be a part of the ROYO Video team?"
Jessica Morrison, the manager of a video store, read from a form.

It had been roughly a week since my appointment with Dr.
Singh, and I'd already landed an interview. Well, technically my mom
landed me the interview through my cousin Devin. He was Jessica's
live-in boyfriend, and when Mom told him I was looking for a job,
he hooked me up.

"I like movies" seemed like the best answer, since I wasn't planning
to disclose that my shrink had prescribed that I enter the workforce.

Jessica jotted down my answer. "What sort of movies are you
into?"

I fixed my eyes on her hands as she wrote, since any other
part of her would've blown my concentration. Jessica was curvy,

doe-eyed, and centerfold worthy, and I, a seventeen-year-old just coming off medication that had suppressed his sex drive for his entire adolescence, was not at all immune to her allure. But since ogling my potential boss was probably not going to help get me this job, I kept my eyes to myself.

"I like all movies—action, horror, comedies." I moved my eyes to the floor and then back to her hands.

Jessica wrote "all" on her form.

"Cool," she said. "Where do you see yourself in five years?"

"I plan to graduate in the spring. Then maybe college." Higher education wasn't exactly on the docket for me, but I said it anyway. After all, it was never too late to become what I might have been.

"Oh, OK. Great." She jotted some more notes. "You know what? Why don't you just fill the rest of this out for me? Devin said you're cool, and you can work nights and weekends. That's all I need to know." She offered me a stack of paperwork, but before I could accept it, she paused. "Wait . . . you're not still sick, are you?"

"Sick . . . ?" I had a feeling I knew where this was going.

"Yeah, Dev said you had leukemia or something when you were younger," she explained. "Is that still going on?"

"Anemia." I corrected her honest mistake with my go-to lie. "And no, it's all cleared up."

Mom had decided on anemia as the ruse for What Was Wrong With Me. She'd needed a serious-but-not-*too*-serious disease to blame my hospitalizations and school absences on, and alphabetically it was the first one in the medical dictionary that seemed believable.

Jessica nodded and handed off the paperwork. Then she pulled out a plastic name badge strung on a lanyard. "You can start tomorrow, right? Come in at five o'clock." She popped the cap off a black Sharpie and poised it beneath the HI! MY NAME IS heading on the name tag. "What do you want to be called?"

"My name is Joel," I reminded her, unoffended that she'd forgotten it. Girls as hot as her couldn't be expected to remember names.

Jessica shook her head, and the lace of her bra peeked above the neckline of her tank top. It was green.

The bra, not the tank top. I don't remember what color the tank top was.

"No. We don't use our actual names at work," she clarified. "My parents' rule."

I knew from Devin that the Morrisons owned the entire city block of businesses that ROYO Video was on, but that was all I really knew about them. It seemed weird that they made their employees take on aliases just to work at a video store, but whatever. This was my first job, and what the hell did I know? "Well, I've always liked the name Mike . . ." Mike was a Normal guy name. I could be a Mike.

"What? No." Jessica laughed. "You have to choose a movie character name. It sets the mood for renting videos. Subliminal advertising."

"Oh." I guessed this made sense. "So does that mean you aren't Jessica here?"

"On the clock, I'm Scarlet." She pointed to her own name badge, which I'd been avoiding looking at because of its proximity to her breasts. "As in Scarlett O'Hara."

I'd never watched *Gone with the Wind*, but now I was tempted to.

"We've also got Dirty Harry—my stupid little brother, Scott. Then there's The Godfather, Mary Poppins, Hannibal, and Baby."

"Baby?"

"It's from *Dirty Dancing*." Jessica-Scarlet looked disgusted, the way all girls did when you didn't know something about *Dirty Dancing*.

"Oh. Never seen it."

"You're missing out."

I doubted it. "So, is there, like, a list of names to pick from?"

9

"No—you just can't have one someone else is using," she said impatiently, indicating the Sharpie. "So, what'll it be?"

I tried to think fast. James Bond, Rocky Balboa, and RoboCop flew through my head, but they all seemed too audacious for a guy like me, fresh out of the psych ward. Jack Nicholson's character from *One Flew Over the Cuckoo's Nest* was maybe more apropos, but I couldn't remember his name.

"What's your favorite movie?" Jessica-Scarlet helped me along.

"Star Wars."

She was unimpressed. "So, what? Like . . . Luke Skywalker?"

"No." I suddenly had a strong opinion on the subject. "Han Solo."

"OK." She wrote HANS SOLO in wet black letters, then waved the badge in the air to dry it. "But Skywalker sounds way sexier."

I would have corrected her spelling, but the word *sex* had derailed my thoughts.

"Welcome to ROYO Video, Hans," Scarlet said, handing me my name tag. "Come in tomorrow. Look for Baby. She'll be training you."

"I'll be here."

Chapter 2

The next day when I arrived for my shift, I was greeted by Mary Poppins.

"Just Poppins is fine," she made sure to let me know when she shook my hand. She smiled what I interpreted as a flirty smile.

Poppins was tanning-bed tan and had bleached-blond hair. She also wore a lot of makeup, enough that I couldn't tell what she would look like without it. From my experience, this amount of eyeliner and lipstick signaled insecurity, and also from experience, it was a bad idea to pursue anything beyond pleasantries with insecure girls.

I smiled back, but just to be nice. "I guess you can call me Han Solo."

Poppins laughed. "Don't you mean 'Hans'?" She pointed to the superfluous *s* on my name tag.

"Jessica wrote it that way. I didn't want to offend her by fixing it."

"Jessica?" Poppins raised an eyebrow. "You're on a first-name basis with the boss lady?"

"Oh, sorry. I mean *Scarlet* wrote it. I thought the fake names were just for customers."

She shrugged. "You can do what you want, but most of us like not having to be ourselves at work."

When she put it that way, I liked the idea of the pseudonyms. A lot.

Poppins pulled out a bottle of nail polish remover and some cotton balls from a cabinet. "So, Han Solo, where do you go to school?" She reached for my badge. "I'm at Kimball."

"I live in Dondero district." This was true, though I didn't bother telling her that I didn't attend high school. My string of hospitalizations meant I was years behind in school, so I had quit going to avoid the public humiliation of being the only fifteen-year-old in seventh grade. Instead the school district sent a tutor to my house—a recent college grad named Mr. Moser. I called him Tim. Academics weren't as hard for me as other things in life, though, so I didn't really need much instruction. Usually Tim just watched me take tests, and then we'd talk about *Seinfeld* and play *Tekken*.

Over the last two years, I'd caught up on enough credits to be the senior I was supposed to be, which meant I technically could've gone back to school in the fall if I'd wanted to. I didn't, though.

"Isn't Dondero's mascot an oak tree?" Poppins asked.

I actually didn't know this, but I didn't want to explain *why* I didn't, so I just said, "Sure."

"That's super lame."

I didn't disagree and handed her my name tag.

From the back of the store, a door slammed. It was followed

by the unmistakable sound of someone puking their guts out.

Her guts out, I decided. It sounded like a girl's guts.

Poppins poured the acetone onto a cotton ball. "Don't worry about it. It's just Baby."

"How do you know?" This seemed like an odd talent — identifying someone by the noises they made while throwing up.

"Because it always is, *Hans*." She rubbed the cotton ball over my name tag until the Sharpie disappeared. "There. Clean slate."

We heard the door slam again, and the puker emerged from the hallway.

"Hey, Poppins," a pale girl with flushed cheeks said as she approached the counter. "Hey . . . new guy."

Before I could introduce myself, Poppins lowered her voice and said, "We could totally hear you, you know . . ." She trailed off and mimed sticking her finger down her throat.

The girl glanced at me. "So what? Eating disorders are all the rage right now, and you know how I like to be hip to the times."

This girl wasn't wrong — I knew from years of group therapy that eating disorders were indeed en vogue. Most people I knew who had them didn't brag about it, though.

"Baby, I'm starting to worry about you. You really are thin enough already," Poppins assured her. "You should really just be happy with the body you have."

This was the typical supporting-actress-in-an-after-school-special advice you'd expect from someone who knew nothing about the complexities of eating disorders.

The puker, now confirmed to be Baby, replied with a sarcastic "Gee, thanks, Poppins! I never thought about it that way. I guess I'll go eat a sheet cake!" and started scanning in videos from the returns bin.

Poppins shrugged and dropped the subject. "Have you been formally introduced to Hans yet?"

13

Baby narrowed her eyes. They were green, which was a note-worthy detail. To me, at least.

"Hans? As in Alan Rickman's character from *Die Hard*?" she asked.

I shot Poppins a sideways look. "No—Han Solo, actually."

"His name is not *Hans*," Baby scoffed. "It's *Han. H-a-n*."

"We know that, Baby—Scarlet spelled it wrong on his name tag."

This information was met with a dramatic eye roll. "Oh, you mean Scarlett O'Hara, who misspells her own name? Doesn't surprise me."

Poppins whispered, "FYI—Baby hates Scarlet."

"What's to like?" Baby grabbed a lanyard from a cupboard and slipped it over her head. The name BABY was written in slanted bold capitals across her name tag. "Seriously, if she's gonna claim Scarlett O'Hara's her favorite movie character, she should have the decency to spell her name with both *t*'s."

This was a valid point, though maybe a weak justification for hating someone.

"I doubt Scarlet's ever even watched *Gone with the Wind*," Baby went on. "It's based on a book that has no pictures in it, and you know she's not a reader. She probably just saw Vivien Leigh's tits busting out of her corset on the movie poster one day and thought, *She looks like me!*"

Poppins looked at me. "See what I mean, *Hans*? Baby hates her."

"Oh my god, enough with the Hans!" Baby snatched my freshly blank name badge from my hand. In the empty space, she printed SOLO in capitals and tossed it back to me.

Solo. I liked it. It was better than Hans. And Han. Also Mike.

"Hey, thanks," I told her.

"Solo." Poppins frowned. "Sounds lonely."

"Yeah, well, Poppins sounds like one of those strippers who jumps out of a cake" was Baby's answer to that.

Poppins smiled passive-aggressively. "Your name makes you sound like an infant."

Baby didn't look up from her scan pile. "Ouch. I'll be feeling that burn for weeks."

Poppins sighed. Her shift officially over, she collected her things to leave. "Good luck tonight. Baby's always unpleasant after a purge."

Baby let Poppins have the last word and waved her off.

Poppins left, and then the store was quiet, save for a scowling Baby slamming movies around on the shelves. I waited for her to talk to me, but she didn't. She just worked around me like I wasn't even there.

"So, anything in particular I need to know about video clerking?" was my attempt to remind her I existed.

In response, Baby rummaged through a cabinet, pulled out a worn three-ring binder labeled NEW EMPLOYEE ORIANTATION in Scarlet's handwriting, and set it on the counter in front of me.

"Read this," she instructed me.

I waited to see if she'd direct me further, but she didn't. "So, that's it? I just read what's in the binder, and I'll know all there is to know about the world of video rentals?"

She took a deep breath and blew it out. "Listen, Solo, I'm not in the mood to hold anyone's hand today. This job is a fucking walk in the park. You'd actually have to work harder to fuck it up than to do it right." She returned to shelving. "Heads up: I swear a lot."

"It's fine," I told her. Then, to prove it, I said, "I mean, it's fucking fine."

I thought she might smile at this, but she didn't.

She did, however, relent a little. "Honestly, the biggest challenge of this job is how boring it can be. With the exception of weekends and bad weather, we're usually pretty dead."

"Great. I'll finally have time to write my novel." That joke fell flat, too.

Baby untied her brown hair from the knot it had been sitting in on top of her head, and it fell down her back, ending just below her waist when she shook it out. She ran her fingers through it a few times before tying it back up on her head, just as it had been before.

Most people I knew who binged and purged didn't have old-time-religion long hair, because when your body is starving, your hair is one of the first things it gives up on. No joke, I'd seen kids with bulimia lose it by the handful. To have hair like that, Baby must have been new to the world of eating disorders.

I considered warning her about the potential hair loss in her future. Maybe if Baby realized she could barf herself bald, it would be the deterrent she needed to get her life right before it was too late. But on the other hand, it probably wasn't a Normal thing to tell a girl you'd just met about the side effects of eating disorders. Normal guys didn't know about that stuff, probably, so I decided to stay out of it.

"I guess I'll get to it, then" is what I said instead, flipping to the first page in the binder.

"All right." Baby paused a few beats before adding, "I'm going to go throw up some more, and when we're both done, maybe I'll show you around the store."

"OK."

She stepped by me, and a few seconds later, the back door slammed for a third time, followed by the unmistakable sound of someone puking her guts out.

* * *

16

The employee training binder was stupid long.

Normally I had a unique appreciation for the mind-numbing slog of reading fine print, thanks to The Bad Thing That Happened. In fact, I'd once read the entire quality assurance manual for my car to distract myself from What Was Wrong With Me when no other deterrent was available, and that shit was record-breakingly boring. But since my mind wasn't already idle and the last occurrence of What Was Wrong With Me was two years deep in my past, it was hard to focus on things like late-fee reports and inventory procedures.

Still, while Baby alternated between waiting on customers and bathroom barf breaks, I soldiered on.

The first section of the manual was basic safety info I already knew—numbers to call in an emergency, where the nearest hospital was located, etc. Since ROYO Video was only a few miles from my house, I was already familiar with the area. I'd driven by here hundreds of times while coming and going from other places; I'd just never set foot inside the store until my interview.

It's not like I didn't rent movies, but I'd just always gone to Blockbuster. Downtown Royal Oak wasn't really my scene. Royal Oak, or "ROYO," as everyone called it, was where groups of kids my age hung out, usually at Coney Island or the Main Art Theatre. Since I was currently between friends (a dry spell spanning more than a decade now), I had little reason to be there.

I could tell right away that ROYO Video was a different kind of store than Blockbuster. I mean, yeah, there were shelves of VHS boxes, movie posters plastered to the walls, racks of candy, and a Coke fridge—your basic video store staples—but it had a different vibe. More hometown, less corporation, I guess. There were handwritten signs, community advertising bulletin boards, and even a Dondero football schedule posted by the door. (Their mascot really *was* an oak tree. Amazing.)

The floors and walls of the store were cluttered, but I liked that. I was at home in tight spaces. Until The Bad Thing, my family lived in a small Sears bungalow in one of those mostly white (like us), middle-class (also us) neighborhoods in Fairfax, Virginia. After The Bad Thing, we moved into a similar house in the same kind of neighborhood in Michigan.

I ended up skimming most of the manual. As I pretended to read, I kept an eye on Baby, hoping to learn what I really needed to know about the job from watching her. From what I could tell, when she wasn't puking, she was pretty good at it.

"Hi, Mr. Jansen! Ooh, you're going to love *Seven*. The ending totally freaked me out."

"I'm sorry, Ashley. *Toy Story* isn't out on video until October. Do you want me to call you when it comes in?"

"So, Wayne, isn't this, like, your fifth time renting *Jumanji* this month? Do you want me to just order you your own personal copy? It might save you money."

"I'm really sorry, Mrs. Schwartz. You have a fifteen-dollar late fee from your husband keeping *Heat* an extra week. Do you want me to remove him from your account?"

Baby knew everyone who came into the store that night, and they all seemed to like her, even Mrs. Schwartz, who did end up kicking her husband off her account after she paid the fine.

First impression, I wouldn't have guessed customer relations would be Baby's strong suit. She was a natural, though, despite throwing up for half her shift.

Strangely, Baby's puking gave me hope for myself. If she could be a successful video clerk when she had Something Wrong With Her, I should be able to hack it now that I didn't.

"How's it going?" Baby checked in with me during a lull between customers. "Bored to death yet?"

"Actually, I have a concern." I held up the binder. "It says in here that employees should 'be clean-cut and dress in business casual attire.'" I shook some long brown strands of hair into my eyes and indicated my grunge-inspired ensemble of faded T-shirt and holey corduroys. "That might be an issue for me."

Baby sat on a stool. "Oh, nobody enforces the dress code. You can wear or not wear whatever you want here. You've met the boss, right? She comes in half naked most days."

So I had noticed.

I closed the binder. "I appreciate you waiting until after I read it all to tell me it doesn't matter."

"You're welcome," she said, and then sat there quietly with her eyes closed.

Just like I wasn't sure I'd recognize Poppins without the inch-thick makeup she wore, I imagined that Baby would look different on a day she wasn't puking every twenty minutes. Like, maybe she wasn't usually so pale, and maybe she didn't typically wear tank tops with sweatpants cut off at the knees. Or maybe she did. It really didn't matter to me. Just like I wasn't interested in insecure girls, I was done hooking up with girls with eating disorders.

Baby perked up again when the bells on the door announced a customer, and after waiting on him, she gave me a rundown of ROYO Video's computer system and rental procedures. By the end of the night, I was waiting on customers myself and using the in-store database to locate movies on the shelves without her help.

I recognize that in the grand scheme of life, these are small feats to master, but given that What Was Wrong With Me had prevented me from mastering a lot of small feats, I was proud of myself. Even if the job was "a fucking walk in the park."

My shift ended at ten o'clock that night, which on Sundays was also when the store closed. Around a quarter to ten, Baby grabbed a checklist of closing procedures, and together we completed it.

"Hey, um . . . Baby?" I started to thank her for showing me the ropes, then stopped. "Sorry, but isn't it weird being called that? It feels like I'm hitting on you."

She made a face. "I know. In hindsight, I shouldn't have settled for that name. I'm so fucking sick of being told 'Nobody puts Baby in a corner.'"

"That's random. Why do people say that?"

She looked surprised. "You know. From the movie. *Dirty Dancing*."

"Oh, right," I said. "I've never seen it."

Unlike with Scarlet, this impressed Baby. "Really? Me neither."

"Wait, *you've* never seen *Dirty Dancing*, yet you still named yourself Baby?"

She pulled her hair down again and this time left it loose after running her fingers through it a few times. "Hardly. Indiana Jones named me."

I waited for her to elaborate. She didn't.

"What an honor," I told her. "I wasn't given the option of being christened by a bona fide action hero. Congratulations."

"Indiana Jones was the manager before Scarlet."

"That makes a lot more sense."

"Does it?" Baby asked. "When I got hired, Indy told me to pick the name of a character from my favorite movie. How can someone have just *one* favorite movie?" She dug her hand into the quarter section of the register and divided the coins into dollars. "Anyway, we fought about it, and he told me to stop being a baby and just pick a name. So I said, 'Maybe I want to be a baby about it,' because I don't know which hills are worth dying on. Then he wrote 'Baby' on my name tag and said, 'Fine, be a baby.'" She made a face. "I had no idea about the *Dirty Dancing* Baby because I'd never seen the stupid movie, and after everyone started up with the corner crap, I lost any desire to."

"Yeah," I said. Then, not wanting to kill the conversation, I added, "It was hard to pick a name. Scarlet said I should be Luke Skywalker."

"Why?" Baby asked as she dropped the coins back into the drawer. "It's not like that would have been any easier for her to spell."

I laughed. "I could've gone with Darth Vader. It's spelled how it sounds."

"Ugh. I'm *so* glad you didn't pick Darth Vader. When people name themselves after villains, it's usually only to compensate for how uninteresting they truly are."

I considered this. "I can see how it would be a letdown to work with a boring guy named Freddy Krueger who doesn't actually try to murder you in your sleep."

"The nerve of some people." Baby smirked, but then her eyes narrowed. "Hold on a sec. You aren't the guy who's supposedly related to Scarlet's boyfriend, are you?"

"Why?"

Baby shrugged. "I've met Scarlet's boyfriend. It's hard to imagine anyone in that meathead's gene pool walking upright."

If I dug deep enough, this felt like a compliment. "Oh. Well, then, supposedly that's me."

"Oh. Sorry for insulting your gene pool."

"No worries. Devin's my cousin on my mom's side. I take after my dad more. His gene pool is relatively meathead-free."

Baby huffed a small laugh and smiled, and it felt like my greatest achievement of the night.

I should probably explain here that while What Was Wrong With Me was psychological, there wasn't anything so fucked up about my personality that I couldn't have had traditional teenage friendships had it not been for The Bad Thing That Happened. Therefore I was proud of making Baby laugh the way any Normal guy would've been proud of it. Not the way a pariah of society like Frankenstein's monster might've been, feeling the first glint of human acceptance after a lifetime of being ostracized, if that's what you're thinking. I'd worked hard for that laugh, and Baby had a good smile — crescent shaped with satisfyingly sharp corners — so I was going to enjoy it.

After Baby finished counting up the money, we locked it in the safe in Scarlet's office. Then we punched our time cards and killed the lights, thus ending my first official shift at ROYO Video.

Our cars were parked a few spaces apart in the employee lot behind the store. Baby unlocked the driver's side of a black Accord while I did the same to my LeBaron.

I felt really good at that moment. One of the side effects of being on meds to help you cope with the lows in life is that they also dull the highs. I'd been off my medication for a few months, and every emotion I felt was pure again. I was downright giddy that I'd made it through my first day on the job like a real live Normal person.

As I pulled out of the parking space, I started to wave at Baby, but then I realized she wasn't in her car. Instead I saw her in front of it, facing the wild shrubbery that lined the edge of the lot.

I rolled down my window.

"Everything all right?"

Instead of answering, Baby bent over at the waist and threw up into the bushes.

I put the car back into park. It wouldn't have been Normal to just abandon someone in a situation like this, but it also probably wasn't Normal to do what I did, which was to get out of the car and jog up behind Baby while she finished heaving.

When she was done, Baby collapsed onto a cement parking

stopper and said what every person says when they vomit in front of someone else: "I'm sorry."

I replied with what everyone wants to be told by the person they've puked in front of: "Don't worry about it. It's no big deal."

"I thought I could make it home before throwing up again." Baby wiped her mouth with her sleeve.

"You were super wrong." It was a long shot, but I was hoping she'd smile at this. She didn't.

Neither of us had anything else to say, so I thought about taking off, but it didn't feel right to leave Baby alone yet. Plus she seemed like the kind of person who would tell me to go away if she wanted to be alone.

"I ruined my tabula rasa," she eventually said.

"Did you get puke on it?" I asked. "I have it on good authority that ammonia can get out even the toughest vomit stain."

"What? No. Tabula rasa means blank slate." Baby pulled a bottle of water out of her purse and took a drink. "You know how it is when you first meet someone and they know nothing about you? There's only a short window of time before they start filling in all the blanks." She screwed the cap back on and sighed. "I just met you a few hours ago, and you've probably already written 'puking psychopath' all over my tabula."

"I don't think you're a psychopath," I told her truthfully. I'd met a few psychopaths in my day, and as far as I knew, vomiting was not a symptom of that particular mental illness.

"Thanks." Baby looked at me.

We sat in silence for a few minutes more, during which a Normal person might have asked Baby some follow-up questions about why she was throwing up so much. However, I understood that just because I knew one thing about Baby, it didn't entitle me to everything else. Which was fine with me, honestly. It's a lot of responsibility, knowing the entire truth about a person, and I was too busy trying to become what I might have been to get involved in What Was Wrong with someone else.

She took a few more sips of water and kept them down, and we both got up to leave. I watched Baby get into her car and successfully exit the parking lot without getting sick again.

I was going to leave, too, but something stopped me. I suddenly got the feeling I wasn't alone, which was not an unfamiliar feeling. As I checked to make sure no one was hiding between the cars or in the dumpsters or within the (now puke-sodden) shrubbery, I thought about the idea of tabula rasas.

I sometimes forgot that The Bad Thing That Happened wasn't written all over my face, that What Was Wrong With Me wasn't visible to the naked eye. It occurred to me that I really *did* have a blank slate at this job. No one at ROYO Video knew a damn thing about my past, and if I played my cards right, I could keep it that way. I really could be someone else at work.

This realization was thrilling.

I got back into my car and started the engine. Of course there was no one else in the lot. Why would there be? There was nothing Wrong With Me. Not anymore. I was Han Solo, and my tabula was rasa.

I adjusted my rearview mirror and drove home.

Chapter 3

At my mom's request, I waited until after my first day of work to tell Dr. Singh about the job.

"There's no sense in celebrating too early" were her words. "Something could go wrong, and we'll be back at the drawing board, trying to figure out what to do with you."

When I finally told my doctor, he was overly congratulatory the way people are when someone they have no expectations of manages the smallest achievement. After a long string of accolades, he turned to my parents and issued a warning.

"The video store is off limits to you," he decreed. "If you want Joel to build independence, he'll need space. No helicoptering, no checking up on him there, understand?"

Before Mom could protest, Dad said, "Whatever it takes to keep Joel healthy."

Mom reluctantly agreed that ROYO Video would be a no-fly zone as long as I kept her reasonably informed about the small part of my life she and Dad weren't at the center of.

Since I wasn't scheduled to work again until Friday, I passed the days as I always did—video games, homework, Tim the tutor. Things felt a little different, though, now that I had work to look forward to.

I'd liked Sunday night at ROYO Video with its steady trickle of renters, the soothing hum of the Coke fridge, and the movies playing on the in-store televisions for background noise. It was calming.

As I soon learned, though, Fridays at a video store weren't anything like Sundays.

From the moment I clocked in, the store was packed. We were so busy that Poppins barely had enough time between customers to introduce me to the rest of my coworkers. They were busy, too, but I noticed some things:

First of all, The Godfather was a girl. She was Asian and had bluntly cut short black hair and dark eyes. She looked like Tia Carrere from *Wayne's World*, though The Godfather's beauty wasn't what I found intimidating about her. She wore all black in a luxe (not goth) way and made zero facial expressions throughout our introduction. Instead of shaking my hand, she just squeezed it and stared straight into my soul. Right away, it was clear that The Godfather had presence in the way someone ballsy enough to call herself "The Godfather" should.

On the other hand, I wasn't at all intimidated by Hannibal. Baby's assertion about people who name themselves after villains applied to him exactly. Since I had *Wayne's World* on my mind, at first glance Hannibal reminded me of a heavier version of the guy riding bitch in the AMC Pacer during the "Bohemian Rhapsody" scene. He had to be at least twenty-five and wore a ponytail and a metal band T-shirt (Pantera), all of which seemed to confirm that his choice of Hannibal was an overcompensation for something. His real name was probably something much less intimidating. Like Glenn.

Dirty Harry was more like what I was expecting. Not because he looked anything like Clint Eastwood, but because Scarlet had called him her stupid little brother. He had the same basic elements that made up Scarlet—hair, height, profile—but repackaged in a scrawny fifteen-year-old-dude body. He was dressed head to toe in Nike clothing, presumably because he was rich and spoiled, not because he was athletic. When he greeted me with "'Sup?" I kind of wanted to punch his face.

After the introductions, Poppins thrust a fishbowl full of plastic tags into my hands. She pointed to the racks of movies. "Good luck, Solo. Customers are crazy tonight."

I knew from Sunday that the way the movies were arranged was twice as confusing as the Dewey decimal system. The tags were both color coded and numbered, and they hung on little hooks beneath the corresponding VHS boxes, signaling to customers which movies were available at any given time. The colors differentiated between new releases and older movies, and the number assignment was for the computer database. Despite these overcomplications, I'd managed to put out a handful of tags correctly on Sunday after Baby showed me how.

But it bears repeating that this wasn't Sunday.

The moment I stepped out from behind the counter, a dozen customers descended on me.

"Hey, do you have a 4589 tag in there?" a mustached man asked, indicating the fishbowl. "I call dibs."

"Um, I don't know—"

27

"I need 4676," a woman with a ponytail interrupted. "And I also want 4589."

"If you just let me sort through—"

"He's not going to have two 4589s." The mustache glared at the ponytail. "It just came out on Tuesday. Sorry, lady."

A third voice joined in—an indignant pair of sunglasses. "Why should you get 4589? I was here first."

"You snooze, you lose," Mustache said. Then to me, "Here— let me see what's in there." He reached for the fishbowl.

Ponytail grabbed for it, too. "I think I see a 4589 in there . . ."

I held the bowl tightly and swatted hands away. These people *were* crazy.

Luckily, crazy was in my wheelhouse.

"Hey!" I yelled. "Everybody step the hell back, or you'll all be getting late fees!"

My assertiveness surprised even me. However, twenty-four eyebrows raised in unison, and the crowd dissipated.

I liked being Solo. People respected him.

I put out the tags, and in the second bowlful of returns, I discovered a 4589. It turned out that number represented *The Juror*, starring Demi Moore and Alec Baldwin, the hottest ticket of the night. Instead of hanging it on a hook, I offered it to a customer with no mustache, ponytail, or sunglasses. (She was thrilled.) The abuse of power was invigorating.

I stayed on the floor until my dinner break a few hours later, and afterward I returned to a thinned crowd and a trashed store. There were candy wrappers on the floor and half-drunk fast food cups abandoned randomly throughout the shelves. The displays were askew, VHS boxes were out of order, and there was a handful of popcorn ground into the carpet, which was weird, since we only sold it in its unpopped state.

"Did we get looted?" I asked Hannibal.

"It's the weekend, my friend" was his response.

"Nice job fending off the tag-grabbers earlier," Poppins chimed in.

"Yeah, dude," Hannibal agreed. "Someone tackled me for *Dumb and Dumber* once. I don't go out there during rush anymore. You're a natural, though."

I enjoyed these accolades, even if they'd only been given so I'd continue doing the crap work no one else wanted to do.

The Godfather's and Dirty's shifts ended first that evening. Then it was just Hannibal, Poppins, and me. Since there were fewer customers as it got later, Poppins stayed on the register while Hannibal put on a pair of headphones and started up the vacuum cleaner. I was given an empty trash bag, and I began collecting the garbage strewn about the store.

I really enjoyed this, which might sound weird, so let me explain. In the heyday of What Was Wrong With Me, I was party to much less desirable messes. Party to some, victim of some, and responsible for one, I should say. Messes happen pretty often in a psych hospital.

Tantrum messes were the most common, since many of my peers were dealing with rage issues. These were usually limited to throwing things or knocking over tables and were typically resolved quickly with a sedative and some sweeping up. Accidental messes, like someone pulling out an IV and spurting blood across the room, were unfortunate but easily forgivable. Premeditated messes were the worst kind. Since psych patients are absent traditional weaponry, they sometimes resort to using their own body byproducts to enact vengeance. Pissing all over the chairs before group therapy, for example. Smearing shit on the bathroom stalls. Throwing up Mop & Glo all over my room. (More on that later.) The kicker was that most messes were on us patients to clean up, a punishment meant to deter such behaviors from recurring. As a result, over the years, I built up a pretty high tolerance to bodily fluids.

The mess in the video store wasn't caused by a tantrum or an accident or revenge, and I found that refreshing. Sure, the place was a disaster zone, but in an *Animal House* post-frat-rager way. People made this mess while looking to score a flick for the weekend. They were enjoying the spoils of Normal life—a little soda, some Skittles—and so what if they left some trash behind? So what if I had to scrape gum out of the carpet? It was a Normal-people mess, the kind that Normal people have to clean up. Normal people like me.

By the time ROYO Video was back in order, my perspective on my job had evolved a bit. I felt less like a video store clerk and more like a party host. The store was my living room: *Come on in, everybody, and make yourself at home. Grab a movie and have a good time, courtesy of everyone's favorite video guy, Han Solo.*

With about half an hour until closing, I gathered the garbage bags and headed out to the dumpster in the employee parking lot. All that was left to do for the night was to count the money in the registers, so I chucked the bags in and took my time walking back to the store.

It was one of those hot summer nights people complained were swampy, even though Michigan is hardly a swamp. I happened to like this kind of humidity because it equated to warmer weather, and I hated the cold. In Michigan the winters seemed seven months long, and that's a crime against humanity. Virginia winters were warmer and shorter (and technically swampier). Not that I wanted to move back there.

Another reason I liked humidity is because it's a warning that rain is coming. Humidity tells you that change is imminent, and a guy like me appreciates a heads-up when something's about to happen.

Which is why I jumped a mile high when, without warning, I heard someone whisper, "Hey!"

I turned my head, but I didn't see anyone. The moisture in the air made halos around the streetlights. I rubbed my eyes, but it didn't help.

The back lot was long and narrow, and there were many cars parked in it, but I couldn't see anyone inside them. It was unsettling.

"Hey!"

The whisper was louder this time, and the hair on my arms pricked up.

I own that I'm paranoid. What Was Wrong With Me had really done a number on my nerves over the years, and my fight-or-flight response had a sensitive trigger. So when I heard the third "Hey!" and there was still no one in sight, you can understand why I wanted to book it out of there like a track-and-field Olympian. After all, a situation like this would scare even a Normal person.

Of course, a Normal person would've been scared that the voice belonged to a kidnapper or murderer. Whereas I was afraid that the voice meant I was having a relapse of What Was Wrong With Me.

I should explain that What Was Wrong With Me could talk. It had a mouth, and curly brown hair, and green eyes, and all the other parts that make up a sixteen-year-old girl. It also had a name: Crystal. But I wasn't supposed to call her that. I wasn't supposed to engage with What Was Wrong With Me. There wasn't supposed to *be* Something Wrong With Me anymore.

Evidently the whisperer hadn't gotten that memo.

"Wait a minute!" the voice called out to me. The command was followed by the sound of footsteps approaching fast.

You might expect that by this point I'd be running back toward the store with superhuman speed, but instead my body did the most counterproductive thing it could do when needing to escape danger, which was to freeze completely fucking still.

I figure there are three reasons this happened.

The first was shock. You see, I never thought I would actually relapse. I was sure I was cured, healed, and delivered from What Was Wrong With Me. Several doctors had given me the all-clear. Besides, Crystal had promised me that if I ever wanted to see her again, *I* would have to find *her*. Crazy as that may sound, she'd always kept her word, so I was fairly stunned that she was showing up now, just when I was finally Normal. So stunned that my goddamn feet simply wouldn't move.

The second reason I didn't run was that I knew it wouldn't matter. Space did not confine Crystal. *She* could hide from *me*, but that road didn't go both ways. If she was coming back, there wasn't anything I could do to stop it.

The third reason made up only about 1 percent of why I didn't run, but it's still worth mentioning: I *missed* Crystal.

At least 1 percent of me did.

This all sounds crazy because it is crazy. But it's also true, and those aren't mutually exclusive. Crystal was What Was Wrong With Me, and she and I had a complicated history. So when the footsteps drew closer and a hand touched my shoulder, only 99 percent of me dreaded turning around and seeing her face.

And that's why when I turned around and the person standing there wasn't Crystal, only 99 percent of me was completely relieved.

"You're not Crystal" was how I greeted the guy in a T-shirt and camouflage pants.

The vast majority of me was so happy to see a dude I didn't recognize that I had to stop myself from hugging him.

He pointed at the video store door and, no longer whispering, asked, "Do you work here?"

"Yeah," I told him. "It's only my second day. Just getting ready to close up shop." I added these details because I lose all discernment when I'm spooked, including what personal information I should be giving to a guy lurking in the shadows of a parking lot. Had he taken any longer to reply, I might have given him a key to my house and volunteered my Social Security number.

"Oh, yeah?" The guy nodded. "Is Nikki working tonight?"

"The Godfather?" I guessed. Because of the back alley and the cloak of darkness, he struck me as her bird of a feather. "She got off a few hours ago."

"No, not her. Nikki. *Baby*," he clarified. "She in there?"

"Oh. *Baby*. No, she's not here." I pulled out a copy of the work schedule that was folded in my wallet and checked the lineup for Saturday. "She'll be in tomorrow, though. We're opening together."

"Damn." The guy rubbed his face and closed his eyes before asking, "How . . . how is she?"

My wits were coming back enough for me to hesitate before answering. "What do you mean?"

"I don't know." He scratched his head. "I heard she might be . . . unwell."

This question aroused some suspicion. "Who are you, exactly?"

He answered me with air quotes. "'Indiana Jones.' Indy. I used to work here."

Oh. This was the guy who had named Baby. I eased up a little. "Han Solo." I pointed at myself. "Solo."

"Right." Indy dug into his pocket and pulled out a pack of cigarettes. He hit it against the palm of his hand before taking two out and offering one to me. I shook my head. "So she's been OK, then?

Baby?" he asked before lighting up. "She said something was going on, but sometimes people exaggerate." He took a drag and blew it out.

He could've been referring to Baby's eating disorder, but I didn't see how it was any of his business. "I just worked with her the one time."

"Yeah. All right." He seemed disappointed.

"You want to come in? Poppins and Hannibal are inside. Do you know them?"

"I can't." He took a few more drags off his cigarette in silence before flicking it onto the ground. We both watched it burn out. "Look, I know you don't know me. But I need a favor." He reached into his back pocket. "I need to get this to Nikki, but I'm leaving town." He handed me an envelope. It was the standard letter size with Baby's apparent name scrawled across the front. "It's really important."

I took it. "Yeah, sure. I'll leave it for her."

"Actually, you need to hand it to her," Indy said firmly.

"Oh, OK. Is she expecting it?"

He shrugged. "She's expecting something."

A rumble in the distance told me that the humidity was about to make good on its warning.

"I should get back to work," I said. "Sure you don't want to come in for a minute?"

"I really can't." He glanced at the back door and shook his head. "And don't mention that you saw me out here. Cool?"

"Sure." I waited for him to explain, but he didn't.

"Thanks, man," Indy said before turning away. He only made it a few steps across the lot before the rain started.

It ended up being a hard rain. I stood under an awning, breathing in the ozone smell of a summer storm. Then, as I expected them to once Indiana Jones was out of sight, my thoughts returned to Crystal.

Crystal was like Pandora's box. Once she made her way to the forefront of my mind, it was hard to stuff her back where she belonged. Into a diagnosis. Into a label. Into What Was Wrong With Me. This time I knew it would be especially hard to forget her because I'd been scared shitless that she was back, and fear like that tended to linger.

As I watched the rain, I decided that if Crystal were going to reappear, this would be a great setting for it. She could just show up as a shadowy silhouette, materializing in the storm, clouds of steam rising up around her from the cold rain beating against the hot pavement. She'd be wearing her green dress, probably belting out a Bon Jovi song I hated.

But that kind of entrance wasn't really her style. If Crystal came back, she'd just show up somewhere acting all Normal. As if she'd never left in the first place.

I waited until the rain let up, and then—because I knew I'd get no peace otherwise—I ran out to the dumpster. I mean, I *knew* Crystal wasn't in there, but I had to make sure. If I didn't do it now, I'd obsess about it all night and end up driving back here at four in the morning to check. Given those two options, it was less crazy to check now, and the less crazy option is always the right one.

I opened the lid and looked inside. There was nothing there but wet garbage. I also looked underneath my car for good measure. And then four others. And then around a stack of wooden pallets behind the pizza place next door.

"Hey—what are you doing?" Poppins called out to me as I climbed down off the pallets.

She was under the awning, watching me.

I squeezed the rain out of my hair. "I saw a stray cat. I thought it might be hurt, but I can't find it now" was my ready reply. In terms of covering up What Was Wrong With Me, this was not my first rodeo. "It must have run off."

Poppins smiled at me the way girls do when they think you care about animals. "Well, come back inside! You look like an insane person out there!"

I took one last look around the pallets and then followed Poppins back into the store. The last thing I wanted was to look like an insane person.

Chapter 4

Sure, I wanted to know what was in the envelope. Of course I did. If some stranger shrouded in the night asked you to deliver a message, you'd wonder what it said, too. That's just plain Normal.

There was no way in hell I was going to open it, though. Privacy is sacred to me. After spending so much time in psych hospitals, where even your shits are subject to monitoring, you learn to appreciate receiving your mail unopened. I wasn't going to rob anyone of that luxury, even if most people took that sort of thing for granted.

Still, I wondered about the envelope. And why Indiana Jones hadn't just left it for Baby at the ROYO Video counter. And what it was she'd been expecting from him. Despite wanting to keep my distance, I found that I was beginning to wonder a lot of things about Baby.

"You're being quiet," Mom observed the next morning at breakfast. "What are you thinking about?"

Another reason I respected other people's privacy so much was because at home I couldn't even keep my thoughts to myself.

"Work" was my answer.

"Work?" she repeated, then assumed the worst. "Is there a problem? Do you want to quit? Is it too overwhelming?"

My dad looked up from his newspaper, and they both waited.

"I was just thinking about last night. It was busy." This was the truth, but not the whole truth. "A good busy, though. Fun busy. I'm just the right amount of whelmed."

"No unexpected visitors?" Mom asked, lighting a cigarette. She meant Crystal. She never used her name.

"No," I said in between bites of cereal. Indiana Jones had been unexpected, but since I knew what she was really asking, it didn't feel like a lie.

That was enough for Dad to go back to his paper.

"I was thinking." Mom inhaled and blew smoke out her nose. "Maybe you should tell all your coworkers about having anemia. Just in case something happens at work. Let them know that if you start acting weird, someone should call me."

I stared at my mother.

This was the last thing I wanted to do. If my tabula was truly rasa at ROYO Video, I didn't want to spoil it by announcing I had a proclivity for freaking out and needing my mommy.

"Devin's girlfriend kind of knows," I revealed, hoping that would satisfy her. "But she thinks I had leukemia."

"Even better," Mom said. "She'll probably be a nicer boss if she thinks you were *that* sick."

You might think she was joking, but she wasn't. I shot her an annoyed look.

"Don't look a gift horse in the mouth, Joel. People are usually nicer to cancer kids."

Translation: nicer than they are to the kind of sick kid I'd been. I might've taken exception to this comment had I not known it to be true.

"How lucky am I to have survived not one but two fake childhood illnesses?" I asked sarcastically. "Why don't we say I beat polio, too? I'd be a triple threat!"

Mom exhaled some smoke. "I'm sure that would impress the girls."

I finished my cereal, grabbed my car keys, and humored my mother. "It's like I have the Tom Cruise of immune systems."

Mom smiled. "Go get 'em, honey."

Baby's Accord wasn't in the lot when I got to work. Since I didn't yet have a store key, I listened to a CD in my car while I waited for her.

I'd been playing R.E.M.'s *Monster* nonstop for the past month, mostly the first six tracks, because I rarely drove anywhere that took longer than that and my CD player always started over with track one when I turned the car on. I often got on kicks where I'd listen to an album ad nauseam. Lately I'd done this with Aerosmith's *Get a Grip*, Stone Temple Pilots' *Core*, and, in a brief R&B stint, Boyz II Men's *II*.

I listened to half a song before I turned down the music and pulled Baby's envelope out of the glove compartment.

Nikki.

It occurred to me that Indy had probably never intended to hand this to Baby himself. If he had, why would he have written her name on it? He must have been waiting in the lot, hoping to run into someone who could deliver it. And if that was the case, I couldn't imagine the envelope contained good news. People like to give good news in person, not via an intermediary.

I started getting nervous. I was literally going to be the bearer of bad news, and nobody wants to be that guy.

When it was time to open the store, there was still no sign of Baby. There *was* a red Volkswagen parked a few spaces down from me, though, so I decided to try the door in case she was here and had just driven a different car.

The door was locked, but I could see a light on inside, so I knocked. Moments later a shadowy someone emerged from the break room, and then Scarlet, not Baby, stepped into the light, walking toward me barefoot with a toothbrush in her mouth.

Also noteworthy was that she was in her underwear.

OK, so maybe not *just* underwear. It was some sort of pajamas that might as well have been underwear but were probably technically shorts and a tank top. Semantics aside, I wasn't prepared for it and immediately broke out in a sweat.

"Hey," she said after she opened the door. "Sorry, I overslept." Her words were garbled by a mouthful of toothpaste.

"That's OK." I fixed my eyes on her ankles and followed them down the hallway and back into the break room. "Are you covering Baby's shift?"

Scarlet spat into the break room sink. "You think I came to work looking like this?" She pointed to her bare stomach and thighs, two regions of her body I'd been willing myself not to ogle. "I spent the night here."

"You did?"

"I thought you saw me, actually." She cupped her hand under the faucet and rinsed out her mouth. "I passed you leaving on my way in last night."

"I didn't see you," I said, then followed Scarlet to a couch in the corner of the break room. She took a change of clothes out of a dresser that a TV sat on.

"So . . . I'm guessing you crash here a lot?" I sat down on the arm of the couch.

"Only when your cousin's being an asshole," she answered. "So yeah. All the time."

This was news to me. I mean, Devin could definitely be an asshole sometimes; I just didn't know he was one to Scarlet. "I'm sorry."

Scarlet dropped the clothes onto the table where employees ate their lunch and began finger-combing her hair. "What the hell is his problem, anyway?"

I literally knew nothing about Devin's problems. We weren't that close. Our moms were, but not us so much. As far as I was concerned, Devin had zero problems and one very hot girlfriend.

"I wish I knew," I offered.

And then, to my complete horror and utter delight, Scarlet took her shirt off.

This time I'm not exaggerating at all. She seriously completely removed her top and stood before me in only her bra.

"Words words words words words," Scarlet said as she lifted a fresh T-shirt off the pile of clothing. "More words."

She slipped the shirt over her head, and I regained language comprehension skills.

"I mean, I just don't know what to do about him anymore," Scarlet concluded. "What do you think?"

What did I think? Was she kidding? She had to know what I was thinking about right then.

While she waited for me to answer, Scarlet took off her shorts. No joke.

She exchanged them for a skirt, which she seemed to pull up over her legs in slow motion as that "Oh Yeah" song from the Twix commercial blared in my brain.

Now, I was not quite an authority on things Normal people did,

41

but *this* did not feel Normal. Why would a girl (who was my boss, who was my cousin's girlfriend, who was a real-life version of Jessica Rabbit) strip her clothes off in front of me, some dude she barely knew? Was it some kind of power move? Was it an invitation? Was she just really proud of her body and liked to show it off? If our roles were reversed, a guy stripping down to his underwear in front of a girl that way would have been at the very least obnoxious and at most sexual harassment. When Scarlet did it, though, it didn't feel like either of those things. It felt like she was daring me to do something. Or not to.

Regardless, Scarlet's question still hung in the air. The problem was, there was a sudden blood drought in my brain, so instead of coming up with any solid relationship advice, I blurted out the first thing that popped into my head:

"I think . . . it's never too late for you to become what you might have been."

Scarlet paused, and then her forehead creased. "Huh?"

I scrambled for what to say next. "It's true." I nodded slowly, the way therapists always do when they want you to agree with them. "The only person in control of your happiness is you," I added. This was advice I'd borrowed from a second poster that hung in my doctor's office. (This one featured a photo of young man with a mullet, staring pensively into a mirror.)

Scarlet blinked at me.

There was no going back at this point. My mind had become a spinning carousel, except in place of horses, there was a herd of shitty motivational posters and half-naked Scarlets careening in circles. I just started babbling. "Today is the first day of the rest of your life, Scarlet." (A picture of feet standing on a paved road lined with trees.) "Life's greatest fulfillments often begin with a drastic change." (A photograph of a butterfly emerging from a cocoon.) "Tough times seem to last long, but tough people last longer." (Garfield, for some reason.) "Hang in there." (Cat on a clothesline.)

Scarlet stared at me with a factory-setting non-expression. "What are you talking about?"

"I really don't know. I'm an idiot."

Scarlet didn't disagree with me. Instead she scooped up her pajamas and slipped her feet into a pair of sandals. "Well . . . whatever. Thanks for listening, at least." Then, in one continuous motion, she bent down, kissed me on the cheek, and walked out the door. In her wake lingered the scent of Victoria's Secret (a compilation of fruit and flowers and sex pheromones), which I swear was the best goddamn smell on the planet, and I just sat there breathing it in and waiting to be able to stand up again.

Too soon after Scarlet exited the store, Baby entered and replaced the air's sexually charged energy with an altogether different one.

"Hello?" she called out frantically.

I met her in the hallway. "Hey."

"Why are you back here? Why didn't you open the store? It's ten after ten!"

"It is?" I glanced at a clock. I almost panicked, but then I remembered I wasn't the one who was late. "I've never opened before. I didn't know what to do."

"Shit!" she yelled and pushed past me. "Get the lights. I'll unlock the doors. Shit! Shit! Shit!"

I flipped some switches, and the store lit up. "I don't think we missed out on any customers, if that's what you're worried about."

"It's not!" Baby turned the deadbolts on the front door. "I just fucking hate being late." She pushed open the door and looked up and down the street.

"No one'll know," I told her. I refrained from mentioning that Scarlet had just left and hadn't seemed to care that Baby was late, just in case she didn't want Baby knowing she'd been crashing at the store.

"Someone is supposed to come by today. We have unfinished business," Baby explained.

It took me a beat, but I put two and two together. "Oh." I felt for the envelope in my pocket. "Are you talking about Indiana Jones?"

Baby's mouth dropped open. "How did you know that?"

"I ran into him last night in the parking lot." I handed her the envelope. "He asked me to give you this."

She stared first at me, then at the envelope. "What is it?"

I shrugged and walked away. She deserved privacy, and besides, my curiosity about the envelope was suddenly dwarfed by my desire not to get involved in Baby's drama.

I heard the envelope tear, and then there was silence.

And then there was shouting.

"What the hell?" She stormed the register that I was now standing behind. "What is this, Solo?" She threw the envelope down on the counter. Some money slid out of it.

"Money" was my matter-of-fact, don't-drag-me-into-whatever's-going-on answer.

"No shit. What's it for?"

"Beats me. He didn't say."

Somehow this was enough information for Baby to figure out the answer, because a few seconds later she said, "Oh."

It was a sad little word, and despite wanting to keep my distance, I instantly felt bad for Baby.

There was silence for a few more seconds before Baby grabbed the cordless telephone from its port by the computer, clicked it on, and disappeared down the hallway. She left the money on the counter and me in charge of the store on this, my third day of employment.

Baby was gone for a long time. I hid the money out of sight and tried to keep busy putting away returns from the overnight bin, but I ran out of things I knew how to do pretty quickly. Considering Baby was going through some shit, it seemed petty to complain that I was bored, but I hadn't worked at the store long enough yet to know how to kill time productively, and we've already established that an idle mind wasn't good for me.

In the cabinets under the register, I found a roll of paper towels and a can of Pledge. Appearance-wise, the store was still in pretty good shape from the night before, but even in a clean room, there's at least a little dust. I set out to bust it.

I headed to the classics shelves first. Sure enough, there were thick layers of gray fuzz covering the entire collection of rarely rented 1940s musicals, so I shook up the Pledge and got to work.

That is to say, I walked up and down every aisle to assure myself that I was truly alone, and *then* I got to work.

You may be noticing a pattern with this behavior, but I promise you I don't have OCD. The doctors thought I did for a while, but it turned out What Was Wrong With Me didn't include that specific diagnosis, because (according to the DSM-III-R) constantly casing your surroundings in search of the girl you sometimes hallucinate is more in line with a schizoaffective disorder. Which, clinically speaking, was what they thought I had.

I didn't agree with that diagnosis, but when you're a kid and your greatest line of defense against getting thrown in a psych hospital is "I'm not crazy!" you might as well pack your bags, because no one is going to believe you.

I'll admit, at times it seemed like maybe I *was* losing my mind. But honestly, it would have been Normal to after The Bad Thing That Happened. The Bad Thing was an atomic bomb that went off right in the center of my world, vaporizing *everything*. Things like normalcy, stability, and predictability all vanished without a trace. From dust they were formed, and to dust they returned, and there I was at ground zero, covered in fucking dust.

In the fallout after The Bad Thing—amidst the scrutiny, the abandonment, the pity, the finger-pointing, and the questions—a lot of things got ignored. Things that mattered, like dentist appointments (I ended up with three cavities) and home repairs (we never did fix that leak in the roof), and a lot of other things that didn't seem to matter at all. Like, for instance, the mail.

As is proper etiquette after an event like The Bad Thing That Happened, there was an influx of cards and letters sent to the house by the community of Fairfax, Virginia. My parents never opened them, so they just collected in stacks that occupied the countertops and the kitchen table we'd stopped eating at. My parents probably planned to deal with them eventually, but after enough time passed, the piles went from being in the way to being just the way things were. The three of us stopped noticing them until it was time for us to move.

One thing unique to our Fairfax home was the old kiln in our backyard. It was a large brick oven shaped like a teepee, built by a previous owner. Since there were no potters in the Teague family, it mostly got used as a play space when I was young. But eventually, like the piles of mail in the house, the kiln became visual white noise. Then one day, while packing for the move to Michigan, ten-year-old Joel had the bright idea of using the kiln to burn all the condolences cluttering the counters rather than boxing them up to schlep to our new house.

I remember filling a laundry basket full of that mail, dragging it outside into the deepest part of the yard, and chucking it into the kiln handfuls at a time. Then I found a book of matches in the garage, lit three of them, and tossed them at the pile.

Just before the flames grabbed hold, though, I noticed a shoebox wedged under a brick inside the kiln, and I dislodged it with my foot. It had been a long time since I'd stored any of my toys out there. I assumed whatever was in the box wasn't very important if I hadn't missed it after all that time, but that was no reason to set it on fire without checking first.

I removed the rubber bands holding the box closed. Nothing about it seemed familiar, and when I got the lid off, the same held true for what was inside: a cassette tape called *Slippery When Wet*, a Bonne Bell bubble gum Lip Smacker, Wet n Wild nail polish, a rolled-up *Teen Beat* magazine, and — wadded into a dense ball — a green dress. There was also a page of Lisa Frank stationery with a list of names written in cursive, which I've since memorized:

Breanne
Ricki
Carol
Belinda
Tara
Gina
Christine
Crystal

It was all girl stuff.

I examined it, trying to figure out who it belonged to and how it had wound up there. It seemed like it could be important to someone, and for that reason, it became important to me.

It was then, as I was trying to solve the mystery of the kiln box, that I first experienced What Was Wrong With Me.

There she was, plain as day: a girl cowering against the wall of the kiln behind the burning piles of mail.

My heart practically stopped. Then I screamed. "I'm sorry! I didn't see you in there!"

I had two years of Cub Scouts under my belt, and I was prepared in case the fire got out of hand, so I grabbed the nearby bucket of water and used it to douse the flames.

When the smoke cleared, no one was there.

As I was crawling around in the wet ashes, looking for loose bricks or a false wall or really any explanation for how a girl could have secretly entered and escaped the mail inferno, I heard rustling behind me.

I emerged from the kiln covered in soggy filth and called out, "Hello?"

I looked around but saw no one. I also didn't see the shoebox. The list of names, however, was sitting on the ground, exactly where I'd dropped it.

Just then I heard my dad calling to me from the back porch. He was facing my direction and shielding his eyes against the sun.

"Joel!" he yelled, but not angrily. "What the hell are you doing out there?" Then, after a pause, "Where's all the mail?"

My mom was none too pleased. She stripped me down to my Underoos and turned on the hose, muttering about how I'd ruined a pair of perfectly good blue jeans and how she wouldn't know who to write thank-you cards to, since I'd destroyed the notes people had so thoughtfully sent. "Everyone already believes we're horrible people . . . this'll be more proof." There were tears rolling down her cheeks as she puffed on one of those long cigarettes marketed to women, of which she'd smoked three packs a day since The Bad Thing. "What possessed you to do such a thing, Joel?"

"He was doing us a favor," my dad defended me. He was sitting cross-legged on the driveway with a scrubbing brush and a box of Tide powdered detergent, trying to salvage the knees of my pants.

"Joel knew if we'd wanted to read any of those cards or letters, we'd have done it by now. Isn't that right?"

I nodded, even though Dad was giving me more credit than I deserved.

"See?" Dad assured Mom. "And trust me, Maureen, no one is expecting anything from us right now, least of all goddamn thank-you cards."

Mom wouldn't acknowledge Dad's point. "But fire, Joel? How many times have we told you not to play with fire?"

The honest answer to this question was none. All I had ever learned about fire safety came from Cub Scouts, Smokey Bear PSAs, and school during Fire Prevention Month. From what I could recall, my parents had never even told me not to play with matches, despite my access to them in a house with a smoker. I guess they believed that not playing with fire was just one of those things kids are supposed to know without being taught.

"I'm sorry."

Mom turned the hose back on.

"Are you sure you didn't burn yourself?" my dad asked, looking up from my Levi's.

My mom paused her spraying so I could answer. "No, I'm fine," I said through chattering teeth. Then water blasted me again, and sooty trickles flowed down my legs like black rivers on a map.

"What were you thinking crawling around in there, anyway?" Mom demanded. "I've told you a million times not to go in that dirty old kiln."

No, she hadn't, actually. Not even once.

"I thought I saw one of my old toys," I lied. It felt more believable than the truth, so it didn't feel wrong.

"This is why I always say not to leave your toys lying around, Joel. I knew something like this would eventually happen."

49

Obviously no one would ever have predicted a scenario wherein I'd ruin a pair of jeans by burning months of unanswered cards we'd received because of The Bad Thing That Happened. But there was no sense in arguing about any of this, because we all knew (even the youngest of us) that Mom rewrote the past however she needed to in order to keep herself together.

"Calm down, Maureen," Dad said gently. "He got rid of a couple stacks of paper. Let's have some perspective. It's not like anybody d—" He stopped himself.

Mom glared at Dad.

"I'm sorry. What I meant to say was, Joel is fine. We don't need to get worked up about a little thing like this." But it was too late.

"A little thing? Try a warning sign, Craig! Try a cry for help! Your son just lit a bonfire and then rolled around in it. Open your god-damn eyes!" Mom threw the hose down and stormed inside.

The walls of the Virginia house were thin, so we could've easily heard Mom stomp up the stairs and slam her bedroom door from the driveway, even if she hadn't done so extra loudly for our benefit.

I crouched down and hugged my knees to my chest in an effort to keep my ass from completely freezing off. Dad fetched a towel from the beach stuff in the garage we hadn't gotten around to packing.

He wrapped me up in it like I was a little boy. I mean, I kind of still was one, but it hadn't felt like it in a while. The towel he'd picked was my favorite because it was big and hadn't been washed too many times. I'd last used it in Virginia Beach a few months before The Bad Thing, the day we ate so many hot dogs after swimming in the ocean. The towel was primary colors—ketchup, mustard, and sky. I loved that memory, but I was afraid to think about it too often, lest I wear it out.

"I'm sorry, Dad," I told him. It wasn't an apology for the mail, though. Neither one of us cared about the mail, but we were both sorry.

"Me too, Joel," he said. Then he took his finger, pruney from the detergent, wiped it across my forehead, and showed me that it was black. "What happened is hard for you and me, but it's even harder for your mom. It doesn't seem like that's possible, but it is, OK? She's doing the best she can."

"I know," I said, though I didn't.

Dad crossed his legs again to make a lap and pulled me onto it, cradling me like a baby. The impulse to resist him was there, but it wasn't nearly as strong as my need for his comfort. So I just sat there and let him hold me for as long as he would.

Later, cleaned up and ready for bed, I pulled the piece of stationery out of the pocket of my dirty (but not ruined, thanks to my dad and the Tide) blue jeans and slipped it under my pillow. The next day, I decided, I would find the girl from the fire, the owner of the shoebox, and give her back the list. I would ask her to tell my mom she had been in the kiln and that I wasn't crazy.

That was my plan, at least. As it turned out, she had another one.

Three hours and two rolls of Bounty later, ROYO Video's entire inventory had a coat of furniture polish, and I daresay the store looked (and smelled) much fresher.

Meanwhile, at some point during my cleaning mission, Baby had returned. I'd almost forgotten she was in the store, quite possibly because of my contact high from all the lemony aerosol fumes.

"You know," she said as I dumped the final load of dirty paper towels into the garbage, "the whole time I've worked here, no one has ever waxed the movies."

"What can I say? I'm a visionary." Her mood seemed lighter than before, and I took that as a sign that she'd worked out her problem.

Baby glanced at the clock. "Our shifts end in half an hour. Big plans this afternoon?"

I had none to speak of. My social calendar consisted only of doctor's appointments and meetups with Tim the tutor, and neither of those things happened on Saturdays. "I don't know. I might rent a movie, I guess."

"Oh, yeah. Me too. I still haven't gotten around to watching *Get Shorty* . . ." She trailed off. "Fuck it, Solo. I can't do small talk right now." She ran her fingers through her hair and sighed. "I need a favor. A ride, actually, right after work. Can you help me out?"

"Um . . . what?"

"Listen, I know we hardly know each other, but I can't find anyone else to take me," she explained. "Trust me, if I could think of literally anyone, I wouldn't be asking you. I'm stuck."

I was immediately hesitant to help her. Where did she need to go, and why couldn't she take herself there? Obviously this was about Indiana Jones and the envelope full of money, and I'd already been drawn into that shady situation way more than I wanted to be. Willingly inserting myself further into Whatever Was Wrong With Baby seemed counterproductive to my overall goal of having a Normal life.

"Is something wrong with your car? Because you could just borrow mine." This seemed like a compromise that a very generous Normal person would suggest, one who didn't care what happened to his LeBaron if it meant keeping a healthy distance from the not-Normal goings-on of his coworker, that is.

"No, it's not like that." She sighed. "I have an appointment. The kind they don't let you drive yourself home from."

Baby tossed a wadded-up business card onto the counter between us.

I reluctantly smoothed it out and read it:

52

Oh . . . *Oh.*

"I don't have an eating disorder, Solo," she said. "I'm knocked up."

I was surprised. Probably more so because I hadn't considered this as a possibility. Like, at all. I mean, it made sense. If I'd tried, I probably could've connected the dots. I'd watched enough movies to know that when a female character threw up, it usually meant we were in for a pregnancy story arc. In real life, though, especially *my* real life in a psych hospital, habitually vomiting almost always pointed to an eating disorder, which was probably why I'd latched onto that theory even when the clues didn't necessarily add up.

God. *Pregnant.* That was heavy. I didn't know what to say to Baby. This didn't seem like a *congratulations* situation, but I had to say something. After a minute, I ended up going with a casual "I had no idea."

She looked at me like I was a moron, because I was one. "Well, it's a good thing I don't need a detective, Solo," she said. "Just a taxi service."

"Oh, yeah."

Suddenly I wasn't as concerned with keeping my distance. What Was Wrong With Baby was isolated to her. Baby (and Indy, I presumed) might've been dealing with some major drama, but I didn't see how her being pregnant could affect me and my quest for Normal at all.

"Yeah, I'll give you a ride. No problem."

"Thanks." Baby faked a smile. "You're my hero."

I knew she was kidding, but it felt good to be the one giving help for once instead of the one needing it.

Chapter 5

We made it through the first six tracks of R.E.M.'s *Monster* before pulling up at the clinic, ending the drive as "Strange Currencies" faded out. Even though Baby hadn't talked to me the entire ride there, she had adjusted her seat, the stereo volume, and the temperature controls to her liking. This let me know up front that she didn't require my hospitality. Baby could take care of herself, except for this one thing.

By the time I parked, Baby was already getting out of the car. "They said it should take about two hours. I think there's a bookstore around the corner, but I don't know if you like to read. I'm sorry." I watched her in the rearview mirror as she jogged up to the cinder block building, pushed open the glass door, and disappeared inside.

I punched the button with the two left-facing triangles on my stereo six times, and "What's the Frequency, Kenneth?" began playing through the speakers once again.

I'd never personally gotten anyone pregnant, but I thought I had once. Sex between crazy teens is a pretty common coping mechanism, even though medication usually prevents them from enjoying promiscuity to its fullest potential. Doctors say this is an unfortunate side effect, but that in order to hamper whatever chemicals in our brains are causing our craziness, our sex chemicals need to be unplugged, too. This sounds like a convenient attempt to prevent unstable youths from procreating, but I also have a history of paranoia, so take that conspiracy theory for what it's worth.

Anyway, I was at a psych hospital just after a flare-up of What Was Wrong With Me. Several of my previous stays had been on pediatric floors where kids only jonesed for things like sugar or video games to take the edge off their issues. Once puberty set in, though, *Mario Kart* and Mars bars couldn't alleviate the type of blues we got, so we turned to more carnal pick-me-ups to distract us from all the shit we were going through.

Adolescent floors weren't coed, but where there were wills, there were ways, and many of us knew how to hook up on the sly. It was going great for a while, but in a psych hospital, there really is no fury like a woman scorned, and all the fun ended when I scorned a girl named Valerie.

She was getting treated for anorexia, and we had a pretty steady thing going for about a month—twice a week in the broom closet while her roommate played lookout—until Valerie caught wind that I hadn't been entirely faithful to her (I was also fooling around with the roommate) and freaked the hell out.

To punish me for my infidelity, she drank half a bottle of Mop & Glo from the janitor's cart. While I was at a group therapy session, a nurse found her in my bed, surrounded by puddles of vomited-up floor cleaner and a note stating that I'd gotten her pregnant and dumped her. For added fun, she also accused me of stealing pain medications from the pharmacy and selling them to other patients.

The next forty-eight hours were complete hell, though I'll spare you the details. Basically, after her stomach was pumped and she was stabilized, Valerie was put on suicide watch while I got interrogated like a serial killer until all parties involved (doctors, parents, police officers, lawyers) were convinced that all the claims in her note were false.

Eventually Valerie admitted to everyone that I wasn't a pill pusher and that she had never been pregnant, but the damage was done. Valerie's near death triggered a lot of shit for me, which ended up extending my hospital stay by months.

As I was reliving the nightmare that was Valerie, the passenger door to my LeBaron suddenly flew open and snapped me back to reality.

Baby had returned. "You need to come inside."

"I do?"

"Yeah, they have to make sure I'm not alone, and they don't believe that Han Solo is waiting in the parking lot for me." Then she turned around and walked back toward the building.

"OK," I said, even though she was already too far away to hear me.

Baby had taken a chair in the waiting area by the time I got inside. A woman motioned to me from behind a thin pane of plexiglass.

"Han Solo, I presume?"

"Yeah, that's me. I mean, that's not my real name—"

"I don't need your life story, honey—just needed to see you with my own eyes to make sure the patient is accompanied."

"Oh. OK," I said. "Well, she is."

The woman nodded and waved me off.

I sat down next to Baby. Now that I was inside, it felt insensitive to leave unless she asked me to. Baby didn't acknowledge me, but since waiting rooms were something of an old stomping ground for me, I wasn't uncomfortable sitting in silence.

I took in the surroundings. The most notable difference between the Women's Health & Family Planning Center and the waiting rooms I was used to was that this one was significantly pinker. The linoleum floor was pink. The plastic bucket seats that lined the perimeter of the room were also pink. The wallpaper was a pink-and-mauve plaid, and I'm pretty sure that before the years of foot traffic, the sad gray rug in front of the door had also been pink. Shrinks' offices tended to be shades of tan and blue, probably because of some cutting-edge psychology about earth tones curing psychosis. I wondered what the science was behind all the damn pink.

I picked up a nearby *Entertainment Weekly* with Liv Tyler on the cover and pretended to read it.

"I couldn't tell them who was driving me home because I don't know your real name," Baby finally said.

Since she hadn't actually asked me what my name was, it took me a minute to realize she wanted to know.

"Oh. My name's Joel."

"Joe?"

"No — Joel. With an *l*. Like Billy Joel. Only it's my first name. My last name is Teague."

"Oh, OK. Cool. I don't know anyone with that name. Except, you know, Billy Joel. But I don't actually know him." Baby ran her fingers through her hair. "Mine's Nicole. Nicole Palmer."

"Not Nikki?"

"God, no. I hate being called Nikki. Actually, I prefer Baby."

"OK."

She turned a page in a copy of *Mademoiselle*, then suddenly folded it onto her lap. "Oh, god. Our names rhyme. Nicole and Joel."

"Yeah," I said. And then, because a one-word response didn't feel like enough, I added, "Joel and Nicole fell in a hole."

"What?"

"You know. Like 'Jack and Jill went up a hill.'"

"Oh. That's dumb." Baby sounded annoyed.

"I know. I'm an idiot," I admitted. "I was just trying to lighten the mood."

I returned to Liv Tyler, and Baby returned to *Mademoiselle*.

"Then what happened?" she asked a minute later.

I looked up from the magazine. "What happened to what?"

"To Joel and Nicole. After they fell in the hole. What happened then?"

"Oh." I thought for a second. "They met a troll?"

Baby nodded. "And then?"

"They . . . chewed some Skoal."

"And then?"

"They danced on a pole."

Baby paused before adding, "And ate Creole."

I smiled. "Out of a bowl."

I thought Baby almost smiled back. "With Dave Grohl."

"Damn," I said. "I thought my Skoal line was as good as it could get, and then you whip out a Foo Fighters reference for the win."

"You mean I scored a goal." Baby really did smile then. One of her crescent smiles.

It was quiet for another moment before I said, "For the record, I do enjoy reading, and I've been to the bookstore around the corner lots of times. There's an old lady who works there who thinks my name is Jimmy."

"Seriously?" Baby looked at me. "Who's named fucking Jimmy north of the Mason-Dixon Line?"

"I know, right? Obviously if my name were James I'd only answer to Jamie, because that's a cool-guy name."

"Obviously. I've never met a Jamie who wasn't cool."

"Right?"

Baby took a deep breath and held it awhile. "I came here to get an abortion."

"I figured."

"I'm sorry I didn't tell you before you drove me here. I guess I should have in case you objected on moral grounds."

I closed my magazine. "What kind of morals would I have if I made a girl take a cab to her own abortion?"

A few seconds later, a door opened, and a woman wearing pink scrubs and holding a clipboard appeared. "Number 1742?" she read, squinting through her glasses.

Without another word to me, Baby grabbed her purse and stood up.

"I'll wait here," I said.

She nodded, and I watched as she disappeared down the pink hallway.

Chapter 6

Baby was quiet on the drive back from her appointment. In fact, she said nothing at all from the time she emerged until I asked her for directions to her house three songs into *Monster*.

"Just take me back to work," she insisted instead.

This confused me. "Isn't the whole point that you aren't supposed to drive after the procedure?"

"Just take me back to the *fucking* video store. Please."

I did as I was told, and as I watched Baby peel out of the parking lot, I regretted not putting up a bigger fight about her driving.

Because we paranoid people are also hyperbolic, worst-case-scenario people, for the next several hours I worried that Baby had died in a car wreck on her way home. I pictured her car wrapped around a tree, a toxicology report revealing a large amount of anesthesia in her blood, and a crowd of mourners at her funeral lamenting, "If only someone had been looking out for her . . ." I thought about this obsessively until finally I said to hell with it and decided to drive to her house to make sure she'd gotten there alive.

This was a difficult task because, as we've established, I didn't know where Baby lived.

There were ten Palmers in Royal Oak, according to the phone book. I drove by five of the addresses to no avail, but in the driveway of the sixth was a late-eighties Accord with a Pearl Jam sticker in the back window, and I breathed a sigh of relief that I hadn't involuntarily manslaughtered Baby.

Once I knew she'd made it home, I didn't think about her any more that week. Maybe that sounds insensitive, but in group therapy, they teach you to compartmentalize people and their issues. You have to see the two things separately. For instance, someone might drop a bombshell secret on you one moment, then ask if you've seen the latest episode of *Friends* the next, and you want to be able to navigate both of those conversations simultaneously. It's surreal at first, don't get me wrong. I remember going to a session early on in my treatment where this kid Kyle revealed that his mom put window cleaner in his food because she liked the attention of having a child who was always sick. (Munchausen syndrome by proxy—look it up.) All of us in the group thought it was so fucked up that we were crying buckets listening to him talk about what he'd been through. But then, like an hour later, we were all eating spaghetti together in the hospital cafeteria and talking about the MTV VMAs. I mean, this guy had just revealed this completely tragic and personal thing, and here we were eating pasta and discussing how Anthony Kiedis had presented the award for Video of the Year while pretending to give a blow job to a banana. It didn't seem possible that both of those moments could happen in the same day or even that both things could exist on the same planet, but they did, and eventually I came to understand that MTV and child abuse were not mutually exclusive. Everyone was carrying around varying amounts of rainbows and shit with them wherever they went, and you couldn't always focus on the shit.

All that is to say that instead of sitting around worrying about Baby that week, I finished my economics and British lit credits and annihilated a frustrated Tim Moser in *Tekken*. (He claimed he was off his game due to the new school year starting.)

Oh, and I also went to therapy.

I told Dr. Singh about my work duties and assured him that my parents were giving me space. I didn't bring up Baby or the abortion, though, because that was her business and not mine.

"I've gotta say, I'm impressed with how well your job is going." His tone was congratulatory as he scribbled on his clipboard.

"I'm only a video store clerk. It's not like I cured cancer."

"Not yet" was his encouraging response. Then he pointed at the "might have been" poster.

Saturday of Labor Day weekend, The Godfather and I were scheduled to work the morning shift together. We showed up at the same time, and she parked her silver Mercedes next to my LeBaron. She stepped out of the car, black-clad from head to toe, and pulled her sunglasses off.

"Seven," The Godfather said, pointing at my shirt.

I looked down. I was wearing a rec league soccer jersey I'd gotten at a thrift store. Indeed the number seven was featured prominently on the front.

"Yup," I agreed, and then, not knowing what else to say, I added, "That's what number that is."

The Godfather stared directly into my eyes. "It is a lucky number." She spoke crisply, overemphasizing each syllable like an academic who felt contractions were beneath her.

"OK, then," I said.

She walked past me, and I followed her into work, my second impression of The Godfather just as intimidating as the first.

We opened the store, and then I found a list of housekeeping chores Scarlet had left, assuming business would be slow over the weekend since everyone usually headed up north to the lakes on holidays.

"How should we divide this up?" I asked The Godfather. She was seated on a stool, filing her already-perfect fingernails. "Which ones do you want to do?"

"*I* do not do chores" was her answer.

Not one to argue with terrifying women, I just said, "All righty," and got to work on the list. I spent the morning replacing lightbulbs, assembling displays for the coming-soon attractions, and cleaning out the storage closet, the last of which was a considerable job that kept me away from The Godfather for several hours, much to my relief.

The storage closet was a closet in name only, considering it was almost the same size as the break room. It was the place where all the stock (candy, soda, etc.) was kept, as well as a ton of other junk. Things like old movie displays, holiday decorations, office supplies, and a population of spiders. Organizing everything (except the spiders) was fairly simple, though. The biggest job turned out to be clearing out the endless piles of cardboard boxes that needed breaking down before they could go out for recycling.

It was chump work, but I did it anyway. Halfway through the piles, I took a break, sat down on a step stool, and cracked open a completely unrefreshing room-temperature Coke. It was then that I noticed my fingers were bleeding from a thousand paper cuts, which is the kind of injury in line with flattening cardboard boxes with one's bare hands. I put the Coke down and held them out in front of me to get a better look.

63

I used to have nice hands. When I was a kid, my mom was always saying God had wasted good fingernails on a boy. "It's all that Jell-O you eat. It makes them grow in thick because it's made of horse hooves." I didn't fact-check this, but I did eat a lot of Jell-O, and I did have nice nails, so it sounded legit to me.

Crystal backed up this idea as well (about me having nice hands, that is, not about the Jell-O). She loved my hands, for some reason. She was always touching them, holding them, and asking to give me manicures. (I let her a few times.) It was always like that with us, from the first time she visited me, the night after the kiln incident.

After all the excitement I'd caused with the burning of the mail, everyone in the Teague house went to bed early. I couldn't have been asleep for long when noise coming from my closet woke me up. It was the kind of noise most kids attributed to monsters, ghosts, or that fucking *It* clown, but since I'd stopped being scared of pretend things after The Bad Thing That Happened, I was more curious than afraid.

I was happy and somehow not surprised to see the girl from the kiln when I opened the door. She was standing on her tiptoes, rummaging through an old metal lunch box full of baseball cards that I kept on a high shelf.

She had no signs of burns on her. She wasn't sooty, either. She was fresh and clean, with her hair teased high and lots of pink makeup around her eyes.

"I'm so glad it's you!" I exclaimed excitedly.

"Of course it's me!" she replied.

"I'm the one who saw you in the kiln today," I told her, unsure if she recognized me.

"I know." She kept rummaging.

"Why were you in there?"

"I was looking for my shoebox. Thanks for finding it!" she said. "Now, if I could just find my list . . ."

"Oh!" I ran back to my bed and pulled the stationery out from under my pillow. "Is this what you're looking for?"

She stopped digging through the baseball cards. "Oh, thank god," she mouthed before plucking it from my hands and wrapping both arms around me. She was wearing the dress from the shoebox. Her hair smelled like bubble gum and baby powder. "Thank you, Joel! Thank you so much!"

"You're welcome!" I didn't remember telling her my name, but I must have said it. I was positive she hadn't told me hers, though, so I asked her.

"That's exactly why I need this!" She pointed to the list of names written on the paper. "Help me out, kiddo. I need to find a good fit."

"You don't already have a name?"

"Well, I did. But it was the wrong name." She smiled. "Do you ever feel like you have the wrong name, Joel?"

"No. I like my name. It's like Billy Joel, only my first name is Joel and my last name is Teague. I was almost Gabrielle, though. The doctor thought I was going to be a girl."

"That's pretty. Much prettier than my name." The girl sat down cross-legged on my closet floor, and I crawled into her lap. "Which of these do you like for me?" She held up the list.

I read it over again. "Well, Christine is the name of that car that kills people. You might get made fun of for that," I warned her. I'd seen the Stephen King movie the summer before and hated the name ever since.

"That's a really good point, kiddo." She laughed through her nose. "It's off the table."

"And I don't like the name Gina because of that Bon Jovi song," I confessed.

"Really? You don't like 'Livin' on a Prayer'? That's my favorite song!" she said, and then she started to sing it.

"I knew someone else who used to sing it all the time," I interrupted. "It got annoying."

She laughed again and mussed my hair. "All right. Enough with the names you hate. Which names do you *like*?"

"Well, I like Ricki, but people might call you Hickey Ricki."

She smiled again. "Then scratch that one, too!" She pointed at the first name on the list. "What do you think of Breanne?"

I didn't say anything. Of all the names, that one made me the most uncomfortable.

"Joel? Do you like the name Breanne?"

"That's not fair."

"Why not?"

"I already know someone who kind of has that name, and I don't want to know another one."

"You don't think it would help you to have a friend named Breanne?"

"Nope."

"Then my name won't be Breanne," she promised. This made me feel better. "So that leaves us with Carol, Belinda, Tara, and Crystal."

"My favorite is Crystal," I said, turning to look at her. "Crystals are pretty, so that one sounds the prettiest."

"Hi, my name is Crystal," she practiced. "You can call me Crystal. Nice to meet you, I'm Crystal." She grinned. "I think we have a winner."

I smiled, but then I was suddenly nervous. "We're moving to Michigan in a few days. Can you come, too?"

"That depends." She patted the floor next to us, and I moved out of her lap. Crystal refolded the list and stood up. From the shelf above my clothing rack, she pulled down her shoebox and exchanged the list for the nail polish. "Do you really want me to stick around?" She shook the bottle, then sat back down beside me and began to paint her fingernails. The shade was Emerald City, I could see from the cap. "Because if you do, then I'll come. But if it'll be too hard, I'll stay here." She pursed her lips and blew the polish dry.

"I want you to come. I'm tired of playing by myself."

Crystal reached for my hand. "Would you look at these nails?" She rubbed my thumbnail with her fingers. "They're like seashells. Learn to love that about yourself, OK? Not everyone has seashell fingernails, but you do." Then she placed her hand palm-to-palm with mine so that our outstretched fingers lined up. "People don't understand me, Joel. If I'm always hanging around you, they might not understand you, either."

I fanned my fingers out and pulled them in a few times, forcing her to do the same. "Well, I just won't tell anyone about you, then."

Crystal looked at me. Her eyes were green. "I'm really good at hiding." She took a dab of polish and painted the nail of my index finger.

I smiled back. "Michigan won't be as scary now."

By the time the storage closet was clean, I was not.

I was sweaty and covered in the dirt and ink that always accompany old cardboard boxes. I washed up in the bathroom as best I could before heading back out to the register.

I'd been gone so long that there'd apparently been a shift change. Baby was now standing in the place I'd last seen The Godfather.

I smiled, genuinely happy to see her. "How's it going?"

Her eyes narrowed. "Is that . . . blood?"

I looked down at my jersey and noticed several rusty smudge

67

marks from where I must've wiped my paper-cut hands. "Dammit." I showed her my fingers. "I was breaking down cardboard."

"You didn't use the box cutter?"

I stared at her. "There's a box cutter?"

She shook her head at me. "What size shirt do you wear?"

I told her medium, and she rummaged through a cabinet.

I was tempted to fill the silence by asking her how she was feeling, but I wasn't sure if I was allowed to. Any version of "How are you?" feels like overstepping when you're asking how a person's abortion recovery is going.

Baby turned back around with a T-shirt in her hands. "Movie studios are always sending us free stuff." She opened the cabinet door wider, and I could see boxes labeled PROMOTIONAL MERCHENDICE. "It's usually just pens and magnets, but sometimes we get shirts with movie posters printed on them." She unfolded one and held it out. "The only medium we have left is for *Reality Bites*."

"What's that about?"

"You haven't seen it?" Baby unfolded the shirt and showed me a picture of Winona Ryder standing between two dudes. "It's about a girl in a love triangle with a successful dork and a hot slacker." She pointed at the different characters as she described them. "Guess which one she chooses?"

I considered Winona's options. "Ethan Hawke?"

"Yup. Hot slacker." Baby tossed the shirt at me. "I swear, there's a guy like that in every movie nowadays, and he always gets the girl. It's an epidemic."

"An epidemic of hot slackers?" I held the shirt up to my chest. It seemed like it would fit. "That sounds serious."

Baby frowned. "It's a bigger problem than you think, Solo. These movies glorify those dumbasses. Attractive, unmotivated underachievers and the girls who save them—that's the basic plot of every film of our generation. It's ridiculous," she ranted. "Not every lazy jerkoff out there is actually a brilliant, tortured artist with limitless potential. Some guys really are just losers, and it shouldn't be on women to fix that."

I looked again at the shirt. "So it's a shitty movie?"

"No, it's good. It would just be a ton better if Winona Ryder chose herself at the end instead." She ran her hand through her hair. "You should watch it, though. I doubt you'll devolve into a slacker just from watching Ethan Hawke act like one, especially since you seem to be light-years more mature than most guys."

Light-years more mature than most guys. I wasn't sure what I'd done to deserve this compliment. Though if Indy was any indication of what most guys were like to Baby, the bar was probably pretty low. But whatever. Such praise was hard to come by for guys like me, so I wasn't going to question it. In fact, I considered having the words embroidered on a pillow.

"Maybe I'll rent it sometime," I told Baby. Then I went to change.

After this, Baby kept to herself most of that afternoon. I worked on assembling a display for *Multiplicity* in the break room, but then a thunderstorm rolled in and the store got busy. Baby and I hopped on side-by-side registers to keep the lines down.

At some point during the rush, a man dropped three tags onto the counter in front of me, then thumbed through his wallet in search of his membership card. He was maybe in his early forties, with olive skin and dark hair graying at the temples. He had a generic familiarity about him. "Hey, how are you tonight?" he asked me.

"Good. Yourself?"

"Good." He pointed at Baby. "Hey! Was that you who called my house about late fees a while back?"

Baby barely paused in waiting on her own customer to answer him. "Probably. You *do* always have late fees, Mr. Schwartz."

He nodded and turned to me. "One of the pitfalls of working the graveyard shift is that it's hard to keep your days straight."

"I'll bet."

I retrieved his selections from the shelves and typed his account number into the computer. When I hit enter, the screen flashed an error message, so I keyed it in again.

Baby glanced at my screen. "Oh, yeah, I forgot. Your wife kicked you off her account."

Mr. Schwartz grinned. "Are you serious? I thought she was joking about that." He laughed. "What happens now? You have to cut up my card, and I'm banned from the store forever?"

"Solo will take care of you," Baby told him, handing me a new membership form.

"You can open up a new account," I confirmed.

He looked at my name tag. "That's *Han* Solo, right?" he asked, as if there were other Solos out there. "I love *Star Wars*. Great choice."

"Thanks, Mr. Schwartz."

"Call me Marc," he insisted. "How long have you worked here?"

"Just a couple of weeks," I answered as I copied Marc Schwartz's address from his driver's license onto the rental contract. "I'll need to see a second form of ID, too."

"Right," Marc said, reaching into his back pocket. "Where'd you work before this? I think I've seen you around."

"This is actually my first job."

"Oh. Hmm." He handed me a business card. "Will this work? It's all I've got on me."

"Sure," I said, glancing at it. There was a familiar logo on the card—a profile outline of a human head with a drawing of a Band-Aid where the brain would be. Below it, I read:

DR. MARC J. SCHWARTZ

DIRECTOR OF PEDIATRIC PSYCHIATRY

WELLER CLAWSON MENTAL HEALTH SPECIALISTS

Oh, shit.

I hadn't recognized *Dr.* Schwartz. This was understandable, considering all the other times I'd seen him he'd had a mustache, glasses, and was wearing a white lab coat.

I handed back the card.

"Something wrong?" Marc asked.

"Nope." I quickly scanned his videos. "First rental on a new account is free; it'll be five twenty-five for the other two."

He handed me a ten-dollar bill, and I counted back his change. "Due back tomorrow by seven." I slid the cassettes across the counter.

His face changed when he recognized me. Maybe he didn't know exactly who I was, but I could tell he knew *how* he knew me.

"Sorry," he whispered, and then he raised his finger and thumb to his mouth and pretended to zip it closed.

There were more subtle ways to be subtle about this. Still, I was grateful he hadn't said something like "So, is that imaginary friend of yours still causing you trouble?"

He picked up the tapes and started for the door. "See ya later, Baby. Don't let anyone put you in any corners, OK?" He glanced back at me. "Good to know you, Solo."

It had never occurred to me that I might run into people like Dr. Schwartz in the real world, but it probably should have. Between hospital staff and fellow patients, there were likely a hundred people in the area who could have outed me as not Normal, and thanks to the sloppy way Marc had handled our encounter, possibly a hundred and one.

I glanced over at Baby. She didn't seem to have noticed anything.

71

The bullet seemingly dodged, I exhaled the breath I'd been holding. My tabula rasa was still intact.

Later, as I was about to clock out, I saw a video had been left on the counter. I was picking it up to scan it back in before I left when I noticed a Post-it note stuck on the case.

Let me know what you think. — *Baby*

I peeled off the note. It was *Reality Bites*.

"It's due tomorrow by seven." Baby reappeared at the counter. "Don't think I won't charge you a late fee, because I will."

I smiled at her.

"Consider it a thank-you gift," she said. "For the ride and . . . you know, all those dope rhymes you made up while we were waiting for my appointment." Baby got serious then. "For real, thanks."

I could tell the gesture was meant to close the conversation about our time at the clinic, not open a new one, so I nodded and held up the video. "Hot slackers, here I come!"

It was probably the most awkward thing I could have said, but whatever. I was light-years more mature than most guys, so it was fine. Plus it made Baby laugh, which was always a victory.

I watched the movie later that night, carefully analyzing the plot in light of Baby's review. I liked it. It had wit and heart, and unlike Baby, I wasn't bothered that Winona ended up with Ethan. I guess maybe I'm just a sucker for a happy ending.

Chapter 7

"What's your sign, Hannibal?" Poppins asked.

"Capricorn."

She turned a page in her magazine and began to read. "'A new season brings with it a potential romance.'" Poppins raised her eyebrows. "'Autumnal earth tones are your power colors, so be prepared to get noticed. Additionally, you'll want to invest in a new exercise routine this month to maintain that beach body you worked so hard for — why not try Tae Bo?'"

"I did work damn hard for this." Hannibal patted his round stomach. "It would be a shame to see it go to waste."

A loud sigh redirected the room's attention to Baby. "How long do we have to wait?" she demanded, her eyes fixed on the clock. It was ten after nine in the morning on the last Sunday in September, and the entire ROYO Video staff (minus Scarlet) was waiting in the break room before the store officially opened for the "mandetory" staff meeting that was supposed to have started at eight forty-five. "How inconsiderate is Scarlet to bail on a meeting *she* called? Like the rest of us don't have anything better to do."

All around the room, heads nodded. Baby had said aloud what most of us were thinking.

This was the first time I had been with everyone I worked with (again, minus Scarlet) at the same time. It reminded me of group therapy, honestly. A ragtag bunch sitting around a table, waiting for the person in charge to show up. Doctors were always running late to those meetings, too. I guess the more important you think you are, the less punctual you have to be.

The same narrative that emerged in those situations seemed to be happening here. When a doctor was more than ten minutes late, the person least comfortable with silence would attempt to entertain the rest of us to pass the time. In this case, it was Poppins with the horoscopes.

The second personality to emerge in these situations was usually the most indignant, so it didn't surprise me in the least when Baby started complaining.

She drummed her fingers on the table impatiently. "Maybe someone should check the door to make sure she's not outside trying to push when she should pull."

"I'm sure she'll be here in a minute," Poppins said. "What's your sign, Baby?"

"I don't have one."

"Of course you do. Everyone has a sign. When's your birthday?"

"Febtember eleventeenth."

Poppins frowned. "C'mon. I'm just trying to kill time until Scarlet gets here."

Baby refused to play along. "I don't want to kill time, Poppins. At the moment, I only want to kill Scarlet."

Poppins ignored her. "What about you, The Godfather? When's your birthday?"

"That is a personal question" was her reply. She was putting on lipstick while looking in a small mirror. Red lipstick, I'd recently learned, was the only exception The Godfather made to her all-black motif. She made a point to reapply it continuously and seemed to relish telling all who asked (and those who didn't) that her preferred shade was called Kiss of Death.

Poppins sighed. "Seriously. What's wrong with you guys? Doesn't anyone want to know their horoscope?" She glanced hopefully at Dirty Harry.

"Which horoscope symbol looks like a sixty-nine?" he asked her.

"That one is . . . Cancer," Poppins confirmed after consulting the magazine.

"Cool. I'll take that one."

"You don't get to pick your zodiac sign. You just get assigned the one you're born under," Poppins explained. "When's your birthday?"

"I just had it. It was September seventeenth."

"Oh—you're Virgo the virgin, then." She took a breath to read his horoscope.

"Nope." He shook his head. "I'm not playing this."

Poppins tossed her magazine into the center of the table. "Fine, we'll just sit here silently staring at each other until Scarlet decides to show up."

"I'm a Taurus," I told her, scooting the magazine back her way. "And I'm dying to know what's awaiting me in October."

Poppins smiled gratefully, and Baby rolled her eyes.

A few weeks had passed since Baby had introduced me to *Reality Bites*. Since then, she'd also insisted I watch *Mallrats* and *Clerks*, I think to drive home her point about slackers. This was followed by *What's Eating Gilbert Grape* for the same reason, but in a more dramatic setting.

I liked all the movies Baby suggested, and I liked discussing them with her afterward, which had become our "thing." I liked having a thing with Baby, and not just because she thought I was Normal. It wasn't a secret that Baby didn't like many people. At least, that was the way she acted at work. Aside from Scarlet, who reigned supreme on her shit list, Baby didn't seem to *hate* any of our coworkers; she just didn't *like* them. The fact that we got along seemed like a rarity, and rare things always feel valuable.

"Taurus," Poppins said, picking up the magazine. She cleared her throat. "'New opportunities are afoot, though things could get complicated when a blast from the past reenters the scene. Remember, old haunts seem to resurface this time of year, especially ones that were never fully laid to rest.'" She interrupted herself. "Wow — easy on the Halloween imagery, *'Teen*." She continued, "'Try to skimp on desserts this month — Tauruses tend to pack on the pounds this time of year, and the holidays are right around the corner.'"

"You can come to aerobics with me, my friend," Hannibal offered.

"Thanks."

The back door bells sounded, and moments later Scarlet made her entrance, breezing into the room with all the casualness of a punctual boss.

When she noticed our glares, she glanced at the clock. "Didn't I say nine-thirty?"

Baby held up the meeting memo. "Eight forty-five," she read with as much hostility as could be packed into four syllables.

"Oh. My bad." Scarlet shrugged. "Anyway — here you go." She distributed a paper to each of us.

"What's this?" Poppins asked.

"Some decisions have been made," Scarlet explained. "To account for my new college schedule."

Everyone stared at her.

"*You* got into college?" Baby asked on behalf of everyone.

Scarlet ignored this condescension the way only a girl who was completely confident could. "Yes! Beauty college. I'm going to be an aesthetician."

There was a pause in the room.

"What is that? Like, a doctor who fixes ugly people?" Hannibal asked.

Scarlet thought for a second before answering, "Yes." She smiled, pleased with herself. "Anyway, I'm cutting back my hours so I can go to class, so there have to be some changes."

All eyes returned to the paper — the following month's schedule — and there was a short moment of silence before the yelling began.

"You've got to be kidding me!" Baby seethed. "*Solo* is a shift manager now?"

"What?" I asked. Poppins pointed to my name on the schedule. Next to it, the letters *SM* were written so small I probably wouldn't have noticed them. "What does that mean?"

"It means you just got a promotion. You know, the thing it takes most people more than six weeks at a job to 'earn.'" Baby used aggressive air quotes.

"Oh."

"Seriously, what gives?" Hannibal demanded. "This isn't cool. I've worked here for *three years* and never gotten a promotion."

"Same here, Hannibal," Baby pointed out.

"This *is* unfair." Poppins joined the charge. "I mean, no offense, Solo, but I still have to remind you to assess rewind fees. You shouldn't be in charge."

"That happened one time," I defended myself, then felt stupid for doing so. I honestly understood why everyone was so pissed about this, even though I still didn't really know what a shift manager was.

"This is an outrage," The Godfather joined in, but it seemed she wasn't really affected by the news. "Is that it? Is this meeting adjourned?"

Dirty Harry put his hands behind his head and leaned back in his chair. "I couldn't care less who's manager. I already make more per hour than most of you since my parents own the place."

This comment incited more rage.

"What the hell?" Baby looked like she might explode.

"So what? I'm their son," Dirty shot back, as though this were a legitimate reason someone should be paid more than their peers.

"Everyone just shut up and listen!" Scarlet attempted to take charge. Baby closed her mouth, but probably only out of curiosity, not because she respected her authority. "OK, first of all, this was not my decision — it was my parents'. So don't shoot the messenger. Second of all, let me just say something about Solo." She smiled and put her hand on my shoulder.

My eyes widened. I didn't know what Scarlet was going to say, but I had a hunch whatever it was wouldn't make this decision any more popular.

"Since he started working here, the entire store has been *spotless*. It's the cleanest it's ever been! There are no more piles of unfiled papers lying all around. And have you guys seen the storage closet? You can eat off the floor in there."

"You're kidding, right?" Baby glowered. "You're promoting him for being a neat freak?"

"No, for his 'work ethic.'" It was Scarlet's turn for finger quotes, though it was clear she didn't understand how they worked. "He shows 'initiative.' He's not 'lazy,' like a lot of people." She then proceeded to list more exemplary things I'd accomplished in my short tenure that had made me seem like the ideal employee but that I'd actually only done to keep my mind from idling toward Crazy Town.

Normally, I think this sort of recognition would've felt good—especially coming from Scarlet. I mean, I *had* gone above and beyond the (low) expectations for a video clerk, and truth be told, the store did look amazing. It was just hard to be proud of anything in a moment when such accolades were inciting a mutiny.

"I still call bullshit on this," Baby said. "Solo doesn't deserve a promotion."

Even though I agreed, it felt shitty to hear Baby say it.

"If you think that, then you must not know him very well," Scarlet said in my defense. "Not only is he a great worker, he's also a survivor. He beat childhood anemia, which is more than I can say for any of you."

There was a brief quiet moment where everyone tried to connect the revelation about my past health issue to the subject at hand.

"What's anemia?" Dirty Harry finally asked.

"It's like . . ." It was at this moment that it became clear Scarlet didn't know what it was. "A very serious condition. And Solo beat it because he's strong and doesn't give up." She looked at me and smiled, which normally would have been awesome but at the moment made everything worse.

"Anemia is just low blood iron, and it's not that serious," an exasperated Baby explained to everyone. Then, to recap, she added, "Solo gets to be shift manager because he had to take vitamins as a kid? Yeah, that's fair."

Scarlet blew off her point. "Whatever. Solo works hard, Baby."

"So do I!" Baby asserted. "I've been working hard for three years longer than he has."

Scarlet scoffed. "Hardly."

It was only one word, but it was a loaded one.

79

The rest of the staff eased off as Baby stood up. "What's that supposed to mean?"

Scarlet remained unfazed. "All I'm saying is that if you'd put as much effort into your job as you did trying to get into Indiana Jones's pants, you could've already been promoted and spared us this hissy fit."

The room felt the lowness of this blow, and everyone's eyes widened.

The two girls were locked in a stare-down that eventually ended with Baby muttering *"Fuck this"* and storming out of the room.

I stood up to follow her, but Scarlet stopped me. "Just let her go, Solo. She'll be fine."

"That was a really shitty thing to say," I told her. I didn't know how much truth there was to Scarlet's accusation, but that didn't matter. It was cruel.

Scarlet cocked her head at me and said innocently, "Listen, I know you're just trying to be a good guy. But honestly, she needed to hear it. The truth hurts, Solo."

From the parking lot behind the store, tires squealed, sounding Baby's exit.

I looked around the room. For some reason, no one else seemed as ready as I was to jump to Baby's defense, and that lessened my resolve. Ultimately I sat back down.

The meeting continued for another twenty minutes, but I was too upset to listen. This was the first time I'd seen Baby and Scarlet together, and it surprised me that the animosity between them was a two-way street. I figured most people talked smack about their bosses, but Scarlet humiliating Baby in front of everyone felt much more personal.

I was finding Scarlet significantly less hot by the time I followed her into her office to discuss my new position (which was probably something we should have done before she gave it to me publicly).

"So are you excited?" Scarlet asked, handing me a form to sign.

"Should I be?"

"Yeah," she said. "It's ten bucks an hour."

I clenched my teeth to keep my jaw from dropping. I currently made minimum wage, which was less than half that. My mother had been decorating cakes at the Farmer Jack bakery for the last six years, and I was pretty sure she only made twelve. "What exactly do I have to *do* for a job that pays that much?"

"Not much more than you're already doing, honestly." She shrugged. "You've proven how valuable you are. And I'm not just talking about cleaning out the closets."

I signed the form accepting my raise and handed it back to her. "Yeah?"

Scarlet sat in a cleared-off spot on her desk. "Sure. I meant what I said about the store looking great. But also my parents credit you with my decision to go back to school."

"What? Why?"

"When you said it wasn't too late for me to be what I might have been, it really made me think," she explained. "I decided you were right."

I stared at her like a dumbass. "You're serious? *That's* why you're going back to school?"

"It was the push I needed. My parents have wanted me to do something like this ever since high school." She squeezed my arm. "The promotion is their way of saying thanks."

I couldn't believe this.

"I also told Devin that he's on thin ice," Scarlet went on. "Mom and Dad are happy about that, too. They've always thought I could do better than him."

A thought occurred to me. "Wait a minute. Did I get this

promotion for my work ethic or because your parents think I'm some sort of good influence on you?"

"Can't it be both?" she asked. "Give yourself some credit, Solo. You're good at giving advice. You're really put together for someone in high school. Mom says overcoming childhood diseases makes people better at living life." She shrugged. "Maybe if I'd had cancer as a kid, I'd be a lawyer or something by now."

Each of those statements was more ironic than the last.

Scarlet read my face and frowned. "I thought you'd be more excited. What gives?"

"It's great, really," I assured her. "I'm just surprised. And, you know, everyone hates me now, so that's going to take some getting used to."

She waved away my concern. "If anyone gives you shit, fire them. You can do that now."

"That's sure to win them over," I commented, but then Scarlet put her hand on mine, and I worried less about things.

"I hope it counts for something that *I* don't hate you," she said in a low voice. "Don't forget that it's never too late for *you* to become what you might have been, too."

I knew I should have stayed mad at her for what she'd said to Baby, but Scarlet was kryptonite to my righteous indignation. It was impossible to be angry when all I could think about was what it wasn't too late to become with Scarlet.

"It counts for more than it probably should," I admitted, and then I left.

Chapter 8

I went home to tell my parents the good news about my promotion. They'd be as shocked as I was, no doubt, but ultimately proud, because when your son's a guy like me, you don't question silver linings. They're so few and far between that you just let yourself enjoy them.

I knew I'd have some time at home alone before I saw them, though, because Mom and Dad were always busy on Sunday mornings. Mom went to church — Catholic Mass — followed by lunch with Aunt Denise someplace with a salad bar and popcorn shrimp. Dad's version of church was an hour or two at the nearest AA meeting and all-you-can-eat pancakes at Maple Mabel's, followed by bowling or darts with some people he just referred to as "the guys I work with at Chrysler."

Now, before you go assuming, I should say that my dad wasn't an alcoholic. That's not me being naive or anything, either. I mean, he drank beer, but he'd have, like, a few watching a Tigers game on TV one day and then none for six months after that. Alcohol had never been his thing or his escape, not even after The Bad Thing That Happened or all I had put him through since.

He explained to me once that he went to AA because that was the only place he could find "real" people. No one there pretended that their lives weren't screwed up. He never felt judged—not for The Bad Thing That Happened or for what I went through because of it—and he'd never found a church he could say the same about.

Neither Mom nor Dad invited me along on Sunday mornings, which was fine, because I understood this was their time. When you were the parent of a kid as screwed up as I was, time away from me was imperative for your own mental health.

I was in the living room, working on homework and waiting for their return, when I heard the distinct reverberations of a familiar guitar intro, followed by a singer loudly demanding, "What's the frequency, Kenneth?"

I got up and went to the front porch.

A black Accord was parked on my street, a few houses down. I walked over and leaned in the open passenger window.

"This is a great song."

"You seem to think so," Baby said. She appeared to be less angry than when she'd stormed out of work. Not much less, but some.

"In all fairness, you've only ridden with me once, so your knowledge of my musical tastes is limited."

Baby smirked. "Yeah, but then later that day, you drove down my street blaring it out your windows like the alternative ice cream truck, so it seems like a pattern."

I froze. I didn't know she'd seen (and heard) me checking up on her. It had been weeks ago, and she'd never brought it up. "Sorry about that."

"For what? Stalking me?"

"I wasn't stalking. I was . . . concerned. I wanted to make sure you made it home OK."

"Of course you did." Baby ran her hand through her hair. "Since you're such a goddamn perfect upstanding citizen and all."

"What are you talking about?"

Baby stared at me, straight-faced. "You stayed with me while I puked in the parking lot, you chauffeured me to get an abortion — of course you're going to check up on me. That's who you are, Solo. You're the hero, and I'm forever the weak little damsel in distress." She made a disgusted face.

No one had ever called me a hero before (non-sarcastically, at least) but I refused to ignore Baby's bigger point. "I don't see you that way at all."

"Whatever. It feels accurate lately. And god, now you're my fucking boss, too." Baby put her head on the steering wheel. "This can't get worse."

"Congratulations accepted," I told her. "Thanks for believing in me."

Baby groaned. Then she looked at me and asked, "Wanna go for a ride?"

The invitation both surprised and excited me. It wasn't every day (or any day) that I got invited to hang out with someone other than my parents.

"Seriously?" I asked, but I was already getting into the car before she could renege on the offer.

Baby put the Accord in drive, and away we went.

"So how'd you know where I live? Did you look up all the Teagues in the phone book and drive by their houses until you found my car in a driveway?" I asked her.

Baby huffed a laugh. "Um, no. I got your address off your rental account at work." She paused. "Wait—is that how *you* found *my* house? You really are a stalker after all."

I realized too late how not Normal my method sounded out loud. "A hero does what he has to do when a damsel is in distress" was how I played it off.

Baby shot me a dirty look, and then "What's the Frequency, Kenneth?" faded out and the second track on *Monster* started to play.

I changed the subject. "Oh, you have this CD, too?"

She narrowed her eyes. "You mean until right now, you thought 'What's the Frequency, Kenneth?' just happened to be playing on the radio at the exact moment I parked in front of your house?" she scoffed. "Seriously, Solo. The universe would not orchestrate such a convenience for you, even if you are, like, the Doogie Howser of the video store corporate ladder."

I laughed. "Honestly, I don't even know what a shift manager does. I'll probably get demoted in no time."

"Whatever. Scarlet had that job before she was manager, and if she can do it, anyone can. Once her parents fired Indy, they didn't trust anyone else to be in charge, so they just eliminated the shift manager position altogether," Baby explained. "Until now, apparently."

"Am I supposed to know why Indy got fired?" I asked. "Because I don't."

Baby steered the car with her knees while she put her hair up into a ponytail. "It's not a secret or anything. Indy did something *colossally* stupid." She paused. "You know that FBI warning that plays at the beginning of videos? The one that warns against duplicating and redistributing movies at the risk of five years in prison or a two hundred and fifty thousand dollar fine?" she asked me.

This title card was at the beginning of every movie ever rented, so yes, I was familiar with it. "Sure."

"Turns out that's a real threat. Indy was dubbing new releases and selling them. Eventually someone narced on him to the cops. He got arrested at the store." She stopped at a red light and looked at me. "It was pretty dramatic."

Having first met the guy in a back-alley parking lot in the middle of the night, I was less surprised than someone else might have been that he was this kind of criminal. "It sounds like it."

"Obviously he got fired. There were supposed to be court appearances, too. But then he up and joined the army, and the charges somehow got dropped."

"So is that what broke you guys up?"

My question hung in the air for a minute, and I wondered if I'd crossed a line.

Eventually, though, she answered. "Indy wasn't really ever my boyfriend. I mean, obviously we were *together*. Just not in any official capacity. It wasn't like what Scarlet accused me of, though. I didn't just, like, throw myself at him." She flipped the turn signal. "But whatever. I'm over it."

Baby didn't necessarily sound over it, but she did sound finished talking about it.

"So when do I get to hear about *your* sordid past, Mr. Childhood Anemia Video Store Prodigy? You must have one."

I turned my eyes to the road. "Must I?"

"Sure," she insisted. "Everyone does."

I thought for a minute. "Well, I did run a speakeasy in Detroit during Prohibition, but there's a gag order on the case, so I can't say much."

Baby rolled her eyes but also smiled, so it felt like a win. "Who says stuff like that?"

People with Something Wrong With Them say stuff like that all the time. It's how they avoid talking about What Is Wrong.

"So where are we going?" I asked, veering the subject away from me.

"I'm hungry," she said, and then she turned the music up.

After a few more miles, Baby pulled into the shared driveway of an Applebee's and Headlights, a little place known as "Hooters, but with cars." To my surprise, she parked next to the front door of the latter.

"You like boobs, right?"

I shot her a look. "Is that why we're here?"

"No. We're here to eat."

"Why?"

"I told you. I'm hungry."

She got out of the car.

I hesitantly followed her. "For the record, I've never been here," I felt the need to clarify.

"Really? I come here all the time," she said, and held the door open for me.

It was true that I'd never been to Headlights, but I'd heard a lot about it. Even having spent the better part of my postpubescent life in a psych hospital, its reputation had reached me. The building used to be a full-service filling station in the fifties. It was then left vacant for decades, until someone had turned it into a bar and wings place. The new owner kept the mechanic vibe (gas pumps, tool boxes, stacks of tires for decoration) but cleaned it up nice. Still, everyone knew that the true draw of the restaurant was the waitresses—hot women who dressed like pinup models from the calendars you'd see hanging in old garages. A restaurant like that could probably work anywhere in the world, but since Detroit was Motor City, a place where women and cars were lusted after equally, Headlights was practically a landmark.

I won't pretend I was against eating at a place like this because, truth be told, I'd been wanting to see it for myself for years. I just figured that when I finally did, I'd be with my guy friends (assuming I eventually made some) and not a female coworker.

I sat in the foyer while Baby talked to the hostess, a woman dressed like Rosie the Riveter if Rosie the Riveter had been an enthusiastic proponent of cleavage. The ambiance of the restaurant was less skeezy than I'd expected. There were neon signs and old car advertisements on the walls. A jukebox shaped like the grille of a fifty-seven Chevy was pumping out a Bob Seger song. I thought the place was pretty cool (except for the Bob Seger song), and I wasn't even a car guy.

Baby took a seat next to me. "They're getting my table ready."

"You have a table here?"

"This is practically the only place I'll eat." Baby stretched her legs out over the bench seat in the waiting area like she owned the joint. "I asked for the manager so I could tell her about your promotion. We'll see about getting some waitresses to sit on your lap since you're such an important guy."

"You did what, now?" I stared at Baby, dumbfounded. "Please tell me you're kidding."

Baby smiled, crescent and all. "Here she comes."

A woman appeared next to the hostess stand. She was tall and thin and wore a low-cut jumpsuit made to look like mechanic's coveralls. She made eye contact with Baby and walked over to us.

"Hey, Nikki!" The woman was older than us for sure, but not old.

She had dark hair and eyes and wore makeup like a model. A name patch stitched onto her suit read: KAT, MANAGER. "How'd your meeting go this morning?"

"Bimbo Barbie pissed me off, so I left early," Baby explained to the woman she clearly knew on more than a customer level.

"You shouldn't call her that—it's catty" was Kat's reply.

"Whatever. You just want me to be nice to Scarlet so you can borrow her clothes." Baby rolled her eyes. "Can we eat?"

"Of course." Kat nodded and smiled a crescent smile of her own. "Aren't you going to introduce me first?"

"Solo, this is Kat. Kat, Solo," Baby muttered. "Is our table ready?"

Kat gave Baby a look, then turned to me. "I swear I taught her better than that." She extended her hand to me. "I'm Kat, Nikki's mom."

I must have blinked five times before this sank in. Nikki's mom = Baby's mom. *Kat was Baby's mother.* "Hi. I'm Solo—I mean, Joel. Joel Teague. I work with Baby. I mean, Nikki." I pointed at Baby. "Her."

"He's my boss," Baby informed her.

This appeared to confuse Kat. "I thought Bimbo Barbie was your boss?"

"As of this morning, they both are." Baby's smile was plastic.

Kat looked at me, and I said, "Please don't make the waitresses sit on my lap," because I'm a grade-A moron.

"Ignore him, he has low iron in his blood," Baby said, then repeated, "Is our table ready?"

"Should be by now." Kat brushed a strand of Baby's hair that had escaped her ponytail out of her face. "Have a seat, and I'll bring some wings and fries out."

"And Cokes," Baby added.

Kat nodded and walked toward the kitchen.

I followed Baby to a booth just past the jukebox.

"So I guess I'm meeting your mom today," I said along the way.

"The things I do to eat for free" was Baby's reply. "I guess now is when you say how hot she is and how she looks young enough to be my sister."

"I wasn't going to say any of that." I was thinking it, sure, but I never would've said it.

"She had me when she was sixteen." Baby clicked her tongue. "I'm a bastard. Never even met the guy who knocked her up."

She said this like she thought it might shock me, but it didn't. After years in and out of the psych ward, I was hard to scandalize. "She seems pretty cool, though."

"She's Scarlet, fast-forward a few years" was Baby's response. "You know, she's worked here since I was two and a half. Can you imagine still working at ROYO Video fifteen years from now? The mere thought makes me itch."

"She must like it, though, right?" I asked as we sat down.

"I guess. She makes good money. Of course, that's mainly because she's hot and has a nice rack. That won't last forever."

There is literally no right way to respond when someone makes this observation about her own mother, so I let her keep talking.

"I guess I shouldn't knock it, though. Her boobs are going to put me through college." She took down her hair and ran her hand through it. "What schools are you applying to, Solo?"

"I haven't really thought about it."

Baby arched her eyebrows. "Aren't you a senior?"

A waitress set two cups of soda and two straws on our table. I tore off the paper, dropped the straw into my drink, and let it bob up and down a few times before answering her. "Basically."

"What? The anemia thing put you behind in school?"

"Maybe."

"So, like, were you hospitalized?"

"Yup."

"What was that like?"

"Sucked."

"So then what happened? You missed too much school and got held back? Had to quit to get your GED?"

I took a drink. I'd never had to navigate a conversation about this topic with someone who didn't know What Was Wrong With Me. I was answering all her questions honestly, but I still felt like a liar. "I'm on track to graduate in May. I just don't know what happens after that."

"Well, you won't get into college if you don't apply anywhere," she pointed out.

I sipped my soda. "Where do you wanna go?"

Baby looked away. "The plan was Sarah Lawrence. You ever heard of it?"

I hadn't.

"It's in New York," she informed me. "I've never lived outside of Michigan. Have you?"

I paused. "I used to live in Virginia," I said, and it felt really weird to reveal this. It was information I usually didn't share with people, both because no one other than my shrinks asked me personal stuff and because the answer felt lacking in context. Baby didn't know about The Bad Thing That Happened or What Was Wrong With Me, and my life in Virginia was impossible to talk about without those two things.

"I've never even *been* to Virginia" was her reply, and somehow I was relieved, as though she would've automatically known my whole history if she'd ever traveled within Virginia state lines. "Do you want to go to college back there?"

"No," I answered immediately. "I'll probably just stick around here." I'd never considered going away to college, probably because I knew how my parents would react if I tried.

"And I'll probably get *stuck* around here." She frowned.

This sounded like a loaded statement, but before she could elaborate, Kat brought out our food.

"So Joel," she said, easing into the seat next to me and poaching a fry from my plate. "Tell me about yourself."

Baby shot her a look. "He's not going to tip you, so you don't have to flirt with him."

"Who's flirting?" Kat held up her hand and pointed at a ring. "I'm an engaged woman."

"Don't remind me," Baby said.

Kat propped her head up with her hand. "Did Nikki mention I'm marrying Bob? He owns the restaurant."

"Congratulations."

"It only took ten years to get him to leave his wife for you," Baby added.

Kat shook her head but seemed unfazed by her daughter. "I'm sure you're aware of Nicole's sense of humor, so I won't bother explaining how none of that is true." She took a drink of Baby's soda. "So tell me about this promotion, Joel. Are they finally filling the spot left by that last guy? The one who got arrested? I don't remember his name."

"I don't really know much about it, but I guess it's Indiana Jones's old job."

Baby sighed impatiently, but Kat ignored her. "That's right, *Indiana Jones*." She sipped from Baby's cup again. "So what's *your* name at work?"

"Han Solo."

She laughed. "Does every guy name himself after Harrison Ford?" Until that moment, I hadn't made the connection. "Or is it just the cute ones?"

As someone who'd often been called "cute" in an endearing way by psych nurses, it didn't bother me that Kat had just referred to me as such. However, it struck a raw nerve with Baby.

"Mom, I didn't bring him here so you could hit on him!" Baby yelled at Kat.

"All right, hon. I'll leave you two alone." Kat winked at me and touched Baby's cheek. "I'll be around if you need anything." She stood up and walked over to another table, put her hands on her hips, and started chatting up two guys in business suits.

"She's so embarrassing," Baby said once Kat had left.

"She seems cool to me," I said, biting into a wing.

"Of course she does." Baby narrowed her eyes.

"C'mon. I'll bet she's a fun mom."

"Yeah, super fun." Baby rolled her eyes. "I was the only kindergartner whose mother wasn't old enough to drink, and I'll be the only senior with a mom who could still get voted prom queen. I'm living every girl's dream."

I could have responded to this with something negative about my mother as a way of guilting Baby into appreciating how good she had it. But therapy had taught me that interrupting someone's pity party to throw one for yourself didn't help anyone appreciate anything, so I just kept eating and let Baby talk.

"I have to be in the wedding. Like, I have to wear a bridesmaid dress and walk down the aisle in front of everyone. The guy she's marrying has been divorced for, like, five seconds, and he's twelve years older than Kat, so basically she's his midlife crisis." Baby took a drink. "Also his last name has ten letters and only one vowel—*Przybylski*. It bugs me."

"Yeah. Never trust a guy with a really high consonant-to-vowel ratio," I agreed.

She half smiled. "Teague's got, what? Like four vowels in one syllable? What does that say about you?"

"I'm highly trustworthy," I concluded. "Based on the logic we're making up."

On the jukebox, Journey's "Don't Stop Believin'" faded out, and a new song started to play. When I heard the first note, I almost choked on my chicken wing.

Baby noticed. "Something wrong?"

"No." I shook my head, but it was an obvious lie.

"Seriously, what's up?"

My heart was starting to race. "Nothing. Just . . . did you see who played this song?"

"No," Baby answered. "Why?"

I looked around the room as the musical intro built. "Do you see a girl anywhere?"

Baby hesitated, then quickly scanned the room. "Could you be any more vague? What does she look like?"

Headlights was busy, but most of the people there were men and much older than I was. I couldn't see the entire restaurant from our booth, though, so I stood up for a better view.

She's not here, I told myself. *It's a popular song. Anyone could have played it. Not just her . . .*

But then, just as Jon Bon Jovi belted out the first line of "Livin' on a Prayer," my eyes found a brunette standing next to a table with her back to me, her hair pulled into a bun on the top of her head, and my heart stopped.

It was her.

"I'll be right back," I told Baby over my shoulder, and I made a beeline for Crystal.

* * *

I couldn't sleep. It was too cold.

It was my first winter in Michigan—or at least it would be in about a month. Technically it was still fall, but it had already snowed.

My parents had given me the upstairs bedroom. "Heat rises," they told me. "You'll have the warmest room in the house."

Not true.

I pulled my comforter over my head and shivered. I could've put on a pair of sweatpants, but it would've taken forever to regain the heat loss of getting out of bed now, even if I returned in warmer clothes.

I decided to try sleeping with the blanket over my head to warm me up, but a few seconds later, I shivered again. This time, though, it was because I was scared.

"Hey!" a voice whispered. "Hey! Joel!"

Terrified, I lay completely still.

"Hey, kiddo. It's Crystal. Scooch over."

I pulled the covers down. "Crystal!"

There she was, next to my bed.

"Hi, Joel!" She hugged me. "I've missed you so much!"

I hadn't seen her since the move. I'd thought she'd stayed behind after all.

"What took you so long to get here?" I demanded, hugging her back. "I didn't think you were coming!"

"I said I would, didn't I?" She pulled away and tousled my hair. "Did you get bigger while I was away?"

"Probably," I told her. "It's been forever."

"I know. I'm sorry. I'm here now, though!" She smiled.

A weight was lifting off of me. Michigan had been so lonely. I'd been feeling quiet, and kids think that means you're a snob even if you're really just sad.

"I saved some room for your stuff," I informed her. "C'mon. I'll show you!"

I got out of bed, and Crystal followed me to my closet. I pushed some hanging clothes out of the way and revealed a drawer that was built into the wall. "Your stuff should be safe in here."

"You're so thoughtful," she said, smiling at me.

I pulled the drawer open. "Your shoebox is already in here. And I got you some makeup and earrings."

"Really?" She peered inside. "Where did you find those things?"

"I bought them. With my allowance."

Crystal tensed. "Do your parents know?"

"They don't," I assured her. "I ride my bike to the store alone, and I tell the cashiers the stuff is for my girlfriend."

Crystal's eyes narrowed. "Girlfriend? Is that how you think of me?"

"Ew! No!"

She hesitated. "Well, then, how do you think of me?"

I considered this. "I'm not really sure," I admitted. Then I tried to put into words something I'd been trying to figure out since the last time I saw her. "I think of you as mine, I guess."

"Yours?"

"Yeah. Like, people always say 'my cousin' or 'my friend.' I don't really know what you are, but it feels like you're my something."

She looked like she didn't know what to say, so I changed the subject.

"I was going to buy you another tape," I informed her. "But I'm not going to waste my money on Bon Jovi, so you're going to have to tell me another band you like."

"But Bon Jovi is my favorite!" Crystal laughed. She took my hand and rubbed my thumbnail.

"I'm so glad you're here," I told her. It felt good to say it. "I missed you."

"I missed you every single day," she told me. "You should get some sleep."

We closed the drawer and tiptoed out of the closet.

Then Crystal climbed into bed with me, and together we went right to sleep.

I stormed across the restaurant and swung Crystal around by her elbow. "What are you doing here?"

My resolve instantly faded; the woman staring bewilderedly back at me was *not* Crystal.

"Excuse me, honey?" She was just a waitress taking the order of two men sitting in a booth.

"Do you know this guy, Tiffany?" one of them asked her.

The other one stood up so we were eye to eye and glared at me.

"I'm sorry. I thought she was someone else." I apologized to the man, then to the waitress. "I'm sorry."

She forced a smile to defuse the situation. "It happens all the time. I just have one of those faces," she told me, knowing very well that I hadn't identified her by her face. Then she squeezed the biceps of the standing man and said, "I know who I want around if I'm ever in real trouble."

They exchanged flirty smiles, and he returned to his seat.

I started backing away from their table. Bon Jovi was still screaming his lungs out behind me.

I searched the entire restaurant, looking under tables, behind columns, in the bathroom—but I couldn't find Crystal anywhere. She was gone.

Or, I tried telling myself, she was never there to begin with. Just like she wasn't in the ROYO Video parking lot that night I'd met Indy. Or, according to many doctors, just like she wasn't anywhere, because she didn't really exist.

It was a good thing I didn't find her, I reminded myself. If she were there, it would mean there was Something Wrong With Me again, and I was really enjoying life as a Normal person. Normal life trumped life with Crystal. It had to.

I returned to the table where Baby was sitting.

She stared at me.

I took a drink of soda. "What were you saying?"

Baby didn't blink for a solid minute. "What the literal fuck was that all about, Solo?"

I tried to shrug her off. "I thought I saw a girl I knew."

"Who?"

"It's complicated."

Baby did not like this answer. "I'm starting to think *you're* complicated."

As much as I wanted to, I couldn't argue with that. And as much as I didn't want it to be true, I was pretty sure I'd just fucked up my tabula rasa.

Baby and I finished our meal in silence, and then Michael Stipe sang us all the way back to my house without interruption. I spent the entire ride searching for a way to explain my behavior to Baby without having to tell her about What Was Wrong With Me.

"I'm sorry if that was weird for you at the restaurant," I said as she pulled up in front of my house. "I wouldn't call my past sordid, but there was a girl in it. She's not anymore, and sometimes that's hard for me."

She stopped the car and killed the radio. "It feels like there's a lot

99

missing from that story."

I stared at her. I didn't know what to say.

"Well? Aren't you going to fill me in?"

"No," I said flatly. "I'm not."

Baby's eyes widened. She hadn't been expecting that answer, I guess. "Seriously, Solo? You already know a lot of personal stuff about me, and I know dick about you. That's not fair. How are we supposed to be friends if I don't know anything about you?"

I didn't really have a defense for this. The thing was, I completely understood why she was getting pissed. But what she couldn't understand was that What Was Wrong With Me was not your run-of-the-mill secret. If Baby knew the truth, she probably wouldn't talk to me ever again. There are certain kinds of crazy that Normal people want nothing to do with, and What Was Wrong With Me scored way off that chart.

I was finally Normal. I was trying out life, and I was getting good at it. I had spent the last nine years wading through The Bad Thing That Happened, and I'd finally laid it to rest. I was the Doogie Howser of the video store corporate ladder, dammit. No one knew about What Was Wrong With Me, and it had to stay that way.

"I don't have anything to say."

Baby pressed a button on her door, and mine unlocked.

"Then neither do I." She nodded at my house. "Go take an iron pill, Solo."

I got out of the car and walked toward the house. By the time I reached my front door, she'd already driven away.

Chapter 9

My parents were downright *giddy* about my promotion. Like, I'm pretty sure my dad teared up when I told him. Mom said something to the effect of "I knew you could do it!" which I doubted was true, but whatever. They were happy, and I was happy they were happy, so it was a real kumbaya moment for the Teague family.

My shrink was happy, too, and OKed me to go a few weeks without seeing him while I adjusted to my new responsibilities. He did warn me not to get too caught up in the "corporate world" and forget to take care of my mental health, though. On the way out of the office, I looked at the "might have been" poster and smiled.

So everything was peachy keen for me at home for the first time in a long while, and I gotta say, that felt pretty damn good.

It turned out that everyone at work got over their righteous indig-nation about my promotion pretty quickly (except for Baby, but we'll get to that), especially when they realized I was a fairly decent dude to work for. Like Scarlet had predicted, not much really changed around ROYO Video. I mean, I guess I was technically now *required* to do most of the heavy lifting I'd already been doing, but that was fine by me. As you know, I liked busywork.

It turned out that I also enjoyed interviewing people for my old job, which is something Scarlet and I did the week after my promo-tion kicked in.

Conducting interviews was a my-how-the-tables-have-turned situation for me, because when you think about it, a job interview is more or less just a mental health evaluation. Truth be told, what an employer is really trying to find out during a job interview is how likely the candidate is to blow up the building. Having had my men-tal stability assessed on many occasions, I felt up to the task of weed-ing out any unstable applicants.

Fortunately, it seemed no obvious psychopaths had applied for the video clerk job, and Scarlet and I narrowed it down to three young hopefuls, each of them seemingly Normal.

We ended up going with a guy named Andres who wanted to be called Maverick—Tom Cruise's character from *Top Gun*, for those of you playing along at home. He'd actually worked at a Blockbuster before, which gave him a clear advantage over the other candi-dates, neither of whom had experience in the field of video rental. Truthfully, though, it was pretty obvious what gave him an edge with Scarlet: Maverick was tall, tan, and looked like a J. Crew model.

Scarlet took the lead during the interview. "So why'd you quit your last video store job?"

"I just worked there the summers I stayed with my grandma in Puerto Rico," answered the future Maverick.

She jotted down a note on his application. "I didn't even know they had Blockbusters in Mexico!"

Maverick glanced from Scarlet to me, and because I felt obligated to let him know that at least one of his potential bosses knew as much, I interjected, "Puerto Rico is not part of Mexico, Scarlet."

She was unfazed by this correction. "Oh, does that mean you don't speak Mexican, then? We sometimes get customers who do, and it'd be nice if we had someone who could talk to them."

Maverick looked at me again, and I shook my head apologetically.

"Eres pendeja," he answered with a smile. "That means yes, I speak Mexican."

I could tell that wasn't really what it meant. I also had a feeling he would fit in at ROYO Video just fine. Especially with Baby.

I asked Baby to show Maverick the ropes like she'd done for me, which in retrospect was probably not the best way to broach that subject.

"Why? So he can be my boss in a week, too?" she asked. "What's my incentive to train anyone ever again, Solo?"

She had a valid point, but I chose not to acknowledge it.

"Don't you want to make your future bosses look good?" was my answer instead, and let me tell you, Baby did not appreciate that joke.

In fact, after that day at Headlights, Baby didn't seem to appreciate me much at all. She started to treat me the way she did everyone else, and I hadn't realized just how differently that was until I'd lost her favor.

Baby no longer rented movies for us to discuss. We no longer discussed anything at all, really. She was quieter altogether post-Headlights. Withdrawn, even (to use a therapy term). She came to work, did her job, and left. Other than that, I didn't see or hear from her.

Well, I guess I can't say I didn't hear from her. There was one thing I heard about very loudly.

It was a payday in October, and everyone stopped by the store to grab their checks. This week, though, in the envelopes along with our paychecks was a memo about the trick-or-treat event that the Royal Oak Chamber of Commerce was putting on the Saturday before Halloween, an event that suddenly mandated our participation.

"We have to wear costumes?" Hannibal asked.

"Yes. It's absolutely required," Scarlet informed him a little too excitedly. "We're all going to dress up as the characters whose names we go by at work. My parents are positive that customers will *love* this idea!"

Hannibal looked confused. "Your parents legit want me to come to work as a serial killer who eats people?"

"Well, it *is* Halloween" was her answer. "It'll be fun!"

"I approve," The Godfather said, but likely only because she dressed like a gangster every day and would have to put zero effort into her costume.

"I only have a week to put together a Mary Poppins costume?" Poppins sighed, but it was clear she loved the idea. "This should be interesting."

Dirty Harry was less enthused. "If Mom wants me to do this, she'd better make my Bigfoot costume. Otherwise forget it."

"What do you need a Bigfoot costume for?" Hannibal asked, which was the same thing I was wondering.

"Haven't you seen *Harry and the Hendersons*?" was Dirty's condescending response. "Dirty Harry is Bigfoot."

"I *have* seen *Harry and the Hendersons*. But I've also seen *Dirty Harry*," Hannibal explained slowly. "Only one of those movies has a character named Dirty Harry in it, my friend. And it's not the one with the Sasquatch."

"Dirty Harry is a badass cop from the seventies." Maverick, who was only one week into his job and already aware of what a dipshit Scarlet's little brother was, piggybacked off what Hannibal had said. "Literally everyone knows that."

"Whatever. No, he's not," Dirty argued.

"Yes, he is," Poppins, The Godfather, and I all confirmed in unison.

"Fine, so what if he is? Who fucking cares?" Dirty decided. "The point is, my mom better make me a Bigfoot costume."

"Oh my god, you're such a moron," Scarlet muttered.

"Oh, c'mon. Like *you* knew who Dirty Harry was," he replied. "And don't pretend this whole costume thing wasn't your idea. I heard you begging Mom to do it because you wanted to wear some slutty dress you found at the Halloween store at the mall."

Scarlet glared at her brother, which made it pretty obvious he was telling the truth. "Shut up, Scott. This is what we're doing, and it's not up for discussion!"

At this, we accepted our Halloween costume fate, and everyone left or went back to work while Dirty presumably ran home to complain to his mommy.

Baby was the only one who stayed put, willing to fight the battle. "This is fucking ridiculous, and I'm not doing it."

Scarlet ignored her indignation and started to walk away. "Yes, you are."

Baby stepped in front of her. "Dressing up for Halloween is against my religion. So I'm not going to."

Scarlet folded her arms across her chest. "Whatever, Baby. You don't even have a religion."

"You don't know that."

"Fine. What religion are you?" Scarlet demanded.

"I don't have to answer that," Baby responded. "It's an illegal question."

"No, it's not."

"Have you ever heard of the Civil Rights Act?" Baby asked, knowing for certain that Scarlet hadn't. "I could sue you for asking me that."

Scarlet rolled her eyes before looking to me. "You handle this, Solo."

I looked at Baby and then back at Scarlet. "How?"

"You're her boss, too," she reminded me. "Tell her she has to wear what we tell her to."

Baby's eyes widened. Mine did, too.

"I honestly don't think we can tell her that," I said in a lowered voice. "I think Baby's right about it being illegal."

Scarlet looked at me innocently. "So you're taking her side?" Then she leaned in close to me and whispered in my ear, "C'mon, Solo. This really means a lot to me."

Have I ever told you how amazing Scarlet smelled? I mean, I'm pretty sure I have, but it bears repeating. And did I mention she was wearing a plaid skirt that day? Like, the Catholic school uniform kind, only way shorter.

I looked at Scarlet and then at Baby.

Finally I said (and I get if you hate me for it), "C'mon, Baby. What's the big deal?"

The look on her face said "Judas!" but her mouth said, "You can both go to hell." She turned on her heel and stomped off down the hallway and out the door.

Scarlet bounced up and down, gloating. "This is going to be so much fun!"

"Honestly, I'm with Baby on this one," I revealed, albeit too late to score any points with Baby. "I don't really want to dress up, either."

"Trust me, it's going to be great! I can't wait to see what a hot

Hans Solo you make." She winked at me. "And I think you'll really like my costume, too."

I suddenly remembered how Baby had described Vivien Leigh on the *Gone with the Wind* poster.

"Well, I guess if it's going to be good for business . . ."

Scarlet beamed before walking away. "Oh, trust me. It'll be an unforgettable day."

Chapter 10

Our basement was of the unfinished storage room variety, lit only by the gloom of unshaded lightbulbs. It was always cold, dank, and inhabited by hosts of centipedes. I avoided the basement at all costs, but the atmosphere I'm describing wasn't the only reason why. Mostly I stayed out because that was the place we hid the tangible reminders of life before The Bad Thing That Happened, and obviously it was hard to think about that.

But there was other stuff in the basement, too. A lot of Mom and Dad's old junk had been in our Virginia attic for years before the move, and when we schlepped it up to Michigan, it stayed in boxes. I'm talking about things like high school yearbooks, old clothes, and records—you know, the stuff destined for a garage sale. Also, I hoped, the stuff destined to become a Han Solo Halloween costume.

Han Solo's wardrobe was neither flashy nor complicated, for the most part. Pants, jackets, vests, all in regular men's clothing colors. If the Force was with me on this, I would have what I needed and be back upstairs in no time.

I avoided the boxes labeled BAT and sifted through polyester shirts, bell-bottoms, and one unfortunate ruffled cummerbund (seriously, Dad?) located in boxes labeled CRAIG'S CLOTHES. I managed to rummage up an old fishing vest, navy slacks, and a cream-colored button-down shirt with a butterfly collar, which was really all I needed to make my costume.

As I was returning what I didn't need to the boxes, I noticed another stack labeled TOYS shoved over in the corner.

Suddenly I remembered the blaster.

We'd had the official Star Wars licensed one back in Virginia. I could picture it perfectly—black molded plastic with a yellow drill-like twisting mechanism inside. It was my most treasured toy from all my childhood. I had no idea if we still had it, but if we did, it would make the perfect accessory for a Han Solo costume.

I removed the lid from the first box of toys and began searching.

It contained only *Masters of the Universe* action figures and the Fireball Island board game. The second box was full of G.I. Joes and Transformers. I resisted the impulse to reminisce about these toys, lest doing so bring up other memories, too. Plus I was freezing and had already killed four centipedes.

My blaster hopes fading fast, I tried the last TOYS box. I knew it was a long shot that my mom would have held on to anything to do with Star Wars (stay tuned for more on that), so I wasn't surprised when the box was filled with other things. I was, however, surprised by what those things were.

Dolls. Purses. A toy ceramic tea set. Wonder Woman posters.

I had no memory of any of this stuff.

I looked inside the box again. These things couldn't have belonged to my mother. I mean, the dolls seemed old, I guess, but not, like, *my mom* old. The purses could've been hers, but I wasn't convinced they were.

It was weird. As far as I could tell, these boxes had been in the basement unopened, like the others, since Virginia. The only girl cousins I had were born in Virginia after that, so it wasn't like these things could have been theirs. I was stumped.

Until I wasn't.

Crystal. These were Crystal's things.

It made sense, and it didn't. I mean, who else could it all have belonged to? But also, everything that Crystal had owned was stuff I bought for her, and I'd sure as hell never seen any of this before.

Then I remembered the shoebox.

It had just appeared one day, too. I hadn't had anything to do with it.

Maybe that was happening again.

About six months after Crystal arrived in Michigan, Mom went through my room and discovered Crystal's cache in my closet.

I had barely walked through the door after school that day before the shit hit the fan.

"What the hell is this, Joel?" Mom demanded as I stood in the doorway, my hand still on the knob. She held up Crystal's green dress. She was crying.

The entire scene caught me off guard. "Did you go through my closet?"

"I absolutely did," Mom said. "I found your jewelry and makeup, too." She puffed on her cigarette and wiped a tear away with the back of her hand. "So you're into this? This is what you do when you're alone in your room?"

I knew enough to be alarmed by my mom's tone even though I didn't know exactly why she was reacting so strongly. "What do you mean?"

"You wear these things." She was yelling now. "You pretend to be a girl."

The accusation was so ludicrous, I actually laughed. "No. Why would I do that?"

"Stop lying!" my mother screamed, and she threw the dress at me. I dropped my backpack and caught it. "You have to tell me the truth! I won't be lied to about *this*!"

"God, Mom! I'm not dressing up like a girl. Calm down!" My confusion about the accusation gave way to anger. "Why are you going through my things, anyway?"

"So they *are* yours?"

"No, but they were in *my* room."

"Don't lie to me! I know what you do! I know you paint your fingernails! Your dad told me to leave you alone about it. That it's just a phase. That you're just trying to cope with everything. But now I see what's happening. You're sick, Joel! Something's the matter with you! Something deep inside of you is seriously screwed up!" She sobbed uncontrollably.

I was shocked. I couldn't believe she was saying these things. I didn't think moms were allowed to say those kinds of things to their own kids.

"There's nothing wrong with me!" I yelled back at her. "I am just a Normal kid! I swear, Mom!"

"Normal boys don't hide makeup and jewelry in their closets, Joel!" she screamed at me. "Normal boys hide the goddamn Victoria's Secret catalog!"

Hot tears sprung into my eyes. "Leave me alone," I growled at her. "Just leave me the hell alone!" I took Crystal's dress and

111

stormed outside, got on my bike, and rode away as fast as I could.

I was so angry. The angriest I had ever been in my entire life.

I rode fast and far. So far that I didn't know exactly where I was when I finally stopped a long time later.

I had ended up at a park somewhere, with a playground and benches and a bridge overlooking a pond. I threw my bike down on the ground and ran toward the water.

It was April, I think. Still cold, though. The world was only half thawed from the longest winter I'd ever known. The playground was empty, and I was alone.

I walked along the water's edge, my shoes sinking into the muddy shoreline. With each step, I felt water seep into my shoes.

"You're a son of a bitch, Mom," I muttered under my breath. "You're the one who's screwed up. Not me." I picked up a stone and threw it into the water.

Then I did it again. And again.

By the time I was done, I must have thrown fifty rocks into that pond. I might have thrown fifty more if I hadn't seen something splashing around in the water.

I was near the bridge, and I ran halfway across for a closer look.

The commotion stopped, and I could see something floating on the surface of the water. It looked like seaweed at first. Or pondweed, if there's a difference. But on second glance, it seemed to be moving.

Was it . . . hair?

I peered down into the water and saw Crystal's face staring back at me.

Her eyes were open, and a small trail of bubbles leaked from one nostril. She was squirming as if she was stuck, unable to come up for air.

"Hey!" I yelled to her, my heart racing. "Hey! I see you!" I dropped the rocks and banged my hands on the railing to keep her attention. "Crystal, I'm coming! Hang on!"

I pulled off my jacket and shoes and jumped off the bridge feet-first into the pond.

The water was freezing and made my entire body seize. The splash stirred up a murky cloud from the pond floor, making it difficult to see. My eyes burned as I attempted to locate Crystal under the water, but I kept them open anyway. I had to find her.

Minutes that felt like hours ticked by with no sign of her, and then finally I came up for air, and I caught a blurry glimpse of Crystal — not in the water, but sitting up on the bridge with her legs dangling over, dry as a bone in her green dress.

I was so relieved, I started to cry.

Exhausted, I struggled to shore and ran to the bridge, shivering and sobbing all the way.

"What's wrong, Joel?" was Crystal's concerned greeting when I'd sloshed my way over to her.

It took me forever to catch my breath. "I thought you were drowning," I finally managed to get out. "I was so worried!"

She touched my face. "I'm right here, Joel."

"I didn't think I'd ever see you again!" I was crying so hard that I don't know how she understood me, but she did.

"I'm sorry you were scared. Thank you for wanting to help me, Joel." Crystal put her arm around me and squeezed. Then she rubbed her finger over my thumbnail in a circular motion and whispered, "Seashells."

This calmed me down.

"My mom found your things," I confessed. "She was really mad."

Crystal stared into the water and nodded. "Did you tell her they were mine?"

"Of course not," I scoffed. "I don't think she's gonna give them back, though."

"That's OK." She smiled. "I've still got my dress."

I tried to smile back, but my teeth were chattering too hard.

Crystal stood up. "You need to get home, Joel. I know you probably don't want to, but things will be worse if you don't."

"What am I supposed to tell my mom?" I asked. "She doesn't believe me that the makeup and jewelry aren't mine, even though I'm telling her the truth."

Crystal chewed thoughtfully on her lower lip. "That doesn't surprise me." She looked away. "Sometimes when the truth is hard to accept, people prefer a lie."

"So what am I supposed to say? Should I tell her I bought all those things for her? That I wanted it to be a surprise and she ruined it?" I asked. "That might make her feel bad, which is fine. She deserves to feel bad about all this."

"Just tell her whatever it takes to protect yourself, Joel" was Crystal's advice. She sounded really sad when she said it.

I stood up and hugged her for a long time.

Eventually Crystal made me go home, so I got on my bike and started riding back the way I'd come. I didn't exactly remember how I'd gotten there, but I knew I'd find my way somehow.

Within minutes, a police car drove up beside me, and the officer rolled down the window.

"Are you Joel Teague?" he asked me.

I nodded.

He put the car in park and adjusted his hat. "Let me give you a lift home, son. Your parents are awful worried about you."

I took the box of dolls and things down the street to the parking lot of a liquor store. The dumpster behind it was always left open. I tossed the box in and walked back home.

Chapter 11

The day of the Royal Oak trick or treat, I opened the store.

The official start time for the event was two o'clock, so I'm not sure why I went to work at nine in the morning dressed as Han Solo, but that's what I did.

Baby, who was opening, too, brought her costume to work in a bag like a Normal person. She had curled her hair and pinned it up so that it looked something like Jennifer Grey's on the *Dirty Dancing* VHS cover (my only point of reference), but other than that, she still looked like regular Baby.

"You know I had to fucking watch *Dirty Dancing*" was the first thing out of her mouth that morning. She was standing behind the counter, opening bags of candy for the trick-or-treaters and emptying them into a giant pumpkin-shaped dish.

"You could've just looked at the VHS box to find out how Baby dressed," I suggested, though admittedly this was a pointless thing to say after the fact.

She glared at me. "I did, dickhead, but I was hoping the movie contained long scenes of Baby wearing pajamas so I'd have an excuse not to dress up."

"Did it?"

"No," she mumbled. "But there was one part where she carried a watermelon for no goddamn reason." She made a face. "Oh, and a botched abortion. So, you know, that was *great*."

"Seriously?"

"Yes, seriously! But don't worry, boss. I watched it anyway. I didn't want to disobey your orders." She saluted me. "I'll be dressed in my costume at fourteen hundred hours."

I felt like shit. "C'mon, Baby," I sighed. "You know it's not like that."

"It's exactly like that," she snapped back. "You know, it's such a disappointment how damn typical you turned out to be, Solo. You fawn all over Boobs McGee like every other guy in the world. I thought you were better than that." She opened another bag of candy with such force that pieces flew everywhere. "You have to know the only reason you got shift manager over me is that I don't have a dick she can tease, right?"

This struck a raw nerve with me. "So what? So what if I'm like every other guy? I am totally cool with being just like every other guy, Baby." It was basically my dream come true, actually.

Baby didn't disguise her disgust. "Why couldn't you just cut me some slack on this one thing?" She went to run her fingers through her hair, then remembered the curls and stopped. "Why couldn't you trust that I had a good reason for not wanting to dress up?"

116

"I don't know," I said. "I guess because I didn't think it was a big deal."

"But *I* did," she argued. "That should have been enough."

The front door opened, cutting our conversation short. Some kids ran past the counter and straight for the Halloween movie display. "They have it in, Mom!" the boy said, snatching a tag and jumping up and down excitedly. "They have *It's the Great Pumpkin, Charlie Brown!*"

"Good morning!" Baby smiled at the parents as they passed the counter. "Welcome to ROYO Video! Let us know if there's anything we can help you find."

"Thanks," the dad said. Then he pointed at me. "Hey! Nice costume! May the Force be with you."

I smiled and for some reason replied with "And also with you."

When they were out of earshot, Baby turned back to me and muttered, "I don't want a single apology from you today. Remember that. Remember that whatever happens, *you* could have prevented it, so apologies will not be fucking accepted." She shoved the bowl of candy into my arms and stomped off.

I had no idea what this warning meant, but it echoed in my head throughout the morning. Baby didn't strike me as someone who made empty threats, so in whatever way a guy could be sorry for forcing a girl to wear a *Dirty Dancing* costume, I fully expected to be it come two o'clock.

In anticipation of the trick or treat, people flooded downtown Royal Oak early that day, and the store stayed steadily busy — too busy for me to tell Baby about the second (and third and fourth) thoughts I was having about siding with Scarlet. I should've fought for an exception for Baby so she didn't have to dress up. She shouldn't have had to give me a reason. Now that I was away from the kryptonite of Scarlet's miniskirt, it was clear that I'd been a total ass. I wanted to make it right.

"Looking good, my friend," Hannibal greeted me at the start of his shift.

I glanced up from my register. "Thanks," I said. Then I tried to think of a compliment to pay him back. He was wearing an orange prison jumpsuit and a hockey mask cut in half horizontally so that it resembled the thing Hannibal Lecter wore to keep him from biting people. "You look appropriately creepy."

"Mission accomplished" was his reply.

Poppins showed up a few minutes later wearing a white button-down shirt with a red bow tie. Her bowler hat had a feather in it, and she carried an umbrella.

"Do I look practically perfect in every way?" she asked me.

"Sure," I humored her. "Practically."

Minutes later Maverick and The Godfather came down the hall-way together, both having put forth considerable effort on their costumes, too. I mean, The Godfather wasn't dressed much differently than she usually was, but she had added a black bow tie and a rose pinned to her blazer. Her hair was slicked back into a bun like Lilith's from *Frasier*, who also happened to be someone I found very intimidating. Maverick had on a fairly accurate bomber jacket complete with air force patches. But really, on any given day the guy looked enough like a movie star that he could pull off dressing like Tom Cruise unironically.

Baby returned from her break shortly after everyone else arrived, then left again almost immediately to put her costume on. I caught up to her alone in the hallway.

"Hey, Baby. I've been thinking . . . you should go home sick."

She folded her arms across her chest. "Why's that?"

"If you go home, you don't have to wear a costume. And you

won't get any shit from Scarlet about it because I can tell her you had it with you and you were *going* to wear it, but then you started throwing up, so you had to leave."

She looked somewhat amused by this suggestion. "So . . . it's OK to *lie* to Scarlet to get me out of doing this, but it's not OK for me to have a perfectly legitimate yet private reason to not participate?"

"In this case, at this moment, yes," I told her. "I'm just trying to give you an out, Baby." I looked down at her shoes. They were Converse. Green. "Just take it, OK?"

She waited a minute before saying, "OK."

"OK?"

"Yeah. OK."

I breathed a sigh of relief. "Are we good?"

"Yeah, Solo. We're good." Baby forced a non-crescent smile with no satisfying corners and went into the storage closet.

I felt better after this, and with the problem solved, I went back to work.

Kids in costumes had begun trickling into the store, and Poppins was standing near the front door doling out suckers and candy bars.

"Form a line! Spit-spot!" she said in a British accent as I retook my place at the register. "And mind your manners. We are not a codfish!"

Baseball players, fairies, firefighters, and generic monsters fell in line and held out their bags and pillowcases to receive their treats.

With all the extra foot traffic in the store, movies were flying off the shelves, so I wasn't really involved in all the Halloween action. I had to admit, though, that seeing all the kids dressed up made me smile. I hadn't been trick-or-treating since coming to Michigan. After the move, I didn't have anyone to go with, and that's not the kind of thing a kid wants to do alone.

I'd been on autopilot for several customers in a row — scanning their membership cards, retrieving their movies, collecting their money—when the name of a customer popped up on my computer screen and caught my attention.

"Jana Schwartz," I read aloud. "As in Marc Schwartz's wife?"

"Yes," she confirmed, handing me a tag. "Though I'd better not have any late fees on there. My husband shouldn't be renting on my account anymore."

"You don't," I said, and I stepped over to the shelf to find her movie. "And he's not."

I didn't know if Dr. Schwartz had told his wife about me, but I recognized that the potential was there. I mean, it's not like I was so noteworthy a fellow that I thought *everyone* talked about me, but in fairness to Marc, if I had been the doctor who'd had to deal with me after my psych hospital lover attempted death by floor cleaner, I probably would've mentioned it to my wife. And then if I'd run into me years later renting out videos to people like a regular Joe Schmo, I might have also mentioned that to her in a *Where Are They Now?*–type follow-up.

Just in case Jana knew anything about What Was Wrong With Me, I decided to act extra Normal around her.

"Here you go—*The Truth About Cats and Dogs*." I scanned the bar code on the VHS. "You know, 'tis the season to rent something scarier than a rom-com, don't you think?"

OK, so maybe *'tis the season* wasn't super Normal, but I gave myself points for effort.

She grinned. "You're right. I just needed a little fun today. Although *this* is fun," Jana admitted, looking around the room.

"I know, right?" I nodded, making a cool-guy face. "I dig the whole vibe."

"Me too," she agreed casually, and I decided that if she knew anything about me, Jana was good at hiding it. "See that little girl dressed as a pumpkin over there?" She pointed toward the door.

I saw a flash of orange disappear behind a rack. "Yeah. Is she yours?"

"Oh, no," Jana said quickly. "No, I just thought her costume was adorable. I don't have any children."

"Oh, my bad." I'd just assumed she was a mom. All grown-up women I knew were moms.

"Don't worry about it—you didn't know."

"Know what?" I asked.

"Never mind." She picked up her movie. "Thanks for this. And nice costume. It's clever, you all dressing as yourselves. How fun."

"Thanks," I said, no longer making my cool-guy face. Evidently, the more Normal I tried to be, the more awkward I made things for everyone else. "Bring it back tomorrow by seven—I know you don't want a late fee."

Jana nodded and exited the store.

It seemed pointless to try to put tags out with kids blocking all the aisles, so I pulled The Godfather off the floor and put her on my register. I wanted to catch Scarlet before she realized that Baby had gone home, but I hadn't seen her come in yet. I went to the office to check for her.

No Scarlet there. I grabbed a few more bags of candy to refill Poppins's bucket and went back out.

It was then that I ran into Scarlet in the hallway. Literally.

"Sorry!" I apologized automatically before taking a step back. I didn't immediately recognize the person I'd collided with as Scarlet because of the wig she was wearing.

And also the lingerie.

I'm not exactly sure how to describe what Scarlet was wearing, but I'm fairly certain it wasn't an accurate representation of anything

121

featured in *Gone with the Wind*, unless *Gone with the Wind* was a cleverly disguised Civil War–era porno.

She had a green-and-white floppy hat tied under her chin. Her wig was dark brown and curly. My vocabulary is limited when it comes to fashion, so I'm just going to call everything Scarlet had on from the neck down "my wildest fantasy come true." I mean, her outfit was a cross between a bathing suit and whatever ballerinas wear. Her pantyhose (I *do* know what those are) were white, but they stopped at her thighs and were attached to the rest of the ensemble with belty things. She also wore high heels—really tall ones that made her tower over me. In summary, Scarlet looked like a giant layer cake of sex, which is the best kind of cake there is.

She recovered from our collision by holding on to my biceps (I know I could have said arm there, but just let me have this one) to steady herself.

"Hey, Solo. Look at you!" she said, but by the way she propped a hand on her hip, I could tell what she really meant was "Look at me!"

And I *was* looking at her, believe me.

"How are everyone else's costumes?" she asked, peeking around me.

Nothing like yours, I wanted to say. But instead I said, "Fine."

"Yeah?" she asked, then looked directly at me. "Baby's too?"

"Oh, yeah. About Baby . . ." I said, trying to snap out of my sexy-cake fantasy, "I sent her home. She was really sick."

Scarlet's face fell. "Are you serious? She faked sick to get out of wearing a costume? How pathetic."

"No—it was legit. And she didn't want to go. I practically had to force her to leave."

Next to us, the storage closet door suddenly opened. "Dream on, Solo," Baby said casually as she entered the hallway. "Like you could force me to do anything."

If Scarlet's costume had surprised me, then you could have colored me fucking shocked by Baby's.

She was wearing white sneakers (not the shocking part), a pair of jean shorts that ended just above her knees (not the shocking part), and a cropped white shirt (not the shocking part, either). On her bare, exposed, and *very round* stomach, Baby had painted a large green watermelon.

I dropped the bags of candy.

Baby was pregnant. Still.

(OK. Time out for a second.

I know you probably saw this coming. I mean, there were definite signs that Baby hadn't gone through with the abortion. But before you go feeling all high and mighty, just remember that I'm the one telling this story, so it's me you have to thank for those clues. Real life doesn't have a narrator conveniently dropping hints here and there. If that were the case, then maybe The Bad Thing might not have happened and What Was Wrong With Me may never have been. Present day doesn't have the one-linear-event-at-a-time luxury that the past does when we retell it. That's why hindsight is twenty-twenty, why the future is foggy, and why I was blindsided by Baby's revelation.

OK? Good.

Time in.)

"What is that?" Scarlet pointed accusingly at Baby's middle.

"I got fat." Baby shrugged. "I should have thrown up more."

Scarlet stared at her. "You look pregnant."

Baby began a condescending slow clap. "You're a regular Sherlock Holmes, you know that, Scarlet?"

"Baby . . ." was the only word I could say. "Baby . . ."

She turned to me. "I'm sorry—are you saying my name? Or are you talking about *the* baby?" She pointed at her stomach. Then she pretended to laugh. "Just kidding, Solo! You don't even know how long I've been waiting to make that joke! Oh, wait, I could probably tell you." She pretended to count on her fingers. "About twenty-two weeks."

"Stop playing around, Baby!" Scarlet insisted. "Don't you know how serious being pregnant is?"

Baby laughed harder. "I do. The gravity of the situation sank in about four months ago when I pissed on a stick and it turned blue."

"Baby, I am so, so sorry," I told her. It all made sense now why she didn't want to wear a costume. I felt like such an asshole.

She held up her hand. "I told you not to apologize."

I nodded. She had.

Scarlet looked at me wide-eyed. "So it's yours?"

For a moment I'd forgotten she was even there, which again tells you just how shocked I was, considering a sexy layer cake is not something easily pushed from the mind.

I looked from Scarlet to Baby and back again, and I had no idea what to say. I mean, obviously I knew the baby wasn't mine, but for whatever reason, I was ready to claim paternity right then and there if that's what Baby wanted.

But she didn't. "God, no," Baby answered for me. "It's not his, Scarlet. So by all means, you can continue to toy with both Solo's dick and head all you want with no fear of a baby cramping your style." She picked up the bags of candy I'd dropped. "Now, if you'll excuse me, I've got to get to work." Baby turned on her heel and walked away.

"Do you think we should do something?" Scarlet asked me.

"Like what?"

"I don't know. Stop her from telling people?"

"Why?" I asked. "She *is* pregnant, Scarlet. It can't stay a secret forever."

Scarlet shifted her weight. "Well, it's not like she's going keep it, right? What's the point of telling anyone if you're not keeping it?"

"How should I know if she's keeping it? I found out about this at the same time you did."

"She shouldn't keep it," Scarlet immediately decided. "Baby would be a terrible mother."

I glanced at her, then down the hallway toward Baby. "Why would you say that?"

We both watched as she stepped behind the counter and took over a register.

"What? Do you think I'm wrong?" Scarlet asked me back.

"I don't know. What makes someone a good mother?" My eyes were still fixed on Baby.

"Not being in high school, for starters."

A distraught Poppins approached Baby at the counter. I could read her lips—"Is that real?"—as she pointed to Baby's midsection.

"Baby's not going to be in high school forever," I reminded Scarlet.

"So you think she *should* keep it?" Her tone was incredulous.

From behind us, the back door opened and shut, and Dirty Harry stamped his time card.

"What's up, bitches?" he said, interrupting our conversation.

We turned around, and I instantly wanted to punch him in the throat.

Dirty Harry was dressed as neither Bigfoot nor a seventies cop. He was instead dressed head to toe in Nike, just like every other day.

"Where the fuck is your costume?" I demanded, glaring at him.

"Uh, I didn't wear one," he answered.

"Why the hell not?"

He shrugged a shoulder. "I don't know. Didn't feel like it."

"Come on, Scott!" Scarlet scolded him. "Everyone was supposed to dress up!"

He narrowed his eyes at his sister, as though she was the one in the wrong. "So? I didn't want to. Dressing up is gay." Dirty looked at me and indicated my costume. "No offense or anything."

"None taken" was what I said before I said, "You're fired."

He paused a beat before laughing. "You're funny." Then he tried to push by me.

I blocked him. "I know. I'm a *panic*," I agreed. "You're still fired."

Dirty's and Scarlet's eyes grew wide. "What?" they both said.

I glanced back down the hallway, where I saw Baby reaching for a movie behind the counter. When she stretched, her watermelon looked even more pronounced. "You were told to wear a costume for this shift, and you didn't do it. So you're fired."

Dirty smirked at me. "You can't be serious."

"I'm *so* serious."

He looked to Scarlet.

"Your sister already made it clear that I have this authority. As shift manager, I can fire people for insubordination." I used this word because I doubted Dirty Harry knew what it meant, and therefore he wouldn't be able to argue against it. "So you can leave now. I'll have your last paycheck mailed to your house."

"Dude, your authority doesn't apply to me. In case you forgot, my parents own this place," he explained before laughing again. "I could fire *you* if I wanted to."

From out in the store, we heard Hannibal exclaim, "Holy shit! Are you pregnant?" Scarlet's head turned toward the noise, and she frowned. She turned her attention back to her brother.

"No, you can't, Scott," Scarlet said. "Solo's right. You're fired." She snatched his key chain out of his hand and slid the store key off the ring. "Go home." She tossed the rest back at him.

Dirty's face screwed up into a pout. "Whatever. I didn't want to work today anyway." He stomped toward the door. Then he yelled back, "When I tell Mom and Dad about this, they're going to fire you"—he pointed at me—"and you're going to be in huge trouble"—he pointed at Scarlet. "Dumb whore."

Before I could choke him to death, Scarlet took off her shoe and chucked it at the back of his head so hard it almost knocked him down.

"Hey!" He rubbed the point of impact on his skull. Instead of retaliating, though, he picked up the shoe and ran out the back door with it.

"Dammit!" Scarlet tried balancing on her remaining high heel but quickly gave up and took it off. "Guess I'm going barefoot today."

"I'm sorry I didn't run that by you first," I said, though to be honest, I wasn't at all sorry. "It's just that—"

Scarlet held up her hand. "My brother's a spoiled little assclown, and my parents know it—they're not going to care that you fired him. They'll probably want to promote you again, actually."

"Still." I shrugged. "I didn't mean to start all *that* with him."

"I don't care." Scarlet sighed. "But I'd better give my parents a heads-up about what happened so they'll be on my side before he goes crying to them." She gave one more backward glance toward Baby before carrying her remaining shoe into the office and shutting the door.

Once she'd left, I let my mind catch up with everything that had happened in the last ten minutes.

Baby was pregnant, and I'd practically forced her to tell the whole world about it. I'd violated her privacy and her trust. It made me sick to my stomach, really, what an asshole I'd been to her by demanding she wear that goddamn costume.

There were still tons of kids in the store. Down the hallway, I zeroed in on a kid dressed as Batman. He was sitting on the floor, blocking the aisle as he spread out his candy. A much smaller Robin plopped down next to him a minute later and did the same thing.

Batman opened up a fun-size Kit Kat, broke it in half, and gave a piece to Robin. Robin in turn picked out a handful from his pile and dumped it into Batman's bucket. The name JORDAN L. was written in marker on one of the buckets. The same lettering appeared on the other bucket, which said DEREK L.

I didn't notice any parents near them, but the kids didn't seem to mind being alone. I mean, they weren't alone, really. They were together. Together eating fistfuls of Halloween candy without a care in the world.

"Solo, are you OK?" Poppins snapped her fingers at me.

I jumped. I hadn't noticed her come into the hallway. "Yeah, why?"

"Because . . ." She looked concerned. "You're crying."

"What? No, I'm not." I touched my face. My cheeks were wet.

"I saw you from the registers," she informed me. "What's wrong?"

I could feel it now. The sinus pressure, the runny nose, the thick throat.

Goddammit. I *was* crying.

Why was I crying? How did I not know I was crying?

"It's allergies," I lied. "I have a nougat allergy, and I accidentally ate a Snickers." The words just tumbled out of my mouth.

Poppins's eyes got big. "Oh, no! Do you need to go to the hospital? I don't even really know what nougat is! I didn't know people could be allergic to it!"

Neither did I. "I'll be fine. I just need to go home and take my medicine," I told her, and headed toward the back door.

"Let me drive you," she insisted.

"I'll be fine! Tell Scarlet I got sick, will you?"

I made it out to the back lot and drove down the street until I couldn't hold it back anymore. I parked along some neighborhood side road and sobbed my face off for a long, long time, feeling a lot of unmedicated feelings while Michael Stipe screamed "What's the Frequency, Kenneth?" into the void.

Chapter 12

I woke up the next morning with a hangover. Not the kind you get from a night well drunk, but the kind you (or at least I) get from crying too much.

"Do you want to go to AA with me today?" my dad joked at breakfast when he saw how terrible I looked. I don't know if he really thought I'd been out drinking or not. I'd been home and in bed by five thirty the night before, though, so if he did, he probably thought I was a lightweight.

"Can you turn the TV down?" was all I said when my mother offered me breakfast.

Mom punched the remote a few times. "Are you sick?" She held her hand to my forehead. "You're not warm."

"I just don't feel good," I told them.

"So I heard." Mom handed me a Post-it note with a phone number scrawled on it. "A girl from work called here last night. She was worried about you. She said her name was Mary Poppins. I thought it was a prank call."

"Thanks." I stuck the note on the table.

"So that's really her name?" Mom lit a cigarette, set it in an ashtray, and sipped her coffee. "Who would do that to a child?"

"No, that's just her work name." I folded my arms and rested my head on them. "I don't know her real name."

"There are 'work names' at this job of yours?" my dad asked after taking a bite of toast. "What do they call you there?"

"Boss," I said, not really wanting to get into it.

"Like Bruce Springsteen?" Mom puffed on her cigarette.

"No, Maureen," my dad corrected her. "He meant that they call him boss because he's the manager, remember?"

"Oh." She shook her head. "I don't think that's what your dad meant, Joel."

Dad looked back down at his newspaper. "He knows that. He's just being a smart aleck. Sounds like they go by movie character names there."

"Well, that's clever." Mom started scratching my head. "So who are you, Joel? Superman?"

I didn't answer, but I scooted closer so she could reach me better. My mom had the longest fingernails, and I loved it when she did this. She had nice hands, too.

"I'll bet they call you Ferris Bueller," my dad guessed. "Or maybe Marty McFly?"

Since I figured they weren't going to drop the subject, I went ahead and told the truth. "I'm Han Solo, actually."

My mom pulled her hand away like I'd just bitten her. "Really, Joel? Why?"

131

My dad was disappointed, too. "Nobody needs that reminder, son."

"It's the name they assigned me," I lied. "I didn't have a choice."

Mom sighed and looked at Dad. "You'd think they would have let him pick something else, considering." Her lips thinned into a straight line.

Though she wasn't talking to me, I still addressed her comment. "Well, they might have if I'd said something. I just didn't think it was a good idea to air all my dirty laundry straight out of the gate. Besides, it's not like you guys have to call me that, so what does it matter?"

"None of us need reminders, Joel. Especially you," Mom repeated, and ground out her cigarette in the ashtray. "I'm going to church." She stood up, grabbed her purse, and walked out the side door.

"I've got to get going, too." My dad stood up and went to the fridge, then set something on the table. I opened one eye to see a can of Miller Lite next to me. "Hair of the dog." He kissed my head. "Don't tell your mother."

"I won't."

Dad left, but moments later he opened the front door again and tossed something onto the couch. "There was a package for you on the porch, Joel," he said, and then he was gone again.

I put the beer back into the fridge before retrieving my mail.

I tore open the envelope, and out slid a VHS tape in a plastic case. There was a note stuck to it.

You owe me this. — *Baby*

The movie was *Dirty Dancing*.

For the first time that morning, I smiled.

Chapter 13

As it turned out, Scarlet's parents were cool about Dirty Harry, and his firing was ruled fair. However, they got him a job at the pizza place next door since they owned that, too, so I'm not sure any lessons were learned.

When the rest of the staff caught wind of why Dirty Harry had been let go, everyone except for Baby thought I was a hard-ass for firing a guy for not wearing a Halloween costume.

"I know you really did it for me," Baby said a few days later.

"Yup," I admitted. "And because he was a prick."

She smiled crescently. "Normally I wouldn't want any favors, but Dirty was a jerkoff, so this time it's fine. Also, don't hire anyone to replace him, because I want his hours."

Baby considered my penance paid after this, and it seemed we were back on the friend track again. I think it also helped matters that I watched *Dirty Dancing* and found it every bit as torturous as she'd warned me it would be.

In general, Baby was more relaxed now that her secret was out. As someone who hid a lot of shit from people, I can tell you it's pretty taxing to pretend nothing is going on when something is. Even though she didn't discuss her pregnancy much (or really at all), I think she was relieved that everyone knew, and once the initial buzz about it died down, nobody really even brought it up.

Except for Scarlet.

"You know, don't you?" she asked me every day. "You know whether or not she's keeping it."

"I don't know anything," I responded honestly every time. "Why does it matter to you so much, anyway?"

"It doesn't—I just want to know" was the contradiction she always answered me with.

I didn't know what to make of this obsession Scarlet had with Baby's situation, but then it came to light that she was on the rocks with Devin, so I figured she was just fixated on Baby's issues to avoid her own.

My mom was the one who told me about their breakup. "You need to call your cousin," she instructed me one Sunday in November after popcorn-shrimping with Aunt Denise. "He's had his heart broken by that Jessica person."

It took me a second to remember who she was talking about. I looked up from the sandwich I was making. "What happened?"

"I told Denise that girl was trouble," Mom said, slipping out of her coat. "You should see her, that one. She dresses like a prostitute."

"I do see her, Mom. I work with Jessica." It felt really strange to call Scarlet that.

She nodded. "Then you know what I'm saying."

I resumed sandwich-making and tried to downplay just how interested I was in this news. "Do you know why they broke up?"

Mom lit a cigarette. "Denise said Jessica just packed up all her stuff and moved out last night while Devin was having dinner with her and Uncle Jim." She ashed into the sink. "You should steer clear of that girl, Joel. Denise says she's got a few screws loose."

My mother was always quick to point out the crazy in other people. "Don't we all?" I asked, taking a bite of my sandwich.

Mom gave me a look. "Call your cousin. He could use a friend right now."

"All right."

But I didn't call Devin. I did, however, pop over to the video store after I ate my sandwich.

Maybe you think I was trying to be a good guy, that I wanted to check in on Scarlet to see how she was doing. Or maybe you think I went there out of pure self-interest, to use Scarlet's vulnerability to my advantage.

Honestly, I don't know which of these motivations was closer to the truth, but it ended up not mattering, because Scarlet wasn't there.

Baby was, though, and she was instantly suspicious of why I'd come.

"What are you doing here?" she demanded when I emerged from the hallway. She was putting tags out while Maverick waited on a customer.

"I work here" was my answer.

"Not today," she pointed out. "Are you turning into one of those lame bosses who spends all his days off at work because he has no life?"

"Probably," I told her. Then it occurred to me to say, "Actually, I just came to rent a movie."

"Oh," Baby said. Then she walked over to the counter, grabbed something, and came back. "I already took the liberty of doing that for you." She pulled a Post-it note off a video and handed it to me.

I was happy to be resuming this part of our friendship. I enjoyed Baby's taste in movies. At least I did until I read this title.

"*Pretty in Pink?*" I raised my eyebrows. "C'mon, Baby. Wasn't *Dirty Dancing* punishment enough?"

"It's not like that," she assured me. "This is John Hughes."

"So?"

She gave me a look. "*So*, it's a classic. A definite must-see."

"I don't know about that," I told her. "It has the words *pretty* and *pink* in the title, and those words clearly point to this being a chick flick."

"Since when do you discriminate against chick flicks?" she demanded, crossing her arms. "Every movie I've ever rented for you has technically been a chick flick, and you've never said boo about it."

"That's what I mean. I need a little variety," I explained. "When are you going to give me something with explosions and a high body count? Or at the very least a bikini beach scene?"

"Gross. Your chauvinism is showing, Solo."

"Cut me some slack. A lot of perfectly fine gentlemen have never seen this movie, I bet." Then, to prove my point, I called over to Maverick. "Hey, Mav, have you seen *Pretty in Pink?*"

He made a J. Crew face and said, "Of course! It's John Hughes!"

"Well, that backfired," Baby noted.

"Can you just pick an action movie for me?" I handed her back the video.

"OK, fine." She thought for a sec. "There actually *is* an action movie I want to see, but it's only playing in theaters."

"Well, I can't rent *that*," I said.

She looked at the clock. "Do you want to maybe go?"

"To the movies?" I clarified. "Like, together?"

Baby rolled her eyes. "No, Solo. I thought we'd see the same film but in different movie theaters and then meet up after to discuss it. Of course together."

Now I looked at the clock. "When?"

She shrugged. "I'll call and check the times."

"OK," I said, the idea quickly growing on me. I hadn't been to the movies in a long time, and I hadn't been with a friend since my Cub Scout troop saw *Goonies* when I was six.

"You're sure you wanna go?" she asked as she dialed the number.

"I've got nothing better to do," I assured her. "I'm one of those lame bosses who doesn't have a life outside of my job."

Baby smiled. "I've heard that about you."

It turned out the movie Baby wanted to see was playing at the Main Art Theatre just down the street half an hour after her shift ended. We decided to walk there because it was a nice day and Baby wasn't in the mood for R.E.M., which she was sure I'd force her to listen to if we drove.

She got the tickets, and I got popcorn and drinks, and we met back up in line for the ticket taker.

"Theater two, enjoy the show," he said to us, ripping our tickets in half and handing them back to Baby.

"Thanks," I said to him. And I asked Baby, "So, what are we seeing?"

She pointed up at a marquee above theater two. The sign read: WILLIAM SHAKESPEARE'S ROMEO + JULIET.

"Are you kidding me right now? *This* is your action movie?" I felt completely duped.

Baby ate a handful of popcorn. "Chill out, Solo. The play is full of violence and murder. Didn't you read it in ninth grade like everyone else?"

I hadn't read it, actually. Tutor Tim had suggested I read *Julius Caesar* for my Shakespeare credit instead.

"Fine, I'll watch it," I relented quickly. I wasn't going to let this ruin my first social outing since the disaster that was Headlights. "But if nothing explodes, I'll be so pissed at you."

I followed Baby into the theater, and she chose our seats.

The room was surprisingly full for a movie adaptation of a play kids are forced to read. It seemed to be mostly couples, which made sense, since chick flicks are typically date movies.

"What do you think of Tybalt?" Baby asked me.

"What's a tybalt?"

"Juliet's cousin," she informed me.

"Oh. *That* Tybalt!" I pretended to think about it. "He's swell."

"I meant the name—for the baby," she clarified. "If it's a boy."

"Oh," I said, and the question suddenly felt heavy. "Well, it's not very common, so he'd never find one of those premade license plates for his bike, if that's a deciding factor for you."

She didn't seem to be listening to me. Instead Baby ran her hand through her hair and stared at the blank screen in front of us. "I mean, I haven't decided what I'm doing or anything." She started tapping her foot, and it made a sticky peeling-off-a-dirty-movie-theater-floor noise whenever she lifted it. "But either way, the kid needs to have a name, right? Since I'm the one giving birth, I feel entitled to pick it."

I considered this logic. "That's fair. What if it's a girl, though?"

"No clue," Baby admitted.

"Not Juliet?"

"Are you kidding me?" She made a face. "She's not exactly a role model, Solo. Though I guess maybe Tybalt isn't really, either, since he kills Romeo's best friend." She shrugged. "I really hope this baby doesn't turn out to be a murderer."

"Most mothers probably hope for that," I said.

Baby paused, then mumbled, "Mother."

The lights dimmed then, and the previews began.

As I just explained, I had never read *Romeo and Juliet*, though I had an idea of what it was about due to the fact that everyone else in the world had read it and the story had unavoidably seeped into the culture. Here's what I knew: forbidden love between enemies, "O Romeo, Romeo, wherefore art thou Romeo?", everyone dies. That's it.

Turned out there was a lot more to the story.

Like when the gangs blew up the gas station.

OK, so maybe that wasn't how the original play went, but it's how the Baz Luhrmann adaptation started out, and it honestly hooked me. It didn't even matter that the actors were speaking in the original Shakespearean language—the action was solid. There were fight scenes and acid-tripping scenes and drag queens and explosions, and sure, the whole love story thing, but the majority of the movie didn't feel chick-flicky at all.

I ended up getting really into the story. In fact, I was totally invested right up until the priest guy, Friar Laurence, got involved.

Here's where it would've been to my advantage to have read the play beforehand, because had I known how that goddamn story ended, I would have known I couldn't handle it.

You might be thinking, "What do you mean you didn't know how the play ends? You just said that you knew everyone dies."

And yeah, I knew they died. I was aware this wasn't a happily-ever-after scenario. I didn't know *how* they died, though, and that really does make a difference here.

I started getting nervous when the friar gave Juliet the drugs to fake her own death. That was a shady thing to do, and there were about a billion different ways it could have ended badly. So when—surprise!—it did, I started to lose it a little bit.

139

I'm sure you know how the story plays out, but since I didn't, I was barely holding it together by the end of the movie when Romeo and Juliet offed themselves.

"Wow" was Baby's first word as the credits started to roll. "That was incredible."

I didn't say anything.

"The director definitely took some liberties, but it worked." She took a drink of soda, and it made that the-cup-is-basically-empty noise. She shook the ice around and attempted another sip before saying, "Did you like it, Solo?"

"Not really," I muttered.

"Really? Why not?"

"It was terrible."

"Those are strong words." She arched one eyebrow. "Is this the first movie we're going to disagree about?"

"I can't believe they make kids read that in school. It's fucking irresponsible."

Baby put down her cup. "What do you mean?"

I forced my voice to remain steady. "It's about kids killing themselves. And it's a romance. That's a really mixed message."

"It's a *tragedy*, Solo. The play is called *The Tragedy of Romeo and Juliet*. It's not like it's called *Teenage Relationships 101*. It's not a how-to guide."

"It's a love story that promotes suicide. It's garbage."

Baby laughed through her nose. "Just because there's suicide *in* the story doesn't mean it's an endorsement *for* suicide." She ran her fingers through her hair. "If that were the case, then the movie would also be endorsing incest, since Lady Capulet makes out with her nephew."

I couldn't let it go. "Why didn't they just run away together? Isn't that a better ending?"

Baby sucked more air through her straw. "Maybe. But I think the whole point is that when they kill themselves, the feud between their families finally ends."

"Oh, well, great! There's a bright side to suicide! That's what the kids need to hear — killing yourself will solve everyone's problems!"

Baby stood up to leave. "OK, calm down, Solo. I get it. I'm sorry you didn't like the movie." She sighed in exasperation. "You don't have to lose your mind over it."

I probably should have taken a deep breath. Or counted to ten. Or done something else to calm down. But the movie had triggered something in me that had been lying dormant for a long time, and now that it was awake, I couldn't force it back to sleep.

A Radiohead song was playing over the credits. I instantly hated it. I hated everything. The music. The movie. William Shakespeare. Everything.

I was mad. Unmedicated, I-don't-know-what-to-do-with-all-this-rage mad. And because I was so enraged, and because I wasn't on any medication that would mellow me out, I did something really stupid.

I punched a chair.

Now, in all my years as a crazy person, I'd never hit anything. Not a person, not a wall, not even a pillow, like my doctors suggested I do to get aggression out. I just wasn't a violent person, and it had never crossed my mind that I might feel better if I just threw a few punches.

But for some reason, in that movie theater, that's what I did. I balled my hand into a fist, and as hard as I could, I punched the back of the empty seat in front of me.

The chair back was made of flexible plastic, which absorbed the force of the blow pretty easily. I mean, I didn't break it into shards or leave a dent in it or wreak any sort of satisfying damage whatsoever. I just punched the chair and then sat there like nothing had happened.

Baby's eyes got huge. "What the fuck was that?"

I didn't know, so I said, "I don't know."

"No," she challenged me. "I think you do."

"I just really didn't like the movie."

"No, that's bullshit," she said. "Just like Headlights was bullshit." Baby looked at me. "We've hung out twice now, and both times you've majorly freaked out and then pretended everything was cool right afterward when it's clearly not. What's going on?"

"I'm anemic."

She groaned in frustration. "God, I can't do this with you. It's just too hard." Baby grabbed her purse.

"What? Where are you going?"

"If you can't be real with me now after everything you know about me and my life and my *shit*, then I'm out of here, Solo. I refuse to be in a completely one-sided friendship. Especially right now"—she pointed at her stomach—"and especially with someone who's crazy"—she pointed at me. And then Baby stomped out of the theater.

I didn't chase after her. Maybe I should have, but I didn't know what to say. Instead I stayed in the theater alone and let the credits finish rolling, unsure which hurt worse, my hand or the truth.

Chapter 14

"Have a seat, Joel. You're looking well."

"Thanks."

"So let me see. It's been a while since our last session. How are things going?"

"Good. School's good."

"That's great news. Still think you'll graduate in the spring?"

"Yes."

"Have you decided what comes after that?"

"I don't really know. Maybe college. We'll see."

"Fine, fine. How's your mood been? Scale of one to ten."

"Um. I think about a seven, I guess."

"A seven . . . Last time you said eight. Have you noticed a change?"

"Oh. No. I wasn't thinking about what I said last time."

"All right. Can you think of any reason why you might be a seven now instead of an eight?"

"I don't know. Like I said, I wasn't thinking about last time."

"OK . . . Do you want me to prescribe you another anti-depressant?"

"No, I'm good. I mean, I did say seven. Seven is still pretty good. It's not like I said three or anything."

"But you also didn't say eight."

"OK. Got it. Next time, before I answer this question, I'll ask what I said the previous time and factor it in."

"Let's just move on, shall we? How is the new promotion going at work?"

"It's going. I got to fire someone. That was pretty cool."

"Oh? That sounds like it could have been a stressful situation."

"No . . . I mean, the kid was a real punk. He had it coming, so it wasn't that big of a deal, to be honest."

"Very assertive of you."

"Yeah, well, that's why they pay me the big bucks, I guess."

"Has the promotion created any waves for you socially? You mentioned last time that you thought that might be a possibility."

"I mean, not really. Seems like everyone came around OK."

"Does that mean you're making friends?"

"I don't know. Some, I guess."

"Perhaps that should be our next goal."

"You want me to set a goal to make a friend? That sounds like a pep talk you'd give a preschooler, Doc."

"In this regard, there are a lot of similarities between you and a young child, Joel, and that's not meant to be offensive. By nature, what you've gone through has caused you to build up walls to protect yourself from others, which is a stumbling block in terms of forming healthy relationships. Do you have any potential friendships you'd like to foster?"

"Yeah. I guess maybe. One."

"Male, female?"

"She's a girl."

"Are the two of you sleeping together?"

"What? No! No, of course not."

"That wasn't meant to be intrusive, Joel. It's just that you have a history of casual sex, so I thought it was an important question to ask."

"Yeah, well. It's not like that."

"So tell me about her."

"What do you want to know?"

"Why her? What makes this girl the one friend you're interested in pursuing?"

"Oh . . . I don't know. She's interesting, I guess."

"Care to elaborate?"

"Hmm. She swears a lot."

"Is she trustworthy?"

"Yeah. I'd say so."

"Good. Good. So have you told this girl anything? About what you've been through?"

"*Fuck* no."

"That was a strong reaction."

"Sorry, I mean no. Just regular no."

"Why not?"

"Are you serious? You seriously don't know why I wouldn't tell people that I've been in and out of the loony bin for the last few years?"

"Of course I understand why you wouldn't announce the details of what you've gone through to the entire world, Joel. But you have to know that it's going to come up eventually as you work on building healthy relationships."

"No, I don't really think it has to. I like being a tabula rasa."

"A blank slate?"

"Yeah, you've heard of it?"

"Sure."

"I like having a fresh start. I like that no one knows anything about me."

"I see . . . How does this girl feel about that?"

"How does she feel about not knowing how crazy I used to be? I would imagine she feels pretty good about that, considering ignorance is bliss and all."

"All right, but when the two of you talk, does she ask you anything personal? Or is she the type of person who's only into talking about herself?"

"No, she's asked some things. I just didn't answer her."

"And she's OK with that?"

"Not so much, I guess. But that's only because she doesn't know what she doesn't know. If she knew, she'd wish she didn't. So really I'm doing her a favor."

"Let me ask you something. Has she shared any private details of her life with you?"

"Yeah."

"Do you wish you didn't know what you know, or are those things partly what make this person so interesting to you?"

"What's your point?"

"My point is that I think you've misunderstood the whole blank slate idea. We're all in a sort of transient state of impression with one another, not in a fixed, permanently blank one. Blank slates get filled up rather quickly as we get to know a person, whether they tell us truths about themselves or not. When there are gaps in the factual information, our minds tend to fill them in with assumptions until we have a clear picture. Does that make sense?"

"Yeah. Like jumping to conclusions."

"Exactly. Which brings me to my point with this girl. Joel, what you've been through doesn't define who you are, but it has certainly shaped it, and that's not something you're going to be able to hide for the rest of your life—nor should you, necessarily. Which is why I want to encourage you to open yourself up. To the right person, of course. And I'm not saying this girl has to be that person, but it sounds like maybe she could be."

"What would I even say? Do I have to tell her *everything*?"

"You don't *have* to do anything. But if you want to experience healthy intimacy in relationships, you're going to have to be emotionally vulnerable with someone at some point."

"What if I don't want to?"

"I would challenge you on that. I believe that you do want meaningful relationships. It's what you've always wanted. I think that's why you ended up here in the first place."

"To build a meaningful relationship with you?"

"No. Because the only meaningful relationship you had was with someone who didn't really exist."

"Oh, yeah. That."

"That hole in your life that 'Crystal' filled is still there. And if you don't fill it with real, flesh-and-blood friends, I fear you may turn to other things."

"Other things like . . . what? Needle drugs? Or prostitutes? Or illegal organized dogfighting? I guess the world is my oyster, so I *could* try them all out and see what feels the most me . . ."

"Joel."

"Yeah?"

"Be serious, please."

"OK."

"Just think about sharing what you've been through, OK?"

"Fine."

"Fine, you'll do it, or fine, you're willing to think about it?"

"Fine, I'll think about it. Maybe."

"It's a goal."

Part 2

Generally speaking, I'm not a fan of November. It's cold. It's gray. There's too much football happening. Calendar-wise, it's as far as possible from the next time I actually want to be outside again. November is always when I realize I've lost my windshield scraper and that I still don't own a good winter coat. It also marks the beginning of the worst time of the year for me: the holidays.

I know I'm in the minority here and you're probably a huge fan of the holidays, but cut me some slack. Historically nothing has highlighted The Bad Thing That Happened more than the holiday season. Before The Bad Thing, the Teagues were a jolly, happy bunch this time of year, just like everyone else. Back in Virginia, we did a traditional Thanksgiving meal at my dad's parents' house, complete with tree trimming, itchy sweaters, and an annual photo with the grandparents. Then a few weeks later, we'd do it all over again on Christmas Eve.

But then The Bad Thing happened, and we moved to Michigan, away from how things used to be. Now we just go to Aunt Denise and Uncle Jim's for Thanksgiving and Christmas Eve, where we don't participate much beyond just showing up.

This particular Thanksgiving, Dad was in a pair of holey sweatpants in front of the TV while Mom was browsing Black Friday ads in her robe, chain-smoking cigarettes until five minutes before we had to leave. At the last possible second, Dad threw on real pants while Mom put on a turtleneck, and then, with a Sara Lee pumpkin pie in hand, we headed out the door as a family.

Because I'd never followed through on my mom's wishes and checked in on Devin, Thanksgiving marked the first time I'd be seeing my cousin since he and Scarlet had split up. As penance for disregarding her demands, Mom made me promise to be especially nice while he was in mourning over losing the hottest girl on the planet (I added that part). So I was all geared up to pretend to care, but then we arrived, and he was hanging ornaments on the Christmas tree with a bouncy little brunette, and I decided that all bets were off.

Tracey was her name, and aerobics instructing was her game. She was smiley and polite in the way a new girlfriend probably always is. I didn't know if she'd had anything to do with the breakup, but judging by how comfortable they were together, it seemed possible. I found myself glaring at them over a dish of candied yams for most of the meal.

I mean, after a breakup with a girl like Scarlet, I wouldn't have faulted the guy for a rebound fling or a dabble in some unhealthy coping mechanisms, but this felt different. Tracey and Devin were all hand-holdy and cuddly, and for some reason it gave me the overwhelming urge to kick him in the nuts.

Sometime after the pie was served, Devin noticed there were people other than Tracey in the room and finally acknowledged me.

"Hey, dude. How's it hanging, bro?" However you imagine the biggest jock you know talking is exactly how he said this. "How's your blood disease?"

"Great," I said. And then, because I knew he knew nothing about anemia, I added, "The transplant was a success."

Tracey smiled sympathetically at me, and I presumed that meant she was as dumb as Devin.

"That's great, man." He asked Tracey (or "Babe," as he called her) to grab him another slice of pie from the kitchen. When she was gone, he changed the subject. "So you're still working with Jess, right?"

"Yup."

He glanced in Tracey's direction. "How's she been doing?"

"She's fantastic," I lied. "She's loving her new digs." After Scarlet officially moved out of Devin's place, she moved into the apartment above the video store, which was previously a real estate office but had a kitchenette and a working shower.

"Good for her," he said, but I couldn't tell if he meant it. "She ever mention me?"

"No," I lied again. "She's been really focused on beauty school."

"Oh. Do you know if she's seeing anyone new yet?"

"I've seen her with a few guys lately." I was on a roll.

"Really?" He looked confused, which to be fair was how Devin usually looked. "Well, tell her I said hey."

I lied one last time: "Will do!"

Just like when Indiana Jones asked about Baby, it didn't seem right to update Devin on his ex, especially since he'd replaced Scarlet like a roll of paper towels. The truth was that she'd been going through a rough patch since their breakup. Permit me to illustrate.

One day the week before Thanksgiving, I walked into work to the sound of shouting. The noise was coming from the storage closet, so the yelling was muffled, but the words were clear enough that I could still make them out.

"For the last time, it's none of your business, Scarlet!" Baby screamed. "Now leave me the hell alone!"

"How can you even *consider* keeping it?" Scarlet shouted back. "There's no way you can raise a kid, Baby. You would ruin the poor thing's life! Not to mention yours!"

I bolted for the closet and pushed the door open. Inside I found a red-faced Scarlet, scowling and cross-armed, glaring at a fist-clenched Baby, who appeared to be two seconds away from murdering in the first degree.

"What the hell is going on in here?" I asked.

No one acknowledged me.

"You're too young! You'd be a terrible mother!" Scarlet pointed a finger at Baby, and the force with which she extended her arm almost knocked her off balance.

Now that the door was no longer muting her voice, it was evident that Scarlet's speech was slurred.

Baby looked at me. "Solo, you'd better get Bimbo Barbie out of here before I give her a black eye."

I wouldn't have put it past Baby, pregnant or not, to punch Scarlet, so I did as I was told. "Scarlet, can I see you in the office for a second?"

"No!" she yelled. "This is *my* store! I was here first! Make Baby leave!"

Baby shrugged at me. "But boss, you assigned me to take inventory today, and you know how I live to serve you."

I stood between the two of them. "Please, Baby? Can you just give us a minute?"

Baby chucked her clipboard onto a shelf and stormed out of the closet.

Once the door had been properly slammed, I asked Scarlet, "What was that all about?"

"Her!" Scarlet yelled, pointing at the door with the exaggerated gesture of someone three sheets to the wind. She took a drink from a Coke bottle I was positive was not filled exclusively with soda and set it on a shelf.

"Why are you so hung up on Baby being pregnant?" I subtly moved the Coke bottle out of her reach.

"I don't want to talk about it." She pouted and hoisted herself onto a stack of candy bar boxes.

"I'm asking you to reconsider."

"I don't want to," she said in the same way a kid might refuse to eat vegetables. "I want to do this." Scarlet grabbed my belt loop and pulled me close enough that she could wrap her legs around my waist, and before I knew it, her tongue was in my mouth.

OK, so of the many (many) fantasies I'd had about Scarlet, it's possible that a few of them had started out just like this: alone in the storage closet, aggressive her coming on to an unsuspecting me. I mean, you can probably see the appeal of such a scenario, right?

But when you added Scarlet being drunk and acting like a four-year-old, suddenly things weren't so sexy.

"Hey, c'mon." I gently pulled away. "Not like this."

"It's fine. Me and Devin broke up." She squeezed her legs tighter around me and pushed her mouth onto mine again.

Her lip gloss tasted like strawberries, and it took every ounce of restraint I had to resist her.

"I know. You guys *just* broke up, which is on the list of reasons why this isn't a good idea right now." I moved her hands off me, laid them at her sides, and wriggled free of her legs.

Scarlet laughed. "Do you seriously think I give a shit about Devin after everything that happened?" She pulled me close again. "C'mon, Solo. Let's make a baby."

"Whoa, whoa, whoa!" I put my hands up like stop signs and backed clear to the other end of the closet. I'm not sure there are any words in the English language more terrifying to a seventeen-year-old male than those, even when they're said by someone who, primal instinct–wise, is the perfect mating specimen. "I'm going to assume that's the alcohol talking, Scarlet, because that's the worst idea anyone has ever had."

"Why?" She seemed offended. "Baby's having one."

"It's not a competition, Scarlet."

She looked like she might cry. "I hate Devin. I hate his stupid face."

"That's OK! His face *is* really stupid. You can hate him all you want!" I was super relieved the conversation was circling back to my cousin. "You just can't scream at Baby because of it."

Scarlet started drunk-girl crying then, which in my opinion is the worst kind of crying.

I'm not trying to sound insensitive. I know Scarlet was upset, and I of all people know the importance of letting your emotions out. But being a dude around a crying drunk girl is a precarious situation, because no matter how you handle things, you're not going to make anything better (because alcohol voids rational thinking) and there's actually a lot you can do to make things worse (e.g., agreeing to make a baby with Scarlet).

I didn't know what to say to her, so once again I blurted out the first thing that popped into my head. "I know things are hard right now, but the only way to truly get over something is to go through it."

I'd borrowed these words from a poster that hung just outside my room in the Weller Clawson Mental Health Facility featuring a giant boulder with a hole carved out of its center. The picture was real, taken at some national park or something. The rock was on a pathway, and there were silhouetted people walking through the hole.

I hadn't thought about that picture in a long time, though if I'm being honest, it was the only motivational poster that had ever made sense to me. And kudos to my subconscious, because of all the places my brain could have gone—from Garfield to Charlie Brown to all the philosophical comic strip characters in between—this particular poster's advice was actually applicable to the situation at hand.

Scarlet, however, wasn't in the mood for my advice. "Will you just go now, Solo?"

"Yup." I was relieved to have an out. And then, because it was true, I said, "I'm sorry you're in pain."

I left her then and went to check on Baby. She and Maverick were standing behind the counter scanning in returns.

"Hey, are you OK?"

"Peachy keen, jelly bean," she said, but she didn't seem to mean it.

"What was that all about? What set Scarlet off?"

"It beats me, Solo. One minute I'm counting boxes of Junior Mints, and the next minute she's going all psycho hose beast on me."

"I'm going to go put tags out," Maverick offered. He seemed eager to get away from the conversation.

Baby ran her fingers through her hair. "Seriously, Solo. Scarlet just stormed into the closet and demanded to know if I'm keeping the baby. When I wouldn't answer her, she started giving me a million reasons not to keep it, like I would be the world's worst mother or something." Baby was angry, noticeably more so than usual. "Why does she even care what I do? How does this involve her at all?" She folded her arms. "You know, I hadn't decided what I was going to do

157

with the baby, but now I'm thinking I may raise it just to spite her. Then when I do such a fucking bang-up job that my kid wins the Nobel Peace Prize, I can tell her to shut her stupid mouth."

"I hear that revenge is a popular reason people choose to become parents," I said. "For those willing to play the long game."

She ignored my comment. "Scarlet's lost her mind," Baby asserted. "Maverick said she was drinking all day in her office. I guess she tried to throw herself at him earlier."

For some ridiculous reason, it stung to hear that I wasn't Scarlet's first seduction attempt of the day. "She did?"

"He turned her down, though. Thank god."

I glanced over at J. Crew. "Good for him," I said, both because it was the right thing to have done and because I hoped it meant he wasn't interested in Scarlet like that. Not that we were competing for her, but I'm just saying that if we were, I'd lose.

"By the way, I shouldn't need to tell you that it's a big fat no-no for my boss to harass me for being pregnant," Baby stated. "The ACLU would eat this shit up. I could sue."

"Are you gonna?"

She made a face and shrugged. "Sounds like a hassle."

Just then there was a loud crash from the hallway, followed by a scream.

I did an about-face, and both Maverick and I arrived back at the storage closet at the same time. He opened the door to reveal a huge pile of knocked-over two-liter soda bottles and overturned boxes of candy. Somewhere under the mess, Scarlet yelled, "A little help here!"

Together we unburied her, and Maverick lifted her from the floor.

"What happened?" he asked as he carried her into the store. "Are you OK?"

"I was just sitting there, and then the room started moving," she explained. "And then I was on the floor."

Maverick gave her a once-over. "Does anything hurt?"

"My hand," Scarlet complained, her eyes half closed. "I don't feel good."

Maverick sat her on the counter, and she almost slumped over. "Oh, crap. You're bleeding." He pointed to her palm. "Probably got cut by the soda crates. Some of them have jagged—"

Scarlet took one look at her injury and threw up all over Maverick.

Baby took one look at Maverick covered in vomit and ran back to the bathroom. All of us then heard the familiar sound of her puking her guts out.

"Sorry," Scarlet said before falling over on the counter.

Maverick and I stared at each other, blinking in silence.

"I need to change my clothes," he finally said. "You got this?" He pointed at Scarlet.

No, I didn't "got this." I still hadn't even really figured out what "this" was. The ten minutes since I'd gotten to work felt like a scene from *Melrose Place* (Mom watched it, OK?) played in fast-forward. Still, I said, "Sure," and then I watched as Maverick hightailed it out the back door, dry-heaving all the way.

I tapped Scarlet's cheek. "Hey, you have to wake up!"

She groaned but didn't rouse.

I rolled up my sleeves and took a look at her hand. I couldn't tell how deep the cut actually was, but I assumed she needed more medical attention than I could administer. "Hey, Scarlet. C'mon, wake up! I need to get you to a doctor."

"What kind of doctor?" she mumbled.

"What?" I was trying to remember how much blood someone needed to lose before a tourniquet was necessary while also assessing how much blood Scarlet was losing while also trying to remember what a tourniquet was. "I don't know. Just the regular kind."

"I'm a doctor," a voice behind me said. "What's going on?"

It hadn't occurred to me that anyone else was in the store while all this was going on, so when I looked over my shoulder and saw Marc Schwartz standing there with two movie tags in one hand and a box of microwave popcorn in the other, I was really confused.

Just a few minutes earlier, I had been driving to work, listening to R.E.M. like any other day, and now here I was standing over a barely conscious and bleeding Scarlet with my former therapist from the psych hospital. I'd had dreams about talking dinosaurs that had seemed more plausible.

"I meant a regular medical doctor, not a shrink." I indicated the blood.

Marc was unfazed. "Clinical psychiatrists are MDs, Joel," he informed me. "Do you have a first aid kit?"

I grabbed one from the cabinet next to the promotional T-shirts and handed it to Marc. He pulled out a pair of latex gloves and suggested I temporarily close up the store until he had the situation under control, so I locked the front door and flipped over the WILL RETURN AT sign before rejoining him.

We carried Scarlet to the break room and set her on the table. Marc drenched some gauze pads with antiseptic. "How'd this happen?" he asked calmly while pressing them into her palm.

I explained in as few words as possible.

"She on anything? Street drugs? Prescription pills? What's her story?"

"I think she's just drunk."

"Was she at a party or something?" Marc reached for another gauze pad.

"She's going through a breakup," I said, not wanting to get into it.

"OK." He nodded. "Do you have any superglue?"

"Superglue?"

"It's legit, I promise."

Having recently cleaned out the storage closet, I knew for a fact that there was superglue among the random office supplies. Trusting Marc that it was a valid solution for Scarlet's bleeding hand (because why not—this was probably a dream anyway), I went to retrieve it.

By the time I got back, Baby had joined Marc in the break room.

"Hey, boss man, you're going to have to go out there and clean up the puke if you want me to go back to work." Baby was peering over Marc's shoulder at Scarlet's hand, looking as pale as she had the day I'd met her. "Otherwise I'm going to continue throwing up all night, and I can't promise I'll always make it to the bathroom."

I sighed and handed Marc the glue.

"Thanks, Joel," he said. "You'll want to use something with bleach to sanitize the area. And make sure you wear gloves."

Of course I knew all this, but I didn't remind him that in terms of cleaning up other people's bodily fluids, this wasn't my maiden voyage.

It took me a while—I'll spare you the details—but when I was finished, I found Baby standing outside of the break room. She looked more distraught than she had when I left, so I assumed something else had happened.

"Scarlet barf again?"

"No," she said distantly. "I'm just thinking."

I wanted to know what about, but I'd surrendered the right to ask Baby personal questions that day at the movies, so instead I said, "It's all clean out there. You can go back to work if you want. Or home, if you need to. It's a weird day."

"Oh. No. It's fine. I'll go back to work in a minute."

"Are you sure? You seem off."

"Like you said"—she barely looked at me—"it's a weird day."

Baby brushed past me and headed toward the store. I might have

161

followed her, but then Marc called for me from inside the break room.

Scarlet was sleeping on the couch, a trash can on the floor by her head. Marc sat in the chair next to her, writing something.

"Hey, Joel." He didn't look up from his paper but indicated Scarlet. "Can you tell me her name?"

"It's Scarlet," I said. "Wait, is this for, like, a medical form or something? Because then it's Jessica."

"It's not official. I just didn't know what to call her. Maybe you don't, either?"

"She goes by Scarlet here. As in Scarlett O'Hara," I told him.

"Oh, yeah. The movie names." Marc continued scribbling doctor scrawl for a few lines before saying, "You know, that's why I didn't put two and two together the first time I saw you here. I'm better with names than faces. Or names and faces together, at least, so it didn't register right away who you were. But don't worry, I remember you very well, Joel. I don't want you thinking you're forgettable."

"Thanks," I told him. "I mean, I guess it actually would have been better if you didn't remember, though, right? It's pretty obvious how messed up I was if you can still pick me out of a lineup years later."

He gave me one of those *I didn't mean it that way* looks. "In my line of work, every patient is equally unforgettable and completely routine simultaneously." Marc kept writing. "So, how've you been these last couple of years?"

"Well, not in a psych hospital, so I daresay pretty good."

He laughed. "*That's* what I remember the most about you. Your sense of humor." Marc smiled, then clicked his pen closed. He gave me the paper, which included a list of warning signs for alcohol poisoning (he was confident Scarlet was fine, though) and some instructions for how she should take care of her hand. Then he handed me his business card.

"I know you said she doesn't need a shrink, but just in case she wants to know who the quack was who glued her shut, I thought she should have this."

"Thanks."

"It's really good to run into you now and then," he said. "You take care, Joel."

"Yeah. You too."

He left me to rent the movies he'd come in for.

I pulled out a blanket from the dresser drawer and draped it over Scarlet. She was breathing heavy sleep breaths with her mouth open. Her hand was wrapped in a bandage and resting over her eyes, like she was shielding them from the light. I flipped one of the switches to dim the room, then read Marc's instructions for Scarlet. Beneath them on the page was this note:

> *I hear you've hit a rough patch. Should you ever want to talk to a professional about what's going on, feel free to call my office. If not, I'm happy you've got some good people at work looking out for you.*

I smiled.

Maverick returned a bit later, and he and I took turns babysitting Scarlet and restacking the soda bottles in the storage closet. She woke up on her own before closing time, and Maverick offered to drive her to a girlfriend's house for the night so she wouldn't be alone. She assured him she was done throwing up, but he made her take a trash bag with her in his car anyway. I helped buckle her in and then watched them drive away.

One of the things I'd learned from therapy was that for most people who have Something Wrong With Them, rock bottom is unavoidable. Until the cost of not dealing with your shit is greater than the cost of dealing with it, it's easier to just kick that can down the road until the sidewalk ends and you crash-land at the bottom of a pit and have no choice but to start the long, hard crawl back out.

Another thing therapy teaches you is that most of the time, rock bottom is not at the end of a freefall. It's not like you're just walking along one day and then the ground opens up and swallows you. The descent is usually subtler than that.

I guess it's more like quicksand. And you're not usually alone in it when you notice that you're stuck. Most of the time, there are people along the edge, throwing you vines and shit, trying to pull you out before you sink all the way to the bottom. Sometimes those people even come waist-deep into the quicksand themselves trying to save you, and in some cases, when you flail around, you end up dragging them under with you.

In the time leading up to The Bad Thing That Happened, I didn't notice the quicksand my family was standing in. If I had, you can be damn sure I'd have gone under trying to stop it.

I'm not saying that Scarlet was in quicksand. Maybe she was, but maybe she just got drunk to blow off some steam and things got out of hand. If she was headed toward rock bottom, though, Devin was probably at least part of the reason she was sinking.

Which was why at Thanksgiving, while he was talking to our dads about what a crappy season the Lions were having, I walked over to Tracey and warned her that her boyfriend was being treated for several venereal diseases.

Chapter 16

Here's a tip: if you want to make your coworkers miserable around the holidays, one surefire way to do so is by forcing them to participate in something called Secret Santa.

Secret Santa, for those of you lucky enough not to know, is a Christmas workplace tradition in which people are randomly assigned to buy gifts for one another, regardless of whether they know each other at all outside of work.

At least that was the gist of Poppins's explanation at the December staff meeting.

"We'll be hanging stockings in the break room — one for each of us. Between now and the twenty-third, you must leave three presents in your person's stocking — two small gifts and one larger gift that cost no more than twenty-five dollars total," she explained proudly. "Any questions?"

"Yes," Baby said, annoyed. "What if we don't want to play?"

Poppins exchanged a look with Scarlet, who answered the question for her. "Too bad. I asked for help planning a holiday activity this year, and Poppins was the only one who volunteered an idea. So if you don't like it, deal with it."

Poppins smiled. "Any other questions?"

"Wait a second," Baby continued. "You mean to tell me that I'm being forced by my employer to spend my hard-earned dollars on Christmas gifts for a person I may or may not even like?" She looked around the room. "No offense, you guys, but I have more pressing financial obligations right now than buying one of you a bunch of crap." Baby rested her hand on her stomach, which was unmistakably protruding by now. Sometime in the past few weeks, Baby had "popped" (her word) and could no longer easily hide her pregnancy under her clothes. She had taken all the XLs from the promotional shirt shelf to serve as maternity clothes, and that particular day she was endorsing *Black Sheep*, a film starring Chris Farley and David Spade.

Scarlet wouldn't look at Baby. "Yes, that's what I'm saying."

Things between Baby and Scarlet had remained tense after their blowout in the storage closet. I was hoping time would heal whatever wound was there, but so far that didn't seem to be happening.

This time I intervened on behalf of Baby, like I should have done when she was protesting dressing up for the trick or treat. "Hold on. Twenty-five dollars is the *maximum*, right? You don't *have* to spend that much; you just can't go over that amount."

Poppins considered this. "Yeah, I guess so. Though it doesn't really seem fair if everyone gets twenty-five dollars' worth of gifts except for the person who has Baby as their Secret Santa."

"Honestly, I don't really want to drop twenty-five bucks on any of you guys, either," Hannibal spoke up. "Not to be a dick, but my mom started making me pay rent, so I don't have much spare cash these days."

Poppins's face fell. "Come on, you guys. It's Christmas."

"Does the gift have to be physical in nature?" The Godfather asked. "What if we wanted to give someone, like, a favor? Favors have no monetary value, per se, but they can be worth a lot." She pulled out her mirror compact and checked her lipstick. "Priceless, even."

"I guess you wouldn't have to *buy* all the gifts," Poppins conceded. "As long as people still put thought into them, I think it's fine."

The staff seemed to have run out of complaints, so we had no choice but to start drawing names.

Poppins held up a bowl and tossed some slips of paper inside. "Who wants to pick first?"

Maverick, being the good sport he was, raised his hand. He reached into the bowl and pulled out a piece of paper, then smiled and leaned back in his seat.

"Oh, I forgot—if you get your own name, you have to draw again," Poppins said.

Maverick's smile turned into a frown. He put the paper back in the bowl and drew again.

I didn't know whose name to hope for. In the past eight years, I'd bought a total of five presents for people, and four of those were bottles of White Shoulders perfume for my mom.

The fifth gift is a longer story that I'll tell you about later.

I decided to hope I drew a guy's name, because I could likely just shove a couple of issues of *Rolling Stone* or *Maxim* in Hannibal's or Maverick's stocking and be all set, whereas I wouldn't know where to begin coming up with a present for someone like, say, Poppins. Poppins seemed like she was going to put all sorts of effort into the gifts she bought and in return would have really high expectations for her Secret Santa. Drawing her name would be the worst-case scenario, then, since I would almost certainly be a huge disappointment to her.

When it was my turn, I reached into the bowl and had mixed feelings about pulling out The Godfather's name.

"Part of the fun is trying to figure out who everyone's Secret Santas are," Poppins reminded us after all the names were distributed. "So remember, *don't* tell anyone who you have until it's over!"

No sooner had she finished saying this than Baby tapped my shoulder and asked, "Who'd you get?"

This surprised me. Not that Baby wanted to break Poppins's stupid rule, but that she was initiating conversation. I mean, it wasn't like we weren't on speaking terms, but Baby had stated her position at the movies the day I'd punched the chair, and apart from the night of Scarlet's drunken escapades, she'd kept her distance.

Though just because we weren't hanging out, it didn't mean I wasn't thinking about Baby. I was also thinking a lot about what my shrink had said, and I knew he was right. I needed a friend. So much about What Was Wrong With Me was due to being too damn lonely for too damn long. My problem was not in acknowledging that I wanted an emotionally intimate relationship with Baby, though. My problem was that every time I thought about telling her about my past, I imagined her whipping out a black marker and writing NUTJOB on my tabula rasa in the same slanted handwriting with which she'd written SOLO on my name tag the day we met, then telling me to fuck off forever.

I waited for the room to clear out, then showed Baby my Secret Santa paper.

Her mouth dropped open. "I can't believe you fucking told me! You never tell me anything, Solo."

This stung a little. It was meant to.

"Who'd you get?" I asked her back.

She smirked. "Like I'm going to tell you."

"Does that mean you picked my name? Because I'm really hard to shop for."

"What do you get for the guy who has everything? Besides this, I guess." She opened her purse and pulled out a pinkish envelope.

"What's this? A Christmas card?"

"Just open it."

I tore open the envelope and took out a thick card with two cartoon mountain lions wearing formal attire embossed on it. Below the apparent male was the name Bob, and below the female was the name Kat.

"Those are bobcats on their wedding invitations. Because they are Bob and Kat and they call themselves BobKat." Baby shook her head. "It's the worst thing I've ever seen in my whole life."

I pointed at the artwork. "Are you kidding? This is awesome!" I read the card. They were getting married on Valentine's Day.

"Don't feel like you have to come." Baby ran her hand through her hair. "I mean, you're invited, obviously. But seriously, I get it if you don't want to attend a wedding for two people you don't know who call themselves BobKat. I wouldn't even be going if I didn't have to."

"Are you sure they want me there?" I asked her. "I only met Kat that one time. Is it weird for me to come?"

Baby fidgeted. "No. I mean, not if you're there with me."

"Oh," I said. "I'd be coming as *your* guest?"

"You don't *have* to. It's just that I'll be bored as hell if I don't bring anyone," she said quickly. "And it's not like people will be lined up to spend Valentine's Day with *all this*." She pointed at her stomach.

It felt like Baby was offering me an olive branch, and I wasn't about to ignore it. "How are things going with the pregnancy, anyway? I never heard how your mom took the news."

Baby sighed. "I guess the one upside of your mom having you when she was a teenager is that she can't really judge you for getting knocked up in high school."

"Look at you, finding the silver lining," I joked.

Baby rolled her eyes. "Kat asked me if it was your kid. I told her no, obviously. She seemed kind of disappointed."

"Please tell your mom that I'm flattered."

"Gross." Baby made a face. "Anyway, she knows the truth, and she didn't kick me out or murder me when I told her, so I guess things are still good between us."

"I'm glad," I said. Then, because I had to know, I asked, "Does the invitation mean that things are good between us, too?"

Baby shrugged. "We weren't really ever *not* good, Solo. I mean, you and that chair at the movie theater seem to have some unresolved issues, but I guess *we're* fine."

This was a relief. "You're sure?"

Baby nodded. "Yeah. I know you're not going to tell me things about you, so I decided not to care."

"Oh." It surprised me that this hurt to hear, but it really did. "OK."

Baby must've been able to tell. "I'm not trying to be a bitch, Solo. I'm just over it." She leveled with me. "Clearly you don't want me to know your shit. I get it. I wish you didn't know mine, either, but whatever. Besides, if you tell me the truth behind why you freaked out at Headlights, I'll probably want to tell you more of my junk. And then you'll tell me more, and then we'll have this weird, obligatory, codependent need to tell each other everything. And then what?" She paused. "What if one of us majorly pisses off the other one someday, and we're not friends anymore? I don't want to have an enemy who's

170

armed with my deepest, darkest secrets—it's too big of a risk."

I could totally follow this logic. In fact, it was a good defense against everything my doctor had said to me about vulnerable relationships.

Still, though, hearing Baby say all of it bothered me.

She continued, "I don't want to stop hanging out with you, Solo. We'll just keep all our problems to ourselves and stick to talking about superficial stuff. Like movies. I still have a lot to teach you on that front, anyway."

I forced a smile, but I wasn't happy. I was realizing too late how much I didn't want to be *just* superficial with Baby.

"All right, then." I put the invitation in my pocket. "Tell BobKat I'll be attending the wedding. I'll buy them a toaster."

Baby nodded, but she didn't smile back. "Perfect."

Chapter 17

A tube of Chanel Kiss of Death lipstick from the makeup counter at Hudson's cost twenty-eight dollars. I didn't even care that it was more than the total amount I was supposed to spend on The Godfather or that the middle-aged clown-faced woman who sold it to me asked if I wanted to wear it out of the store. It was December twenty-second, and I'd put off buying my final Secret Santa gift until the very last minute. This was the one thing I knew The Godfather would like, and since I'd half-assed her other two presents, I needed to finish strong.

As anticipated, Secret Santa had been a nightmare for me. When it was time for the first round of presents to be put into the stockings, I realized I'd completely forgotten about it, so I grabbed a package of peanut M&M's from the storage closet as my feeble offering. Little did I know, The Godfather had a nut allergy.

"I'm not amused," she announced to everyone that payday at check pickup. "Know that there *will* be consequences for any further attempts on my life."

The second time, I didn't do much better: I ended up giving her the Subway Club card I had in my wallet, which entitled her to a free six-inch turkey sub with the purchase of a medium drink. Turned out The Godfather was a vegetarian.

"My Secret Santa is my sworn enemy," she said before throwing my gift in the garbage.

Strike two.

As if I didn't feel bad enough, whoever drew my name turned out to be a magi of a gift-giver. My first present was a miniature Han Solo stuck in carbonite attached to a keychain. It came to me intricately wrapped in one of those little it's-probably-jewelry boxes with a lot of curled ribbon on top. The second gift was a small but very detailed die-cast model of the *Millennium Falcon*. It was most definitely a collector's item and probably not very cheap. This box, too, looked like it had been wrapped by a goddamn professional and included a calligraphed name tag.

All signs pointed to Poppins.

I was even more relieved I hadn't drawn her name.

I didn't really pay attention to what anyone else was getting in their stockings except for Baby, who was given a package of pacifiers and another of teething rings.

But since Baby and I were only talking about superficial things now, I couldn't ask her how she felt about them, even though I really wanted to know.

There was a lot more I wanted to know about Baby but couldn't ask. Like, had she decided if she was keeping the baby? Had she ever told Indy she hadn't gone through with the abortion? Or even, had she heard back from any of the colleges she'd applied to? But instead we spent most of our time together those few weeks ranking Jim Carrey films and arguing about whether *Die Hard* should be classified as a Christmas movie.

Don't get me wrong—I was glad we were still friends. It just wasn't the kind of friendship that the doctor had (literally) ordered.

The makeup lady insisted on gift wrapping The Godfather's lipstick, and then I made the trek back through the mall to JCPenney (because that's where I had parked, because I didn't know they didn't sell Kiss of Death lipstick there, because I didn't know anything about Chanel, because why would I?).

With only three shopping days left until Christmas, the mall was packed. As I weaved through the crowd, I realized I'd never been to this mall at Christmastime (Mom's perfume was available for purchase at the drugstore down the street from my house), but I had purchased the one and only other gift I ever bought for someone here, at the music store. You've probably already guessed that the gift was for Crystal.

Before you say anything, I don't count the earrings or makeup or any of the other stuff I got for Crystal as gifts. Pretty much all she owned when she arrived from Virginia was the shoebox and the clothes on her back, so the things I got her from the drugstore were necessities. The real present I bought her was concert tickets for Bon Jovi's Keep the Faith tour, which was pretty awesome of me, if I do say so myself.

"Are you for real, Joel?" Crystal's eyes widened, and she put her hand over her mouth. "You're taking me to see Bon Jovi?"

"Well, I'm not taking you because *I* like him," I told her.

"Thank you, thank you, thank you!" she squealed. "I seriously cannot wait! I'm going to wear my green dress!"

The show was at the Palace of Auburn Hills, which presented a challenge, since it was about sixteen miles farther than I was allowed to ride my bike, and there was no way my parents would have been cool with me going to a rock concert without an adult at thirteen years old.

Fortunately for me, Devin had just gotten his license and didn't ask a lot of questions. I gave him the allowance I'd been saving up to buy Crystal a T-shirt at the concert, and he dropped me off at the Palace with a promise to pick me up at ten, when the nearby indoor batting cages closed.

Just after Devin drove off, I met up with Crystal. She'd found her own way there and was wearing her dress without a coat even though it was barely March.

She hugged me. "I cannot believe I'm here, Joel! Can you believe we are going to be in the same room with Jon Bon Jovi and Richie Sambora?"

"I can hardly contain myself" was my response, but honestly I was just really happy that she was happy.

The Jeff Healey Band was the opening act. Then Bon Jovi came out, and even from our seats (which were in the nosebleeds, because that's all I could afford) it was a pretty cool entrance. There was smoke and lasers and explosions and really loud guitars. And then there was Crystal, screaming her head off, loving every bit of it.

I watched her more than I looked at the guys on stage. She seemed to know every word of every song they sang, and she jumped and sang all the lyrics, her brown curls bouncing like cartoon springs. It was one of the rare joys of my life, getting to see Crystal that night. There should be a word for what it's like to see someone you love loving something as much as Crystal loved Bon Jovi. It was a way better feeling, I think, than if I had loved them myself.

I kept looking at my watch, careful not to miss my curfew with Devin. Five minutes before ten, I told Crystal that I had to leave.

"You absolutely can't go before 'Livin' on a Prayer,'" she told me. "You have to stay for that song because it's my favorite!"

"OK," I reluctantly promised. She asked so little of me that I wanted her to have what she wanted. And it wasn't her fault, I kept telling myself, that the band didn't play that song until the very end of the set, at eleven fifteen.

"This was the very best night I've ever had, Joel," Crystal told me when the lights went on. "No one has ever done anything like this for me. Never. I didn't think anyone ever would. I should have given you more credit. I'm sorry." She hugged me and scratched my head with her Emerald City fingernails. "I wish I had more time with you."

"Will I see you soon?"

"Yes!" she said. And then Crystal disappeared into the crowd.

It was a quarter to midnight when I finally found Devin standing under a streetlight just outside the arena. With him was my cross-looking Aunt Denise, a police officer, and my violently angry mother.

The next day I was sent to Weller Clawson.

I don't know if this ever happens to you at the mall, but for the life of me, I couldn't remember where I had parked my damn car. I hadn't paid any attention to which department of JCPenney I'd entered through, so I had no idea which one I should exit from.

Rather than walk around outside in the cold hoping to stumble upon my LeBaron, I meandered around the store, waiting for something to jog my memory so I could retrace my steps. Nothing looked familiar, though — not the Levi's display by the women's department entrance or the mannequins wearing No Fear shirts in the men's. I couldn't even remember if I'd passed a Salvation Army bell ringer outside, which shows you just how focused I'd been on lipstick.

I was about to resign myself to taking up permanent residence at the mall when out of the blue, I saw my dad standing at the jewelry counter.

I did a double take to be sure it was him, but since hardly anyone else was still wearing Members Only jackets in those days, I could easily confirm his identity even from a distance.

It was weird seeing my dad at the mall, even beyond the coincidence of it. For starters, Dad simply did not shop. That was Mom's jurisdiction. He hated it so much that Mom even bought her own Christmas gifts so he didn't have to set foot in a store. He usually didn't even know what he'd gotten her until she showed him Christmas morning.

Also it was Sunday afternoon, which meant Dad should've been at Maple Mable's. He never broke his routine unless he was sick, which he didn't appear to be now.

But whatever. I was glad to see him since he would be able to drive me around the parking lot until I found my car.

"Dad!" I called out, but my voice was swallowed up by the crowd between us.

Dad was standing next to a short-haired blond woman who was trying on a bracelet. I watched as she handed it to my dad, and then, in a move that it took my brain some time to process, she took his hand.

I stopped walking toward them and stood in the middle of the aisle.

Dad laced his fingers with the woman's. She smiled at him, and he leaned down and kissed her on the lips.

177

Chapter 18

When I got home, I told my mom I was sleeping over at a friend's house that night. It was a hard sell.

"This is the first time I'm hearing about a friend."

"Hannibal. From work."

"Is he a good kid?"

"Of course."

"What are you going to do?"

"Play video games."

"Does he have a girlfriend?"

"He wishes."

"Will his parents be home?"

"Sure."

"Is Hannibal his first name or his last name?"

"His work name, Mom."

"Oh. What's his real name?"

" . . . Glenn."

"OK. Leave his number by the phone."

I wrote down my work number. That's where I was really going, anyway. I figured since Scarlet no longer needed the break room as an escape, the couch was up for grabs.

As I pulled out of the driveway, I saw my dad's truck in my rear-view mirror.

I was glad that we'd missed each other. It wasn't clear to me yet what I was supposed to do with what I'd seen at the mall. Until it was, I didn't want to face him.

I mean, I guess I was mad? Maybe not for the right reasons, though, because what I felt the angriest about was that I'd had to find out about this other woman, not that there *was* another woman. If that sounds backward, it probably is, but it's still true.

After everything my dad had been through—The Bad Thing That Happened, *me* after The Bad Thing That Happened—he'd remained solid. Like, superhumanly, impenetrably so. He handled all the details of The Bad Thing, the move to Michigan, and the rebuilding of our lives much better than the rest of us. I'm not saying he didn't emote, because he did, but The Bad Thing That Happened had caused my mom and me to lose our respective shits (in different ways, but still), and I could never figure out how my dad had kept himself together like he had.

Now it seemed that maybe he hadn't. Maybe the Something That Was Wrong With My Dad was that he cheated on my mom.

I didn't want to think about it. Fortunately for my brain, Scarlet's parents had asked for some year-end reports, and when I needed a distraction, busywork worked like a charm.

Maverick and Poppins were closing, but I told them not to worry about locking up. I took care of it before changing my clothes, brushing my teeth, and settling in for the night.

I switched on the TV, but its old antennae couldn't receive any static-free stations, so I just lay there under Scarlet's old covers, watching a fuzzy Jay Leno and becoming increasingly distracted by her lingering scent on the blankets.

Scarlet's just upstairs, you know, the voice in my head reminded me.

It only had to say it once. I jumped up, grabbed my coat, and seconds later, I found myself knocking on the door that led to the apartment above ROYO Video.

I might have had sketchy intentions when I went looking for Scarlet right after her breakup, but *I* was the vulnerable one in this particular situation, so I didn't feel guilty for going to see her. As long as she wasn't drunk, all bets were off. Hooking up with Scarlet was something a Normal guy would want to do, and I make no apologies for being Normal.

"What's going on, Solo?" Scarlet asked when she answered my knock dressed in a salon apron and not much else.

"Sorry to bother you. Do you care if I crash in the break room tonight?"

Her eyebrows raised, then lowered. "It's cold outside. Why don't you come up?"

This was exactly what I hoped she'd say. I didn't hesitate to follow her.

"So what happened?" she asked as we ascended the stairs.

"Stuff at home. You know how it is."

The stairs opened up into a wide space lit by overhead fluorescent lights, the way you'd expect a former real estate office to look. There were a few abandoned desks that Scarlet was using as a TV stand and a place to pile her clothes. In the corner, there was a mattress on

181

the floor next to the windows overlooking Washington Street. To the left was a linoleum-floored kitchenette with a chair positioned in the middle of it.

"Do you want something to drink?" she offered. "I've got pop, wine coolers, and I think there's some beer . . ." Scarlet walked toward the refrigerator.

I followed her. "No, thanks."

She opened the fridge and pulled out a soda. "So I guess I don't really know much about your life outside of work." The bottle hissed as she opened it. "Devin always just said your parents were real strict. They do something to piss you off?"

"Can we maybe *not* talk about my parents right now?" I touched Scarlet's elbow, which I realize wasn't exactly a Casanova-level move, but cut me some slack. "Or anything else?"

Scarlet let my hand rest on her arm, but she looked surprised it was there. "I didn't think you were interested in 'not talking' with me, Solo."

"I am," I confessed. "I would really enjoy not talking to you right now."

It was difficult to read the exact emotion on her face when I leaned in to kiss her, probably because one second later I was interrupted by the sound of a door opening behind us, and I literally jumped to the other side of the kitchenette.

From the hallway, out stepped a man in a towel.

"Hey, Jessica. There were all these little hairs on me, so I had to shower — oh, hi."

"Hi," I said back, feeling ridiculously stupid.

"Chase, this is Solo," Scarlet said. "Chase just stopped by for a trim." She pointed at the chair, which I now noticed was surrounded by piles of hair.

182

Chase walked across the room and shook my hand with the one he wasn't using to keep his towel on. "You must be Jessica's brother."

"Uh, no. We work together."

"Downstairs at the video store," Scarlet clarified.

Chase shrugged. "Right on." And then, instead of returning to the bathroom to get dressed or leaving so Scarlet and I could be alone together, he grabbed a beer from the refrigerator and took a seat—still in a towel—in the one other chair at the kitchen table. "You should stay for a haircut, since you're here. Jessica's really good."

"Oh," I said. "No, I'm good. I didn't realize she was busy." I inched toward the door.

Why had I expected Scarlet to be alone? Girls who looked like her were never alone. There were always a billion Chases at their beck and call. I should've known that, since I was one of the billion.

"Yes! I've been dying to get my hands on your hair, Solo," Scarlet told me. She ran her fingers through it a few times before guiding me to the chair.

"Um . . . OK. Just a trim, all right?" was all I could get in before Scarlet started spraying me in the face with cold water, which I knew was for the haircut but also proved beneficial in other ways at that particular moment.

"So," Chase began, "how long have you worked in video?"

"A few months," I said, inwardly groaning. I hated small talk. And, I was fast discovering, I hated it even more passionately when I was forced to have it with a man in a towel who I strongly suspected was flexing his pectorals. Still, obligatorily, I returned the question. "What do you do?"

"I'm a personal trainer."

Of course he was.

"If that's something you'd be interested in, I could hook you up

183

with some free sessions. You probably bench, what? Seventy, eighty pounds?" I had no idea if this was an insulting guess, but it was probably intended to be, even if it was accurate. "I could definitely help you double that in a few months."

"It's something to consider," I pandered. "New year, new me."

"I'm glad you said that, Solo," Scarlet said. Then she handed me a section of hair she'd just removed from my head. The length she'd cut was significant.

Wonderful. So this was going to be my punishment for attempting to seduce Scarlet: I'd lose all my hair while getting workout advice from a frat boy. Well played, universe.

If given the choice between reliving the next thirty minutes or all the time I spent in the psych hospital, it would be a real tough call. At one point, while Chase was giving me pointers on getting my abs to look like his (and feel like his — he made me touch them), I contemplated looking under the sink for some Mop & Glo. I wouldn't have drunk enough of it to kill me, obviously. Just however much it took to end this goddamn nightmare.

When she finished, I told Scarlet I liked my hair without really even looking at it, since it didn't matter one way or the other. I didn't care if she had shaved me bald as long as I could leave.

I wouldn't make eye contact with her when she walked me to the door. "I'm really sorry. I didn't know you were on a date."

"It's fine." She waved me off. "I'm sure he's not threatened by you or anything."

It was like she was trying to kick my libido in the balls. "Oh. Thanks."

"We aren't serious, is all I'm saying. I'm sure Chase couldn't care less if other guys come over."

"What a relief." I reached for the doorknob.

"Wait." She put her hand over mine. "I know you had a shitty day. And when I have a shitty day, you always say something super smart that makes a lot of sense, so I want to return the favor."

"I'm fine, really," I told her.

"No. I want to inspire you," Scarlet insisted. Her brown eyes grew very serious. It took a few seconds, but then she said, "I've got it—the perfect advice." She licked her lips, cleared her throat, and said, "Don't chase waterfalls."

I stared at her. "Is that a metaphor for something?"

"I don't know." She shrugged. "TLC said it."

"You mean in that song about gangs and AIDS and stuff?"

"Yeah."

"OK." I *guess* that was sound advice? As applicable as all the advice I'd stolen from motivational posters in psychiatrists' offices, anyway. "I shall chase no waterfalls," I promised her.

She smiled, satisfied. And with that, I left.

It had started to snow since I'd gone upstairs, and I left footprints in the thin layer of white that now covered the parking lot. It was colder, too. Or maybe it just felt that way to me because I'd lost all my hair.

It was also quiet the way that winter tended to be. Snow was nature's way of shushing the world, I thought. No crunching leaves, no birds chirping. Everything was soundproofed.

And . . . absent.

My little area of the world was covered. Hidden. There were no footprints in the snow. No tire tracks. No comings or goings. No signs of anyone trying to track me down because they were worried about me. No one who cared enough to keep me company.

I missed Crystal.

I wasn't afraid to admit it to myself this time. I really *missed* her.

More than 1 percent of me. All of me.

I reached into my pockets and pulled on my gloves.

185

Why couldn't she have stayed? She never hurt anyone. If anything, she had helped me. She'd helped me through The Bad Thing That Happened more than anything else ever had, I promise you that.

I pushed together a pile of snow until it was packed into a ball, and then I started rolling it along the ground. At first it was pure white, but the more snow it collected from the pavement, the dingier it became. I rolled it until it was too heavy, and then I left it next to the back door and started another.

I had a feeling I knew where I could find her. I'd long suspected where she'd gone, where she'd stayed all this time. Maybe waiting for me, maybe not. But it was a long drive. And even if she were there, I didn't know what I'd say to her now.

I made the second snowball smaller and the third smaller than that. I stacked them on top of each other to make a snowman. We'd never had snow during my childhood in Virginia, and my childhood had ended by the time I got to Michigan, so technically this was the first one I'd ever built.

I used pebbles for eyes and a mouth but, lacking a carrot, left the face noseless. Then I gave it some stick arms and took off my gloves — they were green — and stuck them on the ends. I stood back to admire my creation.

It was the best I could do.

I went back inside the store and fell asleep.

Chapter 19

ROYO Video was scheduled to open late the next day so that the entire staff could get together for a "holiday extraviganza."

I had my fingers crossed that Scarlet's Secret Santa would buy her a dictionary.

I went out to get orange juice early that morning, since that was what Poppins had assigned me to contribute to our little party. As I shopped, it occurred to me that maybe I should get something for all my coworkers, not just my Secret Santa, since I was technically their boss and it seemed like a thing good (and Normal) bosses did. My dad's boss, for example, always gave him a ham right before the holidays. This was maybe an appropriate gift for my family, but considering how the Subway Club card had gone over, I stayed away from gifts of meat. I ended up going with boxes of Sanders chocolates, then managed to find a peanut-allergy-friendly option for The Godfather.

The staff had already started arriving by the time I got back from the grocery store. When I walked in, Poppins was spreading out a poinsettia-patterned tablecloth on the break room table. She gasped when she saw me.

"Solo! Your hair!" Poppins's exclamation made Maverick's and Hannibal's heads jerk toward me, too. "You look like Brad Pitt!"

"Whatever." I laughed, but I was secretly flattered.

"For real," Maverick confirmed. "That's how Brad Pitt wore his hair in *12 Monkeys*."

Even Baby weighed in. "You look like an entirely different person. In a good way, I mean."

I smiled. "Scarlet cut it for me."

"Never mind. I hate it," she said, but I could tell she didn't mean it.

"Maybe I'll have Scarlet cut mine, too," Hannibal said, flipping his ponytail over his shoulder dramatically.

It was nice to see everybody in such a good mood.

Everyone else arrived soon after, toting either casserole dishes or trays for our spread along with their gifts. It turned out that I wasn't the only one who'd bought a little something for everyone, which made me feel extra Normal. All the employees except for Hannibal and Baby had brought extra presents and passed them out around the table. As we sat eating a potluck breakfast of Hostess donut holes, Maverick's mom's plantains, and fruit kebabs, we opened up the candy canes, homemade holiday brownies, fancy hot chocolate, and pairs of Ray-Ban designer sunglasses (this last one from The Godfather) we'd brought for one another.

"Are you serious right now?" Scarlet asked, trying on her sunglasses. "These are really expensive."

The Godfather clicked her tongue at the mention of money.

"Maybe you will show me how much the gesture means to you later. If and when I need you to." She looked each of us in the eyes.

Despite the usual amount of intimidation I felt around The Godfather, I found myself enjoying the party, and not just because I'd scored a pair of sweet shades.

Maybe this was what Christmas was like for kids with friends, but it certainly wasn't what I was used to. Typically the highlight of Christmas was opening a card with a check in it from my grandparents. This was better.

"Well, I'm not sure if Secret Santa is going to measure up to Ray-Bans, but let's get going on the big reveal!" Poppins announced excitedly. I guessed that she was the only person in the room feeling more holiday spirit than I was at that moment, and not just because she was wearing a dress with strands of functioning Christmas lights sewn onto it. "I'll go first!" she offered, setting a box wrapped in holly-themed paper on the table.

It didn't look as showy as the other two gifts I'd gotten in my stocking, but I wasn't going to hold that against her. It was the thought that counted, and Poppins had put so much thought into my other gifts that if this one was wrapped a little sloppily, so what.

But she slid the box past me and in front of Hannibal.

"Oh, cool. You had me?" he said, half grinning.

"Open it!" Poppins urged him.

Hannibal's enthusiasm was apparent as he pulled out an orange plush bear with a jester's collar around its neck. "Aw! A Grateful Dead bear! I'll name him Jerry."

Poppins practically bounced with glee. "I knew you'd like it!"

Hannibal, who had Scarlet, went next.

As he presented her with a gift in a brown paper bag with a stick-on bow, I tried to figure out who, if not Poppins, would have gone to all that trouble for my Secret Santa gifts.

Could it have been Scarlet? I doubted it. Considering she thought my name was *Hans* Solo, her Star Wars knowledge seemed too limited for her to have understood the coolness of a die-cast *Millennium Falcon.*

"Southern Comfort," Scarlet read from the label on the bottle of alcohol she unwrapped. "Perfect." As she showed it to us, I couldn't help but notice the still-fresh scar on her hand from her drunken fall in the storage closet.

"Here, this is for you." Scarlet set her offering in front of Baby, who eyed it suspiciously.

Baby, I had noticed, had been the quietest among us so far that morning. Now that my attention was on her, she looked tired, maybe even a little sad.

But her face was void of expression as she removed the paper from her gift. "*Beyond Jennifer and Johnny: Fifty Thousand Names for Your New Baby,*" she stiffly read, then looked away from the book.

"I know all the gifts I bought are more for the baby than for you," Scarlet said airily. "I figured that was fine."

"I'm sure you did" was Baby's response.

"I didn't know whether you'd picked a name," Scarlet said. "For the record, I like Taylor for a girl. And Tyson for a boy."

"Noted."

"Don't you like your present?" Scarlet pressed, dissatisfied with Baby's reaction. "I mean, I'm just trying to be supportive."

"Supportive?" Baby repeated. "Of what, exactly?"

"Supportive of you, you know . . . having a baby," Scarlet stated matter-of-factly. "I know maybe I wasn't before. But I've had a change of heart. I realized you'll need all the help you can get."

It seemed like she was trying to be sincere, but Baby wasn't buying it. "God, what is it with you and this baby, Scarlet? One minute you're telling me I'm unfit to bring a life into the world, and the next you want to help me name my child. Meanwhile, I don't recall ever asking you for your opinion."

Scarlet actually looked hurt. "Well, excuse me for caring, Baby. I was just trying to do something nice."

"Since when are you nice to me?" Baby asked.

Scarlet scowled at her. "Why do you have to make everything so difficult? I gave you a present. Why can't you just say thank you?"

"Because I don't like it," Baby said outright. "And I don't like you." She stood up then and slid a package toward Maverick. "Merry Christmas, Mav. I hope you needed a scarf." And with that, Baby left the room and, as the bells on the back door indicated, also the store.

We all looked at one another.

"What the hell is her problem?" Scarlet fumed.

This comment seemed to be directed at me for some reason, and she stared at me expectantly, waiting for me to address it.

I really didn't want to. After all, Baby and I weren't close enough for me to speak on her behalf, but everyone was waiting, so I did my best. "I think Baby's just going through a lot right now."

"Oh, please. Who isn't?" Scarlet rolled her eyes.

This bothered me. There was always at least one insensitive kid who would say something like this in every group therapy session. It was usually the most privileged kid in the room, who thought Whatever Was Wrong With Him was the worst thing anyone could possibly be going through. Not that individual trauma is necessarily comparable, but Scarlet breaking up with her boyfriend and Baby having a kid wasn't really apples to apples.

"Baby is *pregnant*. Do you have any idea how it must feel to be in her situation?"

This was usually how the doctors handled the kids like this

191

(though maybe they said it in a less shitty tone than I did). *An exercise in empathy,* they'd call it—putting yourself in someone else's shoes.

"Hard things happen to everyone, Solo" was Scarlet's defense. "I just don't get why Baby's always so angry. It's not like anyone forced her to have this baby."

Everyone looked at her.

"What? She could have used birth control. Or, you know, that other thing. Abstinence."

"Here's a thought," Maverick (thankfully) chimed in. "Maybe I could give my gift now?" He had opened the scarf Baby got him and was wearing it draped around his neck.

"Yeah, let's keep it going," Poppins agreed.

Needing no further prompting, Maverick stood up and walked over to the couch, retrieved a large box covered in curly ribbons, and carried it to the table. "Merry Christmas, Solo," he said, setting it in front of me.

"Wait. What?" I said.

It took me a few beats to reconcile Maverick as my Secret Santa, since I'd assumed it was a girl this whole time.

"Surprised?" he asked.

"Yeah, actually," I told him. "You really threw me off with all that fancy wrapping. Did your mom do it for you?"

"Oh, yeah." He nodded. "I hope you like it."

I opened the box and pulled out my gift, and then my jaw dropped.

Inside was a framed ink-and-watercolor picture. It was of an outer space, Star Wars–ian scene complete with shooting lasers, X-wing starfighters, and a Death Star (mid-explosion) in the background. In the foreground were the words RETURN OF THE ROYO, sketched out like the title of *Return of the Jedi,* and depictions of several characters huddled together.

"This is amazing . . ." I said, still taking it in.

"Look closer," Maverick prompted me.

I leaned in toward the characters. "Is that . . . me?" I asked stupidly, pointing at what appeared to be my face on Han Solo's body.

"Yeah." Maverick was grinning. "I mean, we're all there, but yeah, Han Solo is you. Before your haircut, obviously."

I couldn't believe how much the drawing resembled me, how it had only taken a few lines of pen and paint to replace Harrison Ford's face with mine.

The rest of the staff crowded around the picture.

"Let me see!" Poppins leaned over. "Oh my god! Am I Obi-Wan?"

"Yeah," Maverick confirmed. "There are surprisingly few women in Star Wars, so I had to draw some of the males as females. And one of the droids."

"You *drew* this?" I asked, completely dumbfounded. That probably should have already occurred to me, but it hadn't.

"Well, yeah. Art's my thing," Maverick explained. "And Poppins said we could make some of the gifts. I thought this would count."

"Hell yeah, dude! I'm Chewbacca!" Hannibal grinned, peering over my shoulder.

"I'm Darth Vader?" The Godfather said curiously. Then the faintest of smiles appeared on her lips. "I approve."

"I guess I'm Princess Leia, then," Scarlet assumed, moving around the table to see.

"No, I think that's you as C3PO." Poppins pointed at a droid with shiny metallic breasts.

"What? Why?" She seemed offended. "Who got to be Leia?"

"Baby," I said, looking at the face of the girl with cinnamon-bun hair and a crescent smile hanging on the arm of Han Solo.

I smiled back at her.

Maverick shrugged. "Like I said, there weren't a lot of options for the girls."

"Aww! You made yourself Luke!" Poppins pointed at the J. Crew Jedi standing next to Han. "He looks just like you!"

The attention was getting to Maverick, and his face reddened.

"Thanks for not making me Jabba the Hutt, my friend." Hannibal patted Maverick's shoulder. "It would have been easy, I know. I'm not going to forget that."

"What do *you* think, Solo?" Maverick asked me eagerly. "Do you like it?"

I was speechless. If I'm being honest, I might've been trying not to cry.

Not that there was a lot of competition, but this was by far the most thoughtful gift anyone had ever given me. It was also the most creative, the most personal, and had probably taken the most time to make. Plus it was awesome. I wasn't as good at anything as Maverick was at drawing. I couldn't stop looking at it.

"It's great," I managed. "Thank you."

"You're welcome."

"Can you draw one for me, too?" Poppins asked.

"Yeah, man. I'll pay you," Hannibal agreed. "That's so damn cool."

There was much less fanfare surrounding the final Secret Santa gifts, which were the lipstick I gave to The Godfather (she seemed moved—for her—that I'd gotten the shade right, and she forgave me for my previous gifts) and a hollowed-out book "for hiding valuables in" that The Godfather gifted to Poppins. People were still passing around the drawing long after the rest of the gifts were opened.

"You guys, we have to hang out more often!" Poppins declared when the exchange was complete. "This is the most fun I've had in forever."

194

I agreed. I was ready to completely eat my words on this whole Secret Santa thing.

We all stayed awhile longer, and then it was time to open the store. Everyone slowly dispersed until it was just me, my drawing, and an unclaimed baby name book left in the break room.

I tried not to feel Baby's absence, but I couldn't help it. I thought she would have really liked the Star Wars drawing, especially since Maverick had made her Leia and it had pissed Scarlet off.

I picked up the name book and started flipping through it.

Not that I'd ever tell Baby this, but I thought Scarlet's gift was kind of thoughtful. I certainly didn't think she'd meant anything bad by giving it to her, though honestly I doubted Baby would have liked *any* gift that came from Scarlet. Baby seemed hell-bent on hating her. If Scarlet deserved it, I didn't know exactly why.

I turned to the *N* section of the book.

Nicole (female): victorious.

I smiled. Baby had never seemed like a Nicole to me. It didn't have enough bite. I was glad her name had a decent meaning, though. *Victorious.* A winner. Well, a fighter and a winner. You're only victorious if you defeat something. You wouldn't call someone who just won the lottery victorious, for example. That kind of person was just lucky. But Nicole? Nicole *earned* her successes. She was a warrior. A combatant. *Victorious.*

I flipped to the *J*'s.

Joel (male): strong-willed.

That wasn't nearly as cool.

Though on second thought, Baby's and my names sort of went together. I mean, victorious people become victorious by defying the status quo, or at least doing something that sets them apart from all the non-victorious people, and that's basically what being strong-willed meant, too. Being stubborn. Not giving in, not giving up.

Strong will leads to victory. Put in SAT prep terms: Strong-willed is to victorious as Joel is to Nicole. If Solo, then Baby.

Damn. I must have really missed Baby if I was making up SAT analogies about her.

I mean, I *did* miss her. I wasn't trying to kid myself about that. If it were up to me, I would have hung out with her every day, at work and outside of it. But considering the restrictions she'd placed on our friendship, that didn't seem realistic.

Although . . .

Technically, it would be a completely superficial move to deliver this book to Baby. It was a book. A reference material. Nothing deep there. So if I were to drop it off with her, it would be well within our surface-level friendship agreement. I could just give her the book, maybe show her Maverick's drawing, chitchat about the weather, and then be on my way.

Plus, what else was I going to do that day? I wasn't ready to go home yet, and I didn't have to work until the closing shift. Unless I was going to be a lame boss and hang out at work for ten hours off the clock, I had to figure out something else to do.

I grabbed my keys.

Keeping my windows up and the volume of R.E.M. low, I drove down Baby's street, looking out for the Accord in her driveway. When it wasn't there, I knew only one other place she might be, so that's where I went next.

The Headlights parking lot was sparsely populated, but there was a black Accord in it, and it had a Pearl Jam sticker on its back window.

I felt pretty victorious when I saw it there.

The pinup hostess led me to a table where Baby was sitting alone, poring over a stack of papers and a plate of wings.

"Hey," I said from behind her.

She turned around and looked at me, surprised. "Hey."

I tossed the baby name book on the table.

"Do you know what your name means?" I asked her.

She kept looking at me. "No."

"Victorious."

"Oh" was her uninterested response. "That's weird. Seems like that's what Victoria would mean. Not Nicole."

This was a valid point. "Maybe Victoria means that, too. I didn't check."

We looked at each other.

"Is that all you wanted?"

"No," I said. "I also wanted to talk to you."

She looked at me skeptically. "About what?"

"Movies" was my answer. "That is on the approved list of things we can still talk about, right?"

"Yeah." Baby looked confused. "But I'm kind of in the middle of something right now, so can it wait until work?"

"I just wanted to know if you caught the film about the girl who got into a fight with her boss at their work Christmas party, because I didn't see the end of it, and I was hoping that everything was OK with the girl."

Baby folded her arms over her chest and gave me a look. "Really, Solo?"

"I'm serious. How did it end? It's really bothering me."

She sighed but eventually played along. "It was a real letdown. I was hoping that the boss was going to get hit by a bus, but she didn't."

"What about the girl?"

"She went and ate chicken at a tits-and-ass restaurant."

I raised my eyebrows. "Sounds like a European ending."

Baby rolled her eyes at me but said, "Siskel and Ebert gave it two thumbs up."

"That's good to hear," I told her. "Because I'm really looking forward to the sequel, where the girl and her much-cooler guy friend pull off a jewel heist that makes them very wealthy and infamous."

Baby wanted to smile at this, I could tell. "You couldn't heist your way out of a paper bag, Solo."

"Don't underestimate me," I defended myself. "According to your book, I'm strong-willed."

She shook her head but then offered me a seat at her table, and I felt victorious yet again.

"I know I said I wasn't going to do this anymore," she began. "But can I talk to you about something?"

This elated me. "Anything."

"For real? Because as much fun as it is withholding all information about myself because *you* never tell me shit about *your* life, I need someone to talk to."

"I'm someone," I confirmed. "You can talk to me."

Instead of saying anything, though, Baby just handed me one of her papers.

It was an official-looking letter from the Office of Enrollment at Sarah Lawrence College.

> *Dear Ms. Palmer,*
> *Congratulations! On behalf of the faculty and staff at*
> *Sarah Lawrence College, we are pleased to inform you*
> *that you have been accepted for admittance to our great*
> *institution beginning in the fall semester of 1997 . . .*

My eyes shot up from the letter. "Holy shit, Baby! You got in!" I smiled at her. "This is amazing! Congratulations!"

Baby wasn't smiling back. "What the hell am I going to do?"

"Uh . . . go to college?"

"With a baby?"

"Oh." I remembered. "Right."

Baby sighed. "I'd decided to keep it. At least I was pretty sure I was going to. Before I got this letter, that is. Now I don't know." She paused. "What does it say about me if I change my mind? What kind of mother does that even make me?"

I recognized this as a question that had no answer. In my experience, there are a lot of those.

She went on. "Kat and Bob said they'd raise it until I was done with college if I wanted them to, but that doesn't seem fair. I would feel really selfish abandoning my six-month-old to go study in New York when there's a community college a few miles from my house." Baby rubbed her temples. "Plus, Bob's kids are grown, and he doesn't want any more. He puts up with me because I'm almost out of the house, but a baby was never part of the deal for him and Mom." She sighed again and ran her fingers through her hair. "I either stay here and keep it or go away and don't, and it feels like no matter what I pick, everyone loses." Baby banged her head on the table. She left it there for a few seconds. "Did Maverick like his scarf?"

I was unfazed by the segue. When people are talking about heavy shit, it usually ends abruptly. It's a healthy coping mechanism for your brain to switch subjects when something's hard to talk about. A good listener will ride it out.

"He put it on right away."

"Yeah, but he's super nice like that. Even if he hated it, he'd pretend not to." She took a drink of water. "What did he end up giving you?"

"You knew he had me for Secret Santa?"

"Yeah," Baby admitted, lifting her head back up. "He didn't know what to get you, so he asked me. I told him probably something related to Star Wars, but he'd never seen the movies." She fiddled with her straw, only half interested in what she was telling me. "I thought he did all right with your first two gifts."

"Yeah," I agreed. "I brought the last present with me. I wanted to show it to you."

"Sure." She shrugged.

I excused myself to my car to grab the drawing.

Halfway there, something Baby said fully sank in: Maverick had never seen Star Wars. This struck me as odd for two reasons.

First of all, what kind of person hadn't seen Star Wars?

Secondly, the drawing was so detailed, and the personalities of the characters were so spot-on that I'd just assumed Maverick was a huge fan like I was. I couldn't think of another way he could have captured everything like he did. Or why he would have tried to. I mean, he could have just given me a Subway Club card for Secret Santa and been done with it.

Weird.

When I showed Baby the drawing, she was as blown away as I was.

"Wow! This is, like, *so* good. Like, he-could-make-a-career-as-an-artist good."

"Right?" I agreed. "I mean, especially having never seen the movies. I can't believe how he still nailed everything like he did."

"Oh, he ended up watching them," Baby said without taking her eyes off the picture. "He told me he needed to for your final gift, but I had no idea he was going to make something like *this*."

"He did?" The weirdness I felt persisted. "I can't believe Maverick went to all that trouble just for a Secret Santa gift."

"I can," Baby said, her eyebrows raised. "Ha! I just realized that I'm Princess Leia and Scarlet's fucking C3PO! Please tell me that made her mad."

"Why doesn't it surprise you that Maverick did this?" I asked, tapping on the picture frame.

Baby looked at me and said, "Come on, Solo."

"What?" I demanded, apparently missing something she thought was obvious. "Does he want a raise or something?" I felt myself getting angry at the idea of Secret Santa being used in that way. Why couldn't people just do nice things to be nice? Why did they always want something in return?

"No, stupid." Baby shook her head at me. "I mean, you *know*, right?"

"Know what?"

"About Mav."

"What about Mav?"

"That he's . . ." Baby drew out the words to see if I'd finish her sentence for her. "*Not* into girls."

"What?" I almost shouted. "No, I don't think so."

Baby just shrugged.

"Did he tell you that? Did he tell you he was gay?" I whispered that last part. Saying the word *gay* in a place like Headlights seemed like a great way to get your ass kicked.

"Do any gay kids say they're gay?" Baby asked me. "It'd be like painting a target on your back. Being gay's the one thing people are more judgy about than pregnant teenagers."

"So you don't know for sure, then," I challenged her. "You're just being mean."

This seemed to offend her. "Why would it be mean to say someone is gay if you really think that they are?"

"Because it *is* mean!" I practically yelled. "An accusation like that can ruin someone's life, Baby."

She was slow to respond. "Whose life would be ruined if Maverick had a crush on you—his or yours?"

"You don't understand." I heaved a sigh. "I absolutely can*not* have him liking me."

"Why not?" Baby's eyes narrowed. "Do you have something against Puerto Rican guys?"

"What? No!" I yelled, then lowered my voice. "I don't want any guy to like me like that."

She looked disgusted. "My god, Solo. I didn't figure you for such a homophobe."

"You just implied Maverick is in love with me. What guy is going to be happy about that?"

"A gay one. Maverick's awesome."

"Well, news flash, *I'm* not gay," I whispered.

"So? What are you so upset about, Solo? Maverick's a great guy. And way out of your league in the looks department. You should be flattered at the very least."

"Well, I'm not," I repeated. "Wait. Did *you* think I was gay?"

Baby shook her head. "With the way you drool over Scarlet all the time? I was pretty sure you were straight. Just with bad taste."

"Well, does *Maverick* think I'm gay?" I demanded. "I don't want him thinking I'm interested *at all.*"

"I don't know, Solo. But it's not like if Maverick has a crush on you, it *turns* you gay. So you can go ahead and calm the hell down about this."

But I couldn't. Instead I said, "My parents are going to lose their *fucking* minds," which was admittedly a very odd thing for a person to be preoccupied with in this situation. That is, unless you are me, and then it makes perfect sense, but only if you know some very specific shit about my life, which Baby did not.

"What do your parents have to do with anything?" was her obvious question.

"Never mind." I was so mad I was shaking. "I gotta go." I stood up to leave.

The problem was that I couldn't leave because I had no place to go. I was already avoiding my house, and now I also had to avoid work, the only other place I went, because my male coworker evidently had the hots for me.

Baby grabbed my arm. "No!"

This got my attention.

"You're not doing this to me again, Solo! I just sat here and opened up to you *again*, and now that it's your turn, you're leaving." With her superhuman pregnancy strength, Baby pulled me down into the booth next to her. "I don't want some half-baked friendship with you anymore. We're either all in, or we're nothing. You know my shit, and dammit, I want to know yours! Even if it's homophobic shit! So spill it. Why is Maverick liking you the end of the world?"

I looked into Baby's eyes. They were green.

You may be wondering why I wouldn't just answer *this* question. I mean, it's not like Baby had asked me about What Was Wrong With Me or The Bad Thing That Happened. But what you need to understand is that I couldn't answer this question without getting into those other things. Everything was tangled together.

It was like one of those place mat mazes they give to kids at restaurants, the ones with all the different starting points where the prize is in the middle. No matter which direction you enter the maze from, if you persist through all the dead ends, you come to the same ending as all the other paths do. All roads lead to The Bad Thing That Happened.

I knew that answering Baby's question meant deciding to tell her everything. I wasn't ready for that. She didn't know it, but neither was she.

"It's complicated."

Baby rolled her eyes. "Whatever you're hiding can't be that bad."

"It completely can."

Baby groaned, but she offered me a plea deal. "Fine. Don't tell me this. Start with something else. Just tell me *one* thing. Tell me about the girl."

I froze. "What girl?"

"The girl! The girl, Solo! The girl you thought you saw here that day when you freaked out about the Bon Jovi song!" Baby threw her hands in the air. "What did she do to fuck you up? Cheat on you? Break your heart? *What?*"

"No." I shook my head. "It wasn't like that."

"Then what *was* it like?"

I swallowed hard and considered what to say. I *could* tell her about Crystal without actually *telling her about Crystal*. It might even put my tabula rasa back on the Normal track. A relationship fucking you up was basically a Normal rite of passage. I didn't have to elaborate that mine was with a girl only I could see.

"Fine," I conceded. "There was a girl I cared a lot about. And she abandoned me. She left me when I needed her the most, and it destroyed me."

The look on Baby's face changed from rage to sympathy in a flash. "Who was she?"

For a moment, we were locked in a stare-down.

I wasn't ready to say any more, but my friendship with Baby was on the line.

So I decided to tell her.

. . . I think.

Ultimately, I don't know what I would've done, because before Baby could force me to give her an answer, there was a loud metallic *bang* in the kitchen. This was followed by screaming, followed by smoke, followed by Kat running into the restaurant from the back yelling "Fire!", followed by the overhead sprinklers activating, followed by a lot of cold water, panic, and chaos.

And as fucked up as it sounds, as Baby and I were running out of the restaurant, all I could think about was how the universe had somehow orchestrated this convenience for me, the Doogie Howser of the video store corporate ladder.

Chapter 20

One of the most noted anomalies in the English language is that the words *flammable* and *inflammable* mean the exact same thing. That is, they both indicate that something can blow up. Unfortunately, this particular language irregularity had not been properly explained to the new English-as-a-second-language line cook at Headlights before he left the *in*flammable can of cooking spray on the in-use gas range.

Miraculously, no one was seriously hurt.

It turned out there were only three people in the kitchen when the accident occurred, since it was still so early in the day. The cook had some first-degree burns, and Kat and a waitress I didn't know had some bruises from falling cookware. But considering how bad things could have been, everyone felt pretty lucky.

People were shaken up afterward, but the actual damage seemed minimal. The sprinkler system had obviously poured water into the place, so there was that clean-up to deal with, but it had also put the fire out before the fire department arrived, so there wasn't extensive smoke or burn damage. Headlights would have to be closed for a few weeks while things were restored, but insurance, Bob reminded Kat (who was a crying mess), would cover all their losses.

I changed out of my wet clothes in the bathroom of the Applebee's next door, putting back on what I'd worn the previous day, since I'd slept at the store and still had everything with me. Because Baby was pregnant, she was made to change into scrubs in the back of an ambulance and then sit under heavy blankets until her vitals stabilized, and then, just to be on the safe side, the paramedics ordered an ultrasound at the hospital.

I told her goodbye, and she handed me back my Star Wars drawing, which she'd made sure to save during the evacuation.

Despite wanting to avoid my parents, I went home. At that moment I was less prepared to see Maverick than I was my cheating father, plus I realized that it was a weekday and the odds of running into anyone at my house were slim.

My luck held, and I was able to take a long hot shower in peace and reflect on what had amounted to a couple of pretty fucked-up days in the life of Joel Teague.

There was a lot swimming around in my head, but for some reason I couldn't take my mind off the fire.

I don't want to say that the kitchen fire at Headlights gave me flashbacks of the kiln, because it wasn't like that. It did jog that particular memory loose, though, and it kept playing on a loop, round and round in my head.

"I didn't see you in there!"

The flames. The water. The ashes.

"I didn't see you . . ."
The hose. The cold.
"I didn't see . . ."
Crystal.
"I didn't see you in there!"
The flames. The water. The ashes.
"I didn't see you . . ."
The hose. The cold.
"I didn't see . . ."
Crystal.
Crystal.
Crystal . . .

"Joel, I don't know how you can stand this hospital food." She stuck a spork into the congealed pasta salad that had maintained the shape of the ice cream scooper with which it was served.

"I'm not supposed to talk to you," I said, closing my eyes. "The doctors say you aren't real, so go away." I opened them a few seconds later. She was still there.

"That's mean," Crystal informed me. "Where exactly am I supposed to go?"

"I don't know," I told her. In the drawer of the bedside table, I found a manual for the Posturepedic hospital bed I was lying on. I was reading it to distract myself from her. "Back where you came from, I guess."

"Well, *that's* impossible." She sighed, stretching out one of her curls and watching it bounce back into place. "I thought we were friends, Joel."

"I want to be your friend, but being your friend means I'm crazy," I explained to her. "I don't want to be crazy."

"Your mom might think you're crazy, but no one else really does," she corrected me. "I'm telling you, Joel, she's the one with the real problem."

I set down the manual and took her bait. "Why?"

Crystal laughed to herself. "She's afraid. The majority of the time someone is the way she is, it's because they're afraid."

It had never occurred to me that my mother was afraid of anything. Angry? Yeah. Critical? You betcha. Paranoid? Definitely. But not afraid. "Of what, though?"

"The unknown consequences of being wrong," she (kind of) explained. "That's what most people are afraid of."

This seemed like it might make sense, but I wasn't sure. Crystal seemed to know a lot of things I didn't. "Not me. I'm just afraid of being crazy," I informed her. "Which is why you have to leave."

"Oh, come on. I have it on good authority that you are afraid of other things."

I gave her a doubtful look. "Like what, exactly?"

She came around the side of my bed and leaned against it casually. "I can name three specific things."

"What are you talking about?"

"You know. *Those* three things." Crystal's green eyes sparkled.

I *did* know, but I didn't believe that she really did, so I called her bluff. "I never told you about any three things."

"Oh, you did. Three Star Wars things, to be precise." Crystal leaned over and whispered in my ear, "Wampas and rancors and banthas."

I felt my cheeks go red. "How do you know about that?"

She took a step back and shrugged. Then she whispered it louder. "Wampas and rancors and banthas!"

"Seriously? Who told you that?" I shook my head at her. "I haven't been scared of that stuff since I was a kid."

She started chanting it, à la "lions and tigers and bears."

"Wampas and rancors and banthas, oh my!"

"All right, enough!"

"Wampas and rancors and banthas, oh my!"

"You're not funny!"

Crystal apparently thought otherwise, because she suddenly yelled "Boo!" in my face and began laughing hysterically when I jumped.

I threw my sheets back and stood up. "That's it! I'm going to tell!" I shouted, and stomped out of the room.

Once I set foot outside the room, however, I was no longer at the hospital. The ground beneath me was sandy, and it was sunny and warm. I was outside. I was at a beach.

"Wampas and rancors and banthas, oh my!" I heard Crystal call again, but when I looked back toward my hospital room, it was no longer there. And I didn't see her anywhere.

These meds are weird, I thought. But then I realized where I was: Virginia Beach.

God, I'd missed this place.

"Mom? Dad?" I called out.

"Wampas . . . rancors . . . banthas . . ." A voice echoed from the ocean.

"She's doing it again!" I yelled across the sand. "Crystal's making fun of me about Star Wars!"

"They are just *puppets*!" her voice teased. "How can he be afraid of puppets?"

The beach was full of people, but none of them was Crystal. Miles and miles of towels and umbrellas. Miles and miles of ocean and sand.

"Because they're monsters!" I defended myself. "They're supposed to be scary, and they *are* scary!" Suddenly, sticking halfway out of the sand on the shore, I found my missing Han Solo blaster. I ran

210

toward it. "*That's* where I left it . . ." The whole time I'd thought it was in the basement, it was here.

"Wampas and rancors and banthas, oh my!" Crystal yelled again.

I picked up the gun and squeezed the trigger. It made the drill sound. "Where are you? Come out so I can blast you!"

Wherever she was, Crystal burst into giggles. "I'd like to see you try it, *Han Solo*!" More giggles. "Wampas and rancors and banthas, oh my!"

I waved my blaster around, aiming it at all the people who weren't Crystal. "Come out, come out, wherever you are, *Princess Leia*!"

"Shhh!" another voice hushed me. It was my mom. "I've told you—you can't play this game anymore!" From behind me, she grabbed my wrist and pulled the blaster from my hand. "No more of this. No more Han and Leia. No more Star Wars! No more!"

"We're just playing, Mom!" I tried to explain. "It's not for real."

She sighed. "You just don't get it!" And with that, she chucked my blaster as far as she could out into the ocean.

"No!" I screamed.

I waded out after it until I couldn't touch the ground, and then I started swimming.

I wanted my toy back. I wanted to keep playing. But it was gone, and I couldn't.

I dunked my head underwater, and that's when I finally found Crystal.

Or at least, I found the half of her that hadn't been swallowed up by the ocean floor. An ocean floor that was, to make matters worse, engulfed in flames.

Her eyes were closed, and she was swaying in the waves, her arms and hair floating with the ebb and flow as she slowly sank deeper into the sand.

Quicksand. Ocean quicksand.

I couldn't stop to ask myself if underwater fires and ocean quick-sand were real things. I had to act fast.

I dove down toward her, pointlessly shouting her name into the water, dodging the flames as they danced around me. I grabbed on to her hair first, but as I pulled, it fell out in my hands. Handful after handful until barely any remained. She looked completely different without her hair. Like she wasn't even the same person.

That's when I realized: it wasn't Crystal who was drowning.

Suddenly his eyes opened, and he grabbed me by the arm just before he completely disappeared into the sand.

Despite my struggle, I couldn't break free of his grip, and within seconds, I had gotten sucked under, too.

I woke up with a start, lying on my bed, still wrapped in a bath towel, my heart racing, covered in a cold sweat.

Chapter 21

I called in sick to work that afternoon, which would have made me a coward if I hadn't actually been sick. The thermometer said 101.5, and who was I to argue with it?

I took some Advil and went back to sleep. I woke thirteen hours later at around four in the morning and showered again, even though all I'd done since the last one was sleep.

I waited until six to go downstairs, since that wasn't an entirely unreasonable hour to be awake and because Mom would already be at work at the bakery by then, so I could continue avoiding everyone. Of course, I'd forgotten that it was Christmas Eve, and we surprised each other when I walked into the kitchen.

"You cut your hair." She greeted me with a kiss on the cheek and a head scratch. "It's about time. You were starting to look like a girl."

Then she grabbed me by the face and looked more carefully at me. "You've got sick eyes, Joel. Did you catch a cold?"

"Yeah, but it's not bad."

She went to the fridge and returned with a can of Vernors, a ginger soda with a local reputation for curing all mild illnesses. "Think you'll be better enough to go to Aunt Denise's tonight?" She pulled a cigarette from her pack and lit it.

"No," I said, thankful I had a legitimate excuse to bail on the family Christmas celebration. I opened the ginger ale and drank some.

"That's too bad." She frowned and blew her smoke away from me. "I hate for you to be all alone on Christmas Eve."

"I'll probably just sleep."

She sipped her coffee. "If you start feeling worse, take yourself to urgent care. I'm making Dad come with me to finish Christmas shopping today, but we'll check in." Mom took a long drag from her cigarette. "Any last-minute requests for Santa? Dad's feeling generous this year."

I frowned, remembering the woman at JCPenney. I bet he was feeling generous. "I don't need anything."

"Nothing?" she pressed. "We want this to be a good Christmas."

"Whatever you get me will be fine."

My dad walked in then, still in his robe, and kissed my mom on the top of her head.

"I think I need to go back to bed," I told my mom, and I went back upstairs.

I fell back asleep for a few more hours. Then I got up, played *Tekken*, ate a Hot Pocket, and finally got dressed. Health-wise, I was feeling a lot better. Otherwise, my head was still pretty full.

I went out to my car to get my R.E.M. CD, hoping that Michael

Stipe might help me clear my mind, but then I saw Maverick's Star Wars drawing. Realizing I had to do *something* with it, I brought it up to my room.

If I was going to keep it (which I still wanted to, honestly), I was going to have to find somewhere to hide it, because Star Wars was forbidden in my house. (As you may have noticed, my parents had some issues with it.) I'd stashed the Han Solo keychain and the die-cast *Millennium Falcon* in my glove compartment, but I knew that hiding something this big from my mom would be damn near impossible.

Even though I'd been out of the psych hospital for a few years now, Mom still snooped through my room. I tried not to let it bother me. I knew that she couldn't help herself. She needed the occasional reassurance that her son wasn't hoarding any more earrings or lipstick for his imaginary friend.

After Mom found the green dress and I jumped in the pond, my parents took me to my pediatrician, who hypothesized that my stash of women's clothing might point to a burgeoning homosexuality, which just so happened to confirm my mother's greatest fear.

To combat my inferred gayness, my parents signed me up for a church-run boys' camp, which was supposed to teach me how to be super masculine.

We started each meeting by reading a Bible story about manly men from the Old Testament, and then we spent the rest of the time chopping wood with axes and climbing ropes and running obstacle courses. I also remember eating a lot of meat with those guys. The leaders' wives cooked us steaks, which was the only thing I liked about the program.

After a few months, when I didn't immediately transform into a bona fide lumberjack, my parents pulled me from the group and signed me up for another one called Preparing Boys for Manhood.

In this awkward-as-hell class, we talked a lot about natural physical attraction and how it was normal to want to kiss girls and touch boobs. I also vividly remember them showing us pictures of an almost-naked woman and explaining a few things we might enjoy doing with one when we were older.

It was humiliating.

Not long after the class ended—or maybe this was part of the final exam, I was never sure—a few pages from the lingerie section of the Sears catalog mysteriously appeared on my bed. When I kept them for private use, my parents must have thought I was out of the woods, because that seemed to put an end to the gay crucible.

All that is to say, knowing what homophobes my parents were, I could only imagine what my mom would do if she found out about Maverick's drawing. While it may not have occurred to *me* why Maverick had given me such a personal gift, you can bet your ass that Mom's gaydar would go off, and I'd be on the next bus to conversion therapy.

I opened the back of the drawing's frame and carefully slid a picture of a scantily clad Yasmine Bleeth that I ripped from a magazine in front of it. Mom would be proud.

But I wasn't.

I wasn't proud that Baby thought I was a homophobe. I didn't see myself as one. If I'd learned anything from all my parents' attempts to make me straight when I already *was* straight, it was that homophobic people were *way* scarier than actual gay people.

However, I was phobic of my mother, and she was definitely homophobic, so via the transitive property of mathematics, I guess that made me afraid of her fear. For some reason—maybe because she was religious, maybe because she was afraid of AIDS, maybe

216

because she saw the shitty ways in which the world treated gay people, maybe for another unknown reason — my mother was terrified of having a gay child. So there we were.

The phone rang while I was flipping channels, looking for something better than talk shows with which to kill the afternoon. I knew before I answered it would be my mom checking in.

"Hey, Mom."

"Were you sleeping? Have you eaten anything?"

"No, and yes. I'm feeling better."

"Good enough to go to Aunt Denise's tonight?"

"Not *that* much better."

"All right. We're at Chi-Chi's having Mexican," she told me. Dad rarely agreed to eat ethnic food. He must have been feeling super guilty. "Want me to bring you home some fried ice cream? It can be for la Navidad." She laughed at her own joke. Mom was in a great mood. She must've had a margarita.

"Yeah, sure."

"We saw someone at the mall. One of your old doctors. Dad said it was him, at least, but I remembered this one having a mustache."

"Neat," I said, ready to get off the phone.

"He was in the food court with his wife and teenage daughter, and guess what — she was *pregnant*," my mom dished. "I guess even shrinks can raise screwed-up kids. How do you like that?"

I didn't like it, but it wasn't worth the argument to point out all the ways that one statement was judgmental. "So you'll be home soon, then?"

"In a bit. I'm going to see how much money I can spend today," she said. Then she let me go.

MTV was playing their most-requested one hundred videos of 1996, and even though I'd already watched the top five videos when they had aired a few days before and knew that Alanis Morissette's "Ironic" would be number one, I left it on.

It was then, as I was mindlessly watching Soundgarden's "Blow Up the Outside World," that something my mom had said on the phone set off a domino effect in my head:

Marc Schwartz is one of my former doctors who used to have a mustache.

During the trick or treat, Marc's wife told me that she didn't have any kids.

That means the teenage girl Mom saw with them couldn't have been their daughter.

Maybe Baby is the pregnant teenager who was with them.

I gave this particular thought some attention.

Marc called me Joel, not Solo, the night of Scarlet's accident.

Maybe Baby figured out that I knew him.

The spiraling continued.

Marc and Baby were alone in the break room that night while I was cleaning up Scarlet's vomit.

Maybe he told her about being a doctor. About what kind of doctor he was.

This made me nervous. It made me paranoid.

Maybe Baby was tired of waiting for me to tell her What Was Wrong With Me.

Maybe our conversation at Headlights was the last straw.

Maybe she went to Marc for the truth instead.

I didn't want to believe this was true, but once the idea entered my head, I couldn't shake it.

Would Baby do something like that? And even if she had, would Marc have told her anything about me?

I hoped not. But I didn't know.

The thing about being paranoid is that the not knowing can drive you *crazy*.

My heart hammered.

I turned the television off.

I paced.

I decided.

I grabbed my keys and walked out the door.

Chapter 22

I drove up and down the rows of parked cars in the mall lot, looking for the Accord. When I didn't find it there, I drove to Baby's house, hoping she was home.

My head was pounding as I drove, and I realized too late that I should have taken more medicine for my cold. But knowing that all the Advil in the world wouldn't stop my paranoid thoughts, I kept going until I got to Baby's. Thankfully her car was in the driveway.

"What are you doing here?" was how she greeted me. "And where's your coat? It's fucking freezing." She pulled me inside.

I hadn't noticed that I was cold. Or that I couldn't see straight. Baby and everything around her looked fuzzy. "Were you with Marc Schwartz today?" I demanded. "Please just tell me you weren't, and I'll leave."

I couldn't focus on her face to read her expression, but she sounded sort of shocked when she said, "What?"

Just then I heard Kat's voice. "Nicole, who was that at the door?"

"I just need to know what you guys were talking about," I pleaded, my voice shaking.

"It's Joel, Mom," Baby called. "There's something wrong with him . . ."

"No, there's not, I swear!" I promised her. "Is that what Marc told you? There used to be Something Wrong With Me, OK? But there's not anymore . . ." The lights in the hallway seemed so bright that I had to squint, but I could make out a bench near the door. I practically fell onto it.

Kat came around the corner just then.

"Joel?" I felt her hand touch my forehead. "Honey, are you sick?"

"I think I'm going blind" was my honest answer. I'd heard of people going blind with rage, but never with paranoia. I was a modern marvel.

"What the fuck?" was Baby's reaction.

It would've been mine, too.

"Is he high, Nicole?" Kat asked sternly. "Is this boy about to overdose right here in my foyer?"

"How would I know that?" Baby asked.

"I don't do drugs," I tried to tell them, but my tongue seemed to have gone numb.

"Let's get him to the sofa," Kat directed. Each of them took one of my arms and guided me into their living room.

"Joel, sweetie, do you have a headache?" Kat asked for some reason.

I nodded.

"OK," she said, and then her voice seemed farther away. "Back in a sec."

221

"I am *so* confused right now," Baby said as she gently pushed me back into the couch and swung my legs up so that I was fully stretched out. "You'd better not fucking die on me, Solo. I will seriously never forgive you if you walk into my house on Christmas Eve just to die on my goddamn couch."

Kat returned moments later with some pills and a cold washcloth.

"Have you ever had a migraine, Joel?" she asked.

"No?" I grunted, unsure exactly what a migraine was.

"Well, after all the stress of the fire yesterday, I had one last night. I know they're coming when my vision gets all blurry," she explained. "Are you under a lot of stress?"

"Yes," I told her, and it felt like an understatement.

"I think you'll be fine in a bit. Most of the time, migraines are intense, but they don't last long. Can you rest here for a while?"

I honestly felt so shitty that it didn't seem like I had a choice. "Yeah."

Kat gave me a blanket, a cold compress, and an empty trash can in case I got nauseated, which she warned me could happen with migraines. Then they turned off all the lights, and it was so quiet and dark and warm that I fell asleep in no time.

I awoke with a start a while later, unsure at first where I was. My memory felt distant and foggy.

"You snore," a voice from the darkness told me.

"Baby?" Everything slowly came back to me.

A dim lamp switched on, illuminating Baby sitting in a chair. "You also drool."

"I'm sorry," I apologized, trying to sit up. A dull ache still pulsed in my head. It was only an echo of the pain I'd felt earlier, but it still made me wince.

"You're going to have a headache hangover," she explained to me. "Mom gets them after a migraine. Caffeine helps."

"Thanks for the tip." Then, because it caught me off guard, I noted, "You're dressed up."

"Przybylski holiday party," she explained as she smoothed her hand over her dress. I wasn't sure if I'd ever seen Baby in a dress before or if it just struck me as unusual now because of how big her stomach looked in it. Somehow Baby's pregnancy never ceased to take me by surprise even though it was right in front of me all the time. "It started an hour ago. Kat left already because she had to take a pie over."

"Oh." I started to stand up. "I can go so you can leave."

"Don't," Baby stopped me. "We need to talk, Solo." Her tone was resolute. She cleared her throat. "How did you know I was with Marc Schwartz today?"

This jarred me out of my stupor.

The thing about being paranoid is that 90 percent of the things you worry about aren't actually true. You can tell yourself this while you're worrying as a reminder of why you shouldn't be worrying, but of course it doesn't stop you. After all, what if it's the act of being paranoid that's magically preventing the thing you're worried about from happening? If it's even remotely possible that's how fate works, then statistically speaking, you're warding off 90 percent of the bad things that would be happening to you otherwise. So, in the spirit of why-fix-it-if-it's-not-broken, you congratulate yourself on a job well done and continue freaking the fuck out about a lot of shit you shouldn't worry about, because *it's working*.

It feels that way, at least, until that one time out of ten you end up being right about something really far-fetched, and then you freak out even more.

"What? You really *were* with Marc Schwartz?" The weight of my confirmed suspicions pressed down on me, and I felt like I'd swallowed a brick. *"Fuck."*

"Hold on. You're surprised now? You literally came to my house yelling about this, and now it's suddenly breaking news?"

"I didn't know for sure that it was you. It was just a guess based on the description of you," I admitted, the brick sinking deeper into my gut. *What did Baby know? What did Marc tell her about me?*

She crossed her arms. "Who described me to you?"

"My mom," I informed her. "She was at the mall. She saw you all together."

Baby was legitimately confused. "Your mom knows me?"

"No, but what other pregnant teenager would Marc Schwartz be talking to?" This clearly didn't seem as obvious to her as it did to me. "I need to know exactly, word for word, what you talked about."

Baby narrowed her eyes at me. "Are you fucking serious?"

"Listen, I know I should've been the one to tell you. I mean, I started to, kind of, at the restaurant. But then the fire happened."

"What?" Baby was flabbergasted, which is a word I don't use often because it sounds ridiculous, but there's no better word to describe her at that moment.

I sighed. "Don't believe everything Marc said until you hear my side of things."

"Your side?" Baby seethed in exasperation. "Why would *you* get a side?"

This hurt. "Listen, just because Marc was my doctor, it doesn't mean he knows everything about what I went through. I'm the one who actually lived it!"

"What the fuck are you talking about, Solo?" she demanded. "Marc Schwartz couldn't have been your doctor. He works at a mental hospital!"

"Yeah. *I know.*"

We stared at each other, both realizing some things.

My mouth went completely dry. "You guys really weren't talking about me today, were you?"

She shook her head slowly. "Why would we have been?"

"Shit," I said as everything sank in.

"Solo." Baby said my name with forced calmness. "What the fuck is going on?"

I knew she was entitled to an answer. Baby had suspected Something Was Wrong With Me for some time, and I'd gone and confirmed it. I couldn't just lie or punch a chair; there wasn't going to be another fire or distraction to delay this conversation. I was backed into a corner this time. My tabula was fucked.

If I was ever going to tell Baby about What Was Wrong With Me, it had to be now. If I left, she wasn't going to give me another chance. After everything I'd put her through, I didn't deserve one.

I weighed my options. Don't tell Baby and lose her. Tell Baby and *probably* still lose her, *and* make her think I was crazy.

My odds sucked. The situation sucked. Having Something Wrong With Me in the first place sucked. But Baby, she didn't suck. Ultimately I knew it was worth the risk to keep her in my life rather than give up and accept a life of guaranteed suckage without her in it.

"How late can you be to Bob's party?" I asked her.

She leaned back in her chair. "I'm listening."

I learned pretty early that when I joined a new group in therapy, I shouldn't be the first kid to share. Kind of like bands had opening acts, I usually let two or three other people go before I introduced myself to the masses, since my story almost always ended up being the headliner.

Unfortunately for Baby, there were no other former mental patients around to warm her up.

I started with the kiln. It wasn't the beginning, but the true origin of What Was Wrong With Me dated back to The Bad Thing That Happened, and there was no way I was about to go *there*. It was not only tortuous to talk about; The Bad Thing was also agonizing to *hear* about, and there was no benefit to putting either of us through that amount of pain.

From the kiln forward, I told Baby pretty much everything you already know: finding Crystal in my closet, her coming to Michigan, how my mom discovered her things, the Bon Jovi concert, the hospital stays. I even threw in Mop & Glo Valerie because Marc Schwartz made a cameo in that story.

I talked for a long time and was interrupted only once when Baby's mom called to check in, a break I extended by calling Aunt Denise's to check in with my parents. Baby didn't ask me any questions throughout the entire saga but instead listened silently as I stared out the window like I was talking to a person on the other side of the glass instead of her.

There was snow on the ground outside, and one by one Baby's neighbors flipped on their Christmas lights. Reds, golds, blues. Greens. I watched cars coming and going down the street, probably full of families with kids in itchy sweaters going to their grandparents' houses for dinner and photographs by the tree just like my family had, once upon a time.

I ended my confession by telling Baby about the last time I saw Crystal, which I know I haven't even told you—be patient. When I finished talking, I was exhausted.

Having never told anyone Normal all this stuff before, I had no expectations for Baby's reaction. It was irrational to hope she wouldn't think I was crazy. I mean, I *was* crazy, so the best I could hope for was that Baby would think my particular brand of insanity was somewhere in the quirky-interesting range and not the get-the-fuck-away-from-me-forever range.

When I finally had the balls to look at her, I was even less sure of how Baby felt. I couldn't really sum up her expression in one word — flabbergasted didn't cover it this time — but imagine someone handed you the Klopman diamond, proof that aliens existed, and the cure for cancer. You'd probably think to yourself, "I know this is all important, but I don't know what the fuck I'm supposed to do with any of it." That was pretty much how Baby looked.

I got it. It was a lot to take in. But she was literally saying nothing, and the longer the silence lasted between us, the worse I felt. People described being vulnerable as feeling naked in front of others, and that totally made sense to me. I'd been naked like that in front of many, many people in therapy. Most of them, though, were also naked, or at least partially so. To torture the metaphor to death, everybody in group therapy had some skin in the game. With Baby, though, it felt more like I had taken off every stitch of clothing while she was bundled up for a ski trip. And then, to make matters worse, I also shit myself and then slipped in the shit so that I was both naked and covered in shit, and in response, Baby put on an extra mitten.

After what had to have been ten excruciating minutes of quiet, I finally asked her, "Do you want me to go now?"

"Do you want to go?" was her immediate — and, I daresay, hopeful — response.

"I mean, I can." The brick in my gut doubled in size. "I guess I'll talk to you later?"

"OK," Baby said, and she stood to walk me out.

I don't remember anything else I said to her as I was putting on my shoes. There was probably an awkward apology involved. Maybe I asked her to relay a message of thanks to Kat. But Baby definitely said nothing else to me. I absolutely remember her silence.

That silence was still ringing in my ears hours later as I lay in my bed, dissecting the evening over and over. All this time I'd been paranoid that if I ever told someone What Was Wrong With Me, they would want nothing more to do with me. Statistically speaking, that should've been enough to prevent that fear from coming true, but it hadn't been. Just like everything else about me, my logic was fucked up, too.

Chapter 23

Christmas morning, I woke up to more presents than I had ever seen.

Mom and Dad were sitting in the living room drinking coffee while some parade played on television. Against the wall was our underdecorated Christmas tree surrounded by a sea of brightly wrapped packages.

There were usually about six presents under our tree on Christmas morning, two of which I immediately disqualified from the actual gift count because I knew they were socks and underwear. So in total, I could typically expect about four real presents from my parents. This year, though, the haul looked to be quadruple that number.

"What's all that?"

"Merry Christmas." My dad was smiling like a used car salesman. "It's about time you got up, lazybones!"

I eyed him suspiciously. "Lazybones" was not something my dad, or anyone under the age of sixty, ever called another person. "What's going on?"

Mom stood up and walked over to hug me.

"Who died?" I asked, immediately feeling panicked. "Is it Grandma?"

"Everything's fine," Dad said. "We're just glad you're finally up so you can see what Santa left for you."

Mom put her hand on my forehead. "Feeling better than yesterday?"

"Yeah, I'm fine," I told her, realizing it at the same time. It seemed I'd sufficiently slept off both my fever and my headache hangover. At the thought of my migraine, though, all the events from Baby's house rushed back to me, and the brick rematerialized in my gut. "Mostly, at least."

"Good to hear!" My dad grinned.

It occurred to me that in the three days since I'd run into my dad at the mall with the blond woman, I had spent almost no time thinking about it, which was saying a lot, since I tended to obsess about much smaller events than catching my dad cheating. My therapist would have told me I was being avoidant, that I was just pretending nothing was going on so I didn't have to deal with the consequences of what I'd seen. But I didn't really think that was it.

Standing there, face-to-face with my dad, I didn't have the urge to kick him in the dick or yell at him or anything. Nor did I feel like outing him to my mom right then and there. I guess what I'm saying is that I felt pretty indifferent to the situation, which on the surface makes me sound like an asshole of a son to my mom.

Realistically, though, I knew that Dad having an affair wasn't the worst thing that had happened to any one of us—not by a long shot. There was a short list of things more earth-shattering than what we'd already been through the past nine years, and while I wasn't minimizing my dad fucking not-my-mom, I had enough perspective to know that maybe it was OK to wait to deal with it until after Christmas.

I shot my dad a smile, and he instantly relaxed.

"C'mon, son," he said. "Let's open gifts."

Something you learn in therapy is to be grateful for the small moments when life doesn't suck. If you go through what my family did, it's pretty damn difficult to find the silver linings in anything from that point on. So if you ever do happen to experience joy, you should probably make note of it so on days when you just want the world to end, you can remind yourself happiness is possible.

That said, Christmas morning was pretty great.

I ended up getting some really awesome gifts from Mom and Dad: an R.E.M. shirt, *Tekken 2*, a ton of new clothes, a pair of Doc Martens, a DVD player, *and* a computer. For a second, I wondered if I had a terminal disease they weren't telling me about and they had cashed in my Make-a-Wish on a shopping spree (paranoid), but then I just forgot about it and let myself enjoy life for a goddamn second.

After presents, Mom baked cinnamon rolls, and then she and I put together a five-hundred-piece jigsaw puzzle of a painted scene of an Italian marketplace that probably didn't exist in real life, Dad popping in and out of the action as he set up my new computer.

These times were rare—Mom, Dad, and me in close proximity, on purpose, having quality time. We all tended to avoid stuff like this, since family togetherness always highlighted what was missing more than what we still had to be grateful for. But for whatever reason, that morning we were all committed to this Normal family activity in body, at least, if not in mind.

As much as I tried to stay present in the moment, assembling that Venetian fruit stand, my thoughts kept wandering off to Baby. How could they not? Less than twenty-four hours had passed since

231

my greatest fear had come true, and that kind of shit tends to haunt you for a long time after the fact.

When it came down to it, though, I knew I couldn't blame Baby for how she'd reacted to learning about Crystal. If the tables were turned, I couldn't say for sure that I'd have acted any differently. Had I never met Crystal, and Baby had told me she'd had a deeply personal friendship with someone no one else could see, I probably would have bolted, too. It's what a Normal person would do.

But still, I wanted things to have gone better. Like, I bone-achingly, stomach-churningly, *mother-fuckingly* wanted it. I should've lied. I should have spun a yarn about an ex-girlfriend who had wrecked me by leaving me for my best friend, or just told her the truth about Valerie, omitting the part about us being mental patients, since that whole deal was enough to screw a person up. Hindsight being twenty-twenty and all, I realized I could have given Baby enough details to satisfy her hunch about What Was Wrong With Me with-out talking about Crystal at all. I could have controlled the narrative instead of letting it control me, for once. But I hadn't, and I knew why.

The truth was, I hadn't wanted to lie to Baby. It turned out I *did* want all those things my shrink had accused me of wanting. Intimacy and crap. I wanted it with Baby. I wanted to be real with someone and have them be cool with what I'd been through, so I'd taken the chance and told her the truth. And she had pulled the football away from me just as I was about to kick it.

Fuck, it hurt.

Going forward, work was going to be tricky. That wasn't lost on me. I considered quitting my job and getting into a new line of work where I wouldn't have to talk to anyone at all. Like, maybe as the guy who wore the mouse costume at Chuck E. Cheese or something. No one talked to that guy. He could be anyone—even an ex–mental patient—and as long as he kept his shit together when he had the suit on, no one would ever know. Also, there were the potential perks of free pizza and Skee-ball to consider, which was nothing to sneeze at benefits-wise.

Quitting ROYO Video really did seem like a realistic solution to this whole mess. I was sure Baby would be happy never to have to see me again, and as a bonus, it would get me out of the whole Maverick situation, too. That was something else I was avoiding thinking about, since I had no idea what to do about it. Maybe if Maverick really was hot for me, Baby telling him just how batshit crazy I was might help him move on. Perhaps this would all work out for the best.

Anyway.

My parents and I finished the puzzle in less than two hours, and then each of us immediately retreated to waste the rest of the afternoon away from each other. Dad napped on the couch, Mom chain-smoked while reading back issues of *People*, and I hid in my room playing *Tekken 2*, which, to my disappointment, wasn't much different from the original.

For Christmas dinner my family always ate Chinese takeout. Metro Detroit was rife with ethnic restaurants run by people who didn't celebrate Christmas, so there were a lot of options for people like us who didn't want to cook on holidays. Since anything beyond chicken, rice, and egg rolls was too exotic for my dad, though, we didn't explore much beyond the most basic non-American cuisine. But Chinese food on Christmas was a Teague family tradition dating back to before The Bad Thing, and since we didn't have many of those left, I never complained about wanting to try Thai or Indian instead.

I could smell the kung pao even before my dad called me down to eat, and I entered the kitchen as he and Mom were taking the white cartons of food out of the to-go bags. We sat down at the table to eat together. Moments later there was a knock at the door.

The three of us froze and looked at each other like we'd been expecting the Gestapo to show up any minute. No one really ever came over to our house except for Aunt Denise, and she never knocked.

"Who the hell could that be?" Dad asked.

"It's probably Jehovah's Witnesses," Mom assumed.

"I think they take Christmas off, Maureen." My dad went to the peephole. "It's probably just carolers." He pressed his face to the door, pulled away, and then pressed it up again. "Or not." Dad shot me a look of concern before opening the door. "Can I help you, miss?"

"Um, yeah," a familiar voice began. "I'm sorry to drop in on Christmas, but is it possible you could give this to Joel for me?"

By the time she'd gotten her question out, I'd joined my dad at the door.

Baby was standing on the front porch, wearing a coat she could no longer zip up over her stomach and clutching an envelope and something wrapped in foil.

"What are you doing here?" I asked.

My dad looked from her to her stomach to me and back again.

"Joel?" he said. "Care to introduce us?"

"Dad, this is Nicole. We work together," I told him, and Baby extended her hand with a smile.

He shook it and held the door open for her. "Let's get you in out of the cold, young lady."

"I'll only stay a minute," she promised, looking at me.

I didn't meet her eyes. "Did you come here to quit? Is that a letter of resignation?" I pointed at the envelope. Baby was beating me to the punch.

"What? No." She laughed. "Kat wanted me to bring you some pie." She handed the foil-covered plate to me, and my mom, who had also joined us at the door, took it off my hands.

"I'm Joel's mother," she said standoffishly.

Baby nodded. "Nice to meet you."

"Won't you come in?" Mom gestured Baby into the house, then whispered to me, "Can I talk to you real quick?"

"I'm not the father, Mom. I swear to god," I whispered back, and she relaxed.

"I seriously didn't mean to interrupt your Christmas. I just had something to talk to Joel about that couldn't wait."

"Nonsense," my dad said. "Do you like Chinese? We've got plenty. Join us for dinner."

Baby looked at me, unsure of what to say. And because I didn't know why she'd come, I didn't know what to tell her.

"Is Kat expecting you home for dinner?" I decided to ask.

"No. She's over at the restaurant with Bob, surveying the damage," she informed me. "It's a mess."

"What happened?" Mom asked Baby. She had batlike hearing when she wanted to.

"There was a fire at the restaurant my mom works at," Baby said, glancing at me. "Didn't Joel tell you?"

"No," my parents said in unison.

"Are you talking about the kitchen fire that happened over at Headlights?" my dad asked.

"Yeah," I confirmed, not wanting to know (but guessing) how he already knew about it.

"My mom's the manager there. Her fiancé owns the place," Baby explained.

"Your mom's Kat?" My dad smiled. "Good for her and Bob!"

Mom and I both frowned.

"How often do you go there, Craig?" Mom looked a little disgusted.

Dad pretended not to hear her.

"Anyway, Mom won't be back until late," Baby continued, looking at me. "So I *could* hang out if *you* want."

I couldn't tell if Baby was trying to ask me something in code with the stressors she put on her words. "Do *you* want to?" I asked.

Her fingers moved over the envelope still in her hand. She slid it into her pocket and nodded.

We had to unbury the fourth dining room chair. Since we never had company, it had become the place where we all set the things we didn't want to put away. Dad grabbed an extra place setting, and Baby sat down next to me.

"So how long have you worked at the video store?" Mom asked Baby, handing her the container of rice.

"Three years," Baby answered. "Since I was fifteen."

"You're eighteen?" I asked her, surprised. For some reason, I'd always assumed I was older than her.

"Yeah. Since October."

"I knew you then," I reminded her. "You never said anything about your birthday."

"Was I supposed to make an announcement? Demand a cake? I'm not five."

This made my parents laugh.

"That's a long time to keep the same job when you're young," Mom commented. Then she paused. "How is Joel already your boss if you've worked there so much longer than he has?"

Baby's eyebrows raised. "Funny that, huh?" She took a bite of food. "You'd have to ask Scarlet that one."

"She's talking about Jessica," I translated for my mom. "Devin's ex."

Mom made a face. "Oh, *her*. I'm not a fan of that girl."

"Really?" Baby perked up. "Me neither."

This seemed to instantly bond Baby and my mom. "She treated my nephew very badly. Broke his heart."

"He seems to have bounced back all right," I reminded her before Baby could issue Devin any undeserved sympathy.

"Thank goodness," Mom said. "I didn't think he'd ever get over losing that baby."

I'd just put a bite of chicken into my mouth and had to chew it a few times before I could ask, "Losing Scarlet?" It wasn't like my mom to call girls "baby," but maybe she was trying to be cool for the sake of our guest.

Mom looked at me, surprised. "You mean you don't know? I thought Devin would have confided in you."

"About what?"

"Maureen," Dad said firmly.

"He's old enough to know, Craig." Mom shot a look at Dad.

Baby shot a look at me.

"That's not the point. They work together," Dad reminded her. "You can't just go spouting off about that girl's personal life."

"I'm not," Mom defended herself. "I'm talking about my nephew's personal life. It took both of them to make that baby."

Baby's eyes widened. "Wait, are you saying that Scarlet was pregnant?"

I swallowed my food and stared at my mom.

She was nodding. "Jessica got pregnant, but she didn't want to be. So . . ." Mom raised her eyebrows and pursed her lips. "Devin was devastated."

"Maureen," my dad tried again. "This is really no one's business."

"Holy shit," I heard Baby whisper, which was the same thing I was thinking.

"You should've seen your Aunt Denise, Joel. She was a wreck."

Mom pointed her fork at me. "You know that would've been her grandchild."

Baby and I were both silent.

"It should be illegal, if you ask me," Mom continued.

"No one did," my dad reminded her.

"Girls today take the easy way out. They get themselves into these messes and don't want to deal with the consequences," Mom stated. "Present company excluded, of course. You should be commended, Nicole. Looks like you're taking responsibility for your actions."

"Mom!" I snapped. "Stop talking about this!" I shot Baby an apologetic look, but it was clear she was still thinking about Scarlet.

"I'll thank you to show me more respect at the dinner table, Joel!" Mom barked back.

"You can't blame the boy for being mad, Maureen," Dad interjected. "You wouldn't want people sitting around their dinner tables talking about things you've been through."

This seemed to gut-check my mother, who, after a brief silence, changed the subject.

Well, kind of.

"So, do you know what you're having, Nicole?"

"Nope," Baby answered.

"Well"—Mom handed Baby the container of beef chow mein— "if it's a boy, you're going to want to eat a lot of red meat. It helps develop their virility, which is very important these days."

"Oh, OK." Baby took the container and put a little on her plate.

"You must think it's a girl, then." Mom smiled, pointing to the small amount Baby had taken. "Lots of pink in your future. Sugar and spice and everything nice."

"Seriously, Maureen." Dad sighed. "What's gotten into you?"

"What? I was only thinking of the baby, and baby boys need certain things if they're going to be healthy." She glared at my dad.

My dad, who had either eaten enough or was just fed up, put his napkin on his plate and took it to the sink. "I'm going to go set up your DVD player, Joel. Maybe you and your friend can take a walk around the neighborhood after dinner. Have some privacy."

Once Dad was out of earshot, Mom kept going. "Have you done any reading on pregnancy?" she asked Baby. "The latest research shows that there *is* a link between a mother's diet and a child's tendencies."

Baby swallowed a bite of food. "I haven't read that." She took a drink. And then, since Baby was always polite to adults, she asked, "What kinds of tendencies?"

Looking at me out of the corner of her eye, Mom said, "You know, girls being tomboys, boys being effeminate. Diet affects those things."

"Oh." Baby made a face. "I've literally never heard anything like that."

"That's because it's not true," I told her, glaring at my mom. I carried my plate to the sink.

"It *is* true," Mom reiterated. "Something to think about if you want to raise healthy children. I'm only telling you what I wish I'd known when I was younger."

I stomped over to Baby. "Are you done?" I asked her, indicating her food.

"Sure," she said, but then she took three more quick bites. I felt bad taking food away from a pregnant person, but not bad enough to sit there any longer while my mom was acting like this.

"We're going on that walk," I said. Then I grabbed our coats.

"I'll warm up the pie Nicole brought for when you get back," Mom called after us, ignoring how obviously annoyed I was with her.

I answered by shutting the door harder than was necessary.

We were a few houses down my street before Baby said, "Did you forget I'm, like, super pregnant?" She was out of breath. "First you

239

practically rip my dinner out of my hands, and now we're running a marathon. What gives?"

"I'm sorry. And I'm sorry about my mom, too."

It took a few breaths before she could get out her response. "It's not your fault. But I *am* starting to understand why you freaked out about Maverick. It's like the woman has gay panic."

"You don't know the half of it."

"I'm sure." Baby pointed at the boulevard where there were some covered picnic tables, and we went over to them.

We sat there for a few minutes without saying anything, but it was clear Baby was trying to work up the nerve to tell me that she didn't want to see me again.

Because I'm a rip-off-the-Band-Aid-all-at-once kind of guy, I made things easy for her. "Just so you know, I'm going to put my two weeks' notice in tomorrow."

Baby's face fell. "You're quitting? Why?"

I leveled with her. "C'mon. Clearly we're not going to be able to work together anymore, and you've worked there a lot longer than I have, so it's only fair that I should be the one who goes."

"Why can't we work together anymore?" Baby demanded.

I looked at her. "Don't act like you're cool with what I told you last night, because I know you aren't. If I just leave, we can pretend last night never happened."

"Is that what you want?" she asked me. Then, before I could answer, she clarified, "That's not what *I* want."

"It's not?"

"No."

"Oh. Then what *do* you want?"

"What do you mean?"

"From me. What do you want from me now, in a post-you-knowing-my-shit world?" I asked. "Like, why did you come over

240

tonight if not to end our friendship?"

"God, Solo, you're so dramatic," Baby said. "There are infinite reasons I could have wanted to see you today, and you automatically assume I made a house call just to kick you out of my life? You exhaust me sometimes."

"Seriously?" I huffed back at her. "After your reaction last night, I'm not crazy for thinking you wanted some space. I mean, I'm crazy for a lot of other reasons, but for sure not that one."

"Stop," Baby said. "Stop calling yourself crazy."

"Why? I *am* crazy. I have literal *years* of crazy under my belt," I reminded her.

She ran her hand through her hair. "I don't think you're crazy." Baby sighed. "I know I acted like an asshole last night, and I'm sorry. I didn't know what to say, because I didn't expect any of the shit you said, and I felt like garbage for making you tell me all of it."

"Wait a sec. *You* feel bad about last night?"

"Of course I feel bad!" Baby practically yelled. "I mean, all this time I thought you were keeping regular teenage shit from me. Like, you wouldn't trust me with basic ex-girlfriend or dysfunctional-family stuff. Meanwhile, you knew so much about me, and I felt completely in the dark about you."

"Oh," I said, the brick inside me starting to dissolve.

Baby frowned. "I mean, it's not like I know how I *should* have responded last night. But probably anything would have been better than saying nothing."

"I don't know," I said, feeling notably lighter inside. "Throwing holy water and trying to exorcize the demon in me would definitely have been worse."

"Did someone actually do that to you?"

"Are you kidding?" I said. "It was among the very first treatments my parents tried." This was true, but it wasn't a very interesting story, which is why I haven't mentioned it. Basically, Mom brought me to a priest, he dabbed me with water and said some things in Latin (I think), and then we left and I met up with Crystal in my closet.

Baby's eyes widened. "See? I have so many questions. But I don't know what I'm allowed to ask or what's too insensitive or whether I even have a right to know anything at all."

I had not expected this. It hadn't occurred to me that Baby might want to know more about What Was Wrong With Me after getting the first taste.

"You can ask me whatever you want, I guess." I rested my arms on the picnic table. "I just can't believe you *want* to know things. For years my parents have been *paying* people to listen to me talk about this stuff. No one has voluntarily chosen to chitchat about it."

"Well, how many friends have you told?"

"Just you."

"That's why," Baby asserted. "Not to make you feel like a carnival sideshow or anything, Solo, but you got about a million times more interesting after you told me about Crystal. Seriously, it's all I've been thinking about since you left my house last night." It was weird hearing her say Crystal's name so casually. "I've always wanted to see a ghost. *You* have."

I half smiled. "You think Crystal is a ghost?"

"Don't you? What else would she be?"

"A mental disorder, according to multiple shrinks."

"Nah. I'm going with ghost," Baby decided. "I mean, granted, I'm leaning heavily on what I know of ghosts from movies, but cinematically speaking, it's the most likely explanation."

"I don't know." A lot of the therapy kids had drawn this conclusion about Crystal. But how was I supposed to know if she was a ghost? The kind of people who saw ghosts and the kind with mental problems overlapped a lot.

242

"C'mon, Solo. There are dozens of movies about ghosts. You don't think any of them were inspired by real events? I mean, I personally always hoped that *Field of Dreams* was a true story. Or maybe, you know, the movie *Ghost*. Or *Heart and Souls* with Robert Downey Jr. Any of those movies could be accurate, for all I know."

"I've seen none of those movies."

Baby closed her eyes and shook her head. "You will," she decided. "You're going to have to watch a lot of movies if we're going to get to the bottom of Crystal." She ran her hand through her hair again. "Which we are."

"After years of therapy and dozens of doctors trying to figure out Crystal, you think *you're* going to do it by watching movies?"

"*We* are going to do it." Baby smiled.

"So you still want to hang out with me?" I verified. "You aren't freaked out about Crystal? Or me? Or any of this?"

"I'm really not." She waited about a minute, then said, "I believe everything you said last night. You'd have to be crazy to make that shit up. And like I said, I don't think you're crazy." Baby shrugged. "Besides, you've probably noticed that I don't like most people. So I'm not going to bail on the best friend I've got just because he's complicated."

When she said this, my heart literally skipped a beat, and I don't fucking care if that sounds dramatic. When you're a guy like me and someone says those words to you, you're lucky if you don't drop dead of shock right on the spot. "You're my best friend, too."

Saying those words back to Baby felt almost as good as hearing her say them to me.

The moment lingered, but then Baby interrupted it. "We can get matching BFF necklaces at the mall later."

"Joel and Nicole, best friends forever."

"Baby and Solo," she corrected me.

243

I smiled.

Baby shivered. "I should probably get going. I'm freezing."

I didn't blame her for not wanting to stay for pie, considering the impression my mother had made on her. Nor was I surprised that we didn't talk about the revelation about Scarlet. Maybe we would later. All I knew then was that it felt like I was living in a completely different reality than I had been twenty-four hours before, and in a good way, for once.

I walked Baby to her car. "Before I forget, here's this." She placed the envelope from earlier into my hand.

"What is it?"

She opened her car door. "Remember how after the fire, the paramedics made me get an ultrasound?"

I nodded.

"Everything was fine. But while they were poking around in there, they found out the baby's sex. I had them write it down." She indicated the envelope. "I want you to have it."

"OK. Why?"

Baby shook her head. "I didn't look at it. I don't want to know." She shrugged one shoulder. "But I want you to."

"Really?"

"I want you to know everything," she said, and then she got in her car. "Merry Christmas, Solo." Baby shut the door and started the engine.

I smiled. "Merry Christmas, Baby."

The snow creaked under her tires as she drove away, and I watched until the Accord disappeared around the corner. Then I opened the envelope.

girl

I wouldn't tell a soul.

Chapter 24

The next few weeks were the best ones of my life.

This is likely not breaking news to you, but life is way better when you have someone to share it with. Especially someone who knows What's Wrong With You and likes you anyway.

After Christmas, Baby and I were together a lot, at work and otherwise. If this were a movie, it would be the point in the story where they played a montage of the two of us laughing at ROYO Video, watching movies together, and hanging out at Buddy's Pizza—Normal-people stuff. Sure, Crystal came up sometimes, but she wasn't the focus of our friendship. It turned out that not having to hide something that big about myself from Baby made it seem like less of a big deal in general. The montage would be set to a peppy

R.E.M. song, obviously. Probably "Shiny Happy People" or "Radio Free Europe." It would be filled with crescent smiles and me being everything I could have been, and you'd get a fucking tear in your eye watching it, because *look how far Joel has come.*

Well, you *might* get a tear in your eye. I assume you've been rooting for me all along. But people aren't always happy for others when things start going their way. Sometimes they get suspicious instead, as was the case with just about everyone we worked with.

"You and Baby are fucking, aren't you?" Hannibal asked me while the two of us were assembling a promotional display for the John Travolta movie *Phenomenon.*

"No," I assured him as I folded cardboard tabs into their corresponding slots. "We're just friends."

"C'mon, my friend. Is the kid yours?"

"No," I said more firmly. *"We are just friends."*

Hannibal handed me another section of the display. "Uh-huh," he said. "Riiiiight."

Was this the kind of thing Normal people lied about? *Not* having sex with someone?

"Seriously, dude. Why would I lie about this?"

He shrugged and made the *I don't know* noise. "Because you're her boss?"

"Does that matter here? This isn't corporate America."

"Nah, probably not." He rubbed his chin thoughtfully. "Maybe the real reason you're keeping it on the down-low is so Scarlet doesn't find out."

"Why would that matter?"

"C'mon, dude. Baby and Scarlet hate each other. If one girl found out you were screwing the other one, you'd probably lose your shot at ever fucking her, too."

I followed this logic. "So you think that I've somehow convinced

Baby to sleep with me and not tell anyone just so I have the possibility of also someday sleeping with Scarlet?"

"We *are* talking about *Scarlet*" was Hannibal's response. "A guy
would go to great lengths to keep that option open."

"Well, still. That's not what's happening."

Later I would address similar accusations from Poppins, Maverick,
and Scarlet.

"You guys are like Zack and Kelly from *Saved by the Bell*," Poppins
asserted. "Just admit it."

"What does that even mean?" I asked.

"You know, on-again-off-again but totally in love," Poppins
explained.

"No, that's not us," I assured them. "We're more like the other
two people on that show."

"Jessie and Slater?" Poppins asked.

"Sure."

"They were also a couple."

"Oh. What about that nerdy guy? Wasn't he just friends with
someone?"

"You mean Screech and Lisa?" Poppins shook her head. "Screech
was super in love with her. It was a major plot point."

Evidently I knew very little about this show. "Hmm. Then how
about . . ." My mind went blank. "I don't know. Name a show with a
guy and a girl who are just friends, and that's who we're like."

"There isn't a show like that, because there aren't people like that,"
Poppins said matter-of-factly. "No one would believe it. Guys and
girls don't act how you guys act unless they're secretly hot for each
other. Or unless one of them is gay."

My eyes automatically went to Maverick, who I caught looking
at me.

I still didn't know whether Maverick was gay, or if he was,

whether he liked me — I'd witnessed no proof of Baby's theory — but why take any chances?

"Well, then I guess we're the world's first non-gay male-female friendship in history."

Poppins looked unconvinced. Maverick looked uncomfortable.

It was at that moment that Scarlet popped her head out of the office to ask me to print a report.

"Hey, Scarlet," Poppins called. "Settle something for us. Solo says he and Baby are 'just friends.' Do you buy that?"

I shot Poppins a dirty look.

Scarlet laughed. "Like anyone's going to be interested in Baby. Who wants to date a pregnant chick?"

Ever since my mom had (intentionally) let it slip about Scarlet's abortion, I'd been less surprised about her obsession with Baby's pregnancy. I didn't know exactly how the two things were related, but I was sure that they were. It just made sense that if two people took opposite paths at the same fork in a road, they might be interested in seeing where the other one ended.

"Right," Poppins acknowledged. "But you *do* know that's a temporary situation, don't you? She's not going to be pregnant for the rest of her life. Eventually she'll probably date someone."

"You don't *like* Baby, do you, Solo?" Scarlet asked, as though the possibility were absurd.

I sighed, annoyed that the topic would not die. "We're just really good friends."

"See?" she said to Poppins. "Guys are only 'really good friends' with girls if they aren't attracted to them."

"Baby's pretty" was Poppins's response. "I mean, she was before she was pregnant, at least. But she's also mean, and I can see how that makes her less attractive."

"And *that's* not mean?" I pointed out.

I could tell Poppins hadn't meant to sound harsh. "I'm just saying that personality affects hotness, that's all."

"Implying that Baby has a bad personality," I noted. Then, because I assumed it was a best friend's duty to defend against this type of thing, I added, "I happen to really enjoy being around Baby."

"But you don't want to have sex with her." Scarlet stated this as fact. "Obviously."

I didn't know how to respond to this without insulting Baby in some way. Whether I confirmed or denied it, it would have sounded bad.

Apparently, though, my hesitation *was* an answer.

"So you do, then?" Maverick asked.

Everyone leaned in as they waited for me to answer.

I started to get angry. "So those are my only two options? Either Baby is a terrible person or I want to fuck her? It's not even in the realm of possibility that she could be a nice-looking, enjoyable person who I'm cool not sleeping with?"

"Not really," Scarlet said. "Would you if she wanted to?"

I finally put my foot down. "I'm not doing this."

"Yeah," Maverick chimed in, apparently having a change of heart. "Baby's not even here. It's not cool to talk about her behind her back."

Scarlet rolled her eyes. "Fine. Then let me put it to you this way." She leaned on the counter. "If you could have any one of your coworkers naked in your bed . . . would you pick Baby?"

I felt my cheeks burn. First because the question was unexpected, and second because Scarlet had just said the words "naked" and "bed."

All eyes were on me, and the longer I waited, the hotter my face got. Since honesty was always the best policy, I went with that.

"It wouldn't be Baby," I told them, and then I glanced up at Scarlet.

She was smiling at me. "I didn't think so."

After work on a Sunday night in mid-January, Baby and I ended up having our ghost movie marathon in the ROYO Video break room. There was no school for Baby the following day because of Martin Luther King Jr.'s birthday, and there was no school for me because, well, I did school when I wanted to.

I'd met with Tim a few days before, and he'd laid out the rest of the coursework I needed to complete before graduation in May. Six credits to go until I'd be everything I might have been. The end was in sight, and I admit it felt pretty damn good to be almost done with that shit.

Tim also reminded me that if I was serious about applying to colleges, I should probably get on it, and even though I wasn't sure I *was* serious about it, I heeded his advice. As much as I loved working at the video store, ten bucks an hour wouldn't cut it forever.

For the past year, I'd been receiving a steady stream of college brochures. (Everyone my age did — I wasn't special or anything.) Since it ran in my family to let mail accumulate, I tossed them all into a plastic crate in my bedroom. After my talk with Tim, I went through the stacks, picked the three closest schools, filled out all their forms, and mailed them in, along with the forty-dollar application fees. (What a racket.) On the sly, I also had Tim acquire an application to a certain school in New York, even though I suspected that I had no shot at getting accepted to Sarah Lawrence. Still, I figured I had nothing to lose, except for the *sixty*-dollar application fee. Besides, you already know that once I commit to something, I'm all in, so it shouldn't surprise you that the moment Baby and I became legitimate best friends, I was ready to move with her to the Empire State and plan out the rest of our lives together.

I didn't mention the application to Baby, though. Or my parents.

It was my little secret. No point in bringing it up, since it probably wasn't going to happen anyway.

"Before we start"—Baby held up three videocassettes as we settled onto the couch—"I have a few more questions about Crystal."

It had become Normal to hear Baby talk about Crystal as though she were a real person. I mean, she was, but until Baby, I was the only one who'd ever treated her like one.

"What do you want to know?"

"So, I've been thinking about this a lot. For Crystal to be a ghost, which as far as I'm concerned is still the only logical explanation, she would have to be the ghost *of* someone," Baby explained. "So the question is, who?"

I looked at her. "Am I supposed to know the answer to that?"

"Think about it," she said as she chewed thoughtfully on a Twizzler. "When you lived in Virginia, did you ever hear about anyone like Crystal dying? Like, an unsolved murder or something? Or a girl-gone-missing-type story? Any urban legends?"

I shook my head. "No. But I was a kid. I'm not sure I would have heard about that stuff, you know?"

"Yeah." She made a face. "It's too bad you didn't meet Crystal in Michigan, where public records about things like this would be easier to access."

"Next time I'll try to meet a local ghost so it's more convenient for you."

Baby hit me with her licorice. "I'm being serious. If we could figure out who Crystal was, we might understand why she chose you to avenge her death."

"Crystal never seemed to need avenging," I clarified. "We mostly just hung out together. I never got the impression she was seeking revenge on anyone."

Baby seemed dissatisfied with this. "It's driving me crazy not being able to figure her out."

"Exactly."

"Oh," she said, running her fingers through her hair. "Right."

After *Field of Dreams* and *Ghost*, Baby and I weren't really any closer to the truth about Crystal than we were when the night had started, but I liked both movies, and as always, it was fun to talk about them with her. I assume I would've said the same thing about *Heart and Souls*, but it was almost three in the morning when we started it, and we both ended up falling asleep.

We probably would've slept there until morning when the openers got to work. It would have been a scandal, no doubt, even though we were both fully clothed and at opposite ends of the sofa.

But that didn't end up happening, because the phone rang long before that and woke us both up out of our dead sleeps.

In my half-awake haze, I tried to locate the cordless but couldn't.

"Why are you answering it? It's the middle of the night," Baby mumbled groggily.

"It might be my mom," I reasoned.

"Tell Maureen I said hello," Baby said, and shut her eyes again. "And that she sucks for waking me up."

I went into the store to answer the desk phone.

"ROYO Video, this is Solo," I said with a yawn.

"Solo?" a voice on the line asked.

It wasn't my mom. "Yeah, who's this?"

"Come upstairs."

"Scarlet?" I was suddenly awake. "What's wrong? Are you OK?"

From the break room, I heard Baby yell, "Dammit! Now I have to pee!" and stomp off to the bathroom.

"Are you with Baby?"

"What? Yes. We fell asleep watching movies," I said. Then I looked at my watch. "It's five fifteen in the morning. Why are you awake?"

"I was out. I just got home," she said. "I'm alone and don't want to be. Come upstairs."

"Out with Chase?" I asked for some reason.

"Does it matter? I want you here."

"Why?"

"Seriously, Solo?" She spoke louder. "I'm asking you if you want to come upstairs. Right now. For sex."

I must have been dreaming, because this was not making sense. "What?"

"Ugh!" Scarlet was getting impatient. "C'mon! Don't act like you're not interested. We both know you were talking about me the other day when I asked who from work you wanted to sleep with. Now's your chance. Get up here."

"Um, I . . ." I started a sentence without knowing what I was going to say.

"I'm giving you five minutes before I lock the door. Don't disappoint me." The line went dead.

You know how in cartoons, they sometimes indicate a character leaving a scene really fast by drawing their outline in dust, which slowly dissipates to reveal said character is long gone? *That* cloud of dust should have been all Baby saw of me when she came back from the bathroom.

But as it was, the shock of Scarlet's invitation prevented me from moving at all.

"What was that all about?" Baby nodded at the phone and yawned.

"It was Scarlet," I said, without thinking about whether it was a good idea to tell her. The same applied to what I said next: "She wants me to come upstairs for sex."

Baby was suddenly wide awake. "Are you joking?"

"No."

"Was *she*?"

"I really don't think so. She said I had five minutes to get up there or I'd lose my chance."

Baby and I stared at each other.

"Are you going?"

"I don't know."

"You don't know?" she parroted.

"Yeah. That's what I said. I don't know."

"Wait. How could you *not* know?" There was an edge to Baby's tone. "It's up to you, so you have to know whether or not it's going to happen."

"Well, she just kind of sprang it on me, so I haven't had much time to think about it."

"But you're considering doing it? You would actually fuck Scarlet?"

"Maybe."

"I didn't think you liked her for real."

"I don't. That's not the point."

"It isn't?" she demanded. "You'd sleep with someone you don't even like?"

I could hear the seconds of my five-minute window ticking away. "It wouldn't be the first time. You know that."

"I'm not holding anything you did in a mental hospital against you, Solo. People do weird sex shit in prison all the time because they have no other options. But things are different now."

"Do you see any other girls offering to sleep with me at the moment? Because I don't."

"So that's it? You'll just sleep with anyone who'll let you? Feelings don't matter at all as long as the girl is hot and ready?" Baby looked disgusted. "I'm learning a lot about you right now, Solo. And I don't like any of it."

"I didn't know you cared so much about who I slept with, Baby." *Tick-tock, tick-tock.* "Shit. Why are you making such a big deal out of this? I'm not even sure I'm going to do it."

That was a lie. I was pretty sure.

"Because I don't want you to sleep with Scarlet," Baby answered me point-blank.

"Why do you care?"

"Have you ever heard the expression 'Just because you can doesn't mean you should'?"

"Yeah," I said. "So why shouldn't I?"

"Because she's awful. And you'll probably get crabs" was Baby's defense. "And, I don't know, shouldn't sex mean something?"

The race against time was on, and I didn't stop to think through what I said next: "Did it mean something when you slept with Indy?"

Baby's face looked pained, like it was a low blow to bring him up. I guessed maybe I didn't know that whole story.

"Just go." Baby pointed at the door. "We both know you want to, so just go."

Time was running out, so I couldn't stay there and try to convince Baby that it was fine for me to sleep with Scarlet without missing my chance to actually do it. So instead I just told her, "You're still my best friend, you know?"

"Got it. Wear a rubber." Baby sounded sorely disappointed in me, but I didn't have time to worry about it.

She turned away, and I left as fast as my feet could carry me.

Chapter 25

The door was open. I locked it behind me before I went up the stairs. Scarlet was in the kitchen, staring out the window into the parking lot, dressed like she'd been out clubbing.

She turned to me and smiled smugly. "I knew you'd come."

I walked over to her, and we started kissing. It was everything I had ever imagined it would be.

She was on the kitchen counter, her legs wrapped around my waist, kissing her way from my mouth to my chest and back up again.

"Take me over to the bed," she whispered in my ear, and I picked her up to follow orders.

This proved more difficult than expected, since Scarlet's apartment was much messier than the night she had cut my hair.

Seriously, it looked like she was a burglary victim. There were shoes, clothes, boxes, an overturned houseplant, and plates of old food everywhere. Not to mention piles and piles of hair she hadn't bothered to sweep up, probably from all the Chases she'd given haircuts to lately.

But whatever—Scarlet's tongue was in my mouth. Who cared if her apartment was a wreck?

When we finally found our way to the mattress on the floor, it had to be unburied before we could use it. We remained intertwined as I threw piles of clothes off the bed. When I thought it was clear enough, I laid Scarlet down and moved on top of her.

"Ouch!" she yelled.

I rolled to the side. "What?"

She reached under her back and pulled out an empty liquor bottle I hadn't noticed. She shoved it away and started kissing my chest.

I looked down at her and watched as her hands slid to my belt. She tugged it loose.

I couldn't believe my luck. All the fantasies I'd had about Scarlet were coming true. Ever since Valerie, I had denied myself opportunities to hook up with girls who had Something Wrong With Them, and fate was rewarding my sacrifice by giving me Helen of goddamn Troy. I was scared to blink in case it was all some sort of sex mirage that could disappear at any moment.

But of course I blinked. I had to. I couldn't just *not* blink.

Scarlet didn't disappear when I opened my eyes like I was afraid she might . . . but something else happened.

"What's the matter?" Scarlet asked me as she unbuttoned my shirt. "Why'd you stop?"

I looked around the bed. There wasn't just one empty liquor bottle next to us. There were lots. More than necessary for a good time. Enough for a really bad time.

I looked over at the piles of hair, the garbage strewn throughout the apartment. This was not how Normal people lived. It really seemed like Something Was Wrong With Scarlet.

And that's when it dawned on me what was happening. Scarlet was going through a really hard time. She was adopting some very unhealthy coping mechanisms to deal with it. *I* was one of them.

It was all too familiar, honestly. I'd done it many times myself, once upon a psych hospital. Meaningless sex as a distraction, as a Band-Aid. I'd been down this road before. It had ended very badly, and I'd promised myself I wouldn't go down it again.

FUCK.

Why did I have to realize this at that exact moment? Couldn't my brain have waited a few minutes until we were finished (I'm a realist) to solve this puzzle? Because once I knew *why* this was happening . . . I couldn't let it happen.

Scarlet stopped kissing my neck and came up for air. "Seriously, what gives?"

I took a deep, sexually frustrated breath, then asked her the question that my goddamn conscience was nagging me to ask her. "Scarlet, are you . . . OK?"

She stiffened. "What do you mean?"

"Like, are you *OK*? You've seemed upset a lot lately."

She looked annoyed. "This is what you want to talk about right now?"

If the sex part of my brain could have staged a mutiny against my conscience, I'm sure it would've shut me up right then before I ruined all chances of getting laid that night.

But since it couldn't, this is what I said:

"I'm worried that you might be depressed."

Scarlet narrowed her eyes. "Are you kidding me right now?"

"Unfortunately, I'm totally serious." I sighed again and sat up.

"I mean, you just went through a rough breakup. You got drunk and hurt your hand. You're living in . . . well, like this." I nodded around the apartment. "I think . . . maybe you should talk to someone."

Scarlet sat up. "I ask you for sex, and you tell me I need therapy?"

"It's not like that." I didn't know how else to say what I was trying to say. "It's just, I know it's hard with Baby being pregnant—"

"What are you talking about?" she interrupted me. "Why would *that* be hard for me?"

Shit.

Have you ever done this? Accidentally said something to a person that made them suspicious that you knew something very personal they weren't aware you knew but that you did indeed know?

"I don't know . . ."

She knew I was lying. I could tell by the murderous look on her face.

"You know. *You know.*"

I slowly nodded.

"Get out!" she shrieked at me. In a split second, Scarlet was on her feet. "Get the fuck out of here, Solo!"

"I'm sorry." I stood up to go.

"Get out!" she yelled again, dissolving into tears. "Just leave!"

I tripped three times trying to get to the stairs. I eventually reached them and let myself out of Scarlet's apartment.

Chapter 26

It was the first time since I'd moved to Michigan that I appreciated the cold. After a few minutes outside in subzero temperatures, my balls retracted into my body, and I was able to think about what had just happened with my brain instead of my dick.

I'd done the right thing, I decided. I kind of wanted to punch myself in the face for it, but it was still the right thing.

Having never actually denied someone sex before (drunk Scarlet in the storage closet notwithstanding, because you should never, ever sleep with someone when they are drunk and asking you to procreate, especially when you're seventeen), I wasn't sure what I was supposed to do next. Like, should I leave her an apology note? Should I call someone to check on her? (Who, though? Her parents? Chase?)

Maybe draw up an IOU for when she was doing better so we could try this whole thing again?

I was getting cold now and couldn't make a decision. I reached into my pocket for my car keys when it hit me that in my haste for sex, I'd left them on the coffee table in the break room.

Also in the break room? My coat.

Shit.

A quick glance at the cars in the parking lot told me Baby had hung around after I'd ditched her, so I went to the back door of the store and knocked.

And knocked. And knocked.

Finally a very annoyed Baby came waddling down the hallway, her pregnant stomach preceding her. She stopped at the door but didn't open it.

"You were gone a whole eight minutes." Her voice (but not her tone) was muted through the door. "Scarlet's one lucky lady."

"Can you just let me in?" I pleaded. "I'm freezing my balls off out here!"

"If you think about it, freezing your balls is probably the best thing for them right now," she told me. "It might kill some of the diseases you just acquired."

"I didn't do anything, OK? We didn't have sex," I told her. "Can you just open the door?"

The look on her face told me that Baby did not believe me. Then she confirmed it. "I don't believe you."

"I'm for real." Seriously, why did so many people assume I would lie about *not* having sex?

"Solo, less than ten minutes ago, you ditched me to go stick your dick in Bimbo Barbie, and now you're telling me you passed on the opportunity?" She shook her head.

"I wouldn't put it that way. But yeah, it didn't work out, OK?

261

Now, please let me in before the hypothermia sets in."

She put her hand on the lock but didn't turn it. "Why should I? You're supposed to be my best friend, and you just bailed on me to screw a girl I can't stand."

I pulled my arms into my sleeves to preserve my body heat. "It was a stupid thing to do. It won't happen again." This seemed like an easy promise to keep, considering Scarlet now hated me. "Please, for the love of god, let me in!"

Baby deliberated a bit longer. "Fine," she said. "But I'm still pissed at you." She then unlocked the door, mercifully sparing me from death by freezing. I ran to the break room and put my coat on, shivering all the way.

Baby followed me. "So what happened?"

"It's complicated."

"What? Was she already having sex with someone else when you got up there?" she asked. "Did you have to take a number?"

"No," I sighed. "She was just kind of a wreck. I felt like I would've been taking advantage of her."

Baby looked at me. I could tell she knew what I meant but didn't want to sympathize with Scarlet on principle. "Whatever, Solo. I don't care, and I don't want to care." She ran her fingers through her hair. "Scarlet is not my problem."

"You're right. She's not."

It was quiet between us for a minute.

"I was going to go get some food. Do you wanna come?" Baby finally asked.

My teeth were still chattering. "You aren't still mad?"

"I'm mad *and* hungry," she clarified. "Anyway, if you're done not having sex with Scarlet, you could come with."

"I am."

"Fine," she said. "Let's get out of here. I'll drive."

Headlights was still being renovated, but Baby had a key, and there was a fridge full of food that would spoil if it wasn't eaten soon, so that's where we went.

We walked in the kitchen entrance and into a room filled with the scent of newness. New wood, new paint, the fresh lemony scent of cleaning products. Baby hung her coat on a hook and then did the same with mine.

"What sounds good?" she asked, opening the door to a walk-in refrigerator. "Steak and eggs?"

This was my first time in a commercial kitchen; everything was metal and shiny and state-of-the-art-looking. Baby moved around comfortably, grabbing bowls from here, knives from there. Kat had worked at Headlights for more than fifteen years, I remembered. This was probably a second home to Baby.

For a moment I envied her. I mean, maybe it wasn't ideal to have grown up at "Hooters, but with cars," but still. The place where Baby had spent her past was also where she was spending her present. There was an ease about being in spaces you were once a kid in. Any equivalent places for me were far away in Virginia and had been off-limits for years. All at once, watching Baby cook in this kitchen, I felt their distance.

When the food was done, we took our plates out to the dining area and sat in the same booth we had the day of the fire. Baby turned on the soda fountain and got us each a Coke.

"The clean-up crew did a good job," Baby noted. Then she pointed to a section of the room where several tarps were still laid out. "They have to redo the floor over there. Bob says everything should be ready in time for the wedding reception, though." She cut into her breakfast.

I was already a few bites in. The food was great. I hadn't realized how much of an appetite you could work up by not having sex with Scarlet. "Speaking of the wedding," it dawned on me to ask, "what am I supposed to wear?"

Baby chewed and swallowed. "A suit, probably. Do you have one of those?"

I didn't. I hadn't worn a suit since The Bad Thing. "I'll find something."

"My dress is pink, if that matters to you," Baby said. "I'm going to be enormous by then. Even more than now. I'll look like a giant marshmallow Peep."

"No, you won't," I said, but she probably would.

"I'm due February twenty-fifth, but the doctor said girls my age usually go late, so who knows when it'll happen."

"Will there be any warning signs?" I asked. It hadn't occurred to me before that I might be with Baby when she went into labor, and I wanted to know what to be on the lookout for.

She shrugged. "I'm assuming the godawful amount of pain will be all the clue I need that the person inside of me is trying to break out."

"That sounds absolutely terrifying," I said before considering whether I should.

Baby glared at me. "I appreciate the encouragement."

A lull in the conversation followed. I wanted to say something reassuring to Baby about childbirth, but as I'd never seen a motivational poster on the subject, I was at a loss.

"Why do you think she did it?" was how Baby broke the silence.

Somehow, even without any context, I knew exactly who and what she was talking about.

I considered my answer carefully. "There's no way for me to know, obviously, but maybe it was for whatever reasons you almost did?"

Baby nodded as if I'd confirmed her own guess. "Do you think Scarlet's so screwed up right now because she made the wrong choice?"

I shook my head. "Just because someone is having a hard time doesn't necessarily mean they did the wrong thing. All of the options were going to be hard, right?"

Baby nodded again, and then there was another lull while we continued eating.

"I decided to go to Sarah Lawrence," Baby eventually announced.

I wasn't sure if I was supposed to congratulate her, considering the juxtaposition of this news to other sensitive subjects in our conversation, so instead I followed up with the most logical question. "Does that mean you decided not to keep the baby?"

Baby picked at her eggs for a few seconds before answering. "I wasn't sure what to do until I found this couple who I know would be kickass parents. They said it would be a dream come true to adopt my baby," she said. "I want this kid to have parents who think it's a dream come true, and I know that won't be the case if I keep it."

"It's every kid's dream come true to be someone's dream come true," I told her. "I would imagine, at least. I can't speak from experience, as I've pretty much been my parents' worst nightmare."

"I know what you mean. Kat didn't aspire to be a single mom working at a place like Headlights," Baby acknowledged. "She tells me all the time that before she got knocked up, her dream was to move to Los Angeles and be a model. Even though she never says it outright, I think she resents me for fucking that up for her."

I wanted to reassure Baby that Kat didn't seem like the type to blame her kid for her own choices, but it probably didn't matter what I said—Baby would've still worried about it. So instead I just said, "Kat never would've made it as a model. She's way too short. You saved her from a lifetime of rejection."

Baby laughed then, and I felt victorious.

"It's going to be an open adoption. That means I'll get to be a part of the kid's life. Like, the cool aunt who comes by every few months." She ran her hand through her hair. "This way I get live my own life and still know my kid."

"It sounds like a win-win."

Baby shrugged, and the conversation was over.

We finished eating and washed our dishes. Then Baby took me back to work to get my car. The sun was just coming up when we pulled into the parking lot.

"We didn't finish *Heart and Souls*," Baby said just as I was about to get out of the car.

"Damn. I guess we'll just have to hang out again sometime."

"Yeah. Damn." She yawned. "I'm going home to sleep for sixteen hours." In the daylight, Baby looked like someone who'd been up the whole night.

I was sure I did, too. "Good night."

I sat in my car while it warmed up. It was so cold that my stereo was sluggish, and I could hear my R.E.M. CD spinning inside the player, producing no sound. I switched to the radio instead.

"You're listening to Planet 96.3, getting your Monday morning commute started with a little Bon Jovi. By request, from the *Cross Road* album, here's 'Always' . . ."

My fingers automatically reached for the dial, but I stopped myself from pushing the power button. I waited a few seconds, and then I turned the volume up instead.

As I pulled out of the lot, I noticed several trash bags piled at the bottom of the stairs to Scarlet's apartment that hadn't been there when I'd left earlier.

I smiled.

If Scarlet trying to initiate sex with me hadn't been her rock bottom, maybe it was me rejecting her that had been the real wake-up call. The fact that she'd immediately started cleaning up her life the moment I'd left made ruining my one chance at sleeping with her worth it.

. . . Probably.

Chapter 27

On a Sunday in early February, Mom and Dad both skipped their Sabbath day rituals to continue the spring cleaning they'd begun the day before even though we were still more than a month shy of actual spring.

When I came downstairs for breakfast, Mom was sitting amid the contents of the coat closet, which were strewn across the living room floor.

"There's fresh coffee," she said when she saw me.

"Do I drink coffee?"

"You're old enough." She muted the television. "What size are you now, Joel? I want to know what stuff I can get rid of."

"It's a safe bet that I've outgrown those Ninja Turtles snow pants," I pointed out. "That's probably true of everything here." I tore open the foil on a package of brown sugar Pop-Tarts and dropped them into the toaster.

"How'd you grow up so fast?" Mom asked, holding up a Bart Simpson hat about four sizes too small for me.

"Time flies when you're having fun." I bent down to look at my reflection in the toaster. I still hadn't completely gotten the hang of having shorter hair and the gel it required to achieve its Brad Pitt-ness. If it had fit, I might've worn the Bart Simpson hat just to cover up my hair.

Mom came into the kitchen. "Anything special I should save if I come across it?"

"I'd like to hold on to the Matisse. But it's cool to sell the Renoir. It's not his best work."

"You little shit." Mom smiled at me before lighting a cigarette. "I'm serious."

I thought for a second. "I'd like to keep the He-Man stuff, if you're talking about throwing out old toys. They might be worth something."

"Are those the army guys?"

"No, that's G.I. Joe. He-Man guys are the bigger ones with muscles. Dad'll know."

She jotted this description down verbatim on the back of a Farmer Jack receipt. "Anything else?"

My breakfast popped up from the toaster. "Oh, yeah." I thought carefully about how I should word my next request. "I remember having this toy gun. It was black with a yellow drill thing inside it. I hear it's a collector's item, so I definitely want to hang on to that."

Mom abbreviated that description when she wrote it down. She didn't seem to realize I was talking about the Star Wars blaster she'd forbidden me from playing with as a kid. "What else?"

"Oh, I need a suit."

She took a drag from her cigarette and looked up at me. "A suit? You want to keep your old bathing suits?"

"No. Unrelated to the cleaning. I just remembered I need a suit. The formal kind."

"For what?"

"For Baby's mom's wedding. I mean, Nicole's mom."

"Like a tuxedo?"

"I don't think so. I'm not *in* the wedding. I'm just Nicole's date, so I have to dress up."

"Date?" Mom's eyebrows rose.

"Guest," I corrected myself.

There were footsteps on the basement stairs then, and my dad emerged from the doorway holding a box. "Oh, hey, Joel!" He was clearly surprised to see me. "I thought you'd already left for work."

"I'm about to."

It had been more than a month since I'd caught my dad with another woman, and we'd both managed not to bring up the subject since. At this point, it was like the mail at the Virginia house—his affair was just there. Not dealing with it had become just the way things were between us. I was strangely OK with this.

"Joel needs a suit for a wedding he's going to," Mom told Dad, which started a somewhat awkward exchange between them. "Is that something you want to buy with him?"

He set down his box. "Not if it's something you want to do?"

Mom put out her cigarette and reached for another one. "I thought it sounded like a father-son thing."

"I'd love to take him." Dad hesitated before adding, "If it's OK with you."

"If that's what you want."

I eyed them both. "Why are you guys being weird?"

270

"We're not." Mom lit her second cigarette. "How about we all go? That way no one's left out."

"Sounds good." Dad fake-smiled.

"Great! We'll go tonight. We can go out for dinner, too. It'll be a special evening," Mom decided.

"Perfect. I'll be there." Dad picked up his box and walked outside with it.

I followed him out of the house, but neither of us said anything more.

It was a slow, uneventful Sunday shift at the video store, but I was working with Baby, so I was happy there was a lot of downtime.

In the days since our all-nighter, we'd watched some more ghost movies, but at her house instead of at work to lessen the risk of late-night booty calls from Scarlet (Baby's words). Not that I was anticipating any such offers ever again, but whatever. Baby's house was fine with me, especially since her fridge was stocked with Headlights food.

I hadn't seen much of Scarlet since I'd left her apartment that night. I couldn't tell which one of us was avoiding the other, or if we both were doing it. The only time she talked to me was to rearrange the work schedule. Scarlet wasn't *not* nice to me when we saw each other, but she wasn't changing clothes in front of me, either, as she'd been known to do. I understood that for the most part, this Scarlet was probably better for me (and for her, too), so I tried to look on the bright side.

Baby and I watched *Truly, Madly, Deeply* and *Chances Are* that week, as well as *Hello Again* with Diane from *Cheers*. None of them really reminded me of Crystal, but then again, less and less of anything—movies or otherwise—was making me think about her much those days. The more time I spent with Baby not actively hiding my past, the less I actually thought about it. I'm not going to lie, it was kind of nice.

That particular Sunday, Baby and I were tasked with setting up a Valentine's Day movie shelf to highlight the romantic titles ROYO Video had to offer. Baby had done this in previous years, so she took the lead on collecting the movies that were sure to be popular rentals during the season of love while I put tape on the backs of paper hearts and stuck them around the display.

"I'm not putting *Dirty Dancing* on the shelf," Baby informed me as she carried a stack of VHS boxes to the counter. "Every time I do, the number of people who tell me that nobody should put me in a corner increases by five hundred percent."

"No argument from me."

She arranged a row of rom-coms. "Hey—who do you think is prettier: Meg Ryan or Julia Roberts?" She held up the boxes for *Prelude to a Kiss* and *Pretty Woman* for my examination.

"Julia Roberts."

"Really? I think Meg Ryan is way hotter."

"I guess we have different tastes in women."

Baby put the boxes down and held up two more Meg Ryan movies from the piles; apparently she starred in all of them. "What about Tom Hanks versus Billy Crystal?" She was now comparing *Sleepless in Seattle* to *When Harry Met Sally.* "Who's the better-looking dude?"

I glanced up at her. "I'm not into guys."

"So? I'm not a lesbian, but I can still tell you that Meg Ryan is more attractive than Julia Roberts," she pointed out.

"Good for you. That's not how it works for me."

"I know, I know. You only get boners for Scarlet," Baby mocked me.

"And Julia Roberts."

"Why is that, you think?" She leaned against the counter and rested her hand on her stomach. "Why do people get hot for certain people but not others?"

"Isn't it up to this guy?" I held up a cardboard Cupid. "He shoots people in the ass with his heart arrows. That's how they fall in love."

Baby disregarded my comment. "There has to be some sort of science involved, right? Biology. Chemistry. It's not fucking magic like in fairy tales or in the movies." She nodded at the display. "So what do you think it is about Scarlet that makes you hot for her?"

"Seriously? You want to talk about why I find your mortal enemy sexually attractive?"

"If I can't understand the disease, how will I ever find a cure?" Her tone was pseudo-serious.

I relented. "Fine. I like her body. And her face."

"Most girls I know have bodies and faces," Baby pointed out. "What makes hers so special?"

"I don't know how to answer that" was my cop-out answer. "Maybe it just boils down to instinct?"

Baby ran her hand through her hair. "I wish we had more control over who we're attracted to. It's not like I *wanted* to be attracted to Indiana Jones."

"Really? Why not?" I still knew very little about the guy.

"I want to want a guy who's smart and ambitious, and Indy was no Rhodes Scholar."

"Why were you with him, then?"

"I don't know," she acknowledged. "It used to piss Scarlet off that he paid so much attention to me. She wasn't used to being in second place. Even though she was with your cousin, she still flirted with every dude who came in here, and she couldn't fucking handle that Indy wouldn't give her the time of day." Baby got quiet then, like she was trying to find some words. "Sometimes I think . . . I think *that's*

273

why I slept with him. I think I did it just to spite Scarlet. I wanted to have something that she couldn't have."

This felt like a confession. "So you didn't even like Indy?"

"I liked that he liked me," Baby admitted. "He was just kind of dim. And immature." She sighed and looked away. "Now I'm having his baby, and I'm super scared this kid is going to be ridiculously mediocre, just like its father, and I will be responsible for inflicting it upon the world. Is there any greater crime against humanity?"

Baby didn't sound like she was joking, so I didn't laugh. "I think you're forgetting that this kid is going to be half you. So, you know. It can't be all bad."

Baby looked away from me then, but I could tell she was smiling. Crescently.

"Do you want to feel something weird?"

Having regretted saying yes to this question more than once in the psych hospital, I hesitated before I answered Baby. "OK."

She took my hand and placed it on her stomach.

"Hold on . . ."

I was pretty sure she meant it in the "wait a second" way and not as an instruction to grab on to anything, so I just stood there with my hand on Baby's stomach, her hand on top of mine.

And then I felt something.

"Was that a kick?"

"Or an elbow. I can never tell."

I was completely amazed. "It has elbows?" I looked down at Baby's stomach and then back at her face. "There are elbows in there?"

"I fucking hope so" was Baby's answer. "I mean, technically by now the kid's supposed to be completely done growing all its parts. The doctor says that at this point, it's just staying in there to get fatter."

I felt another thump against my hand, and my eyes got wide.

"You mean there's a totally complete human inside you?"

"Did they not show you the *Miracle of Life* video in homeschool?"

"Holy shit!" There was more movement, and this time I felt something pushing out all across my hand. "Does it hurt you when it does that?"

She shrugged. "Not usually."

"This is so bizarre. No offense."

"I think I'm going to miss this part," Baby admitted. "I think I'm going to feel lonely afterward, once it's gone." She looked at me when she said this. Her eyes were green.

"I'll be around," I told her. "I can even kick you in the stomach sometimes if it will make you feel better."

She made a face at me. "Thanks." Then Baby lifted my hand away but she didn't let it go.

A few seconds went by, and then she brought it closer to her face and examined my fingers. "Damn, Solo. Has anyone ever told you that you could be a hand model?"

I smiled. "Actually, I have heard that before."

Of course I should have known that my mom would want to look for suits at JCPenney. She only really shopped at two places, the other one being the Farmer Jack supermarket where she worked. As far as she was concerned, if what she needed couldn't be found in one of those two stores, it didn't exist.

It felt like returning to the scene of a crime, going back to that store with my dad. We both kept our heads down as we walked past the jewelry counter to the suit department.

"What do you think of the gray one?" Mom posed the question to no one in particular after I'd tried on three jackets. "Is the navy one better?"

"Either one," I said. Really, it made no difference to me what we bought. I just didn't want to make an ass of myself by showing up to the wedding in a hoodie and jeans.

My dad said nothing, just paced around a rack of pants like he had to take a piss and couldn't find a bathroom.

"Craig?"

"Looks good!" he called over without actually looking at me.

"And what color tie?" Mom held a few up to the gray jacket I still had on. "What color is Nicole's dress?"

"Pink."

"Well, you're not wearing a *pink* tie," she said as though that would be a sin. "How about we go with the gray suit and a navy tie?"

"Fine with me," I said, and I stepped back into the changing room.

I needed shoes, too, which we also bought at JCPenney while my dad shifted nervously among the sneakers. Then we were off to dinner.

My parents and I sat in a booth in the smoking section at TGI Fridays. Dad asked the hostess for a beer before we even met our waitress, which was really out of character for him. JCPenney must have done a number on him.

Our waitress, who was Lindsay H. and who was wearing at least twenty decorative buttons on her suspenders that said things like FREE HUGS! and SAVE THE RAINFOREST! and AS IF!, brought my dad his beer and took our orders.

As soon as she was gone, Mom sipped her water and moved the ashtray closer to her. "Do you have any doctor's appointments coming up, Joel?"

"I'm getting my anemia checked in a few weeks."

Mom grinned at my use of the code word. "Good."

"How've you been doing?" It was the first time my dad had addressed me since we'd left the house.

I tore off my straw paper and tied it in a knot. "Honestly, things are going the best they've gone since . . ." I paused. "Since Virginia, I guess."

Mom and Dad both looked very relieved to hear this.

"We thought you seemed happier," Dad said. "The life of a working man suits you."

"Thanks."

There was a look of getting down to business on Mom's face, and then she started talking. "There's something Dad and I have been discussing, and since you're doing good now, we thought we'd let you in on it." She lit a cigarette and looked at my dad.

"OK . . ." I said slowly. "What's going on?"

Dad took a breath and looked down at his beer. "So, your mother and I were thinking of spending a little time apart. We've both got some things to sort out. Grown-up, married-people stuff. We think space would do us some good."

I was caught completely off guard by this. "What does that mean?"

Dad fidgeted in his seat. "You know . . . it means we're separating."

"Why? What happened?" I kept my eyes on my dad, but he wouldn't look at me. Had Mom caught him?

Mom fielded my question with a non-answer. "This has been a long time coming, Joel."

I was really confused. It did not seem like a long time coming to me. It seemed about as abrupt as a car wreck. "How long is this going to last? Like, a week? Two weeks?"

"It's going to be long-term, Joel." Dad finally met my eyes. "Mom's going to stay with Aunt Denise and Uncle Jim at first. Then, once I get my own place, she'll come back to the house."

"So, like, you're breaking up for good. Like, you're getting divorced?"

Mom sighed. "We are moving in that direction, yes. But we're still going to be friends, Joel. Life won't be much different for you. That's why we waited this long to make a change. We wanted to tell you when you had both feet on the ground."

I was *flabbergasted*. "Exactly how long did you wait to tell me? How long have you been thinking about doing this?"

My parents exchanged a guilty look before Dad answered, "It's actually something we decided a long time ago. I've just been staying in the guest room in lieu of moving out. We wanted to keep things normal for you until we thought you could handle a change."

"Normal?" I practically yelled. "There's nothing Normal about not telling your kid his parents broke up. How long has this been going on?"

No one would look at me.

"Three years," Mom said.

"What the *fuck*?" I was now so far beyond flabbergasted that the light from flabbergasted would have taken a hundred years to reach me. "You've been broken up for *three fucking years* and didn't tell me?"

Lindsay H., sensing she was interrupting something, said nothing as she delivered Mom's coffee and my Cherry Coke.

"We really tried to make it work, Joel," my dad continued when she'd gone. "It was important to both of us not to make anything official while you were going through a rough time."

"Oh. Well, how thoughtful. That makes lying to me for three years completely OK. Thanks for sparing my feelings."

He sighed. "I'm not lying when I say that I love your mother, Joel. I'll always love her. And you. We'll both always love you exactly the same as we always have."

"We stuck it out as long as we could, Joel," Mom broke in to add.

"The odds weren't in our favor. Statistically speaking, we made it longer than most couples who've gone through what we have," Dad admitted.

"Oh, OK. So it's *my* fault?" I said what he wouldn't. That was it. I was ready to throw a bunch of inflammable cans of cooking spray on the stove and burn the mother-TGI-fucking restaurant to the ground.

My dad shook his head adamantly. "No, Joel. This has nothing to do with you. This is not in any way your fault. The vast majority of marriages can't survive something like The Bad Thing That Happened. At some point we had to stop pretending that ours had."

"At some point three years ago, you mean."

Mom finished her cigarette and pursed her lips. "Can you really blame us for keeping it a secret, Joel? You just said this is the best you've felt in years, and you're *still* flying off the handle about it."

I stared at her, dumbfounded. The woman had lied to me for one thousand days about something monumentally important (and then when she finally decided to tell me about it, she did it in a goddamn TGI Fridays), but me being upset was flying off the handle?

"Maureen, let the boy react, for crying out loud," Dad said. "He has the right to be mad about this. Shit, I'm mad on his behalf. We should have told him."

Mom turned her hostility toward my dad now. "We were going to, remember? But then his mental patient girlfriend drank Mr. Clean and almost died! And after what that did to him, neither one of us wanted to be the bearer of bad news. It wasn't just me!"

"It was Mop & Glo, and she wasn't my fucking girlfriend!" I yelled, because if you're going to throw someone's psych hospital highlight reel in his face, you should at least get the details right.

"Keep your voice down!" Mom whisper-scolded me.

A heavy silence followed.

"I'm sorry I didn't tell you sooner, Joel," Dad finally said. "I hated keeping it from you. I just honestly didn't know if you could take it." His voice broke. "I never meant to hurt you."

It was surprising that my dad's apology made a dent in my anger given how (justifiably) pissed off I was, but somehow, it did. I mean, it's not like I wasn't mad at all after he said that—the wound was still fresh—but at least Dad was giving me a Band-Aid.

All my life, when I'd been mad at my parents for things they'd done to me—forcing me to go to masculinity classes, sending me to a psych hospital, etc.—they'd managed to convince me that I'd left them no choice. The burden of proof was always on me to validate my anger, and since they were both judge and jury, I could never do it.

But my dad had just done something neither of them ever had before. He had admitted fault. This made it easier to listen to what else he had to say.

Mom must've noticed me softening toward my dad, and she must not have liked it. I don't know why else she would've said what she did next.

"Are you also sorry for screwing that woman from work? Because if you're issuing apologies, I'll take one, too."

My eyes darted back and forth between my parents.

Dad clenched his teeth. "We agreed it wasn't the time or place to talk about that," he whispered.

"Well, since you feel so bad about not telling our son the truth about what's going on, I figured maybe you'd changed your mind."

"You and I have been living separate lives for years, Maureen" was my dad's . . . excuse? Reason? Explanation? Justification? I don't know which one he intended it to be, but since I already knew about the affair, the only surprising thing was that my mom did, too.

"I'm still your wife" was her trump card. "It's still cheating."

He didn't say anything, but my dad's shoulders slumped, and he looked miserable.

Mom folded her arms across her chest and simpered. She'd always been a no-holds-barred fighter, and Dad always quit arguments early to lick his wounds. This time, though, it felt like Mom had shot her weapon at me to spite my dad. She clearly didn't know I already knew about the affair. It was like she wanted me to fly off the handle now, but only so she could blame Dad for it.

I didn't give her the satisfaction. Instead I said, "I want to live with Dad."

My dad's head jerked up in shock. Mom looked completely betrayed. And for some reason, in that moment, I felt victorious.

Just then, Lindsay H. walked by and set a basket of potato skins on our table, along with four appetizer plates. She must have miscounted us, though I don't know how. It was obvious that the Teagues were only a party of three. We had been for a very long time.

Chapter 28

Though I wasn't sure it marked the official start of her temporary move-out, that night Mom went to Aunt Denise's. As far as I knew, she hadn't come back by the time I left for work the next morning. Dad spent most of the night in the basement; the ruse of "spring cleaning" now blown, he openly began moving the boxes labeled CRAIG'S CLOTHES and CRAIG'S CAR MAGAZINES and CRAIG'S MISC. into his truck. Their future destination was as yet unknown to me.

I tried calling Baby, but it was a school night, and she was asleep already. I didn't leave a message with Kat, deciding I could wait until I saw her at work the next afternoon to tell her about my eventful evening, even though I really wanted to talk to her immediately. In fact, there really wasn't anything else I wanted to do besides run to Baby and relay just how fucked up my night had been. But instead I went to bed early, falling asleep and waking up the next morning to the *Monster* album playing on repeat.

I got to work just before eight in the morning, two hours before the store even opened. I decided I would spend those hours meticulously cleaning out all the cabinets and shelves behind the counter. I needed it more than they did.

By ten, I'd rid the store of old movie screeners and broken VHS tapes, filed away a lot of stray paperwork, and removed every visible speck of dust I'd encountered. Then I put everything back inside the cabinets in an orderly fashion and congratulated myself on another menial job well done. It felt good to accomplish something, no matter how unnecessary. Plus it kept my mind off of things, which was more to the point.

I was so angry about my parents splitting up (who could blame me?), and I was not very good at being mad. You may not realize this, but being good at being mad is a skill you have to refine. I'd learned in therapy that anger can and should be productive—a motivator to confront injustice and ensure that conflicts get resolved. Such was not the case for me, though. Anger bested me more often than not. I was bad at anger the way some people can't hold their liquor. When I was super pissed, I got irrational and incoherent. I raised my voice. I sometimes started awkwardly crying. And now you could add "I've been known to punch a chair" to that list, too.

The less time I had on my hands to think about my parents lying to me, the better, is what I'm saying, and I still had seven hours to kill before Baby's shift started and I'd finally have someone to talk to about this shit.

It's not like I was expecting Baby to fix everything. I knew she couldn't. In fact, she probably wouldn't have any advice for me at all. She would probably just look at me and say something like "Your parents split up three years ago and have just been pretending everything's fine? That's super fucked up, Solo. No wonder you were in a mental hospital if those are the people who are raising you." And I would agree with her.

Really, it was just nice to have someone to tell my shitty news to who wasn't getting paid by the hour to hear it. I mean, technically if I told her at work, Baby would be getting paid to listen, but you know what I'm saying. This was something Baby would want to know no matter where I told her, because we were friends, and that was reason enough for me to look forward to talking to her. That, and it's always nice to have someone validate that something you're going through is fucked up. It helps you feel a little less crazy, which for a guy like me is supremely helpful.

I opened the store and decided to put in a movie to pass the time while I ran the weekend's sales report. Monday day shifts were among the slowest of the week, and I wanted to do whatever it took to speed things up.

After poking around the new releases wall without anything grabbing my attention, I wandered into the older titles. I bypassed the romance and horror sections. I stopped in comedies but eventually moved on from them, too. My brain was restless and uninterested in everything. Maybe I'd feel better if I punched a few chairs.

It occurred to me that an action movie might be the way to go. After all, it could be cathartic to watch a bunch of bad guys get the shit kicked out of them by a Jackie Chan type. Justice for all, served up by some odds-defying, reluctant hero. That's what a day like this called for.

I'd just picked up the VHS box for Jean-Claude Van Damme's *Lionheart* when I glanced at the shelf below it. Three movies practically jumped off the shelf at me.

Star Wars. The Empire Strikes Back. Return of the Jedi.

For real, I shivered.

Even though *Star Wars* was my favorite movie, I hadn't watched it in ten years. There were reasons, of course. Some far deeper than my mom's embargo on the whole franchise. As much as I loved it, though, I can't say I'd really wanted to watch the movies much in the last decade. I hadn't been ready to, honestly. But, I thought, maybe now was the right time.

Before I could talk myself out of it, I grabbed the movie off the rental shelf and stuck it in the VCR behind the counter. A few seconds later, these words appeared on the TV:

A long time ago in a galaxy far, far away . . .

Circa 1984, videocassette recorders cost around five hundred dollars. Not five hundred dollars by today's standards — five hundred 1984 dollars, which is way, way more. We Teagues were not in the upper echelon of Fairfax Virginians, economically speaking, but still we got our first VCR that Christmas, and along with it, our first VHS tape: *Star Wars*.

I was a little kid, and there was Nothing Wrong With Me.

I remember how everything felt special that Christmas. My parents had such reverence for the VCR, having saved for months to buy it. After Dad got it hooked up, Mom ran a cloth over it to remove his fingerprints. Then we lined up on the couch, turned the lights off, and powered up our twenty-five-inch Zenith TV set. We ate Jiffy Pop popcorn out of red-and-white boxes Mom had saved from the movie theater, and I watched *Star Wars* for the first of what would be hundreds of times.

From then on, the movie was always playing at our house. Soon *Star Wars* seeped into our psyches. It became a second language to us. We called each other nerf herders and made like we were using the Force on one another. We punctuated all sorts of requests with "You're my only hope!" "Help me set the table, Joel — you're my only hope!" "You need to take the garbage out—you're my only hope!" "Please hand me the newspaper—you're my only hope!" For months, the first thing anyone said to me when I came down for breakfast in the morning was "Aren't you a little short for a stormtrooper?" And whenever one of us was being a smart-ass, Mom inevitably said, "Laugh it up, fuzzball."

Within two years, we'd added *The Empire Strikes Back* and *Return of the Jedi* to our home library, and our vocabularies expanded to include "Luke, I am your father!" (especially whenever any of us walked by a box fan). From there on out, whenever one of us told another "I love you," it was always met with an "I know," just like we were Han and Leia.

I get that this might seem corny to you, and honestly, that's fine. Your family's inside jokes would probably sound weird to me, too. That's the whole point. You only appreciate shit like that when you're a part of it. When you're included. When you belong.

The Star Wars movies were a *thing* for us Teagues. They were a major ingredient of my childhood. Inextricable from it, really. I can't separate one from the other, as much as my mom insisted I start doing so after The Bad Thing That Happened.

I wanted to give the movies my full attention at work that day—Luke and Obi-Wan and Vader. Han and Leia. I wanted to remember the story I loved so much. The Jedi, the princess, the loner. But the movies were triggering too much. Too many memories.

I was a zombie the whole day. I know I waited on some customers, put away movies, ran a few reports, but I couldn't tell you about any of it. I was at work in body only. By the time Luke and Leia were having their moment on the moon of Endor halfway through *Return of the Jedi*, I was completely lost, my mind traveling back and forth at light speed between Fairfax, Virginia, and a galaxy far, far away.

Which was probably why I didn't hear Maverick punch in for the start of his shift that afternoon.

"I don't really understand this scene." He'd made it all the way to the counter without me noticing him.

"Shit!" I jumped when he spoke.

"My bad. I didn't mean to surprise you," Maverick said.

I played it cool and pressed pause. "No worries. I guess I was just caught up in the movie and didn't hear you come in."

He nodded and turned his attention to the TV. "Since you're the Star Wars expert around here, clear something up for me?" Maverick pointed to the screen, which was frozen on a shot of Luke and Leia. "Those two are related, right?"

"They're brother and sister."

Maverick made a confused face. "Then isn't it weird that they basically made out in the first movie?"

"Yeah. A lot of people have a problem with that." I turned off the TV.

Maverick walked around the counter and grabbed his lanyard. "It looks different back here," he noted. "Clean different."

"I straightened up," I said, distracted. My head was still foggy from a day of too much reminiscing.

He raised his eyebrows. "Everything all right?"

"Yeah, why?"

"I was told you're a stress cleaner. The cleaner the store, the more you've got going on."

I huffed out a laugh. "Who told you that?"

"Baby."

I smiled. I liked that Baby knew this about me. "What else did she say?"

"Nothing else like that. It was just something she warned me to watch out for back when I started working here. She said you brood while you clean, so if the store's suddenly spotless, I should look out."

"She's not wrong," I admitted.

Maverick picked up the fishbowl, then set it back down again once he saw there were no tags to put away. "So what's up, then?" he asked, leaning casually against the counter, tucking his thumbs into his front pockets. "You OK?"

Since he already knew something was going on, it felt like a lie to tell him nothing. "There's just some shit going on with my parents," I said, hoping he'd drop the subject.

No such luck, though. "Yeah? Like what?" His interest felt genuine.

"They're splitting up." I tried to sound nonchalant, but because it was such a serious revelation, the conversation didn't end like I wanted it to.

"Oh, shit, man. I'm sorry. You gonna be all right?"

"Yeah, yeah, yeah, I'm cool" was my unconvincing response.

Maverick looked at me skeptically. Sympathetically.

I felt antsy now. My nerves were exposed. If I couldn't find a way to back out of the conversation, pretty soon I'd start word-vomiting all over Maverick about everything. I could feel it coming.

"You don't *have* to be cool, Solo," he said, which, dammit, was the right thing to say. It made me wonder if Maverick was a therapy kid, too. "This is a big deal."

"Yeah, I know," I said, willing myself to act Normal. "It's been a long time coming . . . They've been through the wringer . . . I mean, most married couples don't survive what our family's been through . . ."

Shit. In my effort to say nothing, I'd somehow alluded to *everything*.

Feelings were welling up inside me. TGI Fridays and Star Wars and everything else were coming to a head all at once, and my vision started to blur.

This time it wasn't a migraine, though. It was worse than that. It was because I was going to cry.

I was tearing up. Right there at work, in front of Maverick.

Of course he noticed. "Hey, Solo . . ." he said gently. "It's OK."

I nodded, managing to swallow a sob I was sure was going to escape. I tilted my head back to drain the still unreleased tears back into my eye sockets. It was a close call, but I'd somehow stopped myself from losing my shit.

Maverick reached out and touched my shoulder, steadying me. "Hey, man. You're going to be all right."

I just nodded. "Thanks."

We stood there for a few seconds before I realized that Maverick hadn't taken his hand off of me.

I looked at it, then back at Maverick.

There was a flash of fear in his eyes before he let go of me and jammed his hands into his pockets. "I'm sorry," he said.

I stood there, frozen and speechless.

Moments later, the back door opened and the timecard machine stamped.

"Hey, guys," Baby said. "It's so fucking cold out there right now." She opened the cabinet to grab her lanyard. "I swear to god, the first chance I get, I'm moving somewhere it doesn't snow. If I wanted to live in these Siberian conditions, I'd live in Russia."

Maverick and I were still stuck in a stare-down.

"What's going on?" Baby asked, sensing the tension. She was standing next to me. "What'd I miss?"

I looked at her, then at Maverick, and then back at her. And then, without thinking, I turned to Baby, grabbed her face, and kissed her.

Like, I *went* for it. I kissed her like I meant it. Like I had something to prove.

And then, as abruptly as I'd started, I stopped and looked at the both of them with complete shock, just as surprised as they were by what had just happened.

"I'm sorry! I don't know why I did that."

Maverick, whose turn it was to tear up, apparently, called out my bullshit. "Yeah, you do." He stormed past Baby and me, headed for the back hallway.

Baby, who'd been staring unblinking with her mouth agape, unfroze. "What the hell?" she shouted. She looked at the back of a fleeing Maverick, then at me again. "What the fucking hell was that for?"

"I'm sorry, OK?" I repeated. "I didn't know what else to do."

"About *what?*" Baby demanded. "In what situation is *kissing me* your last resort?"

"The situation where you were right about Maverick, OK?" I told her. "He made a pass at me, and I freaked out. That's why I kissed you."

"Maverick made a pass at you?" Baby repeated. "Maverick made a *pass* at you?"

"Yeah, all right? He touched my shoulder!" I sighed angrily. "Congratulations on your gaydar."

Baby's eyes narrowed as she pieced things together. "So Maverick *touches your shoulder*—which I'm not sure even constitutes a pass—and to prove that *you're* not interested in *him*, you start making out with *me?*"

"Exactly."

Baby's expression turned murderous. "I don't know if that makes you a bigger asshole to Maverick or to me." She removed her lanyard and chucked it at me. "But it definitely makes you an asshole." She grabbed her coat and started putting it back on.

"Where are you going?" I asked, panicking. I'd been needing to talk to Baby the entire day—she couldn't just walk out now, especially mad. "Please don't go."

"You're giving me cramps" was her response. "I need to go lie down." She started toward the door.

"When are you coming back?" My voice was shaking. I was shaking.

"I'm not," she said, attempting to move around me. "At least not tonight. I'm afraid if I have to look at you much longer, I'll throat-punch you."

I stood in her way. "I'll take a throat punch! Just don't go, please."

She held her ground. "Let me leave, Solo! You're acting like a crazy person!"

It was probably the only thing she could've said to get me to stop begging her not to go. Even though Baby had more proof than just about anyone else that I *was* crazy, I couldn't stand for her to think it was actually true.

I stepped aside. She pushed past me and stormed out the back door.

And then, once again, I was by myself in the store.

Goddammit, did I feel alone.

Chapter 29

I wanted to leave, but no one else could cover the store. Scarlet was in class. Hannibal had no ride. Poppins wasn't home, and the number for The Godfather ended up being for a funeral home. That meant I was stuck at work until the store closed at ten, which was fourteen hours after I'd arrived and several hours past sanity, according to my watch.

It took all of my healthy coping mechanisms to make it through that evening shift. Cleaning more shit. Recleaning more shit. Reading the VCR manual. Vacuuming the store. Reading the manual for the vacuum cleaner. Cleaning the vacuum cleaner.

Still the night dragged. Finally, at ten till ten, I could take no more. I counted the money in the drawers and went to the front door to flip the open sign to closed. If someone wanted to rent a movie in the next ten minutes, well, they were shit out of luck. I was going home. That day needed to die already.

I couldn't think anymore about how badly I'd screwed things up. It was killing me. I needed to sleep for twelve, maybe eighteen hours—however long it took to give me some perspective. I'd even have welcomed a medically induced coma at that point. Knock me out for two or three days until Baby was ready to forgive me and life could go back to Normal. Of course, Normal would still mean dealing with my parents and whatever the hell was happening with Maverick, but give me a break, I couldn't worry about everything at the same goddamn time.

When I killed the lights inside the store, all at once I could see through the windows and out into the streets of downtown Royal Oak. The chaos inside me was not mirrored on the other side of the glass. The world was dark and peaceful beyond the doors of the video store. The stars hadn't had any problem coming out just because *my* day was colossally shitty, and it was oddly refreshing that there was a great big world out there beyond ROYO Video and all of Han Solo's problems.

I was locking the door when I noticed a girl sitting in the coffee shop across the street, looking out *her* window in my general direction. Her eyes felt fixed on me. I wondered if she'd been watching me watching everything.

For a fleeting, naively optimistic moment, I got my hopes up that it was Baby over there. I pressed my face closer to the glass to get a better look, but then my breath fogged it up. The odds were slim to none, I knew, but on the off chance it *was* Baby over there nursing a cup of coffee and keeping an eye on me, I wanted her to know I'd noticed.

As I opened the door, the girl in the coffee shop stood up, slipped on her coat, and headed for *that* door. She stepped outside under a streetlight, where I was able to get a better look at her.

It wasn't Baby. This girl was taller, had curly hair, and (perhaps the biggest giveaway) was not pregnant. Disappointed, I turned around to go back inside, but just then another, more jarring thought occurred to me.

The girl looked a little like Crystal.

I did an about-face.

My heart sped up, and I held my breath.

"Crystal?" I said her name reluctantly. "Is that you?"

"Hey!" The person waved at me. "Hey, come over here!"

I'd been sure it was Crystal the night the person in the back lot turned out to be Indiana Jones. I'd been sure it was Crystal who'd played the Bon Jovi song that day at Headlights. Right now, staring across the street at this person, I *wasn't* sure it was Crystal. But then again, I wasn't sure it wasn't, either.

"Crystal?" I asked, more loudly this time.

"I'll just come to you instead!" was her response.

The more I considered it, the more possible it felt that it *was* Crystal. If there was ever a time for her to reappear in my life, now was as good as any. That day in particular was the most desperate and the most crazy I'd felt in years. Crystal may have been waiting for such a time—when I was headed straight for rock bottom—to show back up.

"Come on over!" I yelled at the girl, and then I braced myself for Crystal's return.

I was lying in a bed at Weller Clawson. Valerie had OD'd two days before (though it's probably not an over*dose* if there's no actual suggested dosage because it's fucking *Mop & Glo*), and as I was being interrogated about all she'd accused me of in her suicide note, I had completely lost my shit and ended up needing to be restrained and sedated.

I don't know how long I was like that, because when you're in the state I was in, time feels like it's flying by and also like it has stopped. But at some point my meds were scaled back, and when Dr. Schwartz came into my room to tell me that Valerie was going to pull through, I was able to understand him.

I remember feeling relieved but also like I wouldn't be upset if a bus accidentally ran her over. I hated that girl. Everything she'd accused me of was bullshit. But like I told you before, when there's Something Wrong With You, you pretty much have no credibility, so of course no one believed me when I denied everything.

But anyway, you already know that Valerie's lies about me were eventually debunked. The part of this whole story that you don't know, though, is how Crystal factored into the whole mess, which was pretty significantly.

Crystal had made herself scarce the first few days after the incident, or at least I thought she had. She could've been sitting by my side the whole time and I was just too medicated to notice. But anyway, once I was back in my old (non-padded) room, having been reevaluated and deemed just regular crazy as opposed to strapped-to-a-bed crazy, she paid me a visit.

The closet door opened after the last rounds of the day, and Crystal tiptoed over to my bed and crawled in beside me. She laid her head on my chest and said, "I'm so sorry, Joel."

"I'm never having sex with another crazy girl for the rest of my life," I vowed.

"That's a great idea" was her reply. "Though please don't blame yourself for this. It's not your fault."

"Valerie said it was," I pointed out. "In her note, she said I ruined her life and she wanted to die because of me. Which is ironic, because now I kind of want to die because of her."

Crystal took a deep breath at the same time I did, and we sighed the same sigh.

"You don't mean that, do you?" she asked me a few seconds later. "About wanting to die?"

I knew enough about mental hospitals to understand that the way you answered this particular question determined a lot of things about the treatment you received, so I whispered my answer, just in case someone was eavesdropping on our conversation.

"Sometimes."

I'd never said that out loud before. I'd never admitted it to anyone. Not my parents, not any medical professional, not even any of the journals I'd been forced to keep. It felt scary saying it. It was also a relief, in a way.

Yes, it was true. Sometimes I didn't want to be alive anymore.

It wasn't only because of Valerie that I felt that way, though what she'd put me through hadn't helped things. The truth of the matter was, I was just really tired of my life. You can't blame me; there was *a lot* for me to be tired of. For instance, I was tired of therapy. I was tired of talking about The Bad Thing That Happened and What Was Wrong With Me. I was tired of white walls and motivational posters and the clinical bleach smell of hospitals. I was tired of my mother's suspicious glances when we walked down the cosmetics aisle in the drugstore and my parents constantly going through my closet looking for god knows what and leaving me lingerie catalogs. I was tired of having both "anemia" and pathetic sex with random girls. But most of all, I was tired of missing Fairfax and Virginia Beach and Star Wars and trick-or-treating and playing with toys in the kiln and every single day of my life before The Bad Thing That Happened.

I was tired of being alone all the time unless I was with Crystal, and I was tired of everyone thinking that she was the problem when it was really everything else that was driving me fucking crazy.

"I was afraid of that," Crystal whispered back. Then she held my hand and rubbed circles into my thumbnail until I fell asleep.

I'll be honest, the next few weeks weren't my best. I'd lost a lot of the motivation I'd had for cooperating with my therapists thanks to the Mop & Glo incident, and since I'd written off sleeping with crazy girls, there was nothing to take the edge off of all the shit I was feeling inside. None of my meds seemed to be working, or maybe they were, but not well enough anymore. Needless to say, I was depressed, and I didn't see that changing anytime soon.

Crystal kept her distance. I noticed her a few times, standing in doorways, peeking out of closets. But she remained in the background, watching me. I was OK with this, because I didn't have a lot to say, and it was enough to not feel alone, knowing she was keeping an eye on me.

Then one day I was coming back from a long session of a new experimental therapy called EMDR that was supposed to help me deal with The Bad Thing That Happened when I found Crystal in my room wearing her green dress, facing out the window.

"Hey," I greeted her, surprised. It wasn't like her to be so out in the open. We both knew that if anyone found out I'd been seeing her at the hospital, shit would hit the fan. "What's going on?"

"It's pretty outside," she said, still looking out the window. "It looks warm. Reminds me of Virginia."

I walked around my bed and joined her and noticed the suitcase by her feet, the one with BAT engraved on the plate.

"Are you going somewhere?" I asked her.

She turned to look at me. "It's time for me to go, Joel."

"Go where?"

297

She took a deep breath and forced a smile. "Away. It's time for me to leave."

I immediately started shaking. "What? Why?"

Crystal sighed. "I'm doing more harm to you than good by hanging around. It's obvious to me now. You're not going to get better with me here all the time. So . . . I'm going to go." There was a determination in her voice that I'd never heard before.

"That's not true!" I argued. "I *am* getting better. The doctors just said I'll get to go home soon. That I'm going to be fine!"

She knew I was lying. "Joel, we both know I can't stay forever. It wouldn't be right. And it wouldn't be good for you."

"You know what else isn't good for me? Being fucking alone, which is what I'll be if you leave me," I reminded her. "Please, please don't go right now, Crystal. I don't think I can handle it. I can't handle one more goddamn thing right now. I just can't."

"I know." She nodded. "That's exactly why I have to go now, while you're here. Where the doctors can keep you safe." Tears spilled from her eyes and down her cheeks. "I couldn't stand it if you hurt yourself, Joel."

"I won't," I told her. "I promise I won't."

"Joel . . ." Crystal sighed. "It's time."

"So that's it? I don't have a say in this? You're just abandoning me?" I started to cry. "Right when I need you most?"

Crystal swallowed hard and set her jaw. "It's not like that. It's for your own good. I'm doing the right thing." She picked up her suitcase.

I grabbed the handle, too. "No, I won't let you leave!"

"Joel. You have to know that you can't stop me. You know that, right? You *know*."

"I don't know anything" was my defiant response.

We were both crying now. "You have to. You have to know that

I'm the reason you're stuck here. *I'm* the reason all of this started in the first place. *I'm* the cause of all of this."

"No." I shook my head. "Stop it! Stop saying that! You can't just leave! Don't you know what it will do to me if you go?"

"Yes," she said. "Trust me, it'll be worse if I stay."

I pulled on the suitcase, trying to break her grip to no avail.

"Right now, you need to save yourself, Joel." She touched my face. "You need to use all your energy to fight to get better, and as long as I'm here, you won't."

"What are you talking about?" I cried. "You're not making sense!"

"Joel," she said sharply. "Stop pretending you don't know who I am." She paused, then lowered her voice. "I know that you see me in here." She pointed to herself. "You always have, and we both know it."

I let go of the suitcase and stared at her. Her eyes were the greenest they'd ever been.

"Where are you going?" I asked.

She wiped her eyes with the back of her hand and sniffed. "You'll know. When you're ready, you'll realize where I am."

Crystal leaned forward then and kissed me on the cheek, and I grabbed on to her with both hands.

She quickly pulled away and ran out of the room without looking back. I could only stand it for a few seconds before I chased her into the hallway, shouting her name. But of course she was gone. Gone for good.

I'd spent a lot of time looking for Crystal since that day. There had been times since she'd left when I was sure Crystal had come back. But if I'm being honest with myself, that was my own paranoia getting the best of me. And maybe, every once in a while, *hope* getting the best of me. The truth was that Crystal was right—I had a pretty good idea where she'd gone. The one place I was sure she'd be was the place I was most afraid to look for her.

That night at work, it was hope, not paranoia, that convinced me it could've been Crystal at that coffee shop. It was hope that kept my feet planted on the pavement as the girl came shuffling across the street toward me. It was hope that kept me waiting there until we were face-to-face before the disappointment sank in when the person turned out not to be Crystal.

The girl looked embarrassed. "From far away, you looked like someone I used to know. When you waved, I just assumed you were him."

"Same here," I admitted.

She nodded. Upon closer examination, this girl looked nothing like Crystal. She was too tall, too old. I could tell by the girl's expression that she was thinking about all the ways I wasn't who she thought I was, too, and how disappointing that was.

We stood there for a few seconds, exchanging comments about the awkward moment. Then, just before we went our separate ways, the girl made a decision.

"I think I'm going to look him up. Give him a call," she said definitively. "You made me realize how much I miss him." She laughed to herself. "Do you think that's crazy?"

I shook my head. "Not at all."

"What about you, then?" she asked me. "Whoever you thought I was—are you going to reach out to her now, too?"

I raised my eyebrows at her. "Now, that would *definitely* be crazy."

She laughed. "I guess you dodged a bullet, then. It's funny how that works. What's serendipity for one person is just a coincidence for another."

"Yeah. So funny."

With a final wave, we parted ways, the trajectory of the girl's night different now than it had been just minutes before (maybe for the better, even) while mine felt the same as ever.

I finished closing up the store and stamped my time card at seven minutes after ten, thus ending what had to be the longest workday anyone had ever had in the history of ROYO Video.

Chapter 30

I didn't sleep for sixteen hours that night, but I did manage to get in about eight before my mother, whose turn it was to be back in the house, apparently, woke me up by vacuuming the stairs right outside my bedroom.

"You're not going to just sleep all day" was her greeting when I opened my door. "There's a lot that needs to be done around here." She didn't bother to turn off the vacuum or remove her cigarette from her mouth when she said this. Since I was fluent in passive-aggressive from living with her my whole life, I knew this meant she was still pissed at me.

I didn't argue that seven a.m. was hardly "all day" or point out that she was dropping ashes all over the carpet she'd just cleaned *or* bring up the fact that she had *never* run the vacuum that early in the morning *and why the hell couldn't she just talk to me about why she was mad instead of being a jerk about things?* Instead I took a shower and got dressed, hoping she'd have left for work by the time I went downstairs.

No such luck, though, because it turned out that Mom had taken the whole week off of work to "get her affairs in order" before she and Dad met with their lawyers on Friday. I guess now that the cat was out of the bag, there was no use in dragging things out.

"Friday is Valentine's Day," Mom informed me as I ate a Pop-Tart. "The lawyer will probably want holiday pay."

I think this was her attempt to be funny. When I didn't laugh, she cleared my place at the table (even though I wasn't finished eating) and told me to go clean her tchotchke shelf. I swallowed what was in my mouth and said, "Yes, ma'am."

The chore of cleaning Mom's knickknacks was probably intended as a punishment—the woman had dozens of figurines she insisted be cleaned with a toothbrush and Pine-Sol because she liked the way it smelled. But I was secretly grateful for the job, since I wasn't scheduled to work that day and there was nothing else to do but wait by the phone in case Baby called me.

Mom's mention of Valentine's Day reminded me that the BobKat wedding was on Friday. That only gave me three days to square things away with Baby, and I wasn't sure if that was enough time to pay for the sin I'd committed.

Even though I'd only slept eight hours, I'd gained some perspective about everything that had happened the day before. Unfortunately, none of it made me feel any better about what I'd done.

I mean, honestly, if *I'd* walked into work and *Baby* had mouth-ambushed *me*, I'd have felt at least confused and at worst betrayed, especially after I'd concluded that the whole motivation behind the kiss was cowardice, which, if I'm being honest with myself, it was.

On the flip side, if I were Maverick, I would completely hate me. I mean, if I had a crush on someone who made out with someone else right in front of me to prove they didn't like me back, I'd think that person was an asshole. And I'd be right.

Though if I get any defense here (and I'm not positive I do), let me remind you that my past was incredibly complicated when it came to homophobia. I'd spent my life homophobe-adjacent, and as you know, I'd suffered as a result. Hopefully you can see that and at least cut me enough slack to try to redeem myself.

I was thinking through my road to redemption when Mom came to check on my progress.

"How's it going?" she asked. I'd finished cleaning two rows of ceramic farm animals wearing overalls and glass bells purchased from sixteen states she'd visited.

"Fine. Though there's not much dust even before I brush them, so I doubt you'll be able to tell a difference."

"Keep going anyway," she instructed me. "The house has to be spick-and-span for the appraiser."

"Appraiser?"

She lit a cigarette. "We want to know how much the house is worth. It's good information to have in case we decide to sell." Mom pulled out a chair and sat down at the table.

I started on a new row of figurines—angels this time, labeled with the months of the year and with inspirational Bible verses printed down their fronts. I made it to March before she spoke again.

"You know, we'd already decided that you'd live with me, Joel."

I avoided her eyes. "*We* didn't decide anything."

Mom pursed her lips. "I can't believe you're taking your father's side. He's the one with a mistress, after all. I gave your dad the best years of my life, and he thanks me by getting a girlfriend and taking my son away from me."

I ignored her pity party. "I thought you guys splitting up was a mutual decision. Or do you not remember all the specifics because you decided so long ago?"

She blew smoke out through her nose. "If you want to live with your father just to hurt me, then fine. But if you think he's going to be easier on you than I will, you're wrong. Your dad and I are on the same page."

"What are you talking about?"

"You're not going to get away with anything no matter which one of us you live with. We've always been in agreement about certain things. That's not going to change just because we're separating."

She seemed to be dancing around a subject I wasn't catching on to. "OK . . ."

Mom ground out her cigarette into an ashtray. "I know you think I'm stupid, Joel. But trust me, I'm not. I know about everything that goes on in this house."

I set down the angel I was scrubbing and looked at her, still confused. "I am well aware that nothing gets past you, Mom. Unlike me, who didn't even catch on that you and Dad were faking being a couple for the last three years, you're a regular Sherlock Holmes." At this point, I dropped all the passiveness in my voice, and the aggression came through more clearly.

She crossed her arms over her chest. "Well, then it should come as no surprise to you that I found your little picture. The one you were trying to hide from me behind the bathing suit girl, thinking I wouldn't notice." Her tone was condescending, like I was five and had foolishly shoved all my broccoli under my napkin at dinner, hoping she wouldn't realize it.

My eyes widened, but I willed myself not to react further; I wouldn't give her the satisfaction of knowing how angry she'd made me. "Why do you assume I was hiding it? Maybe I just wanted to frame a picture of a hot girl. Did you ever think of that?"

She actually laughed at this. "When have you ever put up a picture of any girl in your room? As soon as I saw the frame, I knew there must be something behind it that you didn't want me to see."

"So naturally you looked." I dropped my ruse, since she'd so easily seen through it. "Because evidently I deserve no privacy whatsoever."

"I was right, wasn't I?"

I sighed. "So what? I have a Star Wars drawing. I bet there are millions of parents who'd be thrilled if that was the worst thing they found in their teenage sons' bedrooms."

"Let's not pretend that's the worst thing I've ever found in your bedroom," Mom snapped back. "The fact that you're hiding anything is a red flag. Let alone something like this, which you know is forbidden in our home."

I inwardly groaned. "So let me get this straight. I was supposed to know that a drawing of all my coworkers dressed as Star Wars characters was 'forbidden' in this house?"

Mom gave me a dirty look. "You knew enough to try to hide it."

"Fine," I conceded, picking up the April angel. "I should have set the drawing on fire the moment it was given to me and then doused the flames with holy water. Can we drop it now?"

"No, we can't," Mom argued. "Not until you tell me why you're hiding things again."

"I'm not hiding *things*!" I yelled. "I just didn't want you to see that picture."

"Why not?" she demanded.

"Because you hate Star Wars" was my answer.

"Did the pregnant girl give it to you?" Mom asked, pivoting. "Is that why you hid it? You don't think I approve of your friendship with a loose girl? Because you know I'm not judgmental like that, Joel."

This was way funnier than my mom's previous attempt at a joke, except that she was completely serious. Instead of calling her out, though, I just said, "She has a name." After pausing long enough to remember what it was, I added, "And no, Nicole didn't give it to me."

"Then who did?" she demanded.

I tried to figure out what the point would be of answering this question. Mom's real beef with the drawing was that it was a Star Wars picture; for whatever reason, that in itself was a class-A felony. She didn't know anything about Maverick or why he'd gone to such pains to create it for me or that *that* was the true reason I'd tried to keep her from seeing it.

All that is to say, I could've lied to her about it. I could've said that Poppins was the artist. That she had a crush on me and assumed I liked Star Wars since my work name was Solo. I could have told my mom that I had accepted it because I didn't want to hurt Poppins's feelings and that I'd hidden it from my mom because I didn't want to upset her. Then I could have waxed fucking poetic about how I had feelings for Poppins, too, but that I didn't know how to tell her because of all the bad luck I'd had with Valerie. I could have said all this, played it up, and Mom would've been none the wiser because it was a solid lie. And because it fit an acceptable narrative for my life, there would probably be no further debate about me hiding the picture. There'd be no apology from Mom, of course, for going through my things, but regardless, a yarn like that likely would have ended the conversation and gotten me off the hook entirely.

But I didn't want to lie about this.

I'd like to say it was because I believed that lying was wrong, but I'm not going to bullshit you. The real reason that I wanted to tell my mom the truth was because I knew it would send her through the roof, and at that moment, I wanted to hurt her.

Maybe that sounds like a horrible thing to say about your own mother, but it was also true, so there you go. I hated her for putting me through all she had over the last nine years. So when I said what I said next, it was motivated by pure spite. The fact that it was true was of secondary importance.

"A guy at work drew it for me. A gay guy who has a crush on me. It's my favorite gift anyone has ever given me."

Mom stared at me, speechless, so I went on.

"I mean, I wasn't sure at first that he was gay. But then yesterday he pretty much hit on me, so now I'm convinced." I finished polishing the angel in my hand and set it down. "He looks like a J. Crew model."

I watched my mom's face shift in all kinds of ways, and I wondered if that was what I had looked like the night I told Baby about Crystal. All this time, my mom had been paranoid that What Was Wrong With Me meant I was gay, and for whatever reason, that was her worst fear. Even though I wasn't, I allowed her to sit with this information, letting her feel all the warped satisfaction of being right about something that she was petrified was true.

What I didn't think through was Newton's third law (I'd just completed my physics credit), which says that for every action, there is an equal and opposite reaction.

In terms of my mother's equal and opposite reaction, this is what she said: "You're done at the video store. No two weeks' notice, no going back there at all. You. Are. Done."

"What?" I practically screeched. "You can't do that!"

She held up her hand to silence me. "You're never to see that boy again," Mom declared, lighting another cigarette. "Do you understand me?"

"No, I don't understand! *I never understand you!*" I was indignant. "I'm not going to let you take my job away from me, Mom! I'm not a child, and this isn't a toy! This is my *job*!"

"You're not eighteen yet, mister. So you don't get to decide!" She stormed over to the telephone. "I'm calling your father right now. He'll back me up on this."

As she started to dial, I had my own equal and opposite reaction to my mom's threat, and it was to start throwing her ceramic angels at the wall as hard as I could.

"I'm!" (May.) "Not!" (June.) "Fucking!" (July.) "Quitting!" (August.) "My!" (September.) "Job!" (October.)

She flinched as each one hit a different spot on the wall, shattering into shards and leaving dents at the points of impact, which any real estate appraiser would surely notice.

"Well, now you'll *definitely* have to," she growled at me as she snatched the phone off its receiver. "Because you're going back to the hospital! You've clearly lost your mind, Joel! And I'm not going through this again!"

She was right about one thing: I *was* losing my fucking mind. I was losing it because she was taking it from me.

Over the past nine years, I'd worked damn hard to be a Normal kid, and I was finally there. Or at least I was as close as I could be, considering all the shit I had gone through. I would be damned if I was going to let her steal that from me without a fight.

If I was going down, I was going to take her down with me.

I stomped over to my mother and got so close to her face that I inhaled her smoke. "I am not going back to the hospital." My voice was calm but firm. "And if you try to make me, I'll kill myself."

This, I knew, was the atom bomb. The Death Star, if you will. I'd always known that, but because I'd never wanted to hurt my mother the way I knew those words would, I'd never used them. Now she'd left me no choice.

We stood there, eye to eye. I'd cut her deep, and I was waiting for her to bleed.

Seconds later, she began to sob. "Please, Joel! Please, no!" she cried. "Please, don't! I'll do anything! Just let us get you help!"

I stood above her as she wept, feeling waves of guilt and resolve washing over me, one after another. "You're the one who needs help, Mom."

And then I left.

Chapter 31

I owe it to paranoia that I didn't take my car when I left my house. Somehow, in the midst of everything, I had the foresight to know my mom could make one phone call to the cops and there'd be an APB out for a Chrysler LeBaron being driven by a suicidal ex–mental patient. So instead I made my escape quietly on my dad's ten-speed bike, which was the only thing left of his in the garage, now that he was moving out.

Since I was sure Mom was expecting to hear my car peel out, I figured I'd bought myself some time before she realized I was gone, and I used that head start to get myself someplace she wouldn't know to look for me: Baby's house.

I didn't know if Baby would be able to press pause on her hatred long enough to hear me out, but given that I had no other options,

I was willing to take my chances. I mean, maybe once Baby finally knew about my parents, she might even give me a break for fucking up like I had. Or who knew? Maybe she'd still want to kick me square in the junk. I honestly didn't care. I was going there anyway.

The ride to Baby's house was long and cold on a bicycle in February, and thanks to the three inches of snow we'd gotten overnight and no one shoveling their sidewalks, it was also slow. Luckily, my anger helped me summon the strength to keep going despite it all.

Of course I was furious at my mom, but as I worked the pedals through the slush, I could feel some old stale rage boiling up, too. You see, when something like The Bad Thing happens to a person, it's like getting infected with an incurable disease. No matter how you try to treat the symptoms when they arise (with therapy, with medicine, with time), the virus never leaves your system entirely. It might not kill you, but it's part of you forever, sometimes lying dormant, sometimes flaring up.

The fight with my mom had awoken the illness inside me, compounding the fury I was already feeling, which was probably why when I finally made it to Baby's house and no one was home (because it was a Tuesday, because it was the middle of the day, because she was a high school student), I just about lost my entire shit right there in her driveway.

Somehow I managed to hold things together (after a lot of swearing . . . like, *a lot*), and instead of using all my pent-up rage to twist my dad's bike into a pretzel and hurl it into the street, I rode it the few remaining miles to ROYO Video (where else was I gonna go?), hoping against hope that there'd be no nice men with straitjackets waiting for me there.

Fortunately, the only person in the store was Hannibal, who

barely acknowledged me when I barged through the front door crazy-eyed and nearly hypothermic. I stormed past him and down the hallway to the break room, where I grabbed Scarlet's extra bedding. Then I locked myself in the storage closet and immediately went to sleep on the floor.

There are two types of people in the world: those who can't sleep when they're angry, and those whose brains cut to dead air once they reach the peak of fury. I am the latter, and it's one of the few things about my brain that I'm actually grateful for, especially in that moment because I needed a time-out.

For the next four hours, nestled between the two-liter Coke restock and crates of M&M's, I slept hard. It was a dark and dreamless sleep, and for that I was also grateful.

I woke up on my own to afternoon light streaming through the one glass-blocked window in the closet. Since I'd eaten only half a Pop-Tart that day, I scavenged the snack inventory until I came upon a bag of Combos I was sure no one would miss and chased it with a warm Sunkist (because fruit is important) before figuring out what the hell to do next.

A cooler head now prevailing, I was able to more clearly see the latest mess I was in. I have to say, it felt like the biggest one I'd made in years, maybe even since the Bon Jovi concert. I mean, I'd *threatened to kill myself*, which on a red-flag scale of one to ten was an eleven.

I feel like I should explain that I would never have brought up killing myself if Mom hadn't pushed me over the edge. Please know I wasn't *really* suicidal; I'd just needed her to know how serious I was about not going back to the hospital. Since I had only a few weapons at my disposal to battle my mom, you can't blame me for spearing her Achilles' heel when push came to shove. It didn't occur to me until it was too late that this was also the very thing most likely to guarantee the outcome I was trying to avoid.

It felt inevitable that Mom would have me committed now. It wasn't like I would be able to talk my way out of this one with the doctors. Suicide is psychiatrists' greatest fear because doctors get bad reputations if they can't convince their patients to not kill themselves. Dr. Singh would definitely take Mom's side, too, considering how nervous he was that time I'd said my mood was a seven and not an eight. Threatening suicide was probably equivalent to negative one hundred on the *How have you been feeling?* scale.

Fuck. I really couldn't see a way out of this.

The wheels in my head were turning, struggling to find a resolution to my situation that didn't end with me in a padded room, when I heard someone try the doorknob.

"Why is this locked?" I heard Scarlet ask herself following a second attempt to open the door. "Hannibal?" she called out. "Did you lock the storage closet?"

I opened the door.

"Hey," I said.

I startled Scarlet so badly she nearly fell over. "What the hell, Solo? What are you doing in here?"

I opened the door wider and pointed to the bedding. "Sleeping."

"Why?"

I went with "Why not?"

"OK . . ." Scarlet said. She walked past me and picked up a box of printer paper. Then she paused, something occurring to her. "Does this have something to do with Baby?"

"Not directly," I told her. "Why?"

Scarlet shifted the box from one side of her body to the other. "She called off the rest of the week. She said her mom needed her for last-minute wedding stuff, but I don't know if I buy it. She sounded upset. *Sad*-upset. But whatever. It was weird, and so is this." She indicated the blankets on the floor. "I thought maybe the two were related."

"She didn't even tell me she was taking time off." I sighed. It was *possible* Kat wanted Baby's help with wedding stuff, but I knew the more likely scenario was that she was making a point to avoid me, which made me feel even worse for kissing her.

Scarlet's forehead creased. "I figured you guys told each other everything."

"Guess not."

Scarlet paused. "Does that mean you didn't tell her about my situation?"

I didn't follow. "What situation?"

Scarlet gave me a look like I was supposed to know what she was talking about, and then I figured it out.

"I didn't tell Baby, but she knows. I mean, we found out at the same time. My mom let it slip."

Scarlet paled the way a person tends to do when they learn someone knows shit about them that was supposed to be a secret. "Dammit, Aunt Maureen," she muttered under her breath. "I know she's your mother, Solo. But fuck her! That was none of her business."

"You're right. I'm sorry."

Scarlet went on. "Devin never liked her. He said something about her reaming him out for taking you to a concert once. He thinks she's completely crazy."

"There's a case to be made for that."

Scarlet leaned against the wall. "So, does Baby hate me even more now? Does she think I'm a horrible person?"

"No," I said. Then I clarified, "Her opinion of you didn't change," because Baby had always thought Scarlet was horrible, but it had nothing to do with learning about the abortion.

315

She sighed. "Yeah, right. I'm sure she's waiting for the perfect time to throw it in my face. Probably after she has her baby and she turns out to be the best mother in the whole fricking world."

I hated speaking for Baby, but I was confident she would want me to call this out. "She wouldn't do that. If anything, I think this is the one area in life where Baby relates to you. She's been in your shoes."

"But she's having the baby," Scarlet pointed out.

"Sure, but I think that when someone's in a hard situation, it's pretty easy for them to understand how a person in the same situation could make a different choice than the one they make for themselves."

Scarlet sighed. "I guess. But whatever. It's like they say—if you spend your entire life looking backward, you're sure to miss what lies ahead."

I gave her a look. "Who says that?"

"I don't really know." She paused, trying to remember. "I think I read that somewhere."

Something clicked then. Scarlet was quoting a motivational poster. I could picture it clearly: it was a photo of a guy going the wrong way on an escalator. I could also picture exactly where I'd seen it before: Marc Schwartz's outpatient office. It was hanging in the lobby, or at least it had been two years ago when I'd met with his partners for my follow-up appointments after I was released from Weller Clawson.

Sure, Scarlet could have seen it somewhere else. It's not like Marc Schwartz owned the exclusive rights to the picture or anything. But still, that kind of artwork only hangs in certain kinds of places. Places where people with childhood anemia go.

I was really happy for Scarlet. And proud of her, too. "It makes total sense."

She carried the box of paper to the doorway. "I cleaned up the apartment," she informed me. "You don't have to worry about tripping over anything the next time you come over for a trim." She indicated my hair. "Don't wait too long, or you'll get shaggy."

"I won't," I promised, and then she left.

Chapter 32

Poppins and The Godfather were covering the evening shift, and neither of them asked what I was doing hanging around the store when I wasn't scheduled to be there. Poppins was too busy gabbing on and on about the Valentine's date she was going on after work on Friday (his name was Jeremy, he drove a Camaro, and he was — gasp! — in a band) while the always-dressed-for-mourning The Godfather looked out the window at the snow falling.

Since I had nowhere to go, I attempted to stay busy even though I was off the clock. I needed to kill time until I could go back to Baby's (I would call a cab this time) to grovel on my hands and knees for her forgiveness. Assuming we made amends — this was still a big question mark — together we'd come up with a way for me to keep my job and avoid the hospital while simultaneously smoothing things over with Maverick. According to the last five minutes of any ABC family sitcom, these conflicts could be easily resolved with crazy antics, weak disguises, and/or hugs (all of which I was game to try), because anything is possible when two best friends put their heads together.

The problem was that every time I thought I was ready to go to her house, I got distracted by a movie poster that needed changing or some new membership forms that needed filing (read: I chickened out), and then I had to convince myself all over again that it was a good idea to ambush someone who was practically rearranging her life to avoid me.

ROYO Video had steady customers once dinnertime rolled around, and I ended up covering the registers while the girls went on their breaks. When things finally died down for good, it was nine o'clock, which, in terms of pulling the trigger on going to Baby's house, felt like do-or-die time.

I'd just excused myself to the break room with the cordless phone and the yellow pages to call that cab when I heard a familiar (but completely out-of-context) voice carrying from back in the store.

"I don't remember what you call him here," it said. "Something from Star Wars. I just need to know if you've seen him today . . ."

Was that . . . my *dad*?

Shit. I should've realized Mom would send him out as a one-man search party. I would've called him at work if I'd been sure my mom hadn't already convinced him I'd lost my mind (and therefore credibility) again. It was too late now, though. Now he was here, paying me a first-ever visit at work, and right off the bat, he was about to blow my cover as a Normal person.

I rushed back into the store to see my father waving around a picture of me he kept in his wallet. "He's been missing since this morning," Dad explained to a confused Poppins and The Godfather.

"Was he supposed to work today? Did he show up here at all?"

"I'm not missing," I said, coming up behind him. "I'm right here."

He whipped around, took one look at me, and exhaled a breath it sounded like he'd been holding for hours. "Oh, thank god," he said, and then he repeated it about twelve more times as he pinned my arms to my sides with an awkward hug that squeezed all the air out of me.

"I cannot breathe," I practically squeaked out. My dad was neither a big nor a strong man, but at that moment it felt like he was about to snap me in half.

"I was scared that I'd lost you!" His voice shook as he released his death grip on me.

"Well, you found me," I reminded him, inhaling deeply now that I could again.

Poppins, The Godfather, and I all exchanged glances. Poppins seemed concerned about whatever was happening, The Godfather alarmed.

"Do you know this man, Solo?" the latter asked me in a low voice, slowly reaching inside her purse. "Shall I persuade him to unhand you?"

As curious as I was to find out what this meant, I assured both of my coworkers that everything was OK. I then pulled my dad over to the corner of the store by the dusty classics section no one ever went to and immediately started issuing apologies.

"I'm really sorry, Dad. I didn't mean to worry you. I just got in this huge fight with Mom, and I didn't know what to do." Then I threw in, "I was just picking up the phone to call home when I heard you," for good measure, even though it was a lie.

My dad's expression waffled between angry and relieved. "What the hell happened this morning?" he demanded in a firm tone while affectionately stroking the back of my neck. "Your mother called me completely hysterical!"

I explained my side of everything to him as quickly and quietly as I could so no one else would hear, doing my damnedest to downplay the part where I threatened suicide. "I only said it to hurt her, Dad, which I know was totally wrong. I'm so sorry. I would never actually do it. I swear."

My dad looked tempted to believe me, but given The Bad Thing That Happened, I understood why he was wavering. He did hear me out, though, and when you're a guy like me, anytime someone gives you the benefit of the doubt, you appreciate it.

"So it was the drawing that started it all?" my dad clarified when I was done talking. "Your mother wanted to have you committed because some guy drew you a picture?"

"More or less," I confirmed. Then I added, "And because I hid it," because it seemed fairer to my mom, even if realistically she probably would have freaked out just as much if I'd handed it over to her the moment I got it.

Dad rubbed his face and sighed before muttering, "Goddammit, Maureen." Then he looked at me for a long time (which was awkward, but I dealt with it) before asking, "Joel, can you come out to my truck for a minute?"

Because the *goddammit* had been directed at my mother and not me, I felt pretty confident it wasn't a trap, and I agreed to follow him.

The cab of my dad's truck was still warm when I opened the door. He hopped in the driver's seat and made a place for me to sit among the boxes he'd already moved out of the house.

"I have a lot of regrets in my life, Joel," Dad began when he was ready. "I'm sure that all men my age do, but given the hand that life dealt our family, I would venture to say that I've probably got more than the average guy. I can't do anything to change them, though. All

I can do is try my hardest not to repeat my mistakes." He switched the cab light on, selected one of the moving boxes, and put it on my lap. "Go on. Open it."

When I slid the lid off, my jaw about hit the floor. Inside the box, resting on top of all my old He-Man toys that I'd requested be spared during spring cleaning, was my original Star Wars Han Solo blaster in all its black-plastic-with-yellow-drill-mechanism glory.

"Holy shit, Dad!" I cried with joy. "I can't believe you found this!"

"I didn't find it," he admitted. "I always knew where it was."

I took the blaster out of the box and squeezed the plastic trigger. The drill bit struggled more than I remembered, but it still moved. My hands were much bigger than the last time I'd held it, and the blaster felt lighter than it once had. But somehow its familiarity still prompted an onslaught of memory and emotion, and my vision got blurry. "I was sure Mom threw this away."

"She thinks she did, but I saved it," Dad revealed. "I saved a lot of other stuff she wanted to get rid of, too." He indicated a second box next to me labeled CRAIG'S CAR MAGAZINES. Dad looked at me. "I never collected car magazines," he confessed; then he slid the lid off of that box, too.

All three Star Wars VHS tapes were inside it, along with some action figures, some Bon Jovi posters, and some shirts that weren't mine, most of them green.

"Why did you hold on to all of this?" I asked him, still gripping the blaster.

He shrugged. "I guess for the same reason your mom wanted it gone. It reminds me of how things used to be." Dad cleared his throat of the emotion creeping into it. "I don't want to be afraid of the past anymore. I can't keep living like that, but your mom . . . she can't *not*. That's why we can't be together anymore."

"I get it."

"I know most of that stuff wasn't yours, but I want you to have it," Dad offered. "If you want it, that is. We can keep it at my new place, so you don't have to worry about your mom finding it."

"I do want it," I said. "I want all of it."

Dad nodded, but before he put the lid back on the box, he pulled something from behind his seat. "Do you want to keep this, too?"

It was Maverick's drawing. Mom had no doubt given it to him as proof that I'd taken Maverick as a lover before sending him out to retrieve me.

"I do . . ." I said hesitantly, in case *this* was a trap. "It means a lot to me."

"Sure." Dad set the picture atop the shirts and closed the box. "Whoever drew it is a real artist" was all he said about it.

Dad knew the Star Wars drawing was what had started World War III between Mom and me, and it didn't seem to bother him at all. This reaction gave me the confidence I needed to state my case to him.

"Mom says I have to quit my job and go back to the hospital. I really don't want to do either of those things."

Dad took a breath and held it. "Are you going to hurt yourself?" he asked with painful earnestness. "And please, son. Tell me the truth."

"No. I swear to god, no," I promised him. "I would never, Dad. Aside from today, this is honestly the happiest I've been since . . . well, you know. Besides, now that I have my blaster back, I've got way too much to live for."

He didn't think this was funny. (He was probably right.) Instead he looked very thoughtful. Finally he spoke. "I won't sign off on anything that puts you back in the hospital against your will, Joel. I'm not doing that again. You're basically an adult, and if you don't think you need to go, I'm going to take your word for it." Dad looked worried when he said this, which made me even more grateful that he was taking my side anyway. "Your mother's going to be pissed that I disagree with her," he acknowledged. "But what's she going to do about it? Divorce me?"

We both laughed.

"You may want to lay low for a few days until she calms down, though. I think you two could benefit from some time apart, anyway" was Dad's advice. "I'm staying with a friend right now, so I can't offer you a room yet. Do you have a place to sleep for a few days? That pregnant girl's house, maybe? Or I could check you into a hotel?"

"I can manage something," I assured him. "Maybe I'll just skip town. I mean, what fun is it being on the lam if you don't leave your own neighborhood?"

"That's not a bad idea. You could head down to Fairfax for a few days. I know your grandparents would love that," Dad suggested.

I laughed again. My dad was a regular comedian tonight.

"I'm serious, Joel," he informed me. "It could do you a lot of good. It always does for me."

Since The Bad Thing, my dad was the only one in our family who'd returned to Virginia. He usually went for a week in the summer to see his family. Because of What Was Wrong With Me, my parents had never thought it was a good idea for me to go with him, and I had never exactly protested that decision.

"I'll figure something out."

"All right," he conceded. "Do what you've got to do." Then he gave me a number where I could reach him and fifty dollars for food. "I'll think of something to tell your mom. It's definitely going to be a lie, though, so whatever she says when you get back, just go with it."

I agreed and thanked him.

"Before you go, I got something for you." He reached into his jacket pocket and pulled out a wadded-up plastic bag from JCPenney. "I went a lot of places today looking for you. One of them was the mall. I picked this up while I was there."

I accepted the bag and peeked inside.

"I don't know if you want that or not," Dad said. "I wanted you to have it, though. Just in case."

I reached into the bag and pulled out a pink tie.

"I just wanted to tell you . . ." he began and stopped himself. He took a breath and tried again. "I just want you to know that whatever you want is what I want for you, Joel. I mean it. Pink tie. Blue tie. Purple tie. It doesn't make a difference to me. There's nothing wrong with you, Joel. No matter what color tie you wear." He cleared his throat and paused for a moment. "I love you."

This gesture itself might have been small, but this moment was infinitely big. Big enough to dwarf a lot of moments that had felt big before it. Big enough to swallow up some of my dad's regrets from his past. Big enough to wipe the slate clean and give my dad and me a brand-new tabula rasa.

I nodded at him as I clutched his gift in my hand. "I know, Dad," I told him. "I love you, too."

Chapter 33

As was often the case in southeast Michigan in mid-February, a dump of snow meant school was canceled the next day. The roads didn't get cleared until early afternoon, but once they were, droves of local mothers dragged their tired-of-being-cooped-up-with-nothing-to-do children into ROYO Video with the hope of salvaging a few hours of quiet during the unexpected day off with a movie rental.

At least that's what I guessed was going on when I was woken up by the high-pitched whining sounds of "But *Mom*, I want to watch *The Swan Princess*, not *The Land Before Time*!" echoing down the hall-way. One peek into the store at the mostly under-eighteen crowd on my way to the bathroom confirmed my suspicions. The store was never this busy when school was in session.

My rage nap the day before had thrown off my sleep schedule, and I had ended up watching movies until about four that morning before I finally passed out on the couch in the break room. It was after noon by the time I woke up, and I realized that unlike the day before, when my mom had accused me of it, I really had slept this day away.

I walked back to the break room to scavenge leftover pizza and flat soda, my half-assed attempt at a balanced breakfast, but I didn't really have much of an appetite. My stomach was too filled with guilt, I realized. Now that my mother's threats to take my job away and reinstitutionalize me had been neutralized by my dad, I was less afraid of her and more aware of how fucked up what I'd said to her had been. I don't know if it's the same for everyone, but even though I sometimes hated my mom for all the shit she put me through, I still felt shitty for hurting her. Even if she had it coming.

I knew my dad was right about me needing to lay low, but I didn't know how much time and space was the right amount to put between Mom and me before I went home again. Too much or too little could make things worse, I knew, and I definitely didn't want there to be a sequel to our fight—everyone knows that sequels are always way worse than the originals.

The phone rang as I was finishing my food, and knowing they were swamped out in the store, I answered it on the cordless.

"ROYO Video, this is Han Solo. How can I help you?

"Hey, Solo."

I gasped at the sound of her voice. "Baby?"

"Yeah. It's me."

"How are you?" I was so happy she had called that I couldn't think of anything more original to say.

She ignored my question. "Are you working right now, or are you just there?"

327

"I'm just here," I admitted.

"I should've known."

"Listen," I began, seizing the opportunity while I had it. "I'm really sorry about everything. You were totally right, it was such a dick move to kiss you—"

"Solo, stop," Baby interrupted me. "I don't want to talk about it, OK?"

"Really? But you were right. I completely fucked up."

"I know. But just drop it," she said impatiently. "I don't even care anymore."

This shocked me. I'd probably violated about a million unspoken rules of our friendship when I'd kissed her, and what I'd done definitely warranted a grudge. For Baby to let me off the hook like this was not only surprising, it was suspicious. "Is everything OK?"

"Can you just come get me?" She sounded really tired. "I need to be somewhere, and I don't want to go alone."

At this, I forgot all about my suspicions and embraced the sudden turn of the tide. If Baby wanted me around her, I wasn't going to waste any time questioning it.

"Yeah, of course!" I said, looking for my keys. Then I remembered. "Oh, *fuck*. I don't have my car. I've just got a bike right now. It'll take me longer, but I'll ride over."

"A bike? What the hell, Solo? Where's your car?"

"It's a long story. A lot of shit's gone down since I last talked to you."

"Tell me about it," Baby said. She meant this in a *Yeah, I'll bet* way more than a *Give me details, please* way. "Whatever. Just get here. Hitchhike if you have to, I don't even care."

"Yeah, OK," I said, pulling on my coat. The tone of her voice reignited my original concern that something was up, and I couldn't let her go without checking one more time. "Are you sure everything's all right, Baby?"

"Everything's fine" was her answer. "I'll see you soon." Then she hung up.

Two minutes later, I was pedaling the ten-speed down the slushy sidewalks again. It was an easier ride this time, knowing that at the end of it I'd get to see Baby and that she didn't hate me.

My heart was pounding when I knocked on Baby's door, both because of the record speed with which I'd ridden my bike to her house and because I was really excited to see her.

"Hey," Baby said when she opened the door. She stood in the foyer wrapped in a bedspread, her long hair tied up in a knot on the top of her head and her face void of color.

She was a sight for sore eyes. "Hey!" I said back, my tone much more excited than hers. I resisted the urge to hug her, since it was nonconsensual affection that had caused the rift between us to begin with. "I'm so glad to see you."

"Likewise," she said, but she gave no indication that she was glad about anything.

I slid my shoes off on the rug by the door and followed her into the living room. "Happy you got a snow day today?" was my attempt at small talk.

"Today's a snow day? I had no idea."

"Oh. Are you sick?" I guessed, trying to make sense of both Baby's death-warmed-over vibe and why she was home on what she believed was a school day.

"I'm in the vicinity of sick." She plopped down on the couch, resuming the spot I assumed she'd been in before I arrived.

I took the chair. "So are we taking you to the doctor?"

She pulled her blankets tighter and sighed. "Kind of. I have to go to the hospital."

At this, I grew more alarmed. "The hospital?" I repeated. Then, remembering Baby was pregnant, I asked, "Is it time to have the baby?"

This might have been a stupid question, but I didn't know. I mean, like most seventeen-year-old guys, I had zero experience with childbirth. From what I'd learned from movies, a person sitting on a couch calmly scowling wasn't part of that whole process. In TV and movies, at least, the women having babies were always panting and panicked and screaming for a "goddamn epidural" (whatever that was) while threatening to kill the fathers for impregnating them in the first place because labor hurt so, so much.

"No, it's not time for the baby," Baby assured me. Then, to my utter shock, she threw back her blankets and said, "That ship has sailed."

My eyes nearly popped out of my head. The bulge that had been protruding from Baby's midsection the last time I saw her was gone, and all that remained in its place was a loosely hanging, stretched-out promotional T-shirt for Pauly Shore's *Jury Duty*.

"Holy shit!" I practically screamed. "What happened?"

Baby shrugged. "Those 'cramps' I got the other day when you assaulted my mouth?" She made a face at me. "Turned out those were contractions."

My eyes were fixed on Baby's deflated stomach. "You had the baby already? Like, it's gone? It came out?"

Baby rolled her eyes at me. "With some effort, yeah, it came out, Solo."

"Oh" was my genius reaction to this astonishing news. I mean, it probably shouldn't have astonished me, seeing that this was how typical pregnancies ended, but then again, I didn't expect Baby's pregnancy to have ended already, so I was also dealing with the element of surprise.

Tired of waiting for me to articulate a better response, Baby continued to speak. "After I came home from work, my water broke—which, by the way, was fucking gross. By the time Kat got me to the hospital, I was already dilated six centimeters."

I understood what neither water breaking nor dilating meant, exactly, but I nodded anyway.

"It was a blur, Solo. Everything I read said these things can take up to forty hours, and then sometimes the doctors still have to cut the thing out of you. If that's true, I don't know how anyone survives it, because it only took me like two hours the regular old-fashioned way, and it hurt so fucking bad I thought I was going to die."

It felt surreal hearing Baby describe this, like she was catching me up on an important episode of my favorite TV show: *Tonight, on a special* Baby and Solo, *Baby goes through one of the most epic events in the human experience. Meanwhile, at ROYO Video, Solo polishes the chrome on a vacuum cleaner in an effort to maintain his fragile sanity. Check your local listings for time and channel.*

Baby went on, "It's like, one minute I had the worst cramps of my life, the next minute I was pushing a football out of a hole in my body the size of a golf ball, and the minute after that, a nurse was bringing me pudding like nothing ever happened." She looked at me. "In the meantime, the world's population increased by one whole person, and it didn't seem to really faze anyone."

"Not even you?" I asked. I wasn't sure this was the right thing to say or even a fair question to ask her, but it came out of my mouth regardless. "I mean, was everything OK?"

"I think so. I didn't see the baby" was how Baby, after a long pause, answered me. "I mean, I saw the doctors take it away once it was out of me, but I didn't, like, hold it or look at its face or anything. I didn't even let anyone tell me if it was a boy or a girl. I just had the nurse take it straight to the mom who was adopting it. It seemed like the right thing to do, you know?" Baby took her hair out of its messy knot and let it fall around her. "The first person to hold a baby should be its mom. I know it probably doesn't really even make a difference, but I didn't want to confuse anyone."

By "anyone," I assumed Baby meant the baby but probably also herself.

"So, yeah. I gave birth to a baby that I haven't seen, and I don't know its sex or its name," she recapped. "Is that crazy?"

From experience, I knew that if someone had the wherewithal to ask another person if something was crazy, it usually wasn't. Crazy isn't very self-aware, and it really seemed like Baby had put some logical thought into all these choices she'd made. "No. It sounds like you did what you needed to do."

"Yeah, and now I have to do something else."

"What's that?"

Baby glanced at the clock. "I'm supposed to meet with the adopting family for some official ceremony thing before the baby gets released to them from the hospital."

"What kind of ceremony, exactly?"

"I don't really know, but the baby will be there, and so will I. Which is where you come in." Baby ran her fingers through her hair. "I don't want to be alone when I see this kid for the first time. I mean, Kat will be there, but . . . I don't know. I just kind of want someone else there, too."

I felt honored by this. "I'm really good at being someone else," I told her. "I don't want to brag, but I could probably go pro at not being Kat."

Baby forced a non-crescent smile in my direction. "I'll go get ready, then." She stood up to leave but then stopped. "I know you said that a lot of shit's happened to you the last few days, but I really can't deal with anything other than my own shit right now. So unless

Crystal turned up with some spectacular insight about the afterlife, today's going to have to be just about me, OK?"

"No problem," I told her. "There's been no sign of Crystal, so today's all you."

"Damn," Baby said. Then she left to get ready.

The CD playing on Baby's car stereo on the way to the hospital was Hole, and there was a new coconut-scented air freshener hanging from her rearview mirror. These are details I remember because when something out of the ordinary is happening to you (like going to the hospital to meet your friend's baby that you weren't aware she'd had), your senses go all bionic. I'm not bullshitting you; this is true. There's a strong connection between our emotions and our senses, and our senses and our memories. This is why my mom had to switch from Mop & Glo to Pine-Sol after my last hospital stay—I never want to smell that shit again. It's why I can rattle off the advice from just about every motivational poster I've ever seen in a shrink's office. And it's also why, on any given day, seeing the color green can make or break me.

But anyway, as Baby was driving, I found myself wondering what sorts of connections her brain had been making over the last three days. Like, in the coming years, would she ever be able to hear Courtney Love belt out "Violet" without thinking of the car ride we took the day she met her baby face-to-face? Would she ever eat pudding again without thinking about how it was the first thing she had after giving birth? Would she forever associate me kissing her with labor pains? Let me be clear: I had no plans to kiss Baby again. (I hadn't planned it the first time, either, I should point out.) But the idea that I might serve as a walking reminder of a really difficult experience for Baby was deeply concerning to me, and here's why:

I knew it was selfish even to be thinking about myself since this

333

day was supposed to be all about Baby, but after The Bad Thing That Happened, my parents decided we needed to cut the entire state of Virginia out of our lives because it was just one big, fat reminder of painful things. Don't get me wrong, I know there's a difference between The Bad Thing and Baby giving up her kid for adoption, but both are deeply emotional and potentially scarring. Depending on how things shook out for Baby down the road, she might decide to get rid of her Hole CD and stop eating pudding altogether if those things remind her of how hard this time in her life was. A case could then be made for purging me for similar reasons, and that scared the hell out of me. I hoped that there was enough good about Baby's and my friendship to outweigh any painful memories my presence might dredge up for her, but I had my doubts. After all, there were literally hundreds of cities in Virginia that weren't Fairfax that we could have gone to after The Bad Thing, but instead we moved all the way to Michigan and never looked back.

Halfway through the song "Doll Parts," Baby pulled into a space inside the Beaumont Hospital parking garage. She turned the radio down but didn't kill the engine.

"I think you should tell me if I had a boy or a girl," Baby decided. "I'll have enough to process once I meet this baby that it's probably best to get this surprise out of the way."

"Are you sure?" I'd been careful not to let this slip ever since Christmas, which honestly wasn't very hard considering how practiced I was at keeping secrets.

Baby nodded. "I want to know."

I reached for my wallet, pulled the piece of paper Baby had given me from the billfold section, and handed it to her.

"You kept this?"

Clearly this was a rhetorical question, so I didn't answer it. Instead I just watched her unfold the paper and read the word written on it.

"Girl," she said, nodding and exhaling at the same time. "I had a baby girl."

"You did," I confirmed. "Good job."

She refolded the paper and sat there for a minute with it in her hands. "I hope they picked a good name for her," Baby eventually said. "If they ended up calling her Taylor, I'm probably going to riot."

"I thought you wanted to name her?" I said, recalling our conversation at the movie theater.

She shook her head. "I gave the adoptive parents a suggestion. But I don't know if they took it," Baby explained. Then she said, "I mean, *I* picked *them* to be her parents, so whatever name she ends up with is from me vicariously anyway."

I saw her point. Still, I asked, "Will you tell me what you wanted to name her? Just so when we get up there, I'll know if they went with it?"

"I didn't give them one specific name. More like a recommended meaning." Baby ran her hand through her hair. "I told them that either way, boy or girl, I wanted the baby's name to mean victory."

"Oh," I said, remembering. "Like yours."

"Almost. Mine means victorious," she corrected me. "Which, I don't know, is fine as far as name meanings go, I guess. But it's not necessarily *me*. I mean, a person can't just be born victorious. They have to earn it by achieving something. Like a victory." Baby had concluded the same thing I had about her name. "I don't know. Maybe it's fucking lame, but if the baby's name means victory, it sort of legitimizes me being named Nicole."

To me, nothing would legitimize Baby being named Nicole, but I liked that she saw her baby as a victory despite everything. Every kid should be so lucky as to have their mom think that about them.

"Do you think they named her Victoria?" I asked.

"Oh, probably." She sounded resigned. "If they did, I'm going to

335

call her Tori and not Vicki, though," Baby informed me. "As some-one who spent the better part of elementary school getting called Hickey Nikki on the playground, I refuse to set my kid up for the same ridicule."

"That's a great point." Then something occurred to me. "Though I guess they *could* call her Whorey Tori, which might be worse."

Baby sighed. "I'm not above kicking a bunch of eight-year-old asses if it comes to it."

I agreed. "Are you ready to go inside?"

I expected her to say something like, "As ready as I'll ever be," but instead she just sighed and said, "Fuck . . ." which I guess was kind of the same thing.

Without another word, Baby and I climbed out and shut our car doors, and together we went to meet her daughter.

Chapter 34

Whoever decorated the social services waiting area in the maternity wing of Beaumont Hospital did so without a stitch of pink. In fact, as far as waiting rooms went, this one, with its mint walls, framed paintings of geometric designs, and zero motivational posters, was the most pleasant I'd ever seen.

Of course, I wasn't waiting there for a doctor to shrink my head, so that more than the color scheme was probably why I was calm. The real patient this time (if you want to call her that) was Baby, and she was far too busy pacing to appreciate the soothing powers of abstract art.

"What's taking so long?" Baby whined to Kat. "When something is supposed to start at two o'clock, it should fucking start at two o'clock. I'm ready to get this over with."

"Maybe the baby had to eat," suggested Kat, who had just come from her wedding hair and makeup practice appointment. "Babies don't care about being on time, Nicole. This one already proved that by showing up before your due date." Then she changed the subject. "Oh, by the way, Bob dropped your bridesmaid dress off to be taken in this morning, so you won't be swimming in a maternity gown at the wedding." Kat smiled a crescent smile at Baby. "He had to call six places before he found someone who could alter it last-minute, but it's taken care of."

"What a relief." Baby's voice was thick with sarcasm. "That's all I've been thinking about for three days. Whether or not my bridesmaid dress fits is literally the most important thing I've got going on in my life right now."

"Nicole," Kat replied calmly. "Everything's going to be OK. Please just try to relax. It shouldn't be much longer."

Baby ran her hand through her hair. "I'm going to the bathroom. If they come to get us while I'm gone, tell them *they'll* have to wait for *me*." She rushed off down the hallway.

"She's freaking out," Kat concluded as her daughter accidentally walked into the men's room. "She's completely freaking out."

"Definitely," I concurred. "I get it, though. This is a freak-out-worthy situation if ever there was one."

"Oh, I know it," Kat said, turning to me. "It was more than eighteen years ago, but I remember very clearly what those first few days after giving birth felt like. Your whole body hurts, and you're full of crazy hormones. You don't feel like yourself. And then, you know, add this whole adoption thing on top of that . . ." She trailed off. "I'm just happy you're here, Joel. Her mood has improved significantly since yesterday."

This made me feel better and worse at the same time.

Kat examined her fingernails. "Nicole was a real champ in the delivery room. She swore a blue streak, of course, but she pushed that baby out without any pain meds. Tough as nails, that one."

"She's a badass."

"She is. In most situations." Kat sighed. "Though I'm not sure how she's going to handle this next part. Nicole's never really experienced loss. We've had no deaths in the family. She's never even had a friend move away." Kat's voice started to crack, and she dabbed at her eyes with her knuckle. "I just hope she's able to move on."

Kat was raising concerns I hadn't considered. The little time I'd spent thinking about Baby's baby had been more focused on the inconvenience of her pregnancy and less on the reality of her actually having and giving away a child.

"I'm not saying she's making a mistake," Kat went on. "Nicole has a really bright future. She'd regret not going to college in New York, I know it. That's not going to stop it from hurting, though."

The door to the bathroom flew open, and Baby stepped out.

"Anyway, thanks again for being here," Kat said. "I'm glad Nicole has you."

"Sure."

Baby stormed back over to the waiting area, ready to pitch another fit, when a door behind us opened and an African American woman wearing a lot of eye shadow said, "Ms. Palmer and family? We're ready for you now."

Baby didn't slow down so we could enter together. Kat and I followed.

The woman, whose name was LaDonna, offered us coffee and water, paid Kat a compliment about how nice she looked (and then congratulated her when Kat explained about the wedding), and then started in with the official business.

"In a moment, the adoptive parents will come in. A nurse will follow with the baby, whom all of you are welcome to hold." She turned to Baby. "Nicole, I'm aware you already have a relationship with the couple and that this will be an open adoption, whereby you'll maintain contact with the family moving forward. I understand both parties have agreed to minimal visitation throughout this first year with a reevaluation of those terms after that time. Is all that correct?"

"Yeah," Baby said. "That's what I want."

"Excellent. After you've all welcomed the baby—and you can take as long as you like, you just let me know when you're ready to proceed—we'll move on to the ceremony. Nicole, I'll ask you some questions, then I'll ask the adoptive parents similar ones. Then there will be a document you'll all need to sign, and the witnesses will need to sign, too." She pointed to Kat and me. "Then we'll all say goodbye for now. Do you have any questions?"

No one did, so LaDonna excused herself through a different door, and we could hear her muffled voice say "Everyone's ready!" before she returned.

This whole time, I kept watch on Baby. She was stiff, and her jaw was set, a look of determination about her, the same as on Halloween when she revealed her pregnancy to the world.

It didn't seem like four whole months had passed since that day, but at the same time, it could've been a lifetime. Everything was different now—Baby, me, Baby and me—and it felt like everything was about to become different again.

I was so focused on Baby that I didn't even notice who walked in behind LaDonna. It wasn't until one of them said my name that I remembered Baby and I weren't the only two people in the room.

"Joel?"

My eyes darted to a familiar face that was so out of context, it took me several takes to realize who he was. "Dr. Schwartz? What are you doing here?" I looked from him to Baby to Kat to LaDonna and back again. I started to panic. "Did my mother call you?"

I think he thought I was joking, because he laughed. "No, of course not." He extended his hand to shake mine while grinning ear to ear. "I'm really glad you could come." He side-hugged Baby and kissed Kat on the cheek.

Next to him was a woman I recognized from the video store, but I wouldn't have remembered she was Mrs. Schwartz, who'd kicked her delinquent, late-fee-accruing husband off her rental account, if they hadn't been standing next to each other. She, too, was beaming as she made the rounds with hugs and handshakes.

"Jana," she reintroduced herself, gripping my hand. "Nice to see you again."

"You too," I said back.

It took me a few more times looking back and forth between the Schwartzes and Baby to put together that it wasn't just a coincidence we were all in the same room together. Marc and Jana Schwartz were the adoptive parents.

There wasn't much time for all of this to sink in, though, because once everyone was finished greeting one another, LaDonna called for a nurse to bring in the baby. I had to set aside my shock that the same guy who'd babysat me, drugged and drooling after the Mop & Glo incident, was also going to be the father of Baby's baby because, like I'd promised Baby earlier, today wasn't about me.

I was standing next to her when a woman in scrubs brought Baby's daughter into the room. I looked away from Baby. It was too personal a moment to watch her seeing her child for the first time. Even if I could only give her privacy with my own two eyes, I wanted to do it.

"Here she is!" the nurse said, holding an impossibly small human in her arms.

At first all I could see was this mop of black hair swimming in mounds of white fabric. The baby was wearing doll's clothes, or at least clothes that would have fit a doll. She was in a long lacy dress that flowed far past her feet, like what I'd seen my cousins wearing in photos of their baptisms. Once the nurse, using slow and gentle movements, adjusted the baby's position, I was able to get a better look at the parts of her that weren't hair and clothes. And even though everything about that moment overwhelmed me, my equal and opposite reaction to seeing her tiny face was to smile.

She was still and sleeping, her pink lips slightly parted, with a tiny clenched fist on either side of her face as though even while unconscious, she was ready for a fight. It was all the proof I needed that this was Baby's baby.

"What color are her eyes?" I heard Kat ask from beside me. Her voice sounded thick, like she was talking past a lump in her throat.

"Blue," Jana answered. "But a lot of babies are born with blue eyes, so we don't know if they're going to stay that way or change." She reached out and stroked the baby's cheek.

At this, Baby cleared her throat. "They won't turn brown," she said with a steady voice. "I have green eyes, and the biological father has blue eyes. Those are both recessive genes." She explained this to Jana but was looking at her daughter.

Marc smiled at Baby. "She's right," he said. I wasn't sure if he'd taken genetics in psych-doctor med school or if this was just something he happened to know like Baby did.

After this, the nurse asked Baby if she wanted to hold her daughter, and she nodded. She was handed off to Baby, who was not at all confident about the way to hold such a small person. Jana stepped in to help, and then the room got very quiet as everyone watched Baby holding her child.

"What did you name her?" she asked, looking up from the baby at Marc and Jana.

342

"We honored your request, and we chose a name that means victory," Jana said, beaming. "Nicole, meet Daphne."

"Daphne Palmer Schwartz," Marc clarified.

Baby sighed a deep sigh. "You can hold her now, Mom."

Kat's turn with Daphne was much more tearful than Baby's, and by the time she was ready to hand the baby off to me, there were streams of wedding mascara running down her face.

I don't think I exhaled the entire time I held the baby. Part of me wanted to marvel at the miracle of life and contemplate all the things babies make people think about, but honestly I was so terrified I was going to break her somehow that I quickly handed her back to Jana.

The official adoption ceremony began after this, which was mostly (as LaDonna had described) rote Q&A stuff with some flowery language mixed in. Before ink was put to paper formally relinquishing the baby to the Schwartzes, Marc and Jana had a few things they wanted to say to the mother of their child.

First Jana read from a prepared letter in which she detailed her struggles with infertility. She described Baby as a "selfless angel," among other very nice things, while she cried tears of gratitude that she was finally becoming a mother. Next Marc spoke. He wasn't as prepared but wasn't any less sincere, promising Baby that he would lay down his life for her and for Daphne and that he couldn't wait to be the best dad to this little girl.

Everyone in the room cried at one point or another (including me), except for Baby, who evidently had the willpower of a thousand titans.

When asked if there was anything she wanted to say to the Schwartzes, Baby took a minute before responding that she did.

"I guess I just want you to promise to love her no matter what," she said in a small voice. "No matter who she turns out to be, even if it's different from what you hope. Even when you don't understand her, you always have to love her." Baby paused. "It's the one thing I know I would've gotten right."

The Schwartzes promised.

Signatures were then collected, and goodbye hugs were given. Kat made her quick exit, and then Daphne was ready for a bottle. The Schwartzes reminded Baby to call them when she was ready to visit, and before I knew it, Baby and I were alone again, walking to her car in the parking garage.

Without saying anything, Baby handed me her keys. I unlocked the Accord and she climbed into the passenger seat.

If there was a right thing to say to Baby at that moment, I didn't know what it was. There were lots of things going through my head, but they were mostly variations of the same observation I kept making over and over throughout the adoption ceremony: Baby was being quiet.

If I hadn't had the benefit of a billion hours of group therapy under my belt, I probably would have pointed this out to Baby. I would have mistakenly equated the fact that she hadn't completely lost her shit while signing her child over to a couple who rented videos from us with strength of character. I would have complimented her for being calm. I would have thought it meant she wasn't hurting.

I knew better, though. When it came to emotions, there was usually more to them than met the eye. Just because Baby wasn't reacting outwardly didn't mean she wasn't feeling everything inside.

I knew if I waited long enough, she'd say whatever she needed to say. So I did, and she did.

Though she didn't say it with words.

Suddenly the car was filled with a shrill, eardrum-shattering noise. My immediate thought was that the Accord was about to explode — vehicle explosion is a standard fear for paranoid people —

but then I looked over at the passenger seat and realized that the source of the noise was Baby.

Her face was scrunched, her eyes were squeezed shut, and her mouth was wide open as she emitted the longest, steadiest, loudest scream I'd ever heard. It was so fucking high-pitched, it sounded like a siren was going off two feet away, and it would have left my ears ringing if it had been followed by silence instead of the slew of rapid-fire swearing and punching that ensued instead.

"Goddamn fucking (inaudible) with their motherfucking stupid-ass (inaudible) fucking (inaudible) fucks!" was about all I could make out over the sound of Baby pounding against the dashboard.

As the tantrum continued to escalate, I flattened myself against the door to escape her fists of fury.

Punch, punch, scream! Swear, punch, punch! Swear, swear, punch! Scream, scream, swear! (repeat)

To any passersby, I'm sure the commotion coming from the car looked and sounded a lot like the scene in *Jurassic Park* where Newman from *Seinfeld* gets eaten by the spitting dinosaur. The car was rocking, the windows were steamed, and it sure as hell looked like someone wasn't making it out of there alive.

Somehow, though, I managed to remain physically unscathed. Though I can't say the same for the faceplate of Baby's stereo, which met its end during the grand finale of punches when it snapped off and fell lifeless to the floor.

This resulted in one final and very loud "Fuck!" before Baby finally took a breather.

By this point she looked feral. Baby was red-faced and sweaty. Her knuckles were a little bloody. Her clothes were all askew. She looked like an assault victim, and since I was the only other person in the car and the hospital parking lot security guard would probably be by any minute to investigate reports of a suspected dinosaur attack, I decided it was time to start driving.

Without a word, I turned the key in the ignition and backed the car out of the parking space.

We'd only made it half a mile from the hospital—I had no idea where I was going—when round two of yelling began.

"They could have named her Kelsey!" Baby erupted. "They could have named her Laura! They could have named her Colette! Or Veronica! All of those names mean victory, and they're all better names than *Daphne*!" Baby practically spat the name. "There were more than fifty girl names with the same meaning in that goddamn book Scarlet gave me, and they name my kid after a fucking *Scooby-Doo* character! And not even the smart one! They picked the dumb slutty one!"

I waited to make sure Baby was finished before I said anything. "To be fair, I don't think the *Scooby-Doo* Daphne was meant to be slutty. Yeah, she was always going off on her own with Fred, but even if she was fucking him behind the scenes during commercial breaks, there's nothing to say the two of them weren't in a low-key monogamous relationship."

In response to this, Baby broke down in uncontrollable sobs.

I had never seen Baby cry before. It was ten times more terrifying to me than the screaming fit.

I'd like to take back what I said earlier about drunk-girl crying being the worst kind of crying, because I was forgetting one kind when I said that. There's another kind of crying that is so leaps-and-bounds worse than drunk-girl crying that honestly the two aren't even in the same solar system.

The cry I'm talking about is a hopeless cry. An empty cry. It's a futile, core-shaking, bellowing cry. It's a cry you can't do justice to words.

It's the cry of a mourning mother.

Hearing it shook me so badly that I had to pull off the road. Immediately Baby flung her arms around me and continued sobbing onto my shoulder.

"Why?" she pleaded with me. *"Why did any of this have to happen?"*

I couldn't answer her.

I smoothed her hair. I let her cry. I didn't shush her. I didn't let her go.

A long time later, still through tears, she asked me to start driving again. "I don't care where we go," she coughed out. "I just don't want to be here anymore."

"OK." I nodded. "Do you want me to take you to work?"

"No!" She was adamant. "Somewhere else!"

"OK, OK!" I said. "Try to relax."

Baby curled up into a ball and faced her window. My mind scrambled for the right place to take her.

Suddenly I saw a US road atlas sticking out of the driver's side door pocket, and a thought occurred to me.

"How far is too far away, Baby?"

She sniffed. "Nowhere."

Though she couldn't see me, I nodded again. Then I eased the car back onto the road and started driving.

Part 3

Chapter 35

It's approximately 545 miles from Royal Oak, Michigan, to Fairfax, Virginia. Obeying the speed limit, that's about nine hours of travel by car. I didn't obey the speed limit, but we did have to stop once for gas and once to piss, so when it was all said and done, we got there in eight and a half hours.

We made it to Toledo before Baby cried herself to sleep. We made it to Cleveland before I had to fill the tank, and I also used that opportunity to call work from a pay phone to let whoever was closing know I wouldn't be in for my shift the following day.

"I had to skip town," I told The Godfather.

"I'll cover for you," she immediately offered. Somehow I knew she'd be good for an alibi. "In exchange, if it ever comes up, we were together on November twelfth of last year."

"Deal."

Among the many things I didn't consider before embarking on this journey was that when you leave for a nine-hour trip at close to four p.m., you arrive at your destination around one o'clock in the morning. This isn't an ideal time to arrive anywhere, but it's especially problematic when you haven't planned a place to stay and therefore have nowhere to go once you get there.

In almost any other situation imaginable, I would have hard-passed on the hourly-rate motel stationed on the side of the highway just outside of Fairfax, but by that point I was too exhausted to hold out for a Holiday Inn.

Our night there was just as bad as you'd expect considering the motel was located directly across the street from Fairfax's one and only "gentlemen's club." As Baby and I tried to sleep, we were subjected to a lot of noises from the adjacent bedrooms that neither of us ever wanted to hear again. *A lot* of noises.

We eventually found sleep, and later that morning I awoke to sunlight streaming through our room's dirty window as well as some second thoughts about why I'd come all the way back to Virginia.

I mean, I knew why coming to Virginia had seemed like a good idea when Baby was choking on her grief. Seeing an impenetrable person like Baby reduced to a liquefied state can really do a number on a person, especially if you're a guy like me. In the heat of a moment like that, when a person you really care about is falling to pieces, you're willing to do whatever it takes to keep the quicksand from sucking them under.

The heat of that moment had passed now, though, and I was feeling a lot less like a reluctant hero and more like a fucking moron for thinking I could set foot in this state without losing my mind all over again.

I rolled over on my side and saw that Baby was already awake and watching me, and I willed myself to calm down. Of the two of us, she was the one currently more entitled to freak out.

"How're you doing?" I asked her.

Her eyes were red, and her face had the tired, puffy look symptomatic of too much crying.

"I need to acquire feminine hygiene products or things are going to get super gross very soon." Baby stood up and grabbed the keys off the nightstand.

I asked no questions but was glad she felt up to going out. Already she seemed to be in a more solid state of matter than she had the day before.

"I saw a truck stop next to the strip club across the street," Baby informed me.

I wasn't aware a truck stop sold such things, but I assumed Baby knew better than I did.

We'd both slept in our coats as an extra line of defense against whatever diseases might have been lurking on the bed. As Baby zipped hers up, she asked me, "Where are we?"

"Virginia."

This didn't faze her at all. "OK," she said, and then she left.

While she was gone, I considered a shower. However, I surely would've contracted hepatitis had I used it in its current state. The only housekeeper I found on the premises looked to be in her seventies and had a limp, and I wasn't about to demand that she clean it.

Instead I borrowed a pair of rubber gloves and disinfectant from her cart and scrubbed our bathroom myself.

Yes, it was as disgusting at it sounds, which tells you just how badly I needed a distraction. If I was going to get through the day, I couldn't let myself think too much.

I'd just finished when Baby returned.

"Here." She handed me a bag. There was a pair of boxer briefs and a flannel shirt inside, the kind of clothing you'd expect to find at a truck stop.

"Thanks," I told her. "I'll pay you back."

She just shrugged. "They didn't sell women's clothes. I had to buy mine next door."

"At the strip club? They sell clothes there?" I asked. "Isn't that a conflict of interest?"

"You've got to have something on to take off, I guess." Baby rummaged through another bag. "New, with tags," she assured me, holding up some terrifying-looking undergarments. "They were expensive. I'm glad they took credit cards, though Kat's probably going to have some questions when the statement comes."

I smiled. Baby seemed to be returning to her Normal self in record time, which was a huge relief. If all she needed was a little time and distance to gain some perspective on her situation, then maybe we could just shower, grab a bite to eat, and hit the road back to Michigan.

"Bathroom's clean," I informed her.

Baby insisted I go first, since she needed to call Kat and let her know where she was. Having not bathed in more than forty-eight hours, I didn't object.

I cleaned up quickly and dressed in the truck stop clothes (they fit well enough). By the time I was done, Baby was off the phone. She didn't say a word to me before shutting herself in the bathroom and turning the water back on.

I stepped outside for some fresh air. Virginia February, unlike Michigan February, was an acceptable winter temperature, and if I could be outside without the cold hurting my face, there was no reason to spend another second in that godforsaken motel room.

I walked over to the Accord and sat on the hood facing the highway. I knew that we were in the northwest area of the city, but this particular part of Fairfax didn't look familiar to me, not even in a vague, things-sure-have-changed sort of way. Honestly, though, I wasn't sure how much of Fairfax I would recognize now, considering I was just a kid when I lived here. When you're young, your world is small, and you don't think of places in terms of locations on a map. You only know what you see, and everything else about the world feels hypothetical.

Nothing felt that way now. Being back in Virginia, everything felt extra real. Especially knowing why I'd come back.

I'd decided to tell Baby about The Bad Thing That Happened.

One of the foundations of group therapy is that people heal best together. There's something about knowing we aren't the only people who've been through shit that gives us hope life won't always be so hard. If telling Baby my secret would somehow help pull her up from rock bottom, then so be it. I'd do it for her.

However, I wasn't sure Baby was at rock bottom anymore, and if it turned out she didn't need any help returning to Normal, I was going to keep my mouth shut.

There are some bad things that you can share with other people without it affecting them that much. Like, say you get a speeding ticket. That sucks for you, right? And if you tell someone about it, that's probably even what they'll say: "Sucks to be you." However, from that point forward, the speeding ticket isn't going to redefine your friendship. Your friend's not going to start crying every time he sees you. Simply knowing someone who got a speeding ticket isn't going to cause him to have a mini breakdown. The chances of him falling into a depression over it are slim to none, I'd say. In fact, "Sucks to be you" is probably the first and last thing he'd say to you on the subject before forgetting about it altogether.

The Bad Thing That Happened was not one of *those* bad things. The Bad Thing That Happened was not the kind of thing people tended to forget about once you told them. Instead, they got really sad, then afraid. And sometimes they got really judgmental.

They wanted reassurance that What Happened couldn't possibly happen to them. They wanted you to have missed all the signs that they would've noticed. They wanted you to have somehow *deserved* what happened to you. They wanted to be so much better than you or different enough from you that they were immune from The Bad Thing That Happened possibly happening to them. They wanted the fear of The Bad Thing to go away, and the easiest way to make that happen was to write you off, since your presence alone reminded them of it.

Then they wanted you to move to Michigan so they could get on with things without having to worry about being nice to you anymore.

Now, I'm not saying that was how Baby would have reacted if I'd told her about The Bad Thing That Happened, but at the very least, she would've been sad for me, and she was probably already sad enough that I should spare her more heartache if I could.

I lay back on the windshield of the car and stared at the sky. Not much later, Baby emerged from the motel wearing a T-shirt that read BIG RIGGER BABES GENTLEMEN'S CLUB and a towel on her head the way girls always do after a shower.

"There you are," she said.

"Here I am," I said back, sitting up.

Baby walked over and leaned against the car, facing the same direction I was. "So, is Virginia where you meant to bring me, or is this just magnetic north for you?"

"I don't know" was the short answer to this question. "I just drove to somewhere I knew." This didn't feel like a lie, so I didn't count it as one.

"Is this your childhood home?" Baby asked, pulling herself on

356

top of the car next to me. "A crappy motel across from a strip club?"

"Nope, but I did live around these parts," I clarified. Then, before the questions could go any deeper, I asked, "Feeling better?"

She paused before answering. "Sure," she said, and sighed. "I'm really ready for things to go back to normal. I just want to finish high school and move on to Sarah Lawrence. I've got so much to look forward to." She sounded both unconvinced and unconvincing.

"You've got a bright future, that's for sure" was my generic attempt at encouragement.

"My whole life's ahead of me."

Then we got quiet.

"What are you up for today?" I finally asked her. "We can do whatever you want."

She shrugged. "Kat's pissed I didn't come home last night. It's not like I even told her I was *here*." She nodded toward the motel. "She thinks we went to Bob's cottage in Traverse City. I knew if I told her I'd left the state, she'd report me as a runaway. Then I'd have to deal with all that drama, and it would be one more way I screwed up the week of her precious wedding."

"Right," I said, pretending I hadn't completely forgotten her mom was getting married the following day. "We can start heading back."

"I don't care what we do," she said, and this time her words convinced me. Baby then began to remove the towel from her head. "We should probably eat breakfast at some point, though, because—"

"What the fuck happened to your hair?" was how I interrupted her while simultaneously falling off the car. I quickly got back up and stared bug-eyed at Baby.

Her hair, which before she stepped into the bathroom minutes ago had extended beyond her waist, was now gone. The little that remained on her head barely reached her ears.

"Did it fall out?" I asked. I happened to know that people experiencing traumatic events could spontaneously lose their hair, though typically in those situations the person went bald. Baby looked more like she'd been attacked by Edward Scissorhands.

"Calm down, Solo! God." Baby shot me a dirty look while running her fingers through her (barely run-your-fingers-through-able) hair. "I didn't react like that when you changed *your* look."

"What?" I was incredulous. "You did this on purpose?"

(Time out for a second.

Before you go thinking I'm a dick for getting so upset about this, let me explain that I don't really care what women do with their hair. Seriously—short, long, whatever, I have no preference. I mean, sure, I liked the way Baby looked with long hair, but it was *hers*, and she could do what she wanted with it. That said, what Baby had done to herself did not look intentional. What remained of her hair was crooked and uneven, like it had been hacked off in a fit of rage . . . which, let's be honest, it probably had.

Time in.)

"Yeah, I cut my hair." Baby flipped a few jagged strands out of her eyes. "So what?"

"Why? I thought you liked your hair."

She barely shrugged as her answer.

"C'mon, Baby," I said, nerves beginning to churn in my stomach. "Don't do this. Talk to me. Please."

"What? I just felt like a change."

"No," I said, my concern growing deeper. "No, Baby, that's not the reason . . ."

"What do you want me to say, Solo?" Baby huffed in disgust. "I loved having long hair, OK? I *loved* it. It took me forever to grow it out, and I was going to keep it long for the rest of my life, but then I cut it off, and now it's gone. And there's nothing I can do about it, even if I regret it. Because what's done is fucking done, and I'm just going to have to live with the decision I made and move on with my life." Tears spilled out of her eyes then and rolled down her cheeks. "There. Are you happy now?"

I looked at my friend sitting in front of me, crying but not, empty but still draining. She was sinking, and I had to do something about it. If quicksand was going to suck her under, it was going to have to take me, too, because I was diving in to pull her out.

"Go get your stuff," I told her. "There's someplace we need to go."

Chapter 36

I had to stop for directions twice, but I eventually found the place.

I parked the car just down the street from 1819 W. Ivystone Avenue and was still sitting inside it with Baby five minutes after killing the engine, staring at the white bungalow with black shutters where I'd spent most of the first decade of my life.

The new owners had taken good care of it. I mean, I guess several families could've moved in and out since we'd lived there, but at least one of them had cared enough to replace the broken gate, paint the garage, and plant a few trees in the yard. The house looked kept up, which was more than I could say for how my family had left it. Curb appeal was the last thing on our minds in those days.

"Are we ever getting out of the car?" Baby finally asked me. She'd regained her composure by the time we left the motel and had spent most of the drive fussing over her hair before eventually giving up and putting on a hat she found in her back seat.

"We're waiting." I pointed to a minivan that was running in the open garage. "We can get out once they leave."

"Who's 'they'?"

"Whoever lives there," I said.

She shot me a strange look. "I seriously thought you were taking me to a salon to get my hair fixed. Instead you bring me on a stakeout."

"We're here for a reason," I told her.

Baby sighed but didn't argue, which was a true testament to how little energy she had left.

A few minutes later, the front door finally opened, and a woman and a little kid got into the van. Baby and I watched them in silence, sinking down in our seats and looking conspicuously inconspicuous.

Once they'd driven out of sight, we got out of the car.

"Seriously, Solo. Where the fuck are we?" Baby demanded as she joined me on the sidewalk.

"You asked where I grew up," I reminded her. "There it is." I pointed at the bungalow.

"OK," she said. "What the hell are we doing here?"

What *I* was doing was trying not to puke from the anxiety that was hitting me like ocean waves, but instead of telling Baby that, I just said, "C'mon. Follow me."

She did as requested but added, "I've already experienced enough firsts this week, and I'm not interested in adding breaking and entering to that list."

"We're not going inside," I promised. "Hurry up."

I wasn't really worried about the neighbors catching us as we not-so-stealthily made our way around the side of the house—unless the culture of the neighborhood had changed dramatically, this little part of Fairfax wasn't the kind of place where people looked out for anyone but themselves—but it still felt wrong to be there.

I know it's a cliché, but the yard behind my old house was much smaller than I remembered it. It was still familiar, though, the way that childhood places always are. You remember their idiosyncrasies. Like, I knew exactly where there was a divot in the ground as it sloped downhill. I remembered to avoid the hidden stump from the cedar tree we'd cut down. And when Baby and I reached the kiln, I knew to hit the side of it with a stick to scare out any rodents before crawling in.

Baby was silent as we squeezed into the aging (but still solid) brick structure. With our backs against the wall, we sat side by side, looking back at the house.

"So, this is *the* kiln," she said, as if we were sitting on hallowed ground. "The Crystal kiln."

"Yeah," I confirmed.

"I pictured it bigger."

"I used to be smaller."

After a few more minutes of saying nothing, Baby spoke again. "I know it's a big deal that you brought me here, Solo. But I don't really understand why you decided to do it *now*." She looked at me. "Do you?"

I nodded. Then, maybe sensing that I needed her to, or maybe because *she* needed to, Baby held my hand. It was a small gesture, but it helped me summon the courage to start talking.

"You know, a long time before I burned the mail, I used to play in here. I used to pretend it was the *Millennium Falcon*, actually. I never told you this, but the reason I picked Han Solo for my work name is because they used to call me that when I was little," I said. "My family did, I mean. Sometimes." I paused. "I was Han Solo, and my brother was Luke Skywalker."

362

The words hung in the air for a few seconds.

"I didn't know you had a brother, Solo."

I looked at Baby. Her eyes were green. "That's because I never told you about him," I admitted. "But I'm ready to now."

He was eight years older than me. Mom always joked that one of us was an accident, but she'd never say which.

He was already in junior high in my earliest real memories of him. I wasn't around to know what he was like as a young kid, but everyone always said (back when people still said things about him) that he was a quiet child. Before I came along, he spent a lot of time alone, like most only children do. He liked to read. He loved listening to records. He was a big fan of the beach. And, of course, he was obsessed with *Star Wars* when it came out.

When I was born, my brother took his role as my big brother very seriously, both by teaching me things and by teasing me relentlessly. He's why I can name all the US presidents in order (he taught me this when I was five) and also why I don't smile with teeth for pictures (he used to make fun of the overbite I've since had corrected). That's the thing about older siblings, though: You have to take the bad with the good. And because it's their birthright that you basically worship them, both the bad and the good stick with you always.

Growing up, the two of us spent a lot of time together, which felt Normal because I was a kid, and when you're a kid, however things are seems Normal. It didn't occur to me that not all twelve-year-olds only hung out with their kid brothers. It didn't seem strange that my brother didn't have any other friends besides me. All the guys I knew who were his age seemed like assholes. I wouldn't have wanted to hang out with them, either.

Junior high is a tough time for a lot of kids, but watching my brother deal with the crap he did made me nervous about growing up. There were some fights. ("Boys will be boys," the principal said when Dad picked my brother up from school because of a busted lip.) There was a lot of hazing. (More than once he had his gym clothes stolen and thrown into the girls' locker room.) There were some academic concerns. ("He just doesn't seem interested in school," said all his teachers.) Everyone said not to worry, though, and they used words like *phase* to explain everything away.

Finally, when my brother was in eighth grade, things started looking brighter. He met this kid named Kevin, and the two of them really hit it off. Kevin wasn't an asshole, as far as I could tell. He liked Star Wars, which was important, and even though he and my brother were almost in high school, they still played pretend with me sometimes. They both always wanted to be Luke Skywalker, though, because he was the Jedi and therefore got to use the one and only lightsaber we had. Since Kevin was the guest at our house, my brother usually ended up letting him be Luke and taking on the role of Leia because, as he said, he was too short to be Chewbacca and he didn't want to join the dark side as Vader. This made total sense to me. I was short, too, and honestly Darth Vader scared the shit out of me, so if you couldn't be Han Solo or Luke, Leia was obviously the next-best choice. She was Luke's sister and therefore shared his DNA. Leia was probably a Jedi, too, and who didn't want to be a Jedi, even if it meant having to be a girl?

Kevin was the new Normal for a couple of years. He and my brother were inseparable in high school until things suddenly got weird between our families. Kevin wasn't allowed to come over anymore. My brother wasn't allowed to talk to Kevin on the phone. And then Kevin's parents sent him to Richmond to live with his grandparents. This pretty much destroyed my brother. I couldn't relate to what he was going through at the time, losing his best friend like that. I have a better idea now of what that felt like, and trust me, it's not the kind of loss you'd wish on anyone.

The month Kevin left, my parents made my brother go to a ton of doctors (to help with his sadness, I guess). This was also when they placed their moratorium on Star Wars and banned everything else fun, which made my brother even *more* sad. It sucked for the rest of us, too, of course, but not as bad. While we all had to make some sacrifices, my brother was the one who'd lost Kevin.

There was one day a few months after Kevin moved that my brother took me to the park. I remember this day well because of what I told you earlier—it was out of the ordinary, and therefore my senses recorded the entire experience in hi-def and tattooed it on my brain. I'm glad it did this, too, because in retrospect (which unfortunately is the only way a lot of shit makes sense), that day turned out to be really significant.

It was kind of a cold day, but it was sunny. My brother and I skipped rocks in a pond and screwed around on the monkey bars for a while. Then he offered to push me on the swings, which was weird, because I hadn't needed a push in years, but I let him do it because he was my brother and it seemed important to him.

"Don't push me over the bar!" I warned him once I started going really high. There'd been a rumor circulating at school that a kid in the DC area had swung so high that he flipped all the way around the swing set and his body turned inside out. I was not interested in testing the legitimacy of this story.

"Chill out, I'm not going to," my brother said.

"There are no clouds in the sky today," I observed out loud. "It's really blue."

After a few more pushes, he asked me a question. "What if I told you that the sky wasn't blue? What if I said that to me, the sky was . . . I don't know, green?"

"I'd say get glasses" was my answer. "Because it's blue."

"OK," he conceded. Then he asked another question. "Let's say I went to the doctor, and he said that my eyes seemed fine to him, but I still saw green when I looked up at the sky. What then?"

"Is this a real thing?" I asked him. I'd been trying to figure out why things at home had been so strange lately. It'd never occurred to me that it had anything to do with my brother not knowing what color the sky was, but maybe it did. "Is this something that's really happening?"

"It's just a what-if question, Joel," he explained. "What would you do if your doctor told you the sky was blue, but it looked green to you?"

"But it *is* blue" was still my answer.

My brother tried again. "OK. Imagine that you saw the sky as blue, but everybody you knew saw it as green. What would you do then?"

"I'd tell them they were wrong, because it's *obviously* blue."

"OK. What if *everyone in the whole country* told you that you were wrong about it being blue? What would you do then?"

"I don't know. I guess I'd punch them all," I decided, annoyed. I didn't really like this game my brother was playing. It was making me nervous for some reason.

"Yeah," he agreed. "I'd want to punch them, too." My brother sounded sad when he said that, and it made me sad, too. "Do you think that at some point, you'd start to feel crazy? Like, maybe there was Something Wrong With You? I mean, how long can a person stand being told they're wrong about something they know is true without losing their goddamn mind?" Then he immediately followed up with "Sorry for cussing."

I promised not to tell. Then, instead of answering any of his questions (because I was a kid and couldn't have possibly known what to say), I asked him a question of my own. "Are you OK?"

He slowed my swing down and waited until it stopped before stepping in front of it. "Can you promise me something?" my brother asked. "Promise me that no matter how many people tell you the sky is green, if it's blue to you, you'll say so."

Even though this sounded like something that would never actually happen to me, it felt like a very important decision. "OK, I promise."

My brother picked me up and stood me on the swing so that I was taller than him. Then he wrapped his arms around my middle and hugged me for a long time, which was weird, but it still made me feel special.

While we were standing there, I decided something. "You know, if you told me that the sky was green to you, I'd believe you," I said to him. "I would just think, *Hey, maybe my brother has special eyes that see a green sky. Aren't I lucky to know someone with special eyes?*"

My brother smiled at me and squeezed me harder. "Thank you, Joel."

When you're young, a lot of things go over your head. You don't understand quicksand or warning signs or cries for help or what really happened with Kevin. Everything that happens is what's Normal, even when it's not, and there's Nothing Wrong, even when there is.

That day he talked to me about the sky, I didn't know my brother was drowning. I didn't know he was crying out for help. I didn't know—I couldn't have known—it was the last real conversation I'd ever have with him. But as it turned out, it was.

Four days after my brother took me to the park and pushed me on the swings and told me about green skies, he killed himself.

Maybe you saw that coming. Maybe at some point during this long-ass story I've been telling you, you jumped to that conclusion. If so, good for you. I wasn't trying to shock you, so I hope you were braced for it, because let me tell you, when The Bad Thing happened,

367

I was completely blindsided by it. It wrecked me. It broke me in half. And it ruined my fucking life.

After it happened . . . well, you know pretty much everything that happened after that, don't you? This brings you up to speed. You're aware of how badly losing my brother fucked me up. You know about all the years I've spent trying to fix what broke when he left. You know all about my paranoia, my obsessiveness, my anxiety. You know about all the ways I'm not (and will probably never be) Normal.

Now you finally know why. And so did Baby.

When I finished telling Baby everything I had to say, she didn't ask any insensitive questions (*How did he do it? Who found him? Did he leave a note?*), even though I knew she was curious. That's how you know someone is a good friend — they can want to know details about shit you've gone through, but they won't ask out of respect for your mental well-being. Also worth noting is that Baby didn't seem eager to get away from me like she had when I told her What Was Wrong With Me, which was something I had considered might happen. She wasn't the same person she'd been back in December, though. Baby had been through her own Bad Thing since then, and those had a way of making you a lot more accustomed to emotional nudity.

"I don't know how you lived through that" was the first thing she said after an appropriate silence followed the end of my story. We were both teary-eyed, but I was no longer shaking like I had been before and during all I'd said to her.

I took a cleansing breath (therapy trick) and responded to Baby. "I guess it's just like surviving anything else. You live life a day at a time. And you have a few psychiatric breakdowns along the way."

Baby nodded. "I get that."

"I want you to know that I'm here for you. It might feel like you're drowning, but you're not alone. I've been at rock bottom, and

I'm still standing. You're going to be OK, Baby," I assured her. "And you're a long way from crazy. If you start seeing imaginary people, we'll reevaluate your status, but until then I think you're just experiencing Normal grief."

Baby laid her head on my shoulder. "Crystal wasn't imaginary, Solo."

It was a nice thought.

"You know, there's a part of me that thought she might show up here today," I confessed. "Last time I saw her, she said that when I was ready, I'd know where she was. I always assumed she meant here in the kiln. I was looking forward to introducing the two of you."

"It would've been nice."

Not wanting to press our luck with the homeowners, Baby and I stayed only a few minutes longer. Then we crawled out of the kiln and started the trek back to her car.

I turned around for one final look. I knew this was the last time I'd ever come back here, but this time it wasn't because I was afraid of what I might find if I did. It was because there was nothing left to see.

As I said goodbye to the kiln, something on one of the bricks caught my eye. My brother and I had carved our initials in it forever ago, and there they still were after all this time.

JAT

BAT

I stopped in my tracks.

Sometimes the road to acceptance is short. It can be a direct line, even. Like, I know that if I drop something, it will fall. It's easy to accept gravity. As a concept, it's fairly straightforward.

Other times, acceptance is a longer journey. An odyssey, even. Sometimes even accepting something that you've always suspected in your heart can take you years. Almost a decade. And it can take distance, like 545 miles. It can take lots of therapy, and dreams about sinking in the fiery ocean, and trying to be Normal, and your best friend suffering her greatest loss before you're willing to accept that maybe the sky isn't green for you, but it was for your brother.

And *sometimes* you have to go looking in the wrong place for Crystal to realize that you've known where she was the whole time.

"Hey, Baby. There's one more place I want to go."

"OK." She looked at me. "Lead the way."

Chapter 37

Baby took the wheel when we left the house on W. Ivystone Avenue so I could navigate. Our destination was less than a mile from my old house. That had been my mom's justification for choosing it in the first place and then, paradoxically, for wanting to move away not long after.

The cemetery where my brother was buried was next to a church that also operated a nursery school. I remembered this because during his funeral, as the contraption that lowers the coffin into the ground was clicking away, a bunch of little kids were playing outside as if the whole world hadn't just fucking ended.

Even to my young mind, it seemed really insensitive that kids were playing tag while my family was burying my brother a stone's throw away. I knew it was a stone's throw away for a fact because I picked up a rock and threw it in their general direction (calm down, it only hit a lamppost), which prompted the teacher to herd the kids back inside the church, where she probably made them spend the rest of the morning praying for my soul.

Anyway, it was that very same lamppost that caught my eye as Baby and I drove down Wicklow Street, searching for the cemetery, and when I recognized it, I directed her to turn into the parking lot.

She parked the car and looked at me.

"I'll be back in a minute," I told her.

"Take your time."

The only reference point I had to find my brother's gravesite was the angle from which I'd hurled the rock during his burial. I was glad my brain had thought that was such an important detail to hold on to for all those years, because this memory allowed me to immediately skip several rows of graves and head directly toward the ones closest to the church. I was relieved to see no kids were playing there that particular morning.

I hadn't been back to the cemetery since the funeral. I guess I've never seen much of a point to cemeteries in the first place, other than the fact that dead bodies have to be put *somewhere*. It just seems weird to me that this is what we do with the people we love when they die. We dress them up like they're going to a formal dance, put them in super expensive boxes, and then we dig holes, drop them in, mark the spaces with giant rocks, and return every so often to talk to the rocks as though the dead people underneath can hear what we're saying somehow. It's maddening to me that I got thrown in a psych hospital for talking to Crystal, but thousands of people talk to inanimate tombstones every day and are allowed to roam freely.

Anyway, since I hadn't been back, I'd never seen the headstone my parents had picked out for my brother, so I didn't know what I was looking for. That meant reading a lot of tombstones with meaningless

372

(to me) names and then feeling my stomach drop to my feet when all of a sudden his appeared.

BRIAN ALAN TEAGUE
MARCH 13, 1971–APRIL 29, 1987
BELOVED SON

I looked at the headstone for a long time, my senses on furious hyperdrive.

It turned out that my parents had chosen an upright slanted headstone. I don't know what about that particular look made it the right choice. I don't know how you decide something like that. I mean, I'm sure it's a process. I'm sure there's a salesperson with a binder full of options, that there are attractive names tied to all the colors (slate, steel, gunmetal) and different fonts available (Serif, Lancer, Montenegro). But I can't understand why any of it matters, especially if after you pick the perfect combination, you move 545 miles away.

I knelt down in front of the grave. The words were engraved into the stone, not embossed (another of the choices laid out in the binder, no doubt), and there was moss inside some of the letters, left over from the swampy Virginia summer. I picked it out and wiped it on the dead winter grass.

It was odd to me, seeing his name spelled out like that, all official-looking. I mean, whenever anyone in my family had said it (which they didn't anymore), it'd always come out like "Brine," the same way my name got pronounced like it rhymed with *hole* instead of there being any acknowledgment whatsoever of the second vowel. We weren't Bri-an and Jo-el, like fancy people. Together we'd been one sloppy Brine'n'Jole when being called down to dinner.

I'd forgotten about that, what it was like to be lumped in with my brother like we were one entity. *The boys*, they'd called us. *The sons*, Brine'n'Jole. But I was remembering it now. I was remembering too much right now.

"I miss you," I heard myself whisper.

And then suddenly I was no longer alone.

I was looking at the ground when she approached. The hem of her green dress swayed as she walked right up to me and stopped.

I didn't look up. Instead I glanced over at Baby's car. I couldn't see if she was watching me or not.

"I thought you'd be at the kiln," I said.

Crystal sat down beside me. "How'd you know I was here instead?"

I shrugged. "Somehow I've always known."

"Wait . . . are you serious?" she asked. "Or are you just quoting *Return of the Jedi*?"

I raised my head to look at her. Her hair was down, and against her brown tendrils, her green eyes stood out like sea glass. Crystal looked unchanged from the first day I saw her. She had looked sixteen then, she looked sixteen now. Probably because she was sixteen. Then, now, and forevermore.

"Both, actually." I looked away. "The day I found that box in the kiln, I must've known deep down that it was yours. I mean, you loved Bon Jovi. You were obsessed with the color green—the nail polish, the dress—plus that list of names was in your handwriting. I think it's just taken me a really long time to put it all together because, like my therapist says, I spend a lot of time in denial . . ."

We stared at each other for a moment.

"So you know who I am, then," Crystal acknowledged quietly.

I nodded slowly. "I don't know *how* you are who you are . . . but I'm starting to understand who you are . . . who you've always been. It's both completely confusing and makes total sense to me."

She seemed relieved to hear this. "You know, that's how it always felt for me, too. I knew I was different, but I didn't even understand that people *could* be different the way that I was. I didn't even know the words to describe what it meant to be 'like me.'" She pulled her legs up to her chest and hugged her knees. "Nobody else seemed to, either. They just kept telling me that Something Was Wrong With Me."

"It seems like people just slap labels like that on anyone they don't understand."

She sighed. "No kidding."

It got quiet after that.

When I got up the nerve, I broke the silence. "I'm really pissed at you for leaving me."

Crystal straightened her knees out. She patted her lap for me to lay my head down. "I know you are, Joel." She started scratching my head with her fingernails the way Mom did.

"But more than angry . . . I'm just fucking *sad*," I told her. "I hate knowing how shitty things must have been for you, how lonely and scared you must've felt all the time."

"The fact that you hurt *for* me instead of wanting to hurt me makes you different from a lot of people."

These words were heavy, and they sank in fast.

I thought about all the fights at school. The bullying. I thought about the reprieve that was Kevin, and then I remembered the devastation of his absence. I thought about all the doctors. I thought about our parents arguing.

And then I thought about What Happened.

I told you before that I wished there was a word for how much I loved watching Crystal love Bon Jovi. Well, on the flip side, I also wished there was a word for how I felt imagining the depths of suffering she must've endured in her life. This word needed to connote just the right degrees of devastation, rage against injustice, and helplessness. It needed a lot of syllables. It would definitely be a swear.

But I didn't know a word like that, so I yelled a bunch of other words: "I'm so sorry! I'm sorry I didn't realize what was happening sooner! I'm sorry the world is so goddamn shitty! I'm sorry I couldn't protect you!" The shouting didn't make me feel any better, though, and hot tears spilled down my face.

Crystal gently took my hand and rubbed my thumbnail. "What could you have done, Joel? You were a kid," she reminded me. "We both were."

This made me cry harder. She was right. We were both *kids*.

I wondered how old Crystal was when she first realized that she needed to hide who she was to survive. I wondered if she was so good at hiding the truth that she could even fool herself when she needed to.

It occurred to me that maybe I was really good at that, too.

"You've always felt so real to me, but that's just it, isn't it? You being here . . . that's only ever been real to *me*." I heaved a sigh. "All this time, everyone was right. I just made you up. I *am* crazy."

At this, Crystal cupped my chin in her hand and looked me in the eyes. "Stop saying that you're crazy, Joel. You were just a child trying to grieve." Her tone was firm. "All you wanted was for me to have had a happier life than I actually did."

I stared at her.

In all these years, I'd never thought about What Was Wrong in this way.

It wasn't crazy to wonder what earrings Crystal would've liked. Or to want to take her to a concert I knew she'd have loved. It wasn't crazy to miss what was missing. It wasn't crazy to wish for What Should Have Been.

That, in fact, was pretty damn Normal.

Crystal rested her hand on my cheek. "You didn't get to decide how things turned out for me, Joel. But you do get a say in what you do with your life." She pulled her hand away. "Word on the street is that it's not too late to become what you might have been, Joel, which is what I want for you," she said. "The same way that it's what you always wanted for me."

I sighed, but then I nodded.

"So, I guess this is really goodbye," I admitted, more to myself than to her.

"Just because I'm not with you, it doesn't mean you're alone, you know." Crystal glanced toward Baby's car.

I followed her gaze.

"Do you think she'd like me?" Crystal asked.

"Well, she hates most people, but I think you'd make the short list," I said. "For what it's worth, I think you'd like her, too."

"I'm sure I would," she said.

Just then, Baby started up the Accord. She must've gotten cold.

Crystal noticed. "You probably shouldn't keep her waiting."

I nodded but made no move to get up. "There's one more thing I want to tell you." I kept staring into the parking lot as I spoke. "It's about that day . . . that last time we hung out when you took me to the park. Do you remember?"

"Of course I do."

"Well, I just want you to know that I meant what I said to you," I told her. Then I swallowed past the lump in my throat and forced myself to look at her for what I knew would be the last time. "I feel lucky to have had a sister with special eyes."

I watched Crystal as her face slowly lit up.

She wrapped her arms around me and squeezed me tight, and

when she pulled away, I looked into her eyes. They were the greenest of skies.

"I love you, Crystal" were my final words to her.

She smiled and said, "I know."

I doubted that anyone would visit the gravesite before the next good rain. If someone did, though, I hoped they could use the lamppost as a way-finder like I had. It might've been hard to find it otherwise, since there was only one word on the upright, slanted, engraved headstone that I didn't cover up with damp Virginian cemetery dirt before I left. The only word that mattered.

BELOVED

When I opened the passenger door of the Accord and resumed my seat, Baby was staring out her window in the opposite direction of the cemetery. She'd taken off her hat, and what was left of her hair was sticking up in all directions, reminding me that I wasn't the only one who'd had a rough couple of days.

"There are an Alfred Hitchcock number of squirrels over there." She pointed along the dirt road back toward Wicklow Street.

"An astute observation," I said back. She was right. There were a lot of goddamn squirrels.

"I wasn't watching you." She was still looking out the window.

I don't know that I was relieved by this as much as I was grateful. In the same way I hadn't looked at her the first time she saw Daphne, Baby had wanted to give me privacy.

"I don't think I'm ever going to see Crystal again," I told her. "On the other hand, I plan to be seeing a lot of my therapist in the foreseeable future."

Baby took her eyes off the squirrels and looked at me. "Do you know if he's accepting new patients?" She pointed at her hair.

"I can't tell if you're joking."

"I can't, either."

I reached for Baby's hand and squeezed it.

She sighed. "Not to take away from all this personal growth you're experiencing today, because I'm really glad you told me everything, but I still have to deal with all my shit, and I'm super fucking sad about it."

I nodded. "Is there anything I can do? Like, right here, right now—is there anything that would make you feel even, like, an ounce better?"

Baby thought for a second. "Not unless you can fix my stereo. The prospect of driving all the way back to Michigan without any music is enough to push a girl on the brink over the edge."

I looked at the broken stereo. There were no longer any dials to turn or buttons to push, which meant there was no way it could work. But still I said, "OK."

"OK, what?"

"OK, I'll fix it."

Baby shot me a doubtful look. "How, Solo? Are you gonna use the Force?"

"Han Solo does *not* use the Force," I informed her. "But if he can jerry-rig a hyperdrive, then this should be a piece of cake for me."

This logic was absolutely nonsensical, of course, but you know what? It worked. I fucking *fixed the stereo*. Or at least I stuck a ballpoint pen in the hole where the dial used to be, and when I did that, the FM radio began to play, which was good enough.

And you'll never guess what song was on.

It was "Wannabe" by the Spice Girls.

What? I told you that you wouldn't guess it.

I mean, sure. It would have been poetic if "Livin' on a Prayer" had been on, or even "What's the Frequency, Kenneth?" If either of those

379

songs had come on, Baby and I would've looked at each other with widened eyes, flabbergasted that the universe had orchestrated such a convenience for the likes of us. Not to mention, it would have been the perfect way for me to transition out of the Virginia leg of my story.

But that's not what happened, and I'm not going to pretend it did.

"Fucking hell. This is the worst song in the history of music, Solo," Baby declared before quieting the stereo with a smack to the hole I'd stuck the pen in. "I'd rather listen to nothing than that garbage."

"OK, then." I nodded. "Silence it is."

We switched seats and I drove us out of the parking lot. By the time I merged onto the highway ten minutes later, she'd fallen asleep.

And you know what? This all felt . . . Normal.

Which, if I'm being honest, was its own kind of poetry.

Chapter 38

Baby and I made it back to Royal Oak around midnight. In an effort to avoid Kat's wrath for missing the rehearsal dinner for the wedding, Baby crashed on one end of the ROYO Video break room couch, and in an effort to avoid the inevitable follow-up argument with Mom that awaited me at home, I crashed on the other end. We got up and were on our way out with just enough time to spare before the openers arrived so as not to cause a scandal.

Baby dropped me off at my empty (thank god) house. I spent forty-five minutes in the shower, draining the hot water tank in an effort to erase the motel bathroom experience from my body (and memory), and then I went downstairs for food.

As I ate my way through a sleeve of Fig Newtons and downed a glass of milk, I noticed that the kitchen looked different. Not that our house was ever messy, but the place was *clean*-clean. Like, not-even-any-fingerprints-on-the-oven-door clean. That's when I remembered what Mom had said about the appraiser, and then it all came back to me that today was when my parents were meeting with the lawyers, which was probably why Mom wasn't home.

A sudden pang of sadness stabbed me in the gut, a reminder that while a lot had changed in the past week, more changes were on the way.

Mom had removed the remaining unbroken angel figurines from her tchotchke shelf. She probably thought it would devalue the house not to have the complete set, and instead she had spaced out the farm animals so that no one would know anything else had ever been there.

I also noticed that someone — my dad, presumably — had already repaired the dents in the wall. I felt bad that he'd gotten stuck with that job, but home repairs wouldn't be his problem for long. Not in this house, anyway.

A few minutes later, a car pulled into the driveway. I ran upstairs and turned on my stereo so that Mom would know I was home before having to see me face-to-face; it was probably better for both of us if my sudden reappearance didn't take her by surprise.

Even though I'd made it obvious I was home, Mom was evidently in no hurry to see me, because it took her almost a full hour (or fourteen rounds in *Tekken 2*) to finally come knocking on my door.

"Did you have a good time on the retreat?" Mom yelled over my music.

I powered off the stereo. "Retreat?"

Mom was dressed in business clothing and had on her I'm-going-to-church makeup. "Whatever you want to call that trip your dad sent you on so you could get ahold of yourself," she clarified.

It took me a few beats to realize what the hell she was talking about, but then Dad's words came flooding back: *I'll think of something to tell your mom . . . Just go with it.*

"Oh, the *retreat*," I said. "It was good."

"Did you get it all out of your system?" she asked me, leaning against the doorjamb.

I wasn't exactly sure what "it" was, but it seemed like the right answer to this question was yes, so that's what I went with.

"Good," she said, but thankfully asked for no details. Then she changed the subject. "That wedding's today, isn't it? The pregnant girl's mom's?"

I glanced at the clock and realized that if I was going to buy that toaster I'd promised Kat and Bob, I should probably get dressed. "Yeah," I confirmed. Then, I guess for the sake of accuracy, I added, "She's not pregnant anymore, though."

"Oh." Mom looked surprised, then not. "Girl or boy?"

"Girl," I revealed as I changed into my suit pants.

"How sweet" was her response. "What's her name?"

"Daphne."

Mom's eyebrows rose. "Like from *Scooby-Doo?*"

"Sure," I said, rather than go into details. I slipped my shirt off its hanger, put it on, and then changed the subject. "How'd it go this morning?"

Mom paused and, absent a cigarette to light, picked at her fingernails. "The lawyers said you're too old for anyone to get custody of you. They said you should be able to live with whoever you want." She looked past me and out my window.

"Were you planning to fight Dad for custody of me?"

Mom shrugged. "I didn't know how it worked." Then, after a sigh, she followed up with "I guess I should just give your dad the house, then, since neither of you wants to live with me anymore. I'll just move into a one-bedroom spinster apartment, and the two of you can live here with his bimbo." Her tone was sad, not angry, and she looked defeated.

"Mom, stop," I said as lovingly as I could. "You're acting like I never want to see you again."

"Well, that's how it feels, Joel," she said less patiently. "I've only ever tried to do what's best for everyone, and it always seems to blow up in my face."

"Maybe that's because you don't always know what's best."

Mom gave me a dirty look. "What's that supposed to mean?"

With an uncharacteristic level of calm, I told her, "It means that maybe you're not always right about what people should do. Or how they should act. Or who they should be. Maybe you need to stop trying to control everything all the time."

She looked at me as though I'd just told her the sky was green. "I am *not* controlling," she asserted.

"OK, Mom," I said, exactly the way you think I said it.

Mom heaved the world's longest sigh. "You know, I was hoping you'd come back from this retreat a little more appreciative of everything I've done for you. I don't know what's gotten into you, but I'd put money on it having something to do with that boy who drew that picture."

There's always a final straw, and apparently this was mine.

I'm not talking about the kind of last-straw situation where a person snaps and throws ceramic angels against the wall. I'm talking about the kind of final straw where the person who has held power over you for your entire life is suddenly disarmed because your brain decides that you just can't care what she says anymore.

Just as Mom was about to start in again about Maverick and Star Wars and was-I-or-wasn't-I-gay, all the fucks I had left to give on the topic disintegrated into thin air, and it felt so freeing that I wished it'd happened years ago.

"I'm not talking about this with you anymore," I stopped her. "Don't bring up that drawing with me ever again. And don't say another word about the guy who gave it to me. You don't know him, you don't know anything about him, so drop it."

I didn't raise my voice, because I wasn't mad. I was just done.

I was done being accused. I was done explaining. I was done defending myself. I was done being stuck in the past, and that included reliving the same tired fights with my mother all the damn time.

"You don't know *what* I know, Joel," my mom bit back, hurt.

The way she said it bothered me, but I wasn't going to be baited. "You're probably right, Mom," I said as I rummaged through the pockets of my coat. "Everyone around here is so good at keeping secrets from each other that you're probably keeping a lot of stuff from me that I'll never know."

"I mean that you don't know what it's like to be a mother." I heard her swallow past a lump in her throat. "A mother only wants to keep her children safe, Joel. A mother wants to protect her kids from the cruelty out in the world. A mother only wants what's best."

I found the JCPenney bag my dad had given me and pulled out the pink tie. I put it around my neck before I remembered I didn't know how to tie one, so I improvised a slipknot I'd learned at Cub Scouts. "And all children want is for their mother to love them no matter what," I told her. "It's too bad neither of your children will ever know what that feels like."

Mom looked horrified, maybe because of what I'd said or the color of my tie or the fact that I'd tied it in a way that ended up looking like a lasso hanging from my neck or maybe all three of those things together, but I didn't care. I grabbed my suit jacket and shoes and walked past her. I had a wedding to get to, and I wasn't going to let my mom stop me.

As it turned out, she didn't even try.

Chapter 39

After she sold me a toaster, the silver-haired saleslady at Macy's retied my tie for me, stating that she couldn't allow me to attend a wedding looking like a "ragamuffin cowboy." Then she smoothed out my jacket and sent me over to the gift wrapping department, deeming my plan of giving my gift to the bride and groom in a shopping bag "reprehensibly tacky." This might have embarrassed some guys, but not me. I'd already learned a long time ago to accept help when it was offered and then to say thank you and mean it, so that's what I did.

The wedding started at four, which left me with some time to kill after leaving the mall. Since I had nowhere to kill it, I drove to the address listed on Bob and Kat's wedding invitation, and then I turned up *Monster* while I sat in the parking lot of the White House Wedding Chapel.

I'd only made it about halfway through "What's the Frequency, Kenneth?" before I ejected the CD from my stereo. As I held the disc in my hand, it occurred to me that for the first time in a long time, I didn't want to hear that song.

I didn't know why, but suddenly I didn't care what the frequency was. Or who Kenneth was. Or what the song meant. None of those questions felt pressing anymore. I was all of a sudden OK not having the answers. And just like that, I was ready to listen to something else.

First my mom, and now this. I didn't know exactly what was happening, but I kind of wished I'd gone to the cemetery a long time ago.

I was in that awkward, bent-over-into-the-back-seat position, searching for my Weezer CD, when the passenger door opened.

"Shit!" I snapped upright and came face-to-face with Baby. "Oh, it's you—I thought I was being carjacked."

Baby, who was wearing a scarf wrapped around her head and the most makeup I'd ever seen on her face, slid into the passenger seat.

"Calm down. Nobody wants to steal your damn LeBaron."

Even though she'd freaked me out, I was really glad to see Baby. I hadn't expected to get to talk to her until after the ceremony, and I'd figured it probably wouldn't be much even then since she'd have daughter-of-the-bride jobs to do. I welcomed the chance to check in on her.

"You clean up pretty nice," Baby noted, pointing at my suit. "This is a definite upgrade from truck stop clothing."

"I aim to please," I said. "You look nice, too."

Baby gave me a *whatever* look. "I'm wearing a coat and an old-lady scarf."

"I meant your face," I clarified, "but 'Nice face' didn't sound like a compliment."

Baby shrugged. "Oh, well. Anything to make Kat happy" was her answer. "I warned Scarlet not to make me look like a prostitute clown. I guess she did all right."

"Wait, what? *Scarlet* did your makeup? Like, *Scarlet*-Scarlet? ROYO Video Scarlet? Archenemy Scarlet?"

"That's the one," Baby admitted reluctantly, checking her reflection in the visor mirror. "You and I both know I couldn't let my mom see my hair the way it was—not on her wedding day, at least—and I couldn't find anyone else to go to last-minute. Trust me, I *tried*. So, whatever, I went to Scarlet, and she did my hair. Afterward she insisted on messing around with my face, and I didn't have the will to fight her off when she came at me with her blush."

I found all of this so shocking that I needed her to confirm it again. "You went to Scarlet? For help? On purpose?"

"It's not like I asked her to the prom or anything." Baby rolled her eyes. "I needed hair help, and you know, she cut yours, so I figured, why the hell not let her have a whack at mine. She couldn't have made it look worse than it already did."

"All right . . ." I said, imagining how this scenario had played out. "Did she ask what happened to your hair?"

"Of course she did." Baby looked out the window. "I told her the baby pulled it out. I think she believed me. She'll probably never want to have kids now, so I guess that makes me a humanitarian for sparing the world future generations of Scarlet."

I stared at her.

"OK, fine. I told her *I* cut it," Baby admitted. There was a long pause. "And then we talked about some things."

"Really?"

"Yeah." Baby nodded. "I mean, it's not like I could hide that I'm not pregnant anymore. Even Scarlet isn't that oblivious. So, you know. Certain questions arose."

She didn't elaborate, but she didn't really need to. "How'd that go?"

"Fine," she said with a sigh. "I mean, it's not like we're going to get BFF tattoos, but it turned out we had a lot to talk about."

Baby was downplaying the significance of this, but I could tell she was grateful for whatever had transpired between her and Scarlet. I was, too.

"I'm glad," I told her. "I'm glad for you both, actually."

Baby shrugged. "Scarlet really likes Marc Schwartz," she informed me. "That was nice to hear, even coming from her."

It seemed like that was all she had to say on the subject, so I changed it. "Do I get to see your hair?"

Baby began unwrapping her head. "Scarlet was aiming for Drew Barrymore from *Mad Love*. I don't know if that's what I ended up with, but I'm just happy I don't look like my head got run over by a lawnmower anymore." She dropped the scarf into her lap.

I smiled. Baby didn't look like Drew Barrymore (in my opinion), but she did look like Baby with a really nice short haircut, and to me that was better. "I like it."

"Thanks." She exhaled a sigh upward, blowing short pieces of hair that had fallen into her eyes. "And, you know, while we're on the subject . . ." Her tone got more serious. "Thanks for everything else, too. It helped, I think."

I nodded. "I hope it didn't seem like that whole trip was about me."

"That never crossed my mind," Baby assured me. "Getting me out of here probably stopped me from doing some really crazy shit."

"I don't know," I considered. "It doesn't get much crazier than hacking off all your hair at the Bates Motel while wearing stripper underwear you bought at a truck stop."

Baby smiled a crescent smile with satisfying corners for the first time in a long time. "I guess we'll never know how low I would have sunk without you."

"I guess we won't."

She was quiet for a few seconds. "I had a baby, Solo. I got pregnant, and I had a daughter, and I gave her away, and I'm eighteen years old, and now I have to go to my mom's wedding and be happy for her even though I still feel like I want to burn the world to the ground."

"There's Nothing Wrong With You, Baby," I said. "You're going to be OK."

She took a deep breath. "Are you sure?"

"No," I admitted. "But I'm here."

Baby reached over and squeezed my hand. "Then I'll be OK."

The wedding ceremony was short and sweet, and when it was done, all the guests convoyed over to the reception.

Headlights had remained closed since the kitchen fire, so technically the reception was the "grand reopening," even though the event was closed to the public. After a valet guy took my keys, some bouncer-looking dude checked my name off a list and I walked into the restaurant, the smells of fresh paint and varnish and steak and chicken entrees aggressively greeting me.

On top of everything inside the place looking both the same and new, the restaurant had been completely bedecked with old-fashioned pink-and-white Valentine's decorations as well as all the other makings of a big-time celebration, which in my opinion was a pretty classy look for Hooters, but with cars.

Baby spent most of the reception on daughter-of-the-bride duty, so I sat at my assigned table with several off-duty Headlights waitresses who redefined the meaning of open bar.

After dinner and the first dance of the bride and groom, Baby said I had to dance with her, which I agreed to do without complaint because that's what a good wedding date does.

As she led me to the dance floor, Baby asked a favor. "Let me know if my tits start leaking through my dress, all right?"

"Um" was my flabbergasted response. "Leaking what? Like, blood? Is that a thing you're expecting might actually happen?"

Baby stopped swaying to the song and stared at me like the idiot I was. "My milk came in, and my body still thinks there's a baby around who needs to be fed."

This prompted a lot of questions I didn't want answers to, so I just said, "OK, I'll let you know."

"I'm sorry if my breasts are making you uncomfortable, Solo, but they're making me uncomfortable, too, so it's only fair."

"They're not," I lied. "But it's cool if we stop talking about your milk."

There was an Eagles song playing, and we danced through the whole thing before either of us spoke again.

"I wrote a toast for my mom," Baby revealed. "I just didn't feel like giving it in front of everybody."

"Yeah?"

"It would have been a fucking awesome toast, too. It actually might have gone down in history as the best speech anyone has ever given at a wedding."

"Wow, that good, huh? What were you going to say?" I asked because I was pretty sure Baby wanted me to.

"Well," she began. "It was going to start with a movie quote—as all good toasts do—from *Breakfast at Tiffany's*, because that's Kat's favorite. Then I was going to talk about her and Bob and how in love they are, blah blah blah."

"This is the most moving speech I've ever heard," I said. "I can't believe you robbed everyone of their chance to hear it."

Baby intentionally stepped on my toe to shut me up.

"Then I was going to tell her that I know being a mom is the hardest job anyone can ever have. I was going to say that I finally understand how much she loves me and how all the things she did that pissed me off were probably just because she wanted to protect me. I was going to thank her for giving me the best life she could, even though she doubted herself every step of the way, and even if she fucked some things up," Baby explained. "I wasn't actually going to say 'fucked' in the speech, but you get what I mean. And then I was going to wish her and Bob a billion years of happiness, more blah blah blah, and close with a quote from *Four Weddings and a Funeral* because, well, it's fitting."

"Hmm," I said. "Kat would have loved that, I think."

"It sounds sappy when I say it out loud, and she's already been crying the whole damn day, so I'll just find some other time to tell her."

"Yeah," I agreed. "Good idea."

The song ended, and it was time for the bouquet toss, so Baby was called away, and she ended up staying away the rest of the reception.

I spent the evening drinking too much Coke and eating too many damn heart chocolates before the party started winding down around ten. Baby had long ago ditched her shoes by the time she walked barefoot over to my table and asked for a ride home. She put on the boots she'd worn to the chapel, I had the valet get my car, and we hit the road.

"Who got stuck on the night shift?" Baby asked me as we neared the video store.

"I don't remember. I think I put Hannibal on it. He seemed the least likely to be pissed about working on Valentine's Day."

"Want to give him the rest of the night off?"

I gave her a look. "You want to go to work? In your bridesmaid dress?"

"Why not?" she said. "I lost all my hours this week. And besides, I once came to work with a watermelon painted on my bare stomach. No one enforces the dress code."

"Fair point." I hit my turn signal.

We went in through the back door and tossed our jackets into the break room before walking into the store. It had only been a few days since I'd been there, but I'd missed ROYO Video.

The vacuum was running. We followed the trail of its cord, and sure enough, there was Hannibal, vacuuming with his headphones on.

I tapped him on the shoulder and waited for his attention.

"Well, hello, my friend!" he said in surprise. "Look at you!" Hannibal pointed to my clothes. "Hot date?" He indicated Baby.

"My mom got married tonight, Hannibal," Baby answered for me, and he did a quadruple take before realizing who she was.

"Oh, hey, Baby." He looked her up and down in utter confusion. "Weren't you . . . wasn't there, like, more of you last time you were here? Like, more hair and more . . . other stuff?"

"Yeah" was Baby's one-word explanation. "So, do you want the rest of the night off?"

The offer made him forget all about Baby's transformation. "Are you serious?" he asked, glancing from one of us to the other.

"Sure. We'll close for you." I took the vacuum off his hands.

"You don't have to ask me twice," he said. "The guys down at the tattoo place wanted to play D&D and were looking for a Dungeon Master." He adjusted his ponytail. "Happy VD, you two!"

Hannibal wasted no time clocking out while Baby finished vacuuming the store in her evening gown.

There wasn't a customer in sight, which I took as a sign that romance was alive and well in Royal Oak. As much as I personally loved ROYO Video, a video store wasn't exactly the most romantic date night venue. It was probably a good thing for society overall if people had better things to do on Valentine's Day than rent movies.

I was about to run the daily sales reports when over the hum of the vacuum cleaner, I heard the door to the storage closet open and shut. I don't know why it hadn't occurred to me that Hannibal wouldn't be closing alone on a Friday night—that was never a one-person shift—but it hadn't. I watched the back hallway to see who else was working, and a few seconds later, Maverick emerged, a box of candy restock in his hands.

Oh, right. Now I remembered who I'd put on the schedule.

We didn't make eye contact until he was almost at the counter, and when he finally saw me, I watched his expression run the full gamut from surprised to confused to full of dread in about three seconds flat, which honestly was probably exactly how I looked, too.

"Hey," I said when he was close enough that it would have been awkward not to. "How's it going?"

"Fine" was his cool reply as he set the box down on the counter. "I thought you had the night off."

"It was Baby's mom's wedding," I explained. "We came by after to let the closers go home early."

Maverick unloaded the candy onto the counter and began refilling the racks. "How thoughtful," he said. "I'm good to finish my shift, though. My girlfriend lives out of town, so Valentine's Day is a bust for me."

"I didn't even know you had a girlfriend" was my honest and confused response.

"Of course I do," he said. "She lives in a place where you don't know anyone, goes to a high school you've never heard of, and has a really busy cheerleading schedule, so we don't get to see each other hardly ever. When we do, though, trust me, we have sex all the time, because she's so hot I can't keep my hands off of her. Her name is Jenny, just like every other girl."

"Oh," I said, getting it. "She sounds perfect."

"Thanks," he said flatly. "That's kind of the point."

He continued working while I searched for what to say next.

"Look, I'm not going to tell anyone, if that's what you're worried about," I finally said.

"Wow, that's really noble of you, not putting me at extra risk for a hate crime." Maverick glared at me.

"I just didn't want you to worry is all. Your secret is totally safe with me," I promised him. "Trust me, there are a lot of things about me that I don't want people to know. I get it."

At this point, Maverick gave me a look that I hated. Anyone who's had as much group therapy as I had knows exactly the look I'm talking about. It was a mix of anger, restraint, and hopelessness, and it meant *Don't even fucking pretend you know how hard it is to be me.*

In therapy, this is the alpha look, reserved for use by the person whose situation is the least relatable to the others, and it's directed specifically at whichever moron seems to think their textbook case of whatever makes them equals. I'd given that look to people a hell of a lot of times, but I'd never been on the receiving end of it. Let me tell you, it really makes you feel like an asshole.

"The bottom line is, I'm sorry for the way I reacted," I said, and I meant it. "I guess I'm just not the most considerate guy sometimes."

Now he stopped what he was doing and looked at me. "Except that you are considerate, Solo," Maverick disagreed. "About everything else, at least. That's what sucked the most about the whole thing. For months I've watched you be this stand-up guy with Baby and Scarlet whenever they had shit going on. It seemed like you always knew the right thing to say or do with them. It seemed like you *wanted* to say and do the right things, you know? Like you're one of those rare people who cares about what others are going through." He paused. "Everyone but me, I mean. But whatever. I guess I should have known that someone like me would be an exception, even to a guy like you. People like me are always the exception."

His words hung in the air. They stung. They stung because they were wrong, and they stung because they were right.

Maverick felt like he was the exception because I'd treated him like he was. I wouldn't have started groping Baby the second she walked in the room if Poppins or The Godfather had touched me on the shoulder. I knew I'd only acted that way because Maverick was a guy.

"You're right. I was a total asshole," I confessed. "I completely understand if you never want to talk to me again, but that's not what I want at all. I want to be friends with you. You as you, whoever you are, whatever that means." And then, because I didn't know what else to do, I stuck my hand out for him to shake like we were making a deal on a used car.

Maverick (who, let's not forget, was still the way cooler, more J. Crew of the two of us, despite the fact I'd made him feel like he was an exception) shook his head at the gawky formality of my handshake offer, but he accepted it anyway. "For now it means I've got a hot girlfriend named Jenny," he said. "But thanks."

At that moment, Baby, who'd probably been listening and waiting for the opportune time to make her presence known, suddenly appeared. "Hey, guys," she said. "The floor's all clean."

It took Maverick an equal number of takes as it had taken Hannibal to recognize her. But then, because he was one of those rare guys who cared about what others are going through, he just said, "Cute haircut," and left everything else alone.

396

"Thanks," Baby said. She was standing next to the counter by the Valentine's Day movie display. "Hey, Solo. Want to watch a movie after we close?"

I leaned over the counter. "Maybe. Anything good still available?"

She held out the VHS box for *Pretty in Pink*. "You've still never seen it."

I gave her a look. "And I still don't want to."

Baby rolled her eyes. "Fine. What do you want to watch?"

"*Star Wars*," I told her without having to think about it.

"For real?" she asked. "*Star Wars* is your Valentine's pick?"

"Why not?" I demanded. "It's a love story. Kind of."

"In what way is *Star Wars* a fucking love story, Solo?" She gave me a look.

"It is because I love it" was my answer.

Baby blew her hair out of her eyes. "Ugh. Fine. But you're buying pizza."

"Fine," I said, and then I looked at Maverick. "You in?"

He looked at Baby, who nodded.

"Please say yes," she begged. "I've never watched *Star Wars* with him, but I have a feeling he will deserve to be mocked for how seriously he's going to take it."

Maverick looked unsure at first but ultimately consented. "All right. I'm always up for a good mocking."

"Thank god," she said, and then immediately began to mock me. "I can just imagine him mouthing all the words. And performing lightsaber choreography with a broom." She shook her head at Maverick. "I bet he cries tears of joy when the Death Star blows up."

"Is she right?" Maverick looked over at me. "Because if so, there seriously might be something wrong with you."

It was my turn to laugh. "Maybe she's a little right." I shrugged. "But I assure you, there's Nothing Wrong With Me."

Epilogue

Eight Months Later—The Saturday before Halloween 1997

"Happy Halloween, this is ROYO Video," Hannibal said into the phone after removing his paw. There was a long pause. "No, my friend, she doesn't work here anymore." Pause. "Yeah, it was the weirdest thing. She just disappeared one day." Pause. "Trust me, you're not the only person who's called wondering about her." Pause. "Sorry, I don't have any more info, man." Pause. "Yeah, my friend. You too. Bye."

I looked at him as he hung up the phone. "Someone else looking for The Godfather?"

He slipped his hand back into his paw-glove and nodded, and as he did, the eyes on his costume rattled. "Yeah. You haven't heard anything from her, have you?"

"No," I white-lied. "Nothing."

It'd been more than two months since anyone had seen The Godfather. Well, anyone but me, that is. She'd been MIA since about mid-August, when she ran into the store and quit on the spot.

"I no longer work here, effective immediately," she announced to Scarlet, Poppins, and me, looking over her shoulder. Her dark hair was damp with sweat.

"Are you OK?" Poppins asked her. "Is someone after you? Do we need to call the police?"

"No!" was her adamant response. "I regret that I can give no details or notice. I have had an adequate time working with all of you." She squeezed the girls' hands before pulling me in for a peck on the cheek. "Check your pocket," she whispered. Then she ran out of the store, leaving behind a Kiss of Death lip print on my face and a note in my Levi's.

I'm pretty sure everything turned out fine for her. If you had read the note, you'd probably feel that way, too, but because snitches get stitches (as was detailed in said note), I'll just say that I know how to get ahold of her if ever I need a favor, and after I did what the note requested (wouldn't you like to know), she owed me one.

"Look, Mommy! It's Scooby-Doo!" A little girl dressed as a Power Ranger pointed at Hannibal. "And his friend, that guy in the green shirt!"

"I'm Shaggy," I said to her, taking two tags from her mother.

"Well, isn't that fun" was the woman's reply. She looked around the crowded store and pointed out Poppins and Maverick to her daughter. "And there's Velma, and Fred, and . . ." She glanced back at me as I retrieved her cassettes. "Where's Daphne?"

"Around here somewhere," I said, noting Scarlet's absence. "Probably getting more candy so cool kids like you aren't stuck with Smarties."

The little girl grinned. "Smarties taste like medicine."

"Truth," I agreed, finishing up the transaction with her mom. "Due back tomorrow by seven."

Just then Scarlet appeared from the back hallway in the shortest, tightest purple dress this side of a Virginian truck stop strip club. She also had on a green scarf, hot pink tights, and a bright orange wig, which would have made her a dead ringer for Daphne if she hadn't also taken such creative liberties as adding a push-up bra and about four inches of cleavage to her costume. I didn't bother pointing her out to the girl and her mother—when Scarlet was in the room, she was hard to miss.

I kept the line of renters moving, pulling horror movie after suspense thriller off the shelf like they were going out of style, and I'd just helped my last customer when Poppins called over to tell me the Schwartzes had arrived. I exchanged a look with Maverick, who came over to relieve me of my register. He knew I'd been waiting all day to see the real Daphne.

"Hey, Joel!" Marc shook my hand and hugged me. "Shaggy's a good look for you."

"Shaggy's an easy look for me," I pointed out. "All I needed were some brown corduroys, since I already had plenty of green shirts."

Jana was unbuckling Daphne from her stroller. "I think it's so sweet that your whole staff dressed up together." She kissed the baby on the cheek before handing her off to me. "It shows how close you all are."

After months of practice, I was much more comfortable holding Daphne, and after months of seeing me as much as she had (which was a lot, between her trips to the video store and mine to her house), she was comfortable with me, too.

"Hey, kiddo," I said to her. "I like your costume."

Daphne, who was completely oblivious to the fact that she was

400

dressed as an adorable jack-o'-lantern, smiled a tiny crescent smile with satisfying corners and then grabbed my nose.

"Aww," Jana said. "Let me get a picture of you two." She took out her camera from the diaper bag. "I'm going to take a few so I can send some to Nicole."

She didn't have to tell me to smile. I already was.

The flash of the camera caught Scarlet's attention and prompted a squeal from the other side of the store. As I could have predicted, she rushed over to steal the baby from me. "Ooh!" she cooed, lifting Daphne from my arms. "You are the cutest pumpkin I have ever seen!"

Daphne looked at Scarlet's wig with concern, then reached back for me.

"Daph, it's me," Scarlet said, removing her wig. "I wanted to dress up as another Daphne, just so I could be like you!"

I'd had my suspicions that this was why Scarlet had mandated a *Scooby-Doo* theme, but I didn't say anything. Everyone knew that Scarlet was obsessed with the baby, so there was no reason to keep pointing it out. Some obsessions are healthy.

Now seeing her as the blonde she was used to, Daphne was willing to remain in Scarlet's arms. "She feels bigger," Scarlet said to Jana, hugging the baby close to her face. "She's growing up too fast." This was a clichéd thing to say, and it was also very true.

"I know," Jana said with a sigh. "I've been told that the days are long but the years are short."

After a few more minutes spent playing with the baby, Scarlet readjusted her hair, and the three of us posed for a picture together. Then we gathered the rest of the gang for a few group shots with Daphne. No one could get her to smile for the camera, though, because she wouldn't stop looking at Hannibal.

"Oh my gosh, she loves you!" Poppins squeezed Daphne's toes. "She thinks you're really a dog, Hanni!"

"Hey, hey, little friend!" Hannibal bounced up and down to make the googly eyes on the plush Scooby face rattle, and Daphne let out a belly laugh.

When we were done taking photos with Daphne, there were other families who wanted shots of their kids with us, which was unexpected, but I guess it's not every day that you run into the gang from Mystery, Inc., at your local video store. A few kids even demanded autographs, like we were the real deal.

"Hey, Joel!" Marc eventually pulled me aside. "Daph's getting fussy for her bottle, so we're taking off. But we'll see you next weekend for dinner at Headlights, right?"

"Kat would kill me if I missed it," I said. Then I remembered something. "Oh, yeah—Maverick said he's going to bring Ben this time."

"It's about time we finally get to meet him." Marc grinned. "Anyone *else* bringing a date?"

"No, I'm coming by myself, like I always do."

"Don't you mean you're coming *solo*?" He pointed at my name badge. Then he added, "Oh, hey, when you talk to Baby next time—"

"I'll tell her not to let anyone put her in a corner."

Marc squeezed my shoulder. "You're a good man."

The Schwartzes headed toward the door, and Jana took Daphne's hand and made her blow kisses before they disappeared outside into the throngs of Royal Oak trick-or-treaters.

It was a fun Halloween, though less eventful than the previous year. In fact, nothing really happened that was that different from a normal busy Saturday at ROYO Video, which was nice. But it also felt like something was missing.

To be fair, it always felt that way.

I took my break around four o'clock, once the downtown event had officially ended and the crowds of people had thinned. I sat on the couch in the break room with the cordless phone and my calling card in hand, trying (as I always did) to remember whether Michigan and New York were in the same time zone.

Baby's roommate answered the phone.

"Hey, Kylie—is Nicole around?"

I heard a hand cover the mouthpiece of the phone, then a muffled "Nik! It's for you . . ." More muffles. "It's Star Wars."

This is what Baby's roommate called me, because I guess Han Solo was too hard to remember. I didn't mind, though; as far as nicknames went, it was a pretty cool one.

A few seconds later, Baby came on the line. "So, was I right? Did Scarlet manage to breastify her *Scooby-Doo* costume?"

I smiled, happy to hear her voice. "There were boobs everywhere."

She laughed. "I called it."

"Everyone called that. I think half our customers today came in counting on it," I said. "How're classes?"

"Hard, but fine. It helps that I'm not a moron like a lot of kids here." She pulled her mouth away from the phone and said, "I don't mean you, Kylie. Chill out."

"Glad to hear it."

"How're your classes going?" she returned the question. "You never talk about school."

"That's because it's boring community college. I've slept through composition for three weeks straight, and I'm still pulling a ninety-eight."

"Good. Keep getting those A's so you can transfer."

"You think I should reapply to Sarah Lawrence?" I asked her. "You still want me to?"

"Of course. I want you to be out here right now, Solo," Baby scoffed. "I don't know why you got rejected the first time."

"I didn't get rejected, I got wait-listed and they never called back," I reminded her. "Which I guess is just a nice way of saying rejected."

"Whatever. Just get here," she said before changing the subject back to work. "So, what else am I missing today besides Scarlet's breasts?"

"The Schwartzes came in. Oh, before I forget, Marc says—"

"I know what you're going to say, Solo. Please tell Marc that joke is getting old and ask him not to teach it to Daphne ever."

I laughed. "Speaking of Daphne, she was dressed as a pumpkin. Jana is sending you pictures."

"Aww! I can't wait to see them," Baby said wistfully. "Do you think she'll still remember me when I come home at Thanksgiving?"

"Of course she will. You tend to leave an impression on people," I assured her.

"Shut up."

"It's true. Dad says that Grandma and Grandpa talk about you every time they call," I told her. "They want to know if you're coming back next summer when Dad and I visit."

I could almost hear her eyes roll. "God, Solo. Why's your family so obsessed with me?"

I laughed. "I don't know. I don't get it at all."

Just then, Poppins called my name from the hallway. "Solo! Your interview is here!"

"Shit," I said to Baby. "I forgot I was interviewing someone today."

"That's all right," she told me. "I should be studying anyway. Midterms are this week."

"You're gonna do great."

"Yeah, because I'll study my ass off."

"Solo!" Poppins called again.

"Be right there!" I yelled away from the receiver. "OK, I've got to run. I'll call you again soon."

"Monday?" Baby asked. "No, wait, Monday you've got therapy, right?"

"PFLAG meeting," I corrected her. "Family therapy's on Tuesday this week. Well, for Dad and me, at least."

"Still no Maureen, huh?"

"No," I said. "But I keep inviting her."

"That's all you can do, right?"

"Yeah . . . I'll call you afterward to brief you on the amazing progress I'm making."

Baby laughed. "All right, I'll study at home that night."

"And wait by the phone for me to call?"

"Shut up," she said. "But yeah."

I let a few seconds of silence hang between us. I didn't want to hang up. "I love you, Baby," I finally said to her.

"I know," she said back. "I love you, too."

"I know."

"So, what makes you want to be a part of the ROYO Video team?" I asked Angela Khoury, applicant.

We were sitting in the office, my pen poised and ready to write down her answers, though things were already looking good for her, considering she had availability on nights and weekends, which was really the only requirement that mattered.

"I love movies. And the store is walking distance from my house."

"I appreciate the honesty," I told her. "Where do you see yourself in five years, professionally?"

She gave me a funny look. "I don't know." She shrugged. "I never know how to answer that because it's like, on the one hand, if I say I don't plan to be here five years from now, maybe you won't hire me because I don't seem like a loyal person. But then on the other hand, if I say I plan to still be here, it seems like I have no ambition, which doesn't really serve me well, either."

I tossed the papers down on the desk. "You know what? I have a feeling you'll do just fine here."

"Really?" She smiled. "I've got the job? Just like that?"

"I mean, you have to fill out all this paperwork," I told her. "But if you can handle that, then there's a place for you at ROYO Video."

"Awesome!" She clapped her hands together, then picked up the stack of papers off the desk. "So, what happens next?"

I pulled a lanyard from the desk drawer and attached it to a blank HI! MY NAME IS tag. "Next you pick your work name. Everyone here goes by the name of a movie character," I explained. "What do you want to be called?"

"Oh! Fun! What are my choices?"

"You can pick anything that someone's not already using," I told her, then went down the list of the names in use. "Most people just pick their favorite character from their favorite movie. I'm Solo, after Han Solo. Poppins is named after Mary Poppins. You get it."

"OK." She deliberated. "I have two favorite movies: *Dirty Dancing* and *The Princess Bride*. How do I choose which name to be?"

I looked at Angela and smiled.

"How do you feel about Buttercup?" I asked.

"It's perfect."

I wrote it on her name tag. "Come in tomorrow at five. Look for my buddy Maverick. He'll be training you."

ACKNOWLEDGMENTS

If I ever had to give an acceptance speech, I would blow it. I would likely trip up the stairs on my way to the podium. My wardrobe would probably malfunction in a spectacular way. And in the twenty seconds I had to speak, I would forget almost every word in the English language and say something ridiculous like "Milk. It does a body good!" and then apologize and slink off the stage because I am *terrible* on the spot. This is not self-deprecation. This is me owning who I am. I am not ashamed.

For these reasons, I want to first say that I'm grateful to be writing and not speaking my acknowledgments to the many people who made this storytelling journey possible. The odds of me falling, ripping my clothes, and unintentionally quoting old public service announcements are significantly lower this way. Not zero, but lower.

Stephen Barr, the best literary agent on the planet, would argue with me about this. He'd tell me that of course none of those things would happen, and then he'd say the most perfectly encouraging words ever uttered by a human tongue and I'd believe anything is possible. This is why he gets first billing on my list of thank-yous. Stephen, long before I knew you as an agent, I admired you. Thank you for taking care of my story and of me, but mostly just thanks for being you. The world is fantastically better because you're in it.

To my editor, Kaylan Adair, thanks for fighting to acquire my book and then fighting with me and for me ever since. Thank you for challenging me and struggling through the difficult moments with me, for your compassion, and for being worthy of my vulnerability. Oh, and thanks for being an incredible editor, obviously. (You're super-good at your job. You know that, right?) I'm forever indebted to you for teaching me the difference between gray and grey.

To my team at Writers House, I thank you for your tireless effort on behalf of this book. To my foreign rights and audio rights champions, Cecilia de la Campa and Alessandra Birch, thank you for giving Joel's story a chance to be heard elsewhere around the world. A special thanks also to Andrea Vedder and Nora Long—you two are rock stars!

Thank you to everyone at Candlewick. I couldn't be prouder or more humbled that this book sports the C-Flame! Thank you to Matt Roeser for the amazing cover design and to Sherry Fatla for a fantastic interior. Thank you to Amanda Bellamy, the production controller. To Alison Cherry and Jackie Houton, who copyedited my manuscript, and to Jamie Tan, my publicist—thank you for working tirelessly, despite a pandemic. You amaze me, and I am so grateful for your work.

To my film agent at CAA, Dana Spector—thanks for taking a chance on the gang at ROYO. They would all think you are ridiculously cool. Even Baby.

To Shelley: I knew I liked you from the moment I met you at parent/teacher day. What I didn't know then was that being assigned as your son's teacher would completely change my life. I cherish our friendship and admire you greatly. Thank you for everything you've done for me. Without you, I may never have written a single word.

To my loves JLB. You are the best, and I am the luckiest.

Thank you to my mom, my dad, my siblings, and my extended family (both blood and chosen). Much love to Amy and Shawn, Karen and Roy, Bethany, Shannon, Jen, Kim, Liz, Zeddy, Colleen, Lamia, and Lindsay. I love you all with my whole heart.

Granny, can you believe all this? (Sorry for all the swears.)

Much love to my teachers Laura L., Kathy G., the late Steve K., Dr. Beate G., and Dr. Jonathan W. Each of you was instrumental in shaping me as a writer. Thank you for encouraging me. You are changing the world, one child at a time.

Shout out to the now-defunct Summit Ridge Pharmacy video rental department. Thanks for the memories!

Many thanks to the affirming members of my faith community for catching me when I fall.

And last but not least, thank you, Mark Ruffalo.

Remember, only you can prevent forest fires.

RESOURCES

The National Suicide Prevention Lifeline
The National Suicide Prevention Lifeline is a national network of local crisis centers that provides free and confidential emotional support to people in suicidal crisis or emotional distress twenty-four hours a day, seven days a week. They are committed to improving crisis services and advancing suicide prevention by empowering individuals, advancing professional best practices, and building awareness.

1-800-273-8255

https://suicidepreventionlifeline.org

The Trevor Project
Founded in 1998 by the creators of the award-winning short film *Trevor*, the Trevor Project is a national organization providing crisis intervention and suicide prevention services to lesbian, gay, bisexual, transgender, queer, and questioning (LGBTQ) young people under twenty-five. Counselors on its TrevorLifeline are available twenty-four hours a day.

1-866-488-7386

https://www.thetrevorproject.org

The LGBT National Youth Talkline
The LGBT National Youth Talkline provides a safe space that is anonymous and confidential where young callers can speak on many different issues and concerns, including coming-out issues, gender and/or sexuality identities, relationship concerns, bullying, isolation, anxiety at school, family issues, HIV/AIDS concerns, safer sex information, suicide, and more. The line is staffed by trained volunteers who identify somewhere on the LGBTQ spectrum, from all ages and walks of life and from all over the United States. Along with providing peer support, listening, and affirmation, volunteers can refer callers seeking additional support to local resources from the largest LGBTQ resource database in the United States (www.glbtnearme.org).

1-800-246-7743

https://www.glbthotline.org/talkline.html